MADAME GRAY'S TWISTED TALES

A Collection of Horror Stories
By Gerri R. Gray

A HellBound Books LLC
Publication

Copyright © 2021 by HellBound Books Publishing
LLC
All Rights Reserved

Cover and art design by
HellBound Books Publishing LLC

No part of this book may be reproduced, stored in a retrieval system,
or transmitted by any means, electronic, mechanical, photocopying,
recording or otherwise without written permission from the author
This book is a work of fiction. Names, characters, places and
incidents are entirely fictitious or are used fictitiously and any
resemblance to actual persons, living or dead, events or locales is purely
coincidental.

www.hellboundbooks.com

Printed in the United States of America

Also by Gerri R. Gray:

The Amnesia Girl (HellBound Books, 2017)
Gray Skies of Dismal Dreams (HellBound Books, 2018)
The Graveyard Girls (HellBound Books, 2018)
Blood and Blasphemy (HellBound Books, 2019)
The Strange Adventures of Turquoise Moonwolf (HellBound Books, 2020)
Madame Gray's Creep Show (HellBound Books, 2020)
The Toilet Zone: Number Two (HellBound Books, 2020)
Madame Gray's Vault of Gore (HellBound Books, 2021)
The Toilet Zone: The Royal Flush (HellBound Books, 2022)
Madame Gray's Poe-Pourri of Terror (HellBound Books, 2022)

Contributor to:
Ghost Hunting the Mohawk Valley (Black Cat Books, 2013)
Beautiful Tragedies (HellBound Books, 2017)
Demons, Devils & Denizens of Hell 2 (HellBound Books, 2017)
EconoClash Review (Thrill Hill Bottom Press, 2018)
Deadman's Tome Cthulhu Christmas Special (2018)
Hyper-tomb: Crypt of the Cyber-mummy (Horrified Press, 2018)
Mixed Bag of Horror: Vol. 1 (HellBound Books, 2019)
Trump Fiction (Thrill Hill Bottom Press, 2018)
and others.

CONTENTS

INTRODUCTION

Welcome, friends and fiends, to *Madame Gray's Twisted Tales.*

As a child, monsters and madmen intrigued me. Nothing thrilled me more than a good scare, whether it was from watching films like *Night of the Living Dead* or *The Haunting*, reading the works of Edgar Allan Poe or H.P. Lovecraft, or from listening to a blood-chilling ghost story being told by the crackling flames of a fire pit in the dark of night. As far as I was concerned, the scarier the better! That adage has stuck with me throughout the years.

Fear is a natural and biological condition that all human beings and animals experience at one time or another. Fear is a healthy thing. It's programmed into our nervous systems and provides us with the survival instincts we need in order to keep ourselves safe from danger. Fear, in the correct dose, can also be exhilarating and most enjoyable when we know that we aren't in any real danger. I think that's what draws many people to the horror genre.

I'm often asked why, as an author, I choose to write horror when there are so many "more pleasant" things to write about. For me, as I suspect it might well be for many other writers, tapping into the dark recesses of my mind and creating imaginary horrors is something that helps me to deal with the day-to-day horrors of the real world in which we live. Plus, I enjoy scaring the crap out of people.

Few things bring me greater pleasure than creating strange worlds filled with even stranger characters. Crafting a story out of thin air is like weaving a magic spell. Writing is my religion, and my typewriter is my altar. It's what keeps me sane—or happily insane, depending on which day of the week it is. I have an affinity for dark things, which is evident in everything that I write, whether it be a short story, a novel, a poem or a shopping list. What can I say? Monsters turn me on. And many of the twisted tales in this book feature the most terrifying monster of all—man.

With that being said, I have assembled a collection of twenty-five of my darkest stories. Some can best be described as cautionary tales. Some are gore fests, and some are infused with gallows humor. Within the pages that lie ahead await hellish entities, undead things, and other abominations that dwell in the blackest of shadows and feast upon the souls and flesh of people just like you. If you're prone to squeamish tendencies or are easily offended by violence, bloodshed and that which does not fall under the category of political correctness, I urge you to turn back. But if you appreciate the twisted, proceed at your own risk.

> "Horror is the removal of masks."
> —Robert Bloch

MADAME GRAY'S TWISTED TALES

THE ABSINTHE BOTTLE

The perpetual crashing of waves on the rocks—a sound that at one time provided me accompaniment for romantic interludes and poetic flights of fancy—now serves as a constant reminder of my imprisonment in this never-ending hell. The ghost-white gulls circle overhead; their incessant cries, like harsh, derisive laughter, bring me to the brink of madness. How long I've been walking on this desolate beach, I cannot say with any amount of certainty. It could have been a day or two, maybe weeks, perhaps years. It no longer makes any difference. Time is a meaningless thing to me now. And like the tide that ebbs and flows, only to ebb and flow again, so too does my torment go on and on without end. The sun, like a cruel joke, kisses the golden sand that stretches endlessly to the horizon, but does nothing to warm me. All I feel, within and without, is the paralyzing cold that has entombed every fiber of my being since that fateful day…

I had departed Pentevedra early that morning, the back of my red Renault 16 filled with a bundle of sketchpads and several cases of art supplies. On the seat across from me sat one piece of woebegone luggage packed with an adequate supply of clothes and toiletries to last me for a three-day holiday on the northern coast of Spain. An hour and a half of driving time remained before I would arrive at the hotel in the port city of Santander, where I was to meet up with an old friend from my university days. Like myself, Sergio was an artist and a connoisseur of fine wines from the Basque Country. Our plan was to spend our first day together drinking heavily and reminiscing about the long-lost days of our youth. After a good night's sleep and a hearty breakfast, we would then take off to roam about the city, sketching and painting the interesting people and places we encountered. It was something we had been planning for well over a year.

From the highway that meandered through mountains cloaked by green woods, I could see the sapphire expanse of the Cantabrian Sea shimmering beneath the August sun. It was a breathtaking sight to behold—almost too breathtaking for words. But then, as if by some strange magic, it seemed to beckon to me, whispering my name, urging me to stop and surrender to its call.

I can offer no explanation for what I did next, other than having fallen under the spell of the sea—or of something far greater…and deadlier.

I pulled the Renault off to the side of the road and turned off the motor. Without regard to my personal possessions, I climbed out of the car and headed in the direction of the sea. Like a man taken leave of his senses, I began climbing down a rocky slope leading to an uninhabited, rock-strewn beach below. With salty wind against my face and the roar of the ocean in my ears, I found myself walking along the beach in an easterly direction.

I don't know how far I had walked, or for how long, when I realized that the afternoon sun was approaching the western horizon and would soon begin its descent, painting the sky in hues of fiery red and burnt orange, and turning the sea indigo. I scolded myself for having lost track of the time, as the cocktail hour would be long over by the time I arrived at my destination. I was about to turn and start back to my car when my eyes were suddenly drawn to something green and glittering in the sand up ahead. As I drew closer to the mysterious object, I realized it was nothing more than a glass bottle that had washed up on the beach. I bent down and picked it up. The soggy remnants of a label revealed it to be an old absinthe bottle. The mouth of the container was plugged tightly shut with a cork that someone, for some peculiar reason, had sealed with red paraffin. Upon closer inspection, I saw that a rolled-up piece of paper, upon which a message of some sort had been written, lay inside.

What a curious thing, I thought as I held the bottle up to the soon-to-be-setting sun. In the days of my boyhood, I had been intrigued by stories of messages in bottles, but never had I dreamt that one day I would actually stumble upon such a thing. As I made my way back to my waiting car, my green glass prize in hand, I pondered the unread message inside it. Would the scroll turn out to be a treasure map, or perhaps a romantic letter from some faraway lovelorn damsel? A smile crossed my face and a soft chuckle escaped my lips as I imagined it to be: *Help! I'm trapped on a desert island and I've run out of absinthe!*

The darkness of night had already fallen when I finally reached Santander. The hotel, like an ivory palace overlooking the moonlit bay, was a welcome sight for my travel-weary eyes. I checked in at the reception desk and then adjourned to my upstairs room with my luggage and art supplies. I phoned Sergio's room to let him know I had arrived. He was happy to hear my voice.

"I was beginning to think you weren't coming," he said. "I thought you'd be here hours ago. Were you delayed by car trouble?"

"Actually," I replied, "I stopped to partake of some

anchovy stuffed olives, and was seduced by a voluptuous woman of exquisite beauty. Naturally, she begged me to make mad love to her, for hours!"

"Oh, *Dios mio!*" Sergio cried out.

Holding back my laughter, I continued, "Well, being the courteous gentleman that I am, and not wishing to appear rude, there was nothing else for me to do but oblige her wishes. I ask you, old friend, would you not have done the same?"

Sergio and I both erupted into a bout of laughter. After settling down, I explained to him that I had stopped to take a stroll on a beach and subsequently lost sight of the time. I then told him about the old bottle I had found in the sand.

"An absinthe bottle? With a message in it?" he asked, traces of laughter still attached to his voice. "You and your jokes. I don't believe it."

"It's true!" I asserted. "I swear to you! I have it with me in my suitcase."

"Okay, okay. So tell me, rapscallion, what did the message in this bottle say?"

"I don't know," I answered. "I haven't yet opened it."

"Seriously?"

"Seriously."

Sergio was unable to mask the enthusiasm in his voice. "This is incredible! I must see this bottle for myself. Promise me you won't open it until I get to your room. I'm on my way up with a bottle of Chacoli." He then hung up before I could get in another word.

True to his word, Sergio showed up at my door within the span of minutes, a bottle of chilled wine in his hand. I poured us each a glass and we toasted to old friends. He was anxious to see the absinthe bottle, so I retrieved it from my luggage and handed it to him. He gazed upon it with fascination and then handed it back to me.

"Open the bottle and read the message!" he cried. "The suspense is killing me!"

He watched intently as I broke the wax seal and uncorked the bottle, releasing a musty bouquet that was faint and fleeting. After turning the bottle upside down and giving it a few vigorous shakes, it surrendered its secret, which slid out and dropped into my lap.

"What does it say?" my friend asked, craning his neck to get a closer look.

I unfurled the scroll. Written upon it in an elegant hand was a rhyme consisting of four lines, the ink possessing a peculiar rust-colored quality, not unlike that of dried blood. I felt the hairs on the back of my neck stand on end as I read it aloud:

"Heed this message now unsealed
Secrets wait to be revealed.
Journey past the iron gates
A precious thing awaits."

The riddle-like verse was signed, Nicolas Maldonado, and below the name was inscribed an address.

I handed the scroll to Sergio.

A puzzled expression overcame his face as he tried to make sense of it. "Maldonado…his name means 'ill-favored.' Whoever this guy is, he's certainly not much of a poet. What do you suppose he means by 'a precious thing awaits?'"

I gulped down some more wine as I pondered the cryptic message. "Perhaps it's part of a game, some sort of contest or treasure hunt, and the 'precious thing' it speaks of is a valuable prize or a reward given to whomever finds the bottle?"

"Do you really think so?" Sergio groaned a little as he shook his head. "I don't know about that. There's a chance you could be right, but on the other hand, this bottle and its strange message could simply be a lark…the workings of an impish child. Or maybe something more sinister."

I took the scroll from Sergio's hands. "Well, whatever the true nature of this thing is, I intend to pay Señor

Maldonado a visit tomorrow and find out for myself. That's the only way my curiosity will ever be satisfied."

Sergio's eyes widened. "Surely you aren't serious?" he asked. "Why, the idea is madness! For all we know, this bottle could be an ill omen, a decoy. My advice to you is to toss it back into the sea and forget about it!"

I found Sergio's alarmism rather amusing, and I chuckled. "Don't talk so foolishly, Sergio. You sound like one of those old peasant women who look for signs in tea leaves and the tossing of bones."

"Laugh if you will," he replied. "I'm just concerned for your safety, my friend."

I poured myself another glass of wine. "Your concern is appreciated, but inessential. In the morning I will go and claim whatever precious prize is being offered. My mind is made up so let us speak of the matter no more."

Sergio shrugged his shoulders. "If that is what you want, then so be it."

We spent the next couple hours drinking and talking of such things as art, our romantic conquests, and our travels throughout the continent and abroad. The Chacoli and the long drive up from the Iberian Peninsula were beginning to take their toll on my senses. My eyes grew bleary, and Sergio's words became meaningless murmurs that trailed away like unraveling dreams.

As a distant bell tower tolled like a dirge heralding death, I drifted off into a hazy nightmare. I dreamt that I had awakened from my wine-riddled stupor to find Sergio sneaking from my room, the absinthe bottle and its message clutched in his hand. Outraged, I sprung from my chair and grabbed him before he could pilfer my sparkling, green treasure. A quarrel broke out, and I accused him of trying to steal the bottle in order to claim for himself whatever 'precious thing' it promised. He brazenly denied my accusation. Enraged by what I saw as a betrayal of our friendship, I cursed and took a swing at his face, impacting his jaw. He reciprocated by ramming his fist into my midsection, knocking the air from my lungs. We proceeded to tussle like a pair of punch-drunk, back-alley brawlers until I wrestled the bottle from him and bashed it against the side of his head with all the might I could muster in my inebriety. I watched as my friend, now my mortal enemy, crumpled to the terra cotta tiled floor. I staggered back to my chair, beads of sweat clinging to my skin, my breath heavy. Holding the bottle snugly to my chest, I closed my eyes and smiled at my victory before passing out.

I awoke groggy-headed, and from my window I could see the full moon was well past its zenith. I winced as a sledgehammer of a headache pounded the inside of my skull with the relentlessness of a soul-craving devil. And then I became aware that the front of my shirt was splattered with what appeared to be dried blood. *What the hell happened?* Confusion raced through my mind. *Am I bleeding?* I pulled open my shirt, only to find no wounds on my flesh. As I rose from the chair, my eyes beheld a sight that made me recoil in horror.

Curled up on the floor, in a dark, slimy pool of blood and brain matter, lay poor Sergio. Half of his head resembled a smashed pumpkin, a silent scream frozen upon what remained of his face. The blood staining my shirt was his. The dream I had dreamt was not a dream at all, but reality. The realization pummeled me with a fist of ice.

"My God!" I cried, as I stared at the battered corpse, my hands trembling. "This can't be! What on earth have I done?"

A wave of panic and nausea rolled over me, twisting my gut. I felt gorge rising in my throat. I hastened to the bathroom and retched into the marble washbasin. The acrid taste of soured wine and vomitus brought tears to my eyes.

Never before had I been a man prone to violence. The answer to how, in my drunken rage, could I have murdered a man in cold blood over a message in a bottle eluded me.

I gazed up at the ceiling, and in whispered words, begged God and His angels to right my wrong, to forgive my sin, but I knew deep in my heart that no miracles or divine forgiveness would be granted to me.

After splashing handfuls of cold water on my sweating face, I stared at my reflection in the bathroom mirror—it was now the reflection of a killer. My heart was beating with the rapidity of a scared rabbit, and the urge to bolt from the crime scene overwhelmed me. I took a few deep breaths to calm myself, and then spoke out loud to my reflection as through it belonged to someone other than the monster I had become.

"Get a grip on yourself. You didn't intend to kill him. It was an accident. You hit him in self-defense. Such things happen."

A tiny voice, like the voice of doom, uttered inside my head: *The police aren't going to buy that ridiculous story. You'll be sent to prison.*

I had no desire to live out the remainder of my years rotting away in some filthy, vermin-infested prison cell. As far as I was concerned, a quick death by firing squad or garroting would be a preferable fate to that. However, much to my dismay, Spain had abolished capital punishment many years ago.

"Okay then, maybe take him back to his room and then throw his body off the balcony," I suggested. "Make it look like a suicide."

There'll be an investigation, the voice retorted. *Forensics will know it wasn't suicide. Sooner or later the authorities will figure out who killed him, and then you can say goodbye to your life as a free man.*

"Not if they never find him. No corpse, no crime!"

Very good. Now you're thinking, my boy. Dispose of Sergio's body and no one will be any the wiser. But you need a plan. How will you do it?

I thought long and hard for the answer, but nothing

came to me. Feeling like I had reached a dead end, I cried out, "I don't know! I don't know!"

Use your head, man. Think! Your freedom, your future, depends on it!

And suddenly, like a panacea from Heaven—or perhaps from Hell—the answer surfaced: the water tanks on the roof of the hotel! I remembered catching a glimpse of them when I arrived. Who would ever think to look inside them for a dead man? Dragging Sergio's body up to the roof and depositing it inside one of the tanks was a gruesome plan, but one that I believed would save me from a dismal fate behind bars.

Propelled into high gear by a rush of adrenaline, I wrapped Sergio's lifeless body in the sheet from my bed, and with my heart pumping wildly as though ready to burst, I proceeded to drag the carcass out of my room and into the elevator. With a shaking hand I pressed the button for the top floor and prayed that no one else would get on the elevator. Beads of cold sweat drizzled from my brow and stung my eyes as the lift made its ascent to my salvation.

The ding of the elevator bell sent a chill along my spine, and the door opened with a soft hissing sound. Waves of anxiety pulsed through my body as I peered out. Seeing no one around, I dragged the corpse out of the elevator and down the red carpeted hall and around a corner until I came upon a steel door with a sign that said: STAIRS TO ROOF – AUTHORIZED PERSONNEL ONLY. I gripped the knob, and as I turned it I prayed under my breath, "*Querido Dios*, please let this door be unlocked." The door opened, and I breathed a sigh of relief.

Suddenly, there came the dreaded sound of footsteps and the hushed voices of a man and a woman from the other end of the corridor. Were they hotel staff? Police officers? My heart raced and I froze with terror, unable to move and barely breathing out of fear that they might hear me. Would I be discovered? What would I say? What would I do? I wondered if all killers asked themselves these questions. And then I heard the familiar ding of the elevator and the hissing of its door opening and closing. The voices were replaced by hum of the elevator descending in its shaft. Silence once again filled the top floor of the hotel, and I breathed another sigh of relief.

A peculiar sensation of un-reality spun its web around me as I pulled Sergio's dead weight up the stairs leading to the roof—and the watery grave that awaited him. I opened the door at the top of the stairs and stepped out onto the roof. The crisp night air slapped my sweat-coated face like the hand of a woman in a fit of indignation, plunging me back into reality for a brief moment. Everything took a dream-like quality as I proceeded to deposit the remains of my friend in one of the water tanks with a loud splash. Before closing the heavy lid of the tank, I uttered a prayer for the dead man floating in the water.

My eyes were drawn to the sudden appearance of a falling star. I watched as its bluish-white glow streaked across the sky before burning out into a point of inky blackness, never to be seen again. My mind drifted back through time. A dusty memory resurfaced, and I saw myself as a child sitting next to an elderly nun on a train. Her face, in spite of bearing the imprint of age in every lineament, was kind, and her voice melodic as she told me that a falling star meant a soul, having been released from purgatory, was ascending to Heaven. The memory brought a sad laugh to my lips. I had broken God's commandment against killing, and that was an unpardonable sin. There would be no falling star for my soul.

I returned to my room to clean up the ghastly aftermath of my intoxicated rage, scrubbing and wiping down everything until I felt satisfied that no traces of Sergio's blood remained. Exhausted, I collapsed onto the bed. Sleep came quickly and was blighted by nightmares so horrendous they could only have been forged in the fires of

Hell by the Devil himself. I would never again know a night of tranquil slumber.

I checked out of the hotel in the morning, stuffed my belongings into my car, and drove out of the city, feeling only too happy to see the skyline of Santander in the rearview mirror, gradually growing smaller with each second that passed, until it vanished from sight like wisps of phantasmal ground mist in the noontide sun.

Looking back now, I realize the wisest choice I could have made would have been to withdraw all my savings, meager as they were, and flee to France or Portugal before Sergio was reported missing. It would have been easy to change my name and start a new life. But instead, I chose to let the road take me to the house of Nicolas Maldonado.

Journey past the iron gates; a precious thing awaits. The words from that mysterious rhyme tucked inside the absinthe bottle repeated again and again inside my head, nearly driving me to madness. Whatever this "precious thing" was, I had taken a man's life for it. It was my prize to be claimed.

A light drizzle was falling, misting my windshield, when I arrived at the black iron gates guarding the entrance to the Maldonado estate. "Beyond these iron gates," I whispered to myself, "the precious thing—*my precious thing*—awaits." Through the ornate scrollwork, I could see a cypress-lined driveway meandering its way up to a decaying hilltop villa that, in its heyday, must have rivaled in dignity even the grandest of homes in all of the Basque Country. Now weatherworn and cloaked in desolation, it took on the sinister appearance of an alabaster skull against the swirling, slate-colored sky, its rows of shuttered windows grinning monstrously at the sea below.

Finding the gates unlocked, I pushed them open and then climbed back into my car and continued up to the house. As I drove past the withered remains of a rose garden and the ruins of an old fountain choked in weeds, a strange foreboding crept over me. The closer I drew to the villa, the more derelict it grew in appearance. I began to wonder if the place had been long ago abandoned.

I parked the Renault, and with absinthe bottle in hand, and a flutter of anticipation in my belly, approached the front entrance of the once-grand house, its stucco and brick exterior cracked and crumbling away like the dreams of a defeated man. White marble steps lead me up to a pair of arched doors.

A precious thing awaits.

With bated breath I rapped upon one of the doors. The minutes passed with agonizing slowness—each second rolling by like an eternity. I rapped once more, this time a bit louder, and continued to wait. But still there came no answer. Hard rain was now plummeting down, the grim sky blackening to evil shades. A low growl of thunder rumbled in the distance as cruel thoughts rushed into my brain. *Perhaps Maldonado had long ago died, or moved away, leaving his villa to the mercy of the elements. Or, worse yet, what if the message in the bottle was nothing more than a prank, and poor Sergio's death was all for naught?* If luck were with me, I would awaken to discover the events of the past two days were but a bad dream.

Feeling as though I'd been led on a wild goose chase, I turned to head back to my car. That was when I heard the sound of the arched doors being unlocked. The door on the right opened barely a crack, and in the narrow space the ashen face of a senescent man appeared. A pair of dark eyes, overshadowed by grizzled eyebrows, observed me suspiciously.

"Yes?" he asked in a frail sounding voice.

"Señor Maldonado?" I enquired.

"I am not," the old man replied. "Do you have business with Señor Maldonado?"

"No, not really. Well, in a way, I suppose you could say." I suddenly felt foolish and at a loss for words. I took a deep breath and continued, "This will probably sound crazy to you, and I hope you don't think me mad, but yesterday I came upon a bottle—an old absinthe bottle—while walking along a beach." I held up the bottle for him to see. "Inside of it was a poem…"

"Señor Maldonado cannot be disturbed," the old man interrupted. "He is extremely busy and does not concern himself with such trivial matters as old bottles." His dark eyes shot daggers at me. "Now go away, far away from here, and do not come back under any circumstances. Let this be a warning to you."

My spirits sank, and I tried to hide the crestfallen expression I could feel tugging at my rain sodden face. "I'm sorry to have bothered you. Please accept my humble apologies."

I was about to leave when I heard the sound of footsteps approaching the old man from behind. His eyes spawned a look of trepidation, which I found curious, and he quickly turned away from me. It was then that I heard a man's voice say to him, "That will be all for now, Rolondo. I will take care of this matter. You may return to your duties."

The old man mussitated a humble, "Yes sir," and then scurried away.

The door swung open wide, and a tall, dark-haired man, slender of frame and deep in the throes of middle age, greeted me. A black, pencil-thin moustache embellished his pale upper lip with absolute symmetry, suggesting an air of mystery.

"You must excuse Rolondo," he said. "He is but a mere servant here, loyal and hard working. But, alas, he is getting up in years and is somewhat feeble of mind, you must understand."

"Are you Señor Maldonado?" I asked. "The man who wrote the message in the bottle?"

His lips curved in the barest hint of a smile as he introduced himself to me with a firm handshake. "My name is Alazar. *Doctor* Alazar. I am Señor Maldonado's personal physician." He released his grip on me, and beckoned with his other hand. "Come in out of the rain. Señor Maldonado is waiting for you in the dining room. He's been anxiously expecting your arrival."

"Expecting my arrival?" I echoed, as he took the bottle from my hand. "I'm afraid you have me confused with someone else. I've never met Señor Maldonado before, let alone spoken to him. He had no idea that I was coming."

"Come with me," the doctor said. "I will take you to him."

"Lead the way."

As I followed him down the hall, I paused for a moment to gaze upon a taxidermy raven displayed on a barley twist console table. Wired to a piece of dead wood, under a large glass dome, the dead bird sat, its eyes of black-colored glass fixed in a frozen stare. I couldn't help but to feel that, within those eyes—those terrible, lifeless, black eyes—something ominous dwelled.

I looked away and picked up my pace to catch up to the doctor.

"Señor Maldonado is not a well man," he whispered into my ear as we neared the end of the hall, where there stood a tall, carved door leading to the dining room. "He suffers from an extremely rare condition that requires special treatments. Do not be dismayed by his appearance."

He opened the door and ushered me inside a grand room with walls covered in velvet-flocked wallpaper of crimson and gold. Just below the plaster crown molding, a fleur-de-lis border ran the length of the room. Directly beneath a massive wrought iron chandelier with three tiers of electric candles was an elongated table with ten high-back, carved walnut chairs that looked to be relics from the nineteenth century. Seated in a wheelchair at the far end of the table was a man of average build, the sum of his facial features hidden behind a white molded mask with small openings to accommodate his eyes, nostrils and mouth.

Why anyone would choose to wear such a strange and somewhat grotesque imitation of a human face was a mystery to me, but I presumed it was to hide some sort of deformity, and made no mention of it.

"I am Nicolas Maldonado," the man behind the mask said, his voice possessing a rather jovial quality to it. "Welcome to my home. Please have a seat and be comfortable."

I thanked my host, and sat at the opposite end of the table, facing him.

"So, you are the one who found the bottle I had cast into the Cantabrian Sea. What good fortune!" he rejoiced. "You will join me in a drink to celebrate, yes?"

I responded with a nod of my head.

With a hand encased in a long white glove, he picked up a small brass bell that sat on the table in front of him, and rang it three times, summoning the frail servant from an adjoining room. "Rolondo, bring us two glasses of absinthe, *por favor*." He quickly turned back to me. "Unless you prefer wine."

I had never partaken of absinthe, but was familiar with that liquor's reputation of inducing not only creativity and aphrodisia, but insanity as well. "Absinthe is fine," I answered, not wishing to appear unsophisticated.

While we waited for the servant to return with our drinks, Maldonado remarked, "It may interest you to know that absinthe, or "the Green Fairy" as I like to call it, was the drink of choice among turn-of-the-century intellectuals seeking to push the boundaries of perception. It's true. And Oscar Wilde, the most infamous homosexual of the Victorian era, warned that drinking it could produce visions of monstrous and cruel things. I use it only to toast special occasions, such as this. I disapprove of excessive alcohol consumption. It is bad for the liver."

"Yes," I agreed, despite my all too frequent imbibing of

wine and spirituous liquors, "very bad." I cleared my throat and attempted to steer the conversation back to the important matter. "Señor Maldonado, speaking of absinthe, inside the old absinthe bottle I found on the beach was a poem that you wrote. What does the line, *secrets wait to be revealed,* mean? And what is the precious thing that waits for me? Is it gold? Silver? Something else of great value? I must know! My curiosity demands to be satiated!"

"And so it shall be. But all in good time," came his reply—a reply that ruffled me with frustration and unveiled nothing except his desire to play head games with me. "First, you must tell me about yourself. It's only right that I know who the guests in my home are before they receive what is due to them."

I had no choice but to play the game his way. "There's really not much to tell," I replied. "I'm an artist by trade. I sketch. I paint. Still lives. Landscapes. But portraiture is what I'm principally drawn to, if you'll excuse the pun. My models have been women, men, the young and the old…each one is a work of art in their own right. The majesty of the human face and its multifarious expressions—a mirror that reflects the secret emotions of the soul—is my source of inspiration."

With curiosity I watched as Maldonado's gloved hands reached for the sides of his mask. "Tell me," he began, his voice laced with sarcasm, "does the majesty of *this* face inspire you?" He suddenly ripped the mask away from his face, and the true atrocity of his wretched malady was revealed to me. "Do you not find it a work of art worthy of one of your portrait canvases?"

My horror-stricken eyes, filled with revulsion, yet unable to look away, beheld a face that was all but absent of its humanity, its features covered nearly in their entirety by enormous, ashen-colored growths not unlike barnacles that attach themselves to the hulls of ships. At the center of each of these horrible growths yawned a round aperture containing a series of hellish, claw-like teeth similar in their appearance to those found within the stoma of carnivorous nematodes.

I gasped at the sight, instinctively raising my hand to cover my gaping mouth.

Maldonado seemed unfazed by my reaction. With his unblinking eyes not straying from mine, he removed his gloves, and I saw that his hands displayed the same terrible condition as his face. He then sat motionless, cocooned in silence, and observed me like a player in a game of chess, awaiting his opponent's move.

As if the blood in my veins had suddenly turned to ice, I felt a cold chill flow through me. I was not unaccustomed to the horrendous, having experienced, first-hand, all the bloody spectacles of war, which I felt with confidence now manifested themselves as nightmares in the minds of those who bore witness to them, excluding not even those soldiers possessing the most hardened of hearts. Yet, there I sat at Maldonado's dining table, a tremble on my lips and cold sweat beading upon my brow as the ghastliness of my host filled my vision, leading me to question why any merciful god in heaven above would permit something so abominable. I took in a deep breath and upon regaining my composure I immediately offered apologies to the afflicted man and assured him that I meant not to offend him in any way by my conspicuous shock or staring eyes.

It was then that Rolondo returned to the dining room with a small, silver serving tray holding two cut crystal glasses filled with absinthe. He placed one of the glasses in front of me, and the other in front of my hideous host, and then departed the room. Maldonado raised his glass and toasted "to the Fates that brought us together" before downing his drink in one mouthful.

Following his lead, I lifted my glass to my lips, shut my eyes, and then, with one gulp, swallowed the whole of its sticky, emerald green contents. The bittersweet flavor of wormwood and licorice instantly invaded my taste buds and plunged down my throat like a demon ablaze. My eyes popped open and I began to cough, much to the amusement of my disfigured host, whose howls of laughter cut into me like the razor-sharp teeth of some great predatory beast about to close around its prey. Soon, his laughter turned cruel and mocking.

Anger bubbled up inside of me. "Señor Maldonado. I did not come all this way to be laughed at by a…" I stopped myself before completing my sentence.

Maldonado's laughter came to a screeching halt. "By a what?" he demanded to know. "Say it. Don't hold back your tongue. By a *freak*? By a *monster*?"

I looked away in regret.

"Yes, I am all those things—and more," he admitted, sounding almost proud. "My affliction, as horrible as it is, has bestowed upon me one special gift—the ability to see people for what they really are. I am, on the outside, what you are on the inside."

Insulted, I pounded my fist upon the table, causing my empty glass to jump. "How dare you!" I growled. "Just who do you think you are to speak to me in that way? I've traveled a far distance and put my life in peril, all for the sake of the precious thing that was promised to me! And all you've done since I've arrived in this godforsaken house of yours is hurl insults and sicken me with your nasty absinthe and even nastier face. I demand that you bring the precious thing to me now, Maldonado, or else I will leave! I will not permit you to toy with me any further!"

At that moment, Doctor Alazar walked into the dining room, carrying a small wooden box. Without saying a word, he placed it on the table, next to my empty glass. I saw him give a nod to Maldonado, who nodded back as if they shared some great and portentous secret between them. I don't know why, but I found their silent exchange a bit unsettling. The doctor stood nearby, his arms folded across his chest, his dark eyes fixed upon me, observing my every move.

I looked down at the box. It was unembellished, and I could discern that it had some age to it. *Could it be a trinket box?* I wondered. I resisted the urge to open it. *What small treasures might it hold?* My curiosity blossomed, leading me to ask, "What is this?"

"It's something that will change your life forever," the doctor replied.

Maldonado began to wheel himself towards me, a grin of madness plastered across his subhuman face. "Inside that box is a simple object possessing more worth than any crown worn by the kings and queens of this world. Go ahead and open the box. Feast your eyes upon the precious thing within!"

I took a deep breath and lifted up the lid, unsure of what to expect. Tendrils of dread crept into my soul when I saw what was inside the red velvet lined box...a surgical scalpel! "What kind of sick joke is this?" I demanded to know, fearing the answer I might receive.

"It is the wand of transformation—the maker of miracles!" Maldonado whooped. "In the right hand, it is a work of art! Surely, being an artist, you can appreciate that!" The sickening barnacle-like growths that reigned upon his face and hands began gnashing their tiny, claw-like teeth in unison as though demanding to be fed. "You should feel honored," he added. "It has chosen *you* to be the one!" His foul laughter echoed all around me.

It became clear to me then that Maldonado was undeniably insane, most likely driven into his present state of lunacy by his ungodly affliction. His willing henchman, Doctor Alazar, I suspected of being equally psychotic or driven by evil impulses—perhaps a combination of both.

Fearing for my life, I grabbed the scalpel and sprung from my chair, yelling, "Stay away from me! I'll slash your throats if you try to stop me from leaving! I swear by God

Almighty!"

I suddenly felt quite strange. Lightheaded. Nauseous. A cold sweat beaded on my forehead as my vision began to blur. All at once the room seemed to be tilting and swirling. Panic raced through my veins as I arrived at the realization that my drink—that unsavory absinthe—had been drugged or poisoned. I felt doomed. Like a drunkard on a binge, I stumbled from the dining room into the hall, clutching at the walls for support...walls that seemed to be closing in on me.

The last thing I remember seeing before my dwindling strength abandoned me and I plummeted into the abyss of narcosis was the frozen stare of the raven's black eyes…those terrible, lifeless, black eyes.

As I slowly regained consciousness, my mind unclouded, and I found myself lying naked and supine in what appeared to be an old, subterranean dungeon. The chamber was dank, and lit only by the glow of torches in iron sconces mounted to its stony walls. The sound of dripping water echoed in my ears. *Where am I? Is this a dream?* I asked myself. *Why can't I wake up?* I attempted to move but something prevented me from doing so. I then realized, with horror, that my wrists and ankles had been shackled to a bed with leather restraints—the kind used in psychiatric wards to keep violent patients under control.

"Help! Help!" I cried at the top of my lungs. "Somebody help me!"

I persisted with my cries for help until they left me hoarse. After a while there came the sound of nearing footsteps, followed by the clanging of keys, and then the groan of an iron door opening. Doctor Alazar, wearing a blood-spattered, green surgical gown, approached my bed.

"Alazar! I demand that you release me at once!" I ordered, struggling furiously against my restraints. "You have no right or reason to hold me here against my will!"

"You ask for the impossible," came his reply. They

weren't the words I wanted to hear. "Your destiny has been ordained by the precious thing. You will never leave here alive, so you may as well resign yourself to your fate."

I pleaded with him, "I swear to you I won't go to the police. I won't tell anyone. You have my word of honor. I beg you, just let me go!"

All at once, a searing pain shot through my belly, causing me to yelp like a wounded dog. It was then that I noticed the white gauze bandages wrapped around my midsection, a spot of crimson seeping through. "*Dios mio!*"

"Don't be alarmed. Your surgery was a success," Alazar asserted, his words freezing the current of my blood. "You'll heal quicker if you refrain from distressing yourself. You need to rest. I'll bring you a sedative—chloral hydrate. It will induce sleep and help treat your post-surgical pain."

"Surgery?" My heart rate soared. "What surgery? What the hell have you done to me?" I cried out, horrified to learn I had been operated on. My panic-stricken words echoed off the stone walls of my prison.

"I performed a partial hepatectomy to remove part of your liver," Alazar explained, in a nonchalant doctorly fashion. "The procedure, which I've performed dozens of times on behalf of Señor Maldonado, will in no way compromise your health. Rest assured, you can survive with just under half of your liver, and it will regrow to its full size within a matter of months, in time for your next hepatectomy."

"You're mad!" I bellowed. "Why, for the love of God, would you do this to me? For what possible reason?"

"I will show you, and then you'll understand."

Alazar departed the dungeon, and returned a short while later, armed with a hypodermic syringe and accompanied by a well-favored man possessing a glowing complexion and an imposing presence. Something about him struck a chord of familiarity within me. He stood at my bedside and thanked me for my 'liver donation.' I gasped with shock, unable to believe my own ears. I knew that voice all too well, that cruel, horrible, laughing voice. It belonged to Maldonado! My brain swam with confusion.

"How can such a thing be possible? This has to be the work of the Devil!" I shouted.

Alazar explained to me that he had developed an effective, albeit unconventional, treatment for Maldonado's rare disease—a poultice made from fresh human liver, infused with certain restorative botanicals from the Far East, and a nitrogen-containing polysaccharide extracted from the exoskeletons of anthropods. However, the results were not lasting, and new barnacle-like growths would form on his skin after a few months, requiring additional poultice treatments.

He then injected the sedative into my arm, despite my howls of protest, and my thoughts moldered as a deep, dreamless sleep gradually enshrouded my faculties like a spider wrapping its prey in silk.

As the days slowly drifted into weeks, which slowly drifted into months, and then years. I remained a prisoner in Maldonado's dungeon, supplying him with fresh liver for his infernal poultices, and regretting that fateful day when I laid my eyes on that accursed bottle beckoning to me on the shore of the sea. With no hope for escape, I prayed each night for death to visit me as I slept, only to be cursed at sunrise with another day of agony.

In the autumn of the third year, a slice from Doctor Alazar's scalpel left me with an incision that festered. The poison slowly spread through my arteries and veins, and the hundreds of prayers I had prayed were finally made manifest. I welcomed the final beat of my heart and the last gasp of air from my lungs. I climbed out of my lifeless anatomy like a cicada emerging from a desiccated chrysalis. How odd it was to look upon my discarded shell of bones and flesh lying before me in shackles. It was unsettling at first, but I soon came to accept it. Unlike my previous body, which was bound by the laws of the physical world, I found my new form to be ethereal and unfettered. I was free at last, or so I thought.

Death was nothing at all like I had imagined it to be. There were no angels blowing trumpets, no white light beckoning me into the next world, no spirits of departed loved ones waiting to greet me. I bid farewell to myself, and departed the dungeon, passing effortlessly through the heavy, padlocked door of my cell as if it weren't there. I soon discovered, with delight, that I could pass through solid walls with the same amount of ease.

I ran from the villa, drinking in the sweet taste of freedom. It was intoxicating. The grand roar of the ocean, as it broke and foamed and retreated again, filled my senses like an enchanted drumbeat.

And then I sighted Maldonado at the edge of the cliff, tossing one of his absinthe bottles into the sea below. Hungering for revenge, I dashed towards him, intent on shoving my adversary over the edge of the precipice and watching him plunge to his death on the sharp and jagged rocks below. But, just as I had passed through the doors and walls, so too did I pass through Maldonado's body. I went over the cliff and fell through the air, spinning like a feather in a tempest. It was without pain that I made impact with the rocks below. I attempted to climb my way back up, but as my hands reached for the top, I found myself instantly back on the beach below, as though transported by some mysterious, invisible force. Rattled with confusion, I tried climbing again. The outcome was the same.

I made my way down the strip of golden sand that stretched endlessly to the horizon until I heard the sound of traffic. I tried calling out for help, but found my ghostly mouth emitted no sound. I began climbing up the rocks leading up to the coastal highway above, and as I neared the top, I found myself returned to the beach again. *How could this be?* I began running, desperate to find a way off the beach, but there was none. I ran, and I ran, and I ran. There was nothing else I could do.

Feeling expended, I fell to the sand and gazed out to sea, trying to make sense of things. And then a foamy wave broke on the shore, depositing a corked bottle at my feet. I picked it up and saw that it contained a message. I contemplated tossing the bottle back into the sea, but my curiosity haunted me like a fiend. I smashed it against one of the rocks dotting the beach, unraveled the scroll, and read the message written upon it. Horror rushed through me. I recognized the handwriting. It was Sergio's. His words simply said, "Welcome to eternity." I then realized with terrible clarity that my liberation from my flesh, bestowed by whatever angel of mercy saw fit to release me from my earthly suffering, was actually my descent into Hell.

DUST TO DUST

"You can't see them," I said to the squirming girl. "But trust me, my dear, they *are* there. I know this for a fact. They're all around us— watching… hungering… waiting for their moment to feast upon human skin. Why, a sweet, young thing like you is nothing more than a tasty morsel to them! That's why they need to be destroyed. And I do my best. Don't fool yourself into thinking they aren't there simply because you can't see them with your naked eye. I guarantee you, tonight, as you lie sleeping in the darkness, your mind entangled in the strands of a dream, those things will be crawling all over your body and your pretty little face. Oh, there will be thousands, if not millions of them, feasting on your dead skin!"

The girl's watery blue eyes widened. She opened her delicate pink mouth and emitted a high-pitched shriek before running from the room, terrified.

Humming a tune to myself, I picked up my rag and can of lemon-scented furniture polish and happily resumed dusting the intricately carved antique tables and chairs that lined the walls in the great hall of the English manor house.

A few moments later, I heard loud and hurried footsteps ring out as cantankerous Mrs. Ella Strumpshaw stormed into the room, a scowl upon her perpetually unpleasant face. She marched right over to me, came to an abrupt halt, and crossed her arms. Rage flickered in her beady eyes.

"How dare you upset my granddaughter!" she hissed with caustic fury. "I will not tolerate having that young girl frightened out of her wits by you and your idiotic stories about flesh-eating monsters! Is that understood?"

"Yes, ma'am," I replied to the old harpy in my humblest sounding voice. "But begging your pardon, ma'am, they weren't idiotic monster stories that I told to the child. I was merely explaining to her the facts about dust mites. A child of her age should be made aware of such things. That is, if she's to be raised properly."

"Of all the impertinence!" thundered the old woman, as a vein on her temple pulsed violently. "Need I remind you, miss, that you are nothing more than a paid domestic servant here? You've been in my employ for less than two weeks, and in that short period of time you've demonstrated to me your insolence a number of times. You've traumatized my granddaughter—an impressionable child of refined sensibilities—upset the household on numerous occasions, and managed to unnerve the members of my Ladies Auxiliary Society with that strange behavior you exhibit. I will not tolerate strange behavior in this house!"

Feigning shame, I hung my head and noticed a thin layer of dust had formed on the floor. It appeared to be moving as though it were alive and breathing. Unable to look away from such a peculiar sight, I watched as the dust particles moved about. They seemed to be trying to spell out a message.

"Well?" Mrs. Strumpshaw asked, angrily. "What have you to say for yourself? Can you give me one good reason why I shouldn't terminate your employment? Well? Speak up, girl! I'm a busy woman and haven't got all day for dawdling housekeepers."

"I'm terribly sorry, ma'am. Please don't discharge me," I groveled, my eyes remaining fixed on the moving dust to which Mrs. Strumpshaw was clearly oblivious. "I promise to amend my ways. Honest I will. You won't have any more trouble out of me."

I glanced up and searched Mrs. Strumpshaw's gargoyle face for a reaction. I didn't think it was possible for her sourpuss features to look any sourer than they normally did; but, to my amazement, she proved me wrong. In her disgusted sounding voice, she barked out an order for me to return to my duties and then she strolled away, her persnickety nose high in the air.

After breathing a sigh of relief, my eyes returned to the floor; I could scarcely believe what I was seeing! Incredibly, the dust had formed itself into a single, six-letter word, which I knew was meant for my eyes only. Was it some kind of warning? Was it an omen of things to come? The message was all in capital letters. It said: MURDER.

It was shortly after seven-thirty that evening when I retired to my quarters to knit myself a lovely new dust cloth. I soon felt my eyelids growing heavy. With a yawn, I set my knitting on top of the small table next to my bed, burrowed underneath the covers, and switched off the light. No sooner had the blackness consumed the room, than the back of my head sank into the marshmallow softness of my pillow and I drifted off into slumber.

Being the light sleeper that I am, I was awakened by the sound of heavy, creaking footsteps crossing the floor. My eyes sprung open. I gasped. Slowly creeping toward me in the darkness was a hulking figure! Like a mad piston, my heart began to race. My chest filled with dread. My mouth opened and I attempted to unleash a scream, but no sound escaped my trembling lips. I tried to spring from the bed and make a run for it, but I was unable to move. I was paralyzed from head to toe with fear. I suddenly felt a man's hand clamp itself over my mouth.

"Shhh. Don't make a sound and I won't hurt you. Do we have a deal?"

Darkness masked the man's face, but I recognized the whispering voice. It belonged to none other than Mrs. Strumpshaw's ogre of a husband, Lyle—or 'Vile Lyle' as I surreptitiously referred to him. I could also smell the pungent odor of alcohol on his breath. Holding back my vomit, I nodded my head and he cautiously removed his hand from mouth.

"That's a good girl," he said, as though praising a dog for its obedience. "Now, I've a little proposition to make that I'm confident will benefit the both of us. But my wife must never find out. Is that understood?"

I again nodded my head, too stunned to be able to form words. By now my eyes had adjusted themselves to the dark and I could make out Mr. Strumpshaw's aesthetically unappealing face.

"It seems my wife is rather displeased with your work ethic. You apparently did or said something today that ruffled the old girl's tail feathers, and she's hellbent on having you fired." A muffled chuckle escaped his mouth. "Now, I can see to it that your housekeeping position here is a secure one… *if* you're nice to me."

He began to stroke my hair with his wrinkled hand. His touch made me cringe.

"If you aren't nice," he continued, "then I'm afraid I'll have no other alternative but to let my wife dismiss you. I'm sure you wouldn't want that, now would you? The choice is up to you."

Rage coursed through my veins, negating any fear I had felt up to that point. "I'd rather be fired, or even dead, than to let a vile pig like you touch my flesh! I'm sure your wife would be very interested to hear about your sordid little proposition. And don't think I won't hesitate to tell her.

Now get out of this room at once before I start screaming on the top of my lungs!"

The vile one snickered. "Go right ahead. I'll simply tell her that you're mad—out of your mind. It won't take much to convince her of that. She already suspects you of lunacy and won't believe a word you say. However, *the police* will believe *me* when I tell them that I caught you trying to steal my wife's expensive jewelry."

It was at that moment I reached my breaking point. I slapped Mr. Strumpshaw across the face with all my might. He stood there for a moment, appearing stunned by my physical reaction, before returning the slap. He proceeded to rip the front of my nightgown open, exposing my breasts. I began to scream but he climbed on top of me and covered my mouth with one hand, while hurriedly unzipping his trousers with the other.

My stomach was churning from the stench of his fermented breath panting into my face. I felt so helpless… doomed. And then something snapped deep within me and I was overcome by a strange numbness. I felt as though I were hovering outside of my body, watching my fingers wrap themselves around the sharp knitting needle sitting atop my bedside table and drive it into the grunting man's eye.

As he howled with pain, I pushed him off me and he tumbled onto the floor with blood pumping out his impaled eye. I switched on the light and made a dash for the door. I suddenly felt the drunken man's hand latch onto one of my ankles and he pulled me down to join him on the floor.

"You'll pay for this, dearly, you goddamn bitch!" Mr. Strumpshaw vowed. "I'll see that you rot in prison for the rest of your life!"

I yanked the knitting needle from his eye. "You won't be seeing anything!" I cried out, plunging the needle into the bastard's other eye and then pulling it out, a warm gush of blood staining my hand.

Mr. Strumpshaw howled again and began rolling around on the floor like a man possessed, clutching at his bloody eye sockets and hurling a score of profanities and threats at me that I knew he would never carry out. I felt my fist tighten around the knitting needle, as though it had a will of its own, and I thrust it into the man's heart. It was like driving a stake into a vampire. I watched as his arms flailed and his body spasmed violently. He gasped a final breath and then he was dead.

Reality melted all around me like winter's frosty kiss when the sun's swelter brings its demise. Nothing seemed real. My mind was afloat in a dream-like haze, and I was unable to feel my feet touching the floor as I walked to the bathroom to wash the blood from my hands. I suddenly spotted a figure standing in the doorway that connected my sleeping quarters to the hallway. It was human in its shape, but not composed of flesh and bone as you or I. Rather, it was a composition of millions—perhaps even trillions—of dust mites. I stared at it, mesmerized. Without a word, this horrible creature beckoned me to follow it. I felt like I was in some sort of a hypnotic trance, and I obeyed without resistance. It led me through the dark halls and stairwells of the manor house until we arrived at the master bedroom.

Mrs. Strumpshaw was fast asleep on her king-size bed, an opened hardcover copy of *Genocide for the Masses* resting on her chest. I stealthily crept over to her bed and gathered up the book, taking great care not to wake the snoring she-beast underneath it. Well aware that the deed I was destined to carry out would most likely thwart any chances of a raise, I swung the book with all my might into Mrs. Strumpshaw's face, instantly transforming her persnickety nose into a bloody rubbish heap of shattered nasal bones, fractured cartilage, and mangled mucous membranes. Her eyes flew open and a hair-raising scream vaulted from her lungs. I immediately grabbed one of her satin-encased pillows and pushed it down over her face.

Pillows are ideal breeding grounds for dust mites. Did you know that approximately one-third of your pillow's weight contains dead skin, dust mites, and their poop? It's disgusting, but I assure you quite true.

Gasping for air, Mrs. Strumpshaw thrashed about like a fish against a hook, pounding on my arms with her fists and clawing at my flesh with those perfectly manicured fingernails of hers. The harder that old witch fought against me, the harder I mashed that shiny pillow into her face, relentless in my endeavor to put her out of her misery.

I don't remember exactly how long it took before Mrs. Strumpshaw stopped struggling. It seemed like it took forever to smother the life out of her, and I recall my hands and wrists growing tired from the constant pressure. I read somewhere that it takes the average human seven minutes to die from complete loss of oxygen intake. Mrs. Strumpshaw, however, wasn't your average person; she was rotten to the core. That kind doesn't die easily. You have to work a bit harder to put them down.

I have no clear memory of what happened after that. It's like a light bulb in my brain switched off and everything faded to black.

When the police arrived at the manor house the following morning, they were met by the smell of death. With their guns drawn, they followed a trail of smeared blood leading from the master bedroom down to the drawing room, where they found me diligently performing my daily cleaning duties as usual. I'm proud to say there wasn't a single speck of dust anywhere to be found! The officers, however, were aghast to see Mrs. Strumpshaw's disfigured and decapitated head mounted atop my dust mop's wooden handle. However, did it get there, I wonder?

It took them a little longer to find Mr. Strumpshaw's head, which had mysteriously gone missing. It was eventually located when one of the policemen, who needed to relieve his bladder, raised the lid of the toilet. As soon as

I heard his horrified cry of "Oh my God!" resonate from the bathroom, I knew he had hit the jackpot!

I was arrested, jailed, and put on trial, which was given unprecedented coverage in newspapers from London to New York. The press, in their perpetual pursuit of sensationalism, dubbed me "The Killer Maid." Personally, I would have preferred something with a bit more panache—The Dust Mite Slayer Extraordinaire has a much nicer ring to it, wouldn't you agree? But I digress.

Getting back to the trial, the entire ordeal was a humiliating experience to say the least. Each day, from sun up to sun down, my assertion of innocence fell upon deaf ears; my lifetime devotion to mastering the intricacies of housekeeping impressed not a single soul in the courtroom. It soon became evident to me that everybody involved in the case—from the lawyers to the judge to the men and women of the jury—all deemed me to be insane. *Insane*! How absurd. The truth of the matter is that *those* people are the ones whose sanity must be questioned! I am the sanest person I've ever met.

But, nonetheless, I was sent away to an asylum to live amongst the blathering bedlamites and other pitiable wretches cast out of the so-called "normal" world. It was a dismal place, to say the least. The padded, dungeon-like room, where I was kept in the beginning, reeked of urine, vomit, and despair. Outside the locked metal door with its barred rectangular window, a seemingly endless corridor, the color of green stinkbugs, reverberated with endless sobbing, screaming, moaning and mumbling. I was forced to undergo electro-convulsive therapy, hydrotherapy, insulin coma therapy, and an array of terrifying mind-altering drugs. It was enough to drive anyone stark raving mad! Not to mention all those revolting dust particles floating about everywhere, defiantly clinging to everything in sight, mercilessly taunting me, whispering their foul obscenities in my ears.

But all that is behind me now and envelops me with a feeling of un-reality when I think back upon it. In a curious way, it's almost like the fading fragments of a hazy dream when rays of morning sunlight spill down the narrow streets of the city and furiously break through the cracks of the shutters.

A cold wind tousled my hair as I climbed the brick steps leading to the front door of the massive English Tudor mansion. My hand was reaching for the heavy iron doorknocker when something caught my eye. I paused and looked down, and that's when I spotted the newspaper lying near the door, dead leaves gathered around it. I knelt down to pick it up. A headline on its front page screamed out in bold, black letters: KILLER MAID ESCAPES ASYLUM AFTER GRISLY MURDER RAMPAGE! Below it, the subhead read: Two Doctors, Three Nurses and Security Guard Dead.

Grisly indeed, but I assure you, dear friend, it was most necessary. Dust mites are multiplying in every nook and cranny as we speak.

I've always been a huge advocate for occupational therapy. Point in case: If it had not been for my therapist thoughtfully assigning me to light housekeeping chores around the asylum, heaven only knows how long I might have remained a prisoner trapped behind those high iron gates and walls of moss-covered stone. A shot of aerosol furniture polish in the eyes to induce temporary blindness, followed by a good bashing to the side of the head with the can, works wonders in dire situations.

Whoever would have guessed that furniture polish could be so wonderfully lethal?

Accompanying the lurid news story was a large, black and white picture of yours truly—and not at all a very flattering one, I don't mind telling you. I truly wanted to spare my potential new employer any needless consternation, so as a courtesy to him, I folded up the newspaper and tucked it safely away into one of the compartments of my large handbag. It would have been very inconsiderate of me not to.

With that out of the way, I proceeded to knock on the door. A minute or two passed before the door opened partway and a bespectacled man with a graying mustache and balding head peered out at me.

"Mister Dangledown?" I enquired.

He nodded his head.

I introduced myself, using a fictitious name, of course. "I'm here to apply for the housekeeping position you have advertised in the newspaper. I'm experienced, dependable, and confident that you won't find a housekeeper more dedicated to the ongoing fight against dust than I am."

The door opened fully and the man motioned with his hand for me to enter. My footsteps echoed as I stepped into the expansive foyer. The walls were covered with brown paneling and aged tapestries, and the cold marble beneath my feet was what I envisioned the floor inside a mausoleum to be like. An antique oak table with an octagonal top stood in the middle of the room. Above it, hung a medieval-looking chandelier of black wrought iron like the sword of Damocles.

I could sense there were dust mites lurking about in the shadowy corners.

"My, what a grand old house you have here," I complimented as my eyes scanned the opulent surroundings. "And so tastefully decorated, I might add. I just adore working in these old mansions. They possess such charm and character... and copious amounts of dust. But that, of course, is the reason I'm here... to rid you of your dust problem. You might say I'm on a mission."

Mister Dangledown shut the front door and locked it. "You sound perfect for the job," he declared. "Just the type of housekeeper I've been searching for. Good help is so difficult to find, and to keep, these days! I've gone through

44

so many housekeepers in the past few months I've lost count. You see, they just keep dying and I have to keep burying their bodies in the rose garden. It's turned into quite a cemetery out there! But it's getting to the point where I'm running out of room."

"I just adore roses," I said.

Mister Dangledown informed me that I was hired and shook my hand. That's when I noticed the dried blood underneath his fingernails. My new employer smiled at me, and I smiled back at him. I instinctively knew we were going to get along like a house on fire.

THE MADDENING CRY

England—1647

Matthew opened his eyes and stared into the thick darkness that surrounded him. His slumber had not been peaceful. Despite being the finest witch-finder in all of England and an executioner both feared and reviled by peasantry and nobility alike, he was a man who always slept quite soundly. His dreams were often made pleasant by the recollected sights and sounds of his victims' final agonies. However, this night was different for him. A horrific nightmare, unlike any his deep and soothing sleep had ever given rise to, now tormented his mind with a scene that struck terror within his righteous heart and swathed his body in a cold rigor.

In a frightful and most peculiar dream, he found himself lying still upon a bed with his arms crossed over his chest in the manner of a corpse. Six women, each attired in sweeping gowns of black crepe, surrounded him. Their hands were ashen in color, and veils of black lace covered their faces. They suddenly erupted in shrieks and loud disconcerting wails that sliced through the inky emptiness of the night like the banshees of Irish folklore presaging a death. Matthew was desirous to silence the congregation of noisemakers, for he found their clamor most maddening and abhorrent to his ears.

He attempted to vocalize his objection to their ungodly cries to no avail. He then heard the sound of footsteps and watched as two burly men approached his bed, their faces leathery and expressionless, and the garments covering their bodies void of any color but black. The women made haste to step away from his bed yet persisted in their dreadful wailing as the men took hold of his body with their gloved hands. Without uttering a word, they lifted it up from the straw mattress and then carried it to a waiting coffin.

Filled with terror, Matthew attempted to free himself from their grips but was alarmed to find that the power to move his arms and legs was foregone. He made an effort to open his mouth and cry out; however, his lips would not part for him despite his best efforts. His entire body was frozen and rigid in a paralytic state from which he was unable to snap out of. The sight and sound of the coffin lid closing above him filled his eyes and ears, and then, in the ensuing darkness, he heard shovelfuls of earth raining down upon the top of the lid, one after another after another, until a deathly silence overtook the noise and the nightmare came to an abrupt and merciful end.

Matthew awoke drenched in a cold perspiration that clung to his clammy flesh like droplets of dew on morning leaves and blades of grass. He inhaled deeply and then sighed with relief. It was simply a bad dream, he reassured himself. Nothing more than a mere figment of his imagination. The thought soon crossed his mind that his nightmare could very well have been the doings of some vengeful witch versed in the evil ways of poppet magic or some other diablerie.

He then let out a hearty laugh, confident that he would sooner or later discover the true identity of this creature and, with the purification of a blazing fire, command her corrupted, devil-fornicating soul to an eternal damnation in the fiery bowels of hell.

He truly believed himself to be a pious man, despite the sadistic pleasure he derived from the brutal acts of torture that he inflicted upon the naked bodies of accused witches and warlocks in order to obtain their confessions. It mattered not if their bleeding lips denounced the devil and swore their allegiance to Almighty God, especially if witnesses had presented spectral evidence against the accused. These minions of Old Scratch, as he liked to call the Prince of Darkness, thought themselves to be clever and well-versed in the ways of trickery.

However, the witch-finder prided himself to be a man immune to satanic subterfuge. With each bloodcurdling scream and with each cry of agonizing pain, his heart would pump with frenzied excitement. And even greater would be his arousal, bringing a delicious tingling to his loins whenever his cruel, but necessary, duties as a servant of God to eradicate the scourge of witches from the land led him to pretty-faced young sorceresses possessing succulent bosoms and buttocks.

Often, he would have his way with them before his tortures disfigured their attributes and rendered them repulsive to the sight, despite his vows of fidelity that were spoken when he took Elspeth Goode, the unsullied daughter of the local blacksmith, as his wife.

Elspeth was a hard-working, God-fearing lass who could be found each Sunday reciting her prayers in Church. A comely young woman of amiable nature, she was fair of face with long tresses of pale yellow cascading over her milky-white shoulders. Her eyes, green as those of a water sprite, sparkled with innocence. Her cheeks were pink with a childlike quality, and her lips soft like the petals of roses in early summer.

From the moment he first laid eyes upon her, Matthew was determined to have her all to himself. After a brief courtship that lasted for less than half a year, they were wed.

It was during his third year of marriage to the young Elspeth when a rumor that she used charms to bewitch a neighbor's cow began to circulate throughout the small village in which they resided. She was arrested and made to stand trial, shackled and bearing the bruises, welts, and lacerations inflicted upon her flesh by her very own husband in his determination to force a confession from her.

With tears flowing from her once-sparkling eyes, Elspeth pleaded for him to let her live. "Matthew, please! I beg you, spare my life!" she cried out. "I am no more a witch than you are a warlock! For the love of all that is holy, please end this cruelty! I beg you, my husband! Have mercy! I cannot bear this agony much longer!"

In spite of her rounds of torture, which included whippings, the crushing of her thumbs and big toes with a thumbscrew, and the searing of the nipples of her tender, youthful breasts with a red-hot iron poker, Elspeth refused to confess to being a follower of the Old Religion. Her stubborn refusal to admit that she was in league with the devil infuriated Matthew, and no matter how she wept and pleaded for her life, he took no pity upon her.

Not a single tear did Matthew shed on that dismal day in October when he stood with his torch in hand and calmly watched as his battered wife was paraded barefoot through the muddy, dung-filled streets in a manner unfit for either man or beast. She was then dragged, screaming, to a large wooden stake erected in the heart of the village to meet her gruesome fate.

"Burn the witch! Burn the witch!" chanted the villagers, some throwing stones and clods of mud, and all hungering for slaughter. As the cruel chanting of the men, women, and children grew louder and fiercer, an icy wind arose. It howled frightfully through the branches of the trees as if hundreds of witches were careening on their broomsticks through the air around them.

Elspeth was nearly unrecognizable, bearing little resemblance to the eye-pleasing, young maiden the witch-finder had taken as his bride just a few years prior. Her face, once youthful and radiant with zest, was now haggard and abandoned of all hope. Her eyes were swollen shut, given her the appearance of a pummeled boxer. Her nose was broken, her lips cracked and blistered, her hair matted with sweat and dried blood. Her mouth fell open to reveal a number of chipped and bloodstained teeth. Some were missing altogether, having been pulled out by tongs in the torture chamber. Her torso and all of its appendages bore the lacerations and burn marks inflicted upon her by her once-loving spouse.

After she had been securely strapped to the stake with heavy ropes that bit into her wrists and ankles, drawing blood, Matthew tossed his torch at her, setting ablaze the straw and branches and logs that had been piled around the base of the stake. Elspeth's screams, along with the wild cheering of the bloodthirsty mob that had gathered to watch, could be heard throughout the countryside as the hungry flames of the bonfire engulfed her twitching body and her flesh sizzled and burned. The crisp morning air was soon fouled with a putrid-smelling black smoke.

"Blasphemous heathen witch," Matthew grumbled out loud to himself, his words almost taking on the tone of a hissing snake.

Elspeth's execution solidified Matthew's reputation as a virtuous servant unto the Lord. It also sent a clear message that no disciple of the devil would ever be spared the cleansing fire of God's wrath so long as he worked under the esteemed title of "witch-finder general." And that included any witch brazen enough to cast her wicked glamours over him.

As he watched the charred remains of his wife crumble and fall into the glowing embers, he made the sign of the cross and spewed out, "May God have mercy upon her wicked soul." He applauded himself for keeping a solemn face despite the urge of his mouth to rise into a wide smile.

With their bloodlust satisfied, at least for the time being, the crowd began to disperse. Within minutes, the village square was desolate and quiet, save for the occasional pops and crackling sounds emanating from the dying embers.

With his own bloodlust satiated, Matthew turned and made his way down the muddy streets of the village, stopping at a tavern to indulge in shepherd's pie and ale before returning home. He was quite pleased with himself for dispatching yet another witch in strict accordance with God's laws. As he ate his meal and downed his ale with gusto, he reflected on his career as a witch-finder. He had executed so many people, mostly women, he was no longer able to keep count, but it was fair to say that the numbers were in the hundreds. He knew, however, that the job with which he had been tasked was far from being over. Witches were everywhere, initiating new members into Satan's secret sect, holding Black Masses, and defying the Christian faith. It was his duty to rid England of the scourge of sorcery, he told himself.

No sooner had he left the tavern, his belly content with food and drink, did he get struck on the small of his back by a rotting corn cob hurled at him by a ragged urchin girl. He stopped and turned his angry gaze upon the dirty-faced child and shook his fist. "Filthy little she-devil!" he bellowed, as the frightened girl took flight down the muddy street. "Be gone with you before a charge of witchcraft is leveled against you!"

Throughout the years following his wife's horrific execution, Matthew gave little thought to her as he continued his righteous reign of terror. He had simply done what needed to be done and felt not the slightest amount of remorse. Immersed in his duties, he had even begun to forget what she looked like. That is, until this very night when he suddenly recalled that the face one of the veiled mourners in his nightmare bore a striking resemblance to Elspeth's. For some reason unknown to him, he found that to be rather disturbing. He tried to return to sleep but was overcome by a feeling of unease. He decided to get out of bed and read his Bible. His favorite passage was in Exodus and said, "Thou shalt not suffer a witch to live." Those were words by which he lived and earned his daily bread.

The witch-finder made a move to sit up, but he immediately discovered that he was unable to raise his torso more than a few inches before being blocked by some strange obstruction that hovered above in the pitch-blackness of his room. Puzzled by the queerness of this thing, he then attempted to turn himself but found there to be what felt like walls close to his sides. He banged upon them a number of times with his fists in a fruitless effort to break through their restraint.

The walls and roof that surrounded him and afforded him little movement were solid and felt to Matthew to be a rough-hewn wood of some type. They gave off dull thuds in response to his blows but were steadfast in their refusal to budge. The air was now growing uncomfortably warm and steamy.

"What ungodly manner of witchery have I fallen under?" Matthew shouted from within his solid cocoon of darkness. "In the name of the Lord, I command that this cursed spell be at once broken!"

A harrowing minute of silence passed. It felt like an eternity.

Matthew again attempted to sit up, confident in the power of his command, but he found that the mysterious blockade that surrounded his body was still in place, unchanged. He repeated his command, his words fueled by his growing ire. But to his dismay, it was again met by a grim silence that burned within his ears. He then began to wonder if perhaps he was still asleep and this strange predicament was nothing more than part of his foul nightmare. The thought brought some comfort to him, and he lay still and silently prayed to wake up. And then came a faint voice from somewhere above. It was ghostly in its tones yet possessed a strange familiarity about it. It whispered his name, again and again, until Matthew's recognition of it made him shudder. It was the voice of Elspeth.

Matthew's heart began to pound like the fists of a thousand corpses demanding vengeance. It palpitated with such a violent fury that it battered his eardrums and threatened to explode from his chest.

"Witch!" Matthew yelled, flames of anger reddening his face and making prominent the blue veins on his temples. "Do you deny that this sorcery is your doing? Why do you not leave me in peace, foul spirit?"

Elspeth replied with a burst of mocking laughter and then growled, "I shall never leave you in peace, dearly departed husband of mine. I shall remain by your side in hell for all of eternity! That I promise you!" Her voice, once lilt and sweet as a young bird's song, was now a voice possessed of a harsh and venomous tonal quality.

"Dearly departed? But I am not yet dead!" Matthew cried, his lips trembling. "I am very much alive. My heart within my chest continues to beat, albeit in somewhat of a flurry at present." His voice suddenly took on an audacious tone. "I am a servant unto the Lord, and Heaven has reserved a place for my soul."

"Yes, Matthew," Elspeth agreed. "Indeed, you are not yet one of the dead as I am; that much is true. But your time approaches with haste. As for the soul of which you speaketh, you do not possess one. And the only place reserved for you is in hell!" Her laughter once again arose like a tempest, filling Matthew with a sense of dread.

"Hold your tongue, filthy witch!" Matthew cried out, infuriated by the dead woman's insolence. "You are but a fabricator of untruths. Why do you persist in tormenting me in this manner? Are the fires of hell not hot enough to keep you from bewitching my mind with a nightmare of my own burial?"

"Nightmare?" Elspeth chuckled. She found the witch-finder's incomprehension to be a most amusing thing. "No nightmare has plagued your sleep, my husband... my murderer." She went on to explain, "The mourners your eyes saw were quite real. The undertakers who attended to your seemingly lifeless body were quite real. Your burial, as the passage of time will soon convince you, was no figment of the imagination."

Panic had now set in, and Matthew's mind scrambled to form cohesive thoughts. A petrifying numbness was pervading his limbs, deadening his sense of touch, and he was drawing his breaths in short, stabby gasps like a panting dog in hot weather. "But how can that be possible?" he demanded, now realizing that the wood surrounding him actually was a coffin. "How can I continue to breathe as a living man, yet be buried in the cold and dark of the earth as the dead?"

"Don't you know, Matthew?" asked Elspeth in a taunting manner. "When you condemned me as a witch and took pleasure in watching me burn alive, you forgot to take care to remember that I was the only other person who knew the dreadful secret of your cataleptic curse. I'm afraid you've been mistaken for the dead and buried alive, and no one is wise to that fact, save for you and me. It's just our little secret, my love." She roared with vengeful laughter.

Matthew's maddening cry rang out and echoed inside his ears, nearly deafening him. He furiously pounded his fists on the unyielding coffin lid and frantically tried to claw his way out of the wooden funerary box until his fingers were broken and bloodied. Sweat was flowing with profusion from out of his forehead, running down his face, stinging his eyes and bringing a salty taste to his lips. His chest heaved as he desperately gasped for air.

Six feet above, the sound of Elspeth's laughter echoed through the mist-filled graveyard as her ghost tossed a bouquet of wilted flowers on top of her husband's fresh grave, which was marked only by a small wooden cross that stood slightly bent. With a smile on her vaporous face, she turned and slowly walked away as lifeless brown leaves danced in the icy wind. She paused for a moment to take one final look at Matthew's gravesite.

"Enjoy your eternity in hell," she hissed before vanishing into the ethers.

REINDEER GAMES

Faith stared at the colorful lights strung on the drooping spruce that stood in the corner of the isolated cabin, sap slowly bleeding from its axed trunk. Here it was, Christmas Eve. She had already ripped open her flesh-covered gift, and now, as usual, every inch of her body ached with boredom. "She didn't put up much of a fight, did she?" she said, almost in a yawn. "Not like the two before her. It was almost as if that bitch wanted us to torture and kill her. Some Christmas present."

She lit up a Marlboro and returned her gaze to the string of tiny bulbs, filling her eyes with flashings of green, yellow, blue, and her favorite color: red.

Outside, a light snow had begun to fall upon the mountains, turning white the bright crimson path of bloodstained snow leading from the cabin to the secluded spot in the dense of the forest where Faith's boyfriend, Wayne, had dumped the butchered body of the young woman he called 'the plaything.' That's what he liked to call the women whose lives he took great pleasure in snuffing out: playthings. They had no names, no identities, no relevance or importance. He regarded them as less than human. They were simply playthings to him, existing only to satisfy his brutal and demented desires.

Oblivious to the fevered, baleful barking of a hound that sprung up from somewhere in the near distance, Wayne wrapped his bloodstained hand around the bottle of Jack Daniel's that sat on the counter next to the sink, poured some whiskey into a shot glass, and downed it in one gulp. "The next one will be better, Faith," he promised. "Wait until you see the games I've got planned for her." He drifted into an almost trance-like state, enraptured in dark fantasy, as the frantic fit of barking turned into a single yelp, which silence quickly devoured.

Nuzzling the back of her head into her pillow, Faith shut her eyes and remembered a time, not very long ago, when Wayne was enraptured by her and her alone. But when his brutal undertakings with his female victims graduated to a sexual level, all of that seemed to change. When confronting Wayne about it, his reaction was one of anger and he threatened that she would 'meet the same fate as the others' if she ever attempted to leave him.

Having complete control and domination over others, including his partner in crime, was of the utmost importance to Wayne. He was the one in charge, and he intended for it to remain that way. There was no way he would ever permit any woman to manipulate him or stand in the way of his sexual gratification.

Faith opened her eyes and stared up at the wooden beams running across the ceiling. The steady rhythm of Wayne's raspy breathing danced in her ears, lulling as well as repulsing her, and she felt her eyelids grow heavy and droop like the branches of the dying tree in the corner. The car ride from the city to the cabin had been a long and tiresome one, which was now beginning to catch up to her, not to mention the letdown of a less-than-exciting kill. Time seemed to crawl to a stop as she surrendered to the encroaching drowsiness.

Her delicate, creamy features took on an almost angelic appearance as she slept. One might even use the word innocent if one didn't know any better. However, no visions of sugarplums danced in her head—only brutal scenes of torture and murder most savage.

There suddenly came a loud thump at the cabin's door. It was followed by another loud thump and what sounded like a sharp object scraping against the wood.

The bedsprings creaked as Faith bolted into a sitting position, a startled look on her face. "What was that?"

With his muscles tensed, Wayne picked up the knife he had used to disembowel the plaything. "It sure as hell ain't Santa Claus," he replied, his voice low. He made his way over to the window at the front of the cabin and peered out into the snowy remains of the afternoon. After a few moments, the bloodlust in his eyes subsided and he shut the curtain.

"There's nothing out there. Whatever it was, it's gone now."

He slithered into the creaking bed and gently ran the tip of the knife across Faith's throat, sliding it down to her cleavage and across her left breast, where is teasingly circled her engorged nipple. The chill of the steel brought a shudder of excitement to the naked girl and she shut her eyes and moaned, arousal building in her loins.

Faith was born with killer looks…and killer instincts. She knew Wayne regarded himself to be her mentor; however, her appetite for murder was roused long before he came into her life. She committed her first killing at the tender age of six when she crept up to her baby brother's crib in the dead of night and quietly smothered the life out of his tiny body with a pillow. The death was attributed to sudden infant death syndrome, and no one was ever the wiser. Her parents never once suspected that their sweet little girl with the rose-colored cheeks and ribboned pigtails could be a psychopath. She was sugar and spice and everything deadly.

Another thump, louder and more violent than the previous ones, sounded at the door, obliterating the couple's excitement. Like before, it was followed by an ominous scraping sound. Another thump came, and then another, and another.

Faith gave a gasp as her eyes widened with fear. An icy chill sprouted a multitude of goosebumps on the flesh of her forearms. She pulled the blanket up to her chin in a futile effort to warm herself.

"Wayne," she spoke in a near whisper. "You don't think, that girl…"

"Don't talk like a fool," Wayne snapped as he vacated the bed and proceeded to the door, the knife clutched tightly in his hand. "I gutted that whore like a fish after you suffocated her with that plastic bag. Trust me on this; she's a slab of lifeless meat. She isn't going to come back from the dead and pound on the goddamn door like some kind of flesh-eating ghoul. This isn't *Night of the Living Dead*."

Faith held her breath and watched with eager attention as Wayne turned the knob and pulled the door open. A rush of cold air spilled into the cabin, ruffling Faith's tousled whorls of peroxide blonde and set tinkling the glass ornaments hanging from the boughs of the slowly dying Christmas tree.

And then her ears detected what sounded like a hammer smacking a block of wood, and she felt her heart beating wildly as Wayne's fingers clawed at the crossbow quarrel protruding from his throat. She gasped as her malevolent swain stumbled backward and fell to the floor, blood spurting from his open mouth and a ghastly choking sound gurgling in his throat. His head cocked to one side, and he stared at the astounded girl, the life dimming in his eyes.

The sound of snow crunching under feet fractured the wintry silence, growing louder as each footstep drew nearer to the open door of the cabin. A man in a snow-crusted, camouflage-print, hunting jacket appeared in the doorway, a crossbow in his gloved hand. He gazed down at Wayne's twitching body for a few moments, amused, before his eyes met Faith's. He emitted a deviant snicker and grinned, revealing four upper anterior teeth capped with gold crowns. The words "Merry Christmas" rolled off his tongue.

Faith bolted from the bed and rushed over to the man in the doorway. She threw her arms around him and joyously exclaimed, "Nick! I was starting to think you weren't going to show up!"

The grinning man embraced Faith, the crossbow still in his hand. "You know me better than that, angel. Have I ever let you down before?"

Faith giggled like a prepubescent girl and shook her head from side to side. She then disengaged from the hug and shut the door, her exposed body eager for the softly crackling logs in the fireplace to ward off the chill that had crept into the cabin. She paused to marvel at the puddle of blood slowly spreading out from underneath Wayne's speared neck, finding it rather amusing how the bright red color matched that of the glass ornaments on the tree. A smile tugged at her lips. This was turning out to be a very special Christmas Eve indeed.

"Get yourself dressed and then we'll haul this useless carcass out back to the woodshed." Nick winked one of his brown eyes. "I'll let you give him the first blow of the axe like I promised. That is, unless you've had second thoughts about doing it."

Faith experienced a perverse tingle race through her body as she threw on a heavy turtleneck sweater decorated with a reindeer and snowflakes.

"Are you kidding me? I've been dreaming of this day for almost a year! I can't wait to give that bastard the Lizzie Borden treatment. No one deserves to be hacked into little pieces more than he does!"

Nick laughed. "That's my girl." He looked down at Wayne. "Serial killing is an art, too exalted for a sloppy, rank amateur like him. To be a success in this business, you need to possess brains and cunning, as well as a lust for murder."

He shifted his gaze back to Faith, who was stepping into a pair of jeans with her back turned to him.

"Stick with me, and together we'll wreak havoc upon this stinking world while satisfying our darkest, most sadistic desires. Like a finely tuned killing machine, we'll rack up our victims in record-breaking numbers! You and me, angel—we'll be more famous than Fred and Rosemary West, Charles Starkweather and Caril Ann Fugate, Paul Bernardo and Karla Homolka, Ian Bradley and Myra Hindley…"

Faith was sitting on the edge of the bed and pulling on her boots when there came another loud thump at the door, followed by a scraping sound. The rosy glow in her cheeks paled, and her mouth dropped open.

Nick turned and stared at the door. "What the hell was that?"

"I don't know," replied Faith, a measure of uneasiness in her voice. "It happened a few times earlier, but I just assumed it was you trying to lure Wayne outside so you could…"

Another thump sounded, and Faith held her breath as Nick cautiously opened the door and looked around.

"Relax, angel. There's nothing out there but some hoof prints in the snow." Nick pointed down at the white ground. "Looks like they could be caribou tracks, but I'm no expert."

Faith looked puzzled. "Caribou?"

"Yeah. You know… a reindeer."

"Why on earth would an animal like that be trying to get inside the cabin? Is that something they normally do?"

Nick shrugged his shoulders. "Who knows what makes animals do the things they do? I wouldn't worry about it, though. Let's get this body out to the woodshed while there's still a bit of daylight left."

His hands latched onto Wayne's ankles and he began dragging the lifeless body out of the cabin, leaving a sticky snail-trail of smeared blood on the wooden floor.

Faith followed closely behind, taking care not to step on the slippery gore. Shutting the door behind her, she noticed it was riddled with gouges and deep slash marks. She stood motionless, her eyes transfixed on the scarred wood. A chill, like the icy fingertips of death, snaked its way down her body, and she turned the collar up on her coat.

"Come on, Lizzie Borden!" Nick shouted. "We've got work to do!"

Faith caught up with her lover and helped him drag Wayne through the snow to the back of the cabin. Forgetting about the door, her thoughts turned to the butchering at hand. Anticipating the sight and sounds of the axe blade hacking Wayne's limbs from his torso made her breath quicken, and her loins began to tingle. There was no better aphrodisiac in this world for her than murder and mutilation.

Oh, how her creamy white hands ached to wrap themselves around the handle of the axe and plunge its heavy cutting head into Wayne's skull before dismembering him. Her tongue longed to taste the man's blood splattered on her lips. And the very idea that it would still be steaming with warmth ignited an even greater fire of excitement within her.

Nick opened the creaking door of the woodshed, and the sight of the waiting axe infused Faith with a peculiar urge to do unspeakable sexual things with Wayne's decapitated head. The taboo of it was titillating as well as disturbing to her, and it nearly brought her to an explosive orgasm right there on the spot.

Faith drew back with a start as Wayne's body suddenly gave a mighty heave. His eyes, glazed and empty like the glass orbs of a macabre doll, slowly rolled in their sockets until they were staring at hers. A terrible gurgling noise that sounded like 'you rotten bitch' bubbled up inside his bleeding throat.

"He's still alive!" Faith announced, worriedly.

Nick looked down at Wayne and grinned. "Just barely. But that'll make what we're going to do to him all the more fun! Just think how the look of terror in his eyes as he helplessly watches you raise the axe blade, anticipating that horrifying blow and his inevitable death, will feed your hunger for revenge."

A sudden clicking noise drew the attention of the killers to the sight of a large reindeer standing about eight yards away, a massive thicket of antlers, like sharp blades, protruding from its head. From the corner of its foam-lathered mouth dangled a small, fleshy object. The animal's deep blue eyes stared strangely at Faith and Nick, causing a wave of uneasiness to ripple through their stomachs. All at once, it opened its mouth and emitted a loud, startling noise that sounded like a snort mixed with a bark, and upon doing so, dropped the fleshy object onto the pearly-white snow.

Faith gasped with shock as she realized what the reindeer had dropped was a woman's partially devoured hand, most likely belonging to Wayne's dead plaything out in the woods. "Oh, Jesus Christ!"

Nick looked stupefied. "Holy shit! That's the damnedest thing I've ever seen! I didn't know reindeers were carnivorous."

"They aren't," Faith replied. The sight of the hand in the snow captivated her eyes. "I remember back in school reading that they were herbivores. Their diet is supposed to consist of leaves and grass and other vegetation—not meat."

The reindeer snorted again and began to charge like a four-legged steam engine.

Nick grabbed Faith by the arm and quickly pulled her into the woodshed before slamming the door shut. The sound of feet dashing through the snow grew louder as the reindeer drew closer, and then there came a loud thud and the sound of splintering wood as its cloven hoofs smashed a hole in the door with violent force.

Faith let out a scream, and her body jolted as the reindeer backed up and snorted again as though preparing for another charge. Nick wrapped his hands around the axe, held it up in a position to strike, and waited with bated breath for the berserk beast to come smashing through the door. But instead, there came the sound of wild thrashing, accompanied by a gurgling cry, which endured for nearly ten seconds before sinking into a weak whimper. That soon gave way to a hellish symphony of ripping flesh and the crunching of bone.

Peering through the hole in the door, Faith and Nick watched with disbelieving eyes as the reindeer eviscerated Wayne's body before dragging it away into the snowy wilderness.

With a tone of urgency in his voice, Nick suggested to Faith that they hurry back to the safety of the cabin in case the "rabid" reindeer decided it would return. Faith nervously nodded her head in agreement, and the two psychopaths sprinted through the blood-soaked snow to the cabin. Faith opened the door and rushed inside with Nick trailing close behind, axe still in hand.

A bellowing scream shook Faith to the core, and she turned to catch sight of Nick rising up off the ground, his back impaled on the sharp antlers of another reindeer, considerably larger than the first one. With his arms flailing and his face contorted with pain, he was violently flung forward, his body landing halfway into the cabin.

Faith grabbed hold of his arms and pulled him all the

way inside as the reindeer stood and watched from a few feet away. She quickly shut the door and locked it before attending to her injured lover. Lifting up his torn camouflage hunting jacket and the bloody, perforated shirt underneath it, she grimaced at the multiple puncture wounds on Nick's back. From one of them protruded part of a broken antler covered with blood and gristle.

"Don't worry, Nick," she reassured him, fighting the panic that was rising up inside her as his blood spilled out of his body. "You're going to be all right. I promise."

Nick screamed out in agony as Faith used her fingertips, without success, to extract the slippery piece of antler deeply imbedded in his back. "Jesus Christ! That God damned thing burns like a son of a bitch!"

After several fruitless attempts to remove the antler, Faith rushed to the kitchen and yanked a rusty metal toolbox from out of the cabinet under the sink. She threw it onto the countertop, opened the lid, and fumbled through its contents until she found a pair of pliers. At that moment, a rack of reindeer antlers smashed their way through the window above the sink, showering Faith with shards of broken glass. To her horror, the reindeer poked its head and neck all the way through the window, and its powerful jaws clamped down upon her left wrist, sending pain shooting down into her hand and up her arm. Screaming, she grabbed Wayne's bottle of whiskey from the counter with her other hand and swung it at the animal's snout with all her might, turning its nose red with blood and prompting it to release her wrist and retreat.

Ignoring her throbbing pain, Faith grabbed the pliers and several dishtowels and ran back to Nick, who was groaning in agony. Grasping the jagged end of the antler in the jaw of the pliers, she proceeded to extract the bony shaft with one long and steady pull. Nick screamed out like a madman as blood gushed from the unplugged wound and flowed down his sides and onto the floor, where it merged with Wayne's.

Faith then folded the dishtowels and applied them as a compress in an effort to arrest the spillage of blood from the wounds. However, Nick continued to bleed profusely. His face had gone pale and clammy, and he looked like he was slipping into shock.

"I can't get the bleeding to stop." Faith's attempt to mask the distress in her voice and the dread in her eyes was futile. "I think it's best if I get you to a hospital, right away." Helping Nick to his feet, she added, "We'll take Wayne's pickup truck. It's not that far away. You can make it, baby. Just hang onto me for support."

With a biting wind whipping her face and stinging her cheeks with pellets of ice, Faith peered out from behind the cabin's partially opened door, hiding behind it like a shield. To her relief, not a single reindeer was in sight. She took Nick's arm and draped it around her shoulders. Together they trudged through the ankle-deep snow until they came to the pickup truck.

After helping Nick onto the passenger seat, Faith hurried around to the other side of the truck, climbed in, and started up the engine. Interwoven with static, Gene Autry's voice singing *Rudolph the Red-Nosed Reindeer* faded in and out on the radio. Faith immediately switched it off.

"Don't worry, baby. You're going to be all right," Faith promised her hemorrhaging passenger as she maneuvered the truck down the unplowed road that wound its way through the pine-mantled mountains.

All of a sudden, a pair of reindeer darted out from the trees lining the slippery, twisting road, their eyes reflecting the headlights of the pickup truck with an eerie, greenish glow. Faith jammed on the brakes and swerved to the right to avoid hitting them. The truck spun out of control and slid sideways into a tree with a loud thud. Both reindeer immediately began ramming the vehicle, puncturing all four of its tires with the spear-like tips of their antlers. Six other reindeer joined them—one of which leapt onto the steaming hood of the pickup and smashed out the windshield with its hoofs.

Covered with broken glass, Faith let out a blood-curdling scream as the reindeer bit down on Nick's arm and pulled him out of the truck and onto the hood. Faith fought with all her might to pull him back inside, but her strength proved to be no match for the power of the reindeer, and within a few terrifying moments, Nick was no longer in sight.

In an attempt to scare away the reindeer, Faith repeatedly blasted the horn, but to her horror, the herd gathered in a circle, surrounding the truck—watching and waiting. A bone-chilling wind was blowing snow into the cab through the missing windshield, and as the night grew darker, the temperature dropped.

What a way to spend Christmas Eve, Faith thought as she shivered from the cold.

Her breathing soon became shallow, and a wave of nausea surged over her. She stuck her head out the door to vomit, but all she could do was gag and dry heave. She then spotted the eight reindeer inching closer to the truck. She quickly shut the door and the herd immediately stopped in their tracks. Faith could feel all sixteen of their eyes boring into her—hungry, merciless, savoring every delicious morsel of her fear.

"Sooner or later, someone's got to come along and see that there's been an accident," Faith mumbled to herself, her words slightly slurred. "And then they'll send help and everything will be okay."

A loud snorting sound from one of the reindeer derailed Faith's train of thought.

"Nick?" she called out to the darkness. "Can you hear me? Are you out there? Nick! Please! Answer me! Nick!"

Faith listened for a reply, but her ears heard only the desolate wailing of the wind through the pine boughs. She tried her best to remain hopeful, but knew in her heart she would never hear Nick's voice again. Her instincts told her that he was dead, just like Wayne and the pretty little plaything that he had kidnapped and brought up to the cabin for slaughter.

As the minutes multiplied, a web of confusion enveloped Faith's mind, and she found herself drifting in and out of consciousness, her chills replaced by a strange and irrational sensation that her body was on fire. Succumbing to the final stages of hypothermia, she then slumped over onto the passenger seat, and her body gradually disappeared underneath a pearly white blanket of snow.

Christmas morning brought with it a cloudless sky of sapphire blue and brilliant sunshine that sparkled like diamonds on the snow-covered trees and ground.

Just as Faith had predicted, a passing motorist had spotted the wrecked pickup truck on the mountain road and called the police, who discovered Faith's corpse inside the snow-filled cab. She was frozen solid like a slab of venison in a meat freezer, and she was in death what she was in life—a cold-hearted bitch. Only now, her heart was far more colder…seventy degrees colder, to be exact.

BEAUTY *IS* THE BEAST

Vanity de Milo's obsession with beauty developed as soon as she was old enough to gaze into a mirror. She had always believed that beauty was next to godliness, and that ugliness was an unpardonable sin. Therefore, not one person in her extremely small circle of extraordinarily beautiful friends were particularly surprised when she decided to open up her own beauty salon in the heart of town. Vanity de Milo was not only blessed with beauty; she lived for beauty.

A low rumble of thunder heralded an approaching storm as Vanity filed her sculptured nails and waited for her next client to enter her shop on their eternal quest for beauty. The lights flickered a few times and a hard rain began to beat against the window glass that was partially obscured by pleated pink curtains with red tassel tiebacks. Without warning, a strange uneasiness came over the beautician, and, like a dark omen, the ticking of the clock on the wall began to pound inside her head like the heartbeat of a great and hideous beast. With the tinkling of a bell, the door to the shop opened and Vanity let out a loud gasp as her eyes beheld a most grotesque sight. A feeling of queasiness began to gnaw at her stomach like a rat.

The strange straggly-haired man stood in the doorway for several moments as the lightning flashed angrily behind him and the rumble of the ensuing thunder grew in its intensity, causing the tiled floor of the beauty parlor to shudder. His frightfully disfigured face was covered in huge warts and a week's worth of graying beard stubble. His lanky body was covered from head to toe in soiled, torn clothes that were rain-soaked and forming a small puddle on the spot where he stood. Like some monstrous owl, he slowly turned his head from side to side as if checking out the interior of the beauty salon. As if satisfied to find no one else in the shop, he then focused his stare upon Vanity. His bloodshot eyes were dismal gray and speckled with black. From them, an unsettling madness seemed to emanate.

He was the most hideous man the beautician had even laid her eyes upon. His extreme ugliness represented everything in the world that she despised, and the very sight of him filled her with feelings of disgust and contempt. She feared that if he didn't leave soon, she would become violently sick to her stomach.

"I'm sorry, but I don't cater to walk-ins," Vanity said to him snobbishly from across the room, in the hopes that the man would promptly turn and leave. However, much to her dismay, he remained in his spot in front of the door, his eyes still fixed firmly upon her and growing wilder by the minute. He said nothing.

"Did you hear me?" Vanity asked loudly, a tone of irritation resonated in her voice. "I said I don't take walk-ins here. I see all clients by appointment only, and it just so happens that I'm all booked up for quite awhile. I'm afraid you'll just have to go somewhere else for a shave and haircut, or whatever it was that you came for."

The man's chapped pale lips suddenly stretched into an evil grin and the foul odor of sour wine and halitosis escaped from his mouth. The few dingy yellow teeth that he possessed were crooked and decayed. He shut the door, locked it, and then began to slowly advance toward the repulsed and terrified beautician, who yelled: "How dare you try to intimidate me! If you've come here looking for some sort of handout, you can just turn around and take your ugly face the hell out of here!"

It became apparent to Vanity de Milo that the repugnant man had no intentions of leaving the shop, and an icy cold wave of fear surged through her body. Her heart began to pound rapidly in her chest like that of a terrified sparrow just before it dies from fright. She turned and rushed over to the front counter where an ornate French-style telephone was sitting and grabbed the white and gold plastic receiver. However, before her dainty finger could dial the police, the man made a beeline for the telephone and ripped the cord from the wall. He picked up the phone and threw it to the floor with an animalistic rage, causing it to break apart. Vanity let out an ear-piercing scream as he grunted like a wild beast and stomped on the broken pieces with his foot.

"You're out of your mind!" she shrieked before making a mad dash for the door.

A bright flash of lightning illuminated the sky as Vanity's hand reached for the lock. But before she could open it and escape into the relative safety of the storm that was raging outside, she felt the man's horrible hair-covered hands grab onto her upper arms and pull her away from the door. She struggled to free herself from his grasp but he was too powerful for her.

"Let go of me!" she screamed as another rumble of thunder sounded. "What is it that you want?" Panic was building up inside of her. Her mind was reeling. She could hardly believe that what was happening to her was real. It had to have been a nightmare.

The man still did not utter a word. Instead, he dragged Vanity, kicking and screaming, across the beauty parlor, past a row of swivel chairs with pink and white vinyl seats, and into a small, unlocked supply room, which was located at the back of the shop. He flung her like a rag doll and her body slammed into a white enameled cabinet. The doors flew open and plastic bottles containing shampoo, conditioner, toners, and crème developers toppled from the shelves and plummeted to the floor. His grubby hands viciously ripped at the screaming beautician's pink uniform, popping off some of the buttons, and he began to grunt and drool like an animal in heat.

Fighting for dear life, Vanity kicked and threw punches at her assailant, and during the course of the struggle she clawed at the man's face with her perfectly polished fingernails. To her horror, his skin ripped away like a fleshy rubber mask, revealing his true face that had been hidden underneath all this time. It was dark green in color and completely covered in reptilian scales. He hissed at her and from out of his foul-smelling mouth flicked a long skinny tongue that was forked at the end. He then emitted a strange and rapid clicking noise that was unlike anything Vanity had ever heard before, and proceeded to slowly run his snakelike tongue along Vanity's cheek and across her gloss-covered lips, leaving a glistening trail of clear slime. She let out a terror-filled scream, which only afforded the beast's tongue to dart into the recesses of her mouth, where it slithered past her tongue and explored her tonsils.

The horror was too much for Vanity to bear and she plummeted straight into a state of unconsciousness. When she came to, some time later, she found that her bestial alien attacker was gone, along with all of the money in the cash register and every bit of Vanity's sanity.

She slowly rose to her feet and staggered out of the supply room and back into the beauty parlor. Her body felt oddly numb as though she were floating in a dream. She looked up at the clock; her one o'clock appointment, a snooty Mrs. Snodgrass who never tipped, was due in shortly for a shampoo and a dye job. Thunder continued to rumble as Vanity freshened herself up, fixed her hair and makeup, and changed into a clean pink smock. She gazed at her reflection in one of the mirrors and flashed it a mad grin.

Having been violated in such a violent manner and by a man of such extreme ugliness pushed Vanity over the edge. With her mind now twisted, all she could think about was committing acts of murder. Revenge would not only be sweet, it would be beautiful, she whispered to herself.

Mrs. Snodgrass arrived promptly at one o'clock. Her punctuality, as she often pointed out, was a "sign of refined character and a proper upbringing." As she removed the wet plastic rain bonnet that covered her hair, she complained: "Oh, the weather today is simply horrid! My croquet game had to be cancelled because of the rain, which has left me in a rather foul mood."

No sooner had she been wrapped in a waterproof cape and the back of her head lowered into the shampoo bowl, she emitted a condescending chuckle and remarked: "How silly of me! I don't even know why I'm discussing croquet with you. I'm sure you haven't the slightest inkling of the game. I mean, croquet has never been a pastime of the working class. They simply lack the social graces for it."

With her left hand, Vanity grabbed hold of Mrs. Snodgrass' wet hair and firmly held her head down in the sink while her other hand dipped into the pocket of her smock and retrieved a metal rattail comb.

"Ouch!" yelled an annoyed Mrs. Snodgrass. "You're pulling on my hair, you clumsy incompetent girl! Don't expect a tip from me, Miss de Milo!"

With an expression of insane glee on her face, the beautician howled out a loud and unhinged laugh and then forcefully plunged the sharp pointed handle of the comb into the right side of the woman's neck, puncturing one of her jugular veins. Mrs. Snodgrass let out a frantic scream as blood gushed forth from the stab wound like a fountain of red gore. Laughing wildly, Vanity plunged the rattail comb into the side of her client's neck, again and again, until Mrs. Snodgrass' screams turned into deathly silence and her quivering body was motionless and drained of color.

Filled with exhilaration and a strange sense of accomplishment, Vanity dragged Mrs. Snodgrass' corpse across the shop and into the supply room, where she laid it to rest underneath a shelf of neatly folded white salon towels. She then grabbed a string mop and a bucket filled with warm soapy water and proceeded to clean up the blood smeared sink and floor. After she finished with that, she washed off the blood that had splattered onto her hands and face, changed into another clean smock, and looked up at the clock. Her two o'clock appointment, elderly Miss Crabtree, would be arriving in less than fifteen minutes for a permanent wave. She sat herself down on one of the swivel chairs and waited for the old lady with a savage hunger growing deep inside of her.

The gaudy Hawaiian-print muumuu dress and multi-colored necklace of plastic baubles worn by Miss Crabtree filled Vanity with a feeling of revulsion. "How dare she wear anything so ugly and tasteless to my distinguished salon of beauty," Vanity furiously muttered to herself underneath her breath as she eyed the slow-moving woman making her entrance. "She will pay for it with her life."

After Miss Crabtree was seated comfortably, the beautician took out a long leather belt from a drawer filled with an array of cosmetics and strapped her upper torso to the back of the chair to prevent her from moving.

"What's this all about?" Miss Crabtree inquired, her aged voice sounding quite startled. Her prune-like face bore a look of surprise.

Vanity smiled. "Nothing for you to worry yourself over, Miss Crabtree," she said in a pleasant and reassuring tone as she proceeded to tie her client's wrists to the armrests of the chair with the red tassel tiebacks she had plucked from the curtains. "This new safety procedure is simply to prevent you from falling out of the chair during your perm. I'm merely following the latest beauty industry regulations, which pertain to all senior citizen clients. We can't afford to have any personal injury lawsuits now, can we?"

"No, I suppose not," replied Miss Crabtree, sounding a bit confused as she watched Vanity securely knotting the tiebacks. She began to wiggle her fingers. "I shouldn't think this is good for one's circulation. Especially at my age."

"Relax, Miss Crabtree," said Vanity. "I'm a trained professional and I know exactly what I'm doing. You're in very good hands." She then reached into the pocket of her smock and produced a hypodermic syringe. She gazed at it longingly as she placed the tip of her thumb on the plunger.

Miss Crabtree wrinkled up her nose and squinted as she fixed her eyes upon the odd reflection of the beautician holding the hypodermic syringe in the mirror in front of her. "Oh dear!" she cried. "Is that a hypo there in your hands? Whatever is it for?"

"It's filled with ammonium thioglycolate," answered Vanity. "The chemical used for your alkaline perm. I no longer apply it externally. I've found that internal applications are much more effective and with less damage to the hair!"

Before Miss Crabtree could say a word, the needle of the syringe pierced her skin with a hot stinging sensation and Vanity pushed down on the plunger, injecting the solution into the old lady's arm. The murderous beauty peddler then took a step back and watched intently; her heart racing with anticipation. Miss Crabtree cried out in agony as the scorching chemical raced through her bloodstream and, within a matter of a few seconds, her body began to spasm most violently. Foam came from her mouth like a rabid dog and her eyeballs rolled up into her head.

Her convulsions continued for just over five minutes (Vanity timed them) and then gradually came to a halt. She belched out a loud gasp, which was immediately followed by a gurgling noise, and then she was stone cold dead.

Vanity untied Miss Crabtree's restraints and dragged her lifeless body into the supply room. She laid her onto the floor, parallel to Mrs. Snodgrass, switched off the light, and locked the door behind her. She took in a deep breath and then slowly exhaled with ecstasy. Murder made her feel beautiful.

Her next client, a prissy aspiring actor and male model by the name of Mr. Limpsky, arrived just before three fifteen for a styling and a facial. He strutted like a peacock over to the chair with his nose high in the air, swept away some imaginary dust from the seat with the side of his hand, and then sat down, crossing his legs in a womanly fashion.

"I have an important audition at five today," he said in a deep, yet effeminate sounding voice, while staring at his reflection in the mirror on the wall. "I mean *très* important. Therefore, my hair has to be absolutely perfect. Not one single strand out of place. Do you understand?"

"Of course, Mr. Limpsky," said Vanity as she began clipping away at his golden highlighted shoulder-length locks. "When I get finished with you, your hair will be nothing short of a work of modern art. You won't even recognize yourself!"

The actor gave a slight grunt to indicate that he was clearly unimpressed and then buried his eyes between the glossy pages of a high fashion magazine that he had brought along with him to help pass the time.

When Vanity finished coiffuring her client's hair, she put down her comb and scissors and reached for a sixteen-ounce can of extra-hold hairspray and gave his new hairdo a quick spraying. "*Voila!*" she said, beaming with pride. "And if I do say so myself, you look absolutely fabulous!"

The aspiring actor set his magazine down onto his lap

to inspect his hair in the mirror. As his eyes met his reflection, he immediately let out a horrified scream that sounded like a cow being stabbed in the ass. His fingertips touched his hideously butchered locks, which Vanity had hacked into uneven spiky clumps that resembled crabgrass. Covering his head were at least a dozen bald patches.

"My hair!" he screamed in a voice that was two keys higher than normal. "Look what you've done, you spiteful, substandard, beauty school flunky! You've destroyed my hair! It's beyond repair! You'll be hearing from my lawyer. I'm going to sue you for everything you own. You can kiss this dump of a beauty salon *au revoir*!"

The outraged actor made a move to stand up when Vanity swung the can of hairspray against the side of his head with all of her might. The force of the impact created a loud thud and left a dent in the can. He fell onto the floor in a semi-conscious daze and then Vanity continued bashing in his head with the can of hairspray, over and over, until it was battered and bloodied and his dead body lay at her feet with fragments of his shattered skull and bits of brain matter clinging to his blood-soaked hair.

She huffed and puffed and tiny beads of perspiration gathered on her forehead as she dragged Mr. Limpsky's dead weight along the floor en route to the supply room. She dumped his body next to those of her other two victims and then smiled with satisfaction at her gruesome handiwork. She had one more client scheduled for that afternoon.

"What on earth is that god-awful stench in here?" asked gossipmonger, Wanda Whippleby, waving her hand in front of her nose. "It smells like something died."

"Rats in the walls," Vanity replied in a nonchalant manner as she plugged in the crimping iron. "I saw one in the supply room the other day and called for an exterminator. He came and set out some rat poison for them."

"Well," began Wanda as she shut her umbrella and removed her raincoat, "by the smell of things in here, I'd say your rats took the bait."

Vanity grinned. "Yes, they did," she said, nodding her head. "All three of them."

Wanda gave the beautician a bit of a queer look and then sat down in the chair. "I've never been crimped before," she said, "but I'm anxious to try a new look. My husband and I have been invited to a party tonight at the Finklestein's and you can bet there's going to be a lot of juicy gossip flowing like wine there. Paula Finklestein is the biggest gossip this side of the Mississippi. I can hardly wait to get the latest dirt on everyone and dish some dirt too!"

She opened her mouth to laugh and, at that precise moment, Vanity de Milo thrust the end of the scorching hot crimping iron into Wanda's mouth, trapping her tongue between the heated parallel plates. A loud sizzling sound issued forth from the woman's mouth and she let out an obstructed scream and began to struggle to get out of the chair. Vanity pulled the crimping iron's electrical cord from the outlet and quickly wrapped it around the gossipmonger's throat, cutting off her oxygen. Wanda thrashed about for some time, flailing her arms, kicking her legs, and frantically twisted her head back and forth and to and fro, but Vanity vigilantly kept a tight grip on the garrote. Finally Wanda's body went limp as the beautician's death toll climbed to four and she slumped against the back of the chair with her eyes bulging from their sockets and her crimped and blistered tongue dangling from her mouth. Minutes later, her corpse joined the others in the supply room.

And so the crazed beautician continued to exact her revenge on those who came into her shop to be preened and pampered, day after day, thinking up new and creative ways to use the beauty supplies she had at her disposal to inflict pain and death upon her unsuspecting clientele. The number of corpses in the supply room was mounting, as was the gut-wrenching smell from the rotting flesh, which she tried to mask with air fresheners and scented candles. There seemed to be no end to Vanity de Milo's cold-blooded killing spree. That is, until one afternoon when Babs McDroolson, an undercover policewoman investigating the beautician's missing clients, strolled into the beauty salon under the false pretense of a French manicure and began asking a lot of nosy questions.

"Don't you think it's a rather curious coincidence," McDroolson asked as she eyed Vanity with suspicion, "that over a dozen people in this neighborhood have mysteriously gone missing without a trace in just this past week, and every single one of them have been clients of yours?"

"Oh?" asked Vanity as she escorted the policewoman to the manicure table, avoiding eye contact with her. Her voice was emotionless and her words monotonal. "I wasn't at all aware of that. How very strange. There must be a lunatic running amuck."

"Yes," replied McDroolson, still eyeing Vanity. "There must be. But sooner or later the police will catch him… or her." Her words had an ominous ring to them.

Vanity went silent.

"If you don't mind me asking, what exactly is that room over there at the back of your salon used for?" McDroolson asked, pointing her finger towards the locked door of the supply room.

"It's just a big closet where I keep all the supplies for the beauty shop," Vanity replied. "There's nothing special about it. Why do you ask?"

"There's a very peculiar odor coming from it. Or haven't you noticed?"

"It's just a bunch of rats that ate poisoned bait," said Vanity, still avoiding eye contact, "and they died inside the walls. The exterminator said the smell could linger for months."

"Really?" asked Babs McDroolson as she started towards the supply room. "How very interesting. You wouldn't mind if I took a peek in there, would you?"

Wielding a large metal nail file with a razor-sharp edge, the bloodthirsty beautician suddenly burst into maniacal laughter and lunged at the female officer from behind, attempting to slit her throat with it. McDroolson's hand latched onto Vanity's wrist and she attempted to wrestle the file from her while delivering a swift mule kick to her shins.

"Drop the nail file, de Milo!" shouted the policewoman. "I'm an undercover police officer and you're under arrest!"

Vanity ignored McDroolson's order, and during the ensuing struggle, the sharpened nail file accidentally slashed a three-inch long gash in Vanity's cheek. A horrendous burning pain surged through the side of her face and she screamed as blood spurted from the wound, staining her pink smock and dripping onto the floor. She dropped the deadly manicure implement and pressed the palm of her hand against her cheek to quell the river of blood.

The policewoman immediately extracted a pair of handcuffs that she had hidden in her back pocket and turned to place them on Vanity's wrists. However, her feet slipped on the slick puddle of blood that covered the floor in front of her and she lost her balance and fell backwards. With a loud thud, the back of her head made a less-than-pleasurable contact with a stainless-steel shampoo bowl and she was knocked into unconsciousness.

A combination of pain and rage bubbled within Vanity like a foul and poisonous witch's brew in a cauldron. She handcuffed McDroolson's wrists together behind her back and then snatched the nail file from the floor and began plunging it multiple times into the officer's body while screaming: "Die! You ugly bitch! Die! Die! Die!"

Using the sharpened nail file and a pair of cuticle scissors, Vanity began the gruesome, albeit enjoyable, task of hacking off the policewoman's head. The entire decapitation process took her exactly twenty-five minutes (she timed it), and when she completed what she set out to do, she picked up McDroolson's head by her long hair, which was matted with blood, and shouted at it: "Ugly people don't deserve to live!" She then flung it across the beauty salon as though it were a bowling bowl and howled with laughter.

Slowly, she rose to her feet and gazed at her blood-splattered reflection in the mirror that hung on the wall. "Oh God!" she shrieked in horror. "My face! My beautiful face!"

Driven to further madness by the sight of her disfigured face, the beautician rushed to the corpse-filled supply room and retrieved an industrial-sized bottle of nail polish remover from the white enameled cabinet. With tears streaming down her cheeks, she hesitated for a moment and then proceeded to douse herself with the nail polish remover. The chemical burned as it made contact with the open wound on her cheek and tears streamed from her eyes, mixing with the blood of the beheaded policewoman. She then lit a match and smiled as the flames engulfed her with a beautiful glow.

VOW OF OBEDIENCE

"**K**ill her!" it demanded in a voice that sounded very much like Sister Benedicta's; only it possessed a disturbing tone of cruelty – an insatiable bloodlust driven by pure evil, if you will. "I need blood, and she needs to die. *Tonight.* There's plenty of room in the vineyard for one more girl. Don't turn away from me, sow, when I'm speaking to you!"

Sister Benedicta's instincts told her not to look. She felt the urge to flee, to keep on running, and to never look back. But she knew it would follow her. It always did. She recalled the day when it first made its evil presence known to her. It was when she took her Vow of Obedience – the same day that her sister died in a house fire. Naturally, she had feared for her sanity in the beginning, and even considered consulting a psychiatrist or having herself committed, but she soon came to realize that the voice that sounded like hers came not from her own lips or from within her own mind.

It came from the deepest, darkest bowels of Hell.

She reluctantly turned her head back to look at it, as it

had instructed her to do. She felt compelled to obey its commands, no matter how diabolical they were. Her stomach swam with queasiness as she made eye contact with it… a face she had come to fear. A face that was but her own reflection in the old mirror that hung on the wall in her cold and sparsely furnished sleeping quarters.

"But, I can't do it," the dark-haired nun whimpered softly to her reflected image. Tears welled up in her dark brown eyes. "Please. Not anymore. I just can't."

"You must!" the voice that sounded like hers insisted. Its tone had become even more vicious than before. It reverberated inside the nun's head, bringing her to the edge of vertigo.

"But, she's like a daughter to me. So young... so very innocent," the disconcerted nun pleaded, while trying to maintain her balance. Her hands and lower lip trembled. She knew that her words were futile, her begging in vain, as it had always been. But, nevertheless, she clung to a shred of hope that the thing that disguised itself as her reflection in the mirror would be merciful this time.

It was not.

"I don't care one bit about that!" the voice that sounded like hers hissed. "If you choose to disobey me, sow, I'll destroy this convent with fire. And everyone in it, including you, will die. You know I can make it happen, and there's not a God damn thing you can do to stop me."

Sister Benedicta picked up the large wooden crucifix that sat atop her small, beat-up chest-of-drawers beneath the mirror and tenderly caressed it, hoping to garner some comfort from the object. "I realize that," she said, tearfully. "I won't disobey you. I swear."

"Good," commended the voice that sounded like hers. "Then you must carry out your dark deed tonight… and you must kill that girl in the same way that you exterminated the other three. Did I ever tell you how delicious they were? Oh, stop your sobbing, Benedicta. Your religion is nothing but a death cult. You and your ilk turn your backs on life and concern yourselves more with what happens after your physical bodies die. And is not that crucifix you clutch in your murdering hands a symbol of execution? You might as well pray to a noose or an electric chair." It roared with laughter. "After three exsanguinations, you should be used to killing by now."

"I'm not," declared Sister Benedicta. "I will never get used to ending innocent lives and draining their blood for you. It's wrong. It's sinful! You've made me break one of God's Ten Commandments: Thou shalt not kill. You've corrupted my soul."

"Silence your tongue, nun!" angrily barked the voice that sounded like hers. "I don't want to hear anymore of that twaddle! You know I need the blood of your kind to sustain me—to sustain *us*. Warm, sweet, fresh human blood. And, like it or not, you are the chosen sow to do my bidding."

The nun's mirrored image displayed a look of hunger. The pupils of her eyes dilated, turning the irises almost completely black. Her lips grew a deep shade of scarlet-red and stretched into a frightening, demonic grin.

Sister Benedicta shut her eyes. She could no longer bear to gaze upon her own reflection in the mirror. She gripped the crucifix and then began to pray out loud. "Almighty God, I have sinned against you, through my own fault, in thought, and word, and deed."

"Stop that blasted praying!" the voice that sounded like hers screamed inside her head. It then growled like a dog. Vicious. Rabid. And then it snorted and squealed like a wild boar. "I'm warning you!"

The mirror began to rattle and soon the lower half of its wooden frame pulled away from the wall, as if by invisible hands, and then violently slammed back against it. It pulled away and slammed again and again; each time, causing a grenade of excruciating pain to detonate inside the praying nun's head.

"Heavenly Father," Sister Benedicta continued, ignoring the pain and defying the demonic voice and the contorted face that glared at her from the reflective surface of the mirror. "I ask that you hear my prayer and grant me forgiveness of all my sins. I ask that you grant me the grace and comfort of the Holy Spirit." She then opened her eyes and swung the crucifix at the mirror with all of her might as she cried out, "Amen!"

With a loud smashing sound, the mirror's glass shattered into thirteen jagged pieces, some of which landed on top of the chest-of-drawers, and some of which landed on the floor. A sudden cold wind rushed through the room and then it was gone.

Sister Benedicta smiled and felt enraptured. She was sure that the demon that willed her to kill had been cast out and no longer exerted any control over her body, mind and soul. She felt in her heart that God had truly answered her prayer and delivered her from evil. She was free, at last.

All at once, she experienced a great tightness in her chest, similar to a fist clenching. She dropped the crucifix, which broke in two upon hitting the floor, and clutched at the left side of her chest with both hands in a feeble attempt to quell the intense pain. She began to stagger like a drunken woman, knocking into the chest-of-drawers and stepping upon some of the pieces of shattered glass. Her eyes filled with panic. She struggled to call out to God, but her mouth was unable to form words. As a cold sweat poured out of her skin and a feeling of impending doom overpowered her, she let out a loud, horrible gasp and then collapsed onto the floor. She was dead from cardiac arrest.

The gruesome discovery of Sister Benedicta's discolored and bloated corpse was made the following morning. Sister Maria and Sister Agnes had been sent to check up on the nun when she failed to appear for breakfast. Upon entering her room, they were horrified to find her lifeless body on the floor. They immediately crossed themselves and offered up a prayer to God for the repose of the dead nun's soul.

From the thirteen pieces of the broken mirror, Sister Maria's reflection peered up at her, wearing a strange grin that unsettled her. Goosebumps sprung up along her arms. Without knowing why, she was suddenly overwhelmed by the urge to pick up one of the shards of glass and slash Sister Agnes' throat with it. And then a voice that sounded very much like her own, only cruel and bloodthirsty, whispered inside her head, "Kill her!"

THE GREEN-EYED MONSTER

"Goddamn it, Wendell! Must you always slurp your soup like that?" Beverly asked her bespectacled husband. "You have absolutely no idea how revolting the sounds are that you make when you eat. Or maybe you do it deliberately just to get under my skin. That's it, isn't it?"

"I'm sorry, dear," Wendell replied. "I would never dream of getting under your skin. In fact, Beverly, I can assure you in all sincerity that under your skin is not a place that I would care to venture." He returned to his soup slurping.

"You strive to make my life as miserable as possible," Beverly declared as she checked with her fingertips to ensure that her pink hair curlers were still in place. "It's like your mission in life. And you know what, Wendell? You succeed in doing it on a daily basis!"

"I'm sorry, dear," Wendell replied, meekly. He removed his glasses that were fogged up by the steam of the hot soup and wiped the lenses clear with his paper dinner napkin.

"Oh don't give me that crap," snapped Beverly as she lit up a cigarette. "You and I both know that you aren't sorry about a damn thing."

Wendell put down his soupspoon. "Well," he began, sounding rather cautious, "that isn't quite entirely true, dear. There are one or two things that I *am* sorry about."

"Oh? And I suppose marrying me is one of them?" asked Beverly, glaring at her husband from across the small kitchen table.

Wendell wiped a dribble of soup from his bottom lip with his napkin, and then exhaled a tired-sounding sigh.

Beverly took a deep drag on her cigarette and blew the smoke out in one big puff in Wendell's direction. She then smashed out the cigarette into the seashell-shaped ashtray on the table.

"Well, let me tell you something," she said. "If anyone in this kitchen should be sorry about that, it's me!" she shouted, pushing her chair away from the table. "I wasted the best years of my life on you with high expectations that you were going to make it as a world-renowned anthropologist. But your ludicrous treatises on the mating habits of Bigfoot got you laughed right out of the University. And to think, I could have married an architect!"

She sashayed over to the window overlooking the seemingly endless forest. Rays of afternoon sunlight filtered through the pine needles and danced upon the leaves of the locust trees, which were hinting of golden yellow as a reminder that autumn was on the horizon.

All at once the chirping of the birds outside died away and an eerie hush fell over the woods. Beverly thought she saw a dark hulking figure run through the forest, weaving in and out of the trees. And then it vanished from sight. She dismissed it as some kind of wild animal, perhaps a large bear.

"Every other month you drag me up to this spider-infested cabin in the middle of the godforsaken wilderness," Beverly complained, turning back to glare at her husband. "I'm almost positive that you do it just to drive me out of my mind with boredom. Well, here's a news flash, Wendell. Sitting around in this dump a million miles from civilization with only you for company isn't exactly my idea of a rip-roaring good time. Why can't we ever go on a real vacation like the Sinclairs? This past summer they spent three whole weeks on the French Riviera. And the Goldfarbs, they just got back from an African safari!"

Beverly's nostrils were suddenly assaulted by a strange and putrid stench that sent her stomach reeling with nausea.

"What on earth is that revolting smell?" she asked, waving her hand in front of her nose and contorting her face in disgust. "Oh my god! Is that coming from you, Wendell?"

"No dear," Wendell answered. His lips cracked a slight smile.

"Ugh!" Beverly groaned while wrinkling up her nose. "Whatever that rancid smell is, it's simply ghastly and it's making my stomach turn. Oh, I need to open the window to let some fresh air in!"

Beverly unlatched the lock that secured the window and threw open the sash. However, her expectation of fresh air was not fulfilled, as the foul stench grew even stronger now and appeared to be emanating from outside of the cabin.

"Oh my god!" she vociferated. "It smells like something died out there! I don't know why I always let you talk me into coming up here all the time. This place is appalling. Did you hear what I said, Wendell? It's appalling!"

Just as Beverly was about to pull down the sash, a monstrous hair-covered face with large glowing eyes of green appeared outside the open window and curiously peered in at her. Beverly's eyes widened in terror and from her mouth was generated a loud scream.

"Wendell!" she cried out as she slowly backed away from the window. "There's some kind of huge hideous animal outside the window staring at me! Do something!"

The creature began to emit loud grunting sounds, which triggered another scream from the terrified woman. Beverly's body shook with fear, causing one of her pink hair curlers to loosen and fly from her head.

"Wendell!" she cried. "Don't just sit there! Get the rifle! Quickly! This thing is getting ready to attack! Wendell!"

"There's no need for you to panic, dear," Wendell stated with the utmost calmness in his voice. He lit up his pipe like he did after every meal, and took a few puffs on it. The tobacco smoke tantalized his taste buds with its sweetness. "That 'thing' as you call it is just a female Sasquatch. You see, Beverly, they do exist. She won't harm you. Unless, of course, you insist on making her feel threatened, which is a propensity that you've become quite masterful at over the years."

"Well," said Beverly in a huff, "if you aren't going to do anything about it, then I most certainly will!" She then rushed across the cabin and retrieved the loaded hunting rifle that was hanging on the wall over the mantel of the stone fireplace.

Wendell's calmness instantly evaporated into thin air and he jumped up from his seat, clearly agitated. "What on earth do you think you're doing?" he asked in a rather loud voice. "Put that gun down, Beverly! Put it down right this instant!"

"Like hell I will!" Beverly yelled, returning to the window with the firearm in her hands. She then aimed it at the Sasquatch, which continued to peer in. It looked into her eyes and let out a deep growl.

"I forbid you to shoot her!" yelled Wendell. His normally meek-sounding voice was now tinged with outrage and rang with an unusual assertion that took his wife aback. "She's with child and due to give birth any day now!"

"Oh?" said Beverly with curiosity. "And just how do you know so much about this… this… knocked-up monster and its baby?"

"Because I'm the father," Wendell replied emphatically.

"You're the what?" said Beverly in an exaggerated tone of disbelief. "This is no time to be cracking jokes, Wendell! You've never been any good at delivering a punch line. Have I ever told you that the only funny thing about your jokes is your inability to be funny?"

"It's no joke," said Wendell. "I'm afraid I'm quite serious. If you must know, I impregnated her last December. I've been closely monitoring the progress of her gestation, and when my documentation on the first successful interspecies mating between human and Sasquatch knocks the world on its ear, I'll finally be awarded the recognition due to me from that pretentious university!"

Beverly began to cackle with uncontrollable laughter.

"Are you seriously expecting me to believe that you screwed a Bigfoot?" she asked in between cackles. But her laughter soon faded away as she came to realize that Wendell's confession of infidelity had been spoken with sincerity. Rage began to bubble up inside of her and then erupted like a volcano spewing molten lava. She turned the gun on her unfaithful husband and his face went pale.

"You bastard!" she screamed as she squeezed the trigger.

The handle of the rifle kicked back and knocked another one of Beverly's pink curlers off her head as a loud shot rang out and a bullet exploded through Wendell's abdomen, leaving a gaping hole. It struck the knotty pine wall behind him and became lodged in the wood. Clutching his blood-gushing bullet wound with his hands, he collapsed onto the floor. A puddle of blood began to quickly spread around his twitching body.

The green-eyed creature let out an ear-piercing wailing noise that made Beverly's blood run cold as ice. She aimed the gun at the Sasquatch and fired, but the bullet missed its mark and hit the frame of the window instead. The creature took off running and despite its advanced state of pregnancy, it moved with great agility and speed. Beverly rushed back to the window, took aim and fired the gun once more, but again she missed.

"Damn it!" she growled as she watched the fleeing creature disappear into the shadows of the forest.

Beverly plopped back down in her chair in the kitchen and reached for her pack of cigarettes that sat on the table. Annoyed to discover there was only one cigarette remaining in the pack, she cursed her bad luck underneath her breath, lit up her last smoke, and then pondered what to do about her husband's dead body.

She suddenly remembered the shovel and pickaxe that were out in the shed behind the cabin. She decided she would go out into the woods and dig a grave as deep as she could. Once Wendell was buried, she would then burn the cabin to the ground and drive home. She would also fabricate a story that Wendell packed his bags and left her. It was a tale she felt sure nobody would have any trouble believing, as the couple's contempt for each other was well known within their small circle of friends.

Beverly located a spot in a small clearing off the path near a babbling brook that she felt would make an ideal gravesite. With the loaded rifle and a kerosene lantern by her side, she began the task of digging.

"God damn you, Wendell," she said out loud in an irritated-sounding voice as she paused to catch her breath and to blot the beads of perspiration from her face with a handkerchief. "You always make work for me."

Beverly toiled away into the night and sighed with relief when she finally had the hole completely dug. She then made her way back to the cabin by the light of the kerosene lantern and was looking forward to a well-earned rest and a glass or two of blackberry brandy before dragging her husband's corpse through the woods, rolling it into the waiting grave, and filling it back in with dirt. As she neared the door, she heard several loud knocking noises coming from somewhere in the forest, which sounded like a rock being struck against a tree.

She hurried to get back inside the cabin, quickly shutting and locking the door behind her. She placed the rifle and kerosene lantern upon the table and set off to retrieve a bottle of brandy from the kitchen cupboard. A loud gasp escaped from between her lips when she discovered that Wendell's body was no longer on the floor where she had left him earlier. From the large pool of dried blood that marked the spot where his body had landed after sustaining his gunshot wound, a long trail of smeared blood led across the floorboards to the bedroom door. Beverly was aghast.

"Wouldn't that just be typical of Wendell," she mumbled to herself, "to be alive after I just spent over eight grueling hours digging a grave for that man?"

She followed the trail up to the bedroom door and called out, "Wendell? Are you in there? Are you still alive?"

No sound came from the other side of the door.

Beverly placed her hand upon the knob and turned it as a flutter of anticipation spread from the pit of her stomach to the tips of her fingers. She opened the door very slowly; unsure of what would be waiting for her inside the room. All at once, an all-too-familiar putrid stench assailed her sense of smell, and she gasped with horror and cringed at the nightmarish sight that unfolded before her eyes.

She initially thought that her eyes were deceiving her, but as she realized that what they were showing her was indeed real, fear slashed through her body like a hot blade and she felt herself trembling like the ground when fault lines release their built-up tension. She felt a scream rising up in her throat but no sound would issue forth from her mouth.

There upon the blood-soaked mattress of the bed lay Wendell's body, unmoving and slightly bluish in color. His eyes and mouth were gaping just as they had been when Beverly left the cabin to dig his grave. At his side was the pregnant Sasquatch, and gathered around the bed as if in silent vigil stood half a dozen more of the gigantic humanoid creatures. Their massive bodies were covered by glossy black hair and their heights ranged from seven to eight feet tall. They all turned their grotesque faces in Beverly's direction, bared their sharp yellowish teeth, and growled with such volume and ferocity that Beverly was sure she could feel the floor beneath her feet vibrating.

The scream that had been stuck in her throat now managed to find its way out of her mouth and she turned and ran towards the door leading outside. The growling Sasquatch creatures bolted after her, clawing at the air with their black and leathery paw-like hands.

Beverly's adrenalin was pumping like an oil well in Texas as she frantically fumbled with the latch. She managed to unlock it and flung open the door, fleeing from the cabin into the pitch-blackness of the forest. Without the kerosene lantern, she had to rely solely on the pale rays of the waning moon that shone down through the dense canopy of the treetops to light her way. She could hear the frightful sounds of the creatures growing louder as they gained on her, and she ran as fast as she could. Her feet stumbled over jagged rocks and gnarled roots. Tree branches that impeded her path, invisible within the dark cloak of night, clawed her face and arms.

Panic-stricken and with her vision obscured by night blindness, Beverly had no idea where she was or in what direction she was heading. All she knew was she had to keep running to avoid being captured by the growling creatures pursuing her.

As she ran through the forest like a frightened deer, she began to wonder what horrible things the Sasquatch would do to her if they caught her. Would they tear her apart and devour her flesh until all that remained were her skull and bones? Or would they gang rape her and impregnate her with some sort of hellish half-human monster? Would that be their retribution for Wendell having impregnated one of their own?

Beverly's pondering came to a quick end as the solid ground underneath her feet suddenly disappeared without warning. She felt herself plummeting, and within a matter of seconds she landed with a thud on the hard ground at the bottom of the deep hole she had dug for her husband's body, and several more pink curlers flew out of her sweat-drenched hair. Upon impact there came a loud snapping noise from her left shin, followed by excruciating pain. With her fingers she could feel the broken end of her tibia bone protruding through the skin. Blood ran like a river from the wound, dampening the ground under her leg. Beverly battled with herself to keep from crying out from the agony. She clenched her teeth tightly and contorted the muscles in her face. Tears were rolling down her cheeks.

Realizing that it would be impossible for her to outrun the Sasquatch with her leg in the sorry state it was now in, she figured the only thing she could do at that point was stay hidden in the hole and try to keep as quiet as possible so they wouldn't be able to locate her. She reassured herself that it would be sunrise in just a few hours and she would make an attempt then to pull herself out of the hole.

Just then, she heard the sound of twigs snapping nearby. It was soon followed by the dreaded putrid stench, which wafted ominously into the hole. Beverly held her breath and feared that the pounding of her heart would give her away. She then saw the faces of the Sasquatch peering down at her from the top of the hole. They grunted and wailed, and then, to Beverly's astonishment, they were gone. She exhaled a sigh of relief.

However, minutes later they returned with armloads of large rocks, which they began dropping into the hole. One hit Beverly's broken leg and she howled in pain. And then, using their large hands as shovels, the hairy creatures began filling in the hole with the mound of soil that Beverly had piled up next to it. The terrified woman screamed hysterically and struggled fruitlessly to climb out of the hole as it rapidly filled in with dirt and rocks, burying her alive.

The dawn kissed the dew-drenched forest with its soft rays of golden light while spiders diligently spun their silken webs between the branches of shrubs. The waking birds sang their chirping songs and the meandering brook gurgled as water flowed over its slick and shiny stones. Chipmunks scurried across paths paved with last autumn's fallen leaves. Purple morning glories bloomed, butterflies fluttered and bees buzzed. And not far from the mound of a fresh grave in the middle of a small clearing, there came the sound of a baby's first cry.

DON'T GO INTO THE CELLAR

Bobby Weldon had been chasing tornadoes with his video equipment for well over ten years. It was in his blood. The thrill he derived from observing the power and the fury of Mother Nature up close was like no other he had ever experienced. He lived every waking moment of his life for it.

His wife, Chelsea, on the other hand, took a rather dim view of his storm-chasing obsession—to put it mildly. No sooner had she said, "I do," she began demanding that Bobby give up cigarettes and his passion for vortices of violently rotating winds, but to no avail. Her demands soon transformed into heated arguments, and ultimately were accompanied by threats of divorce. One morning, during a late-season tornado outbreak that tore through six states, Chelsea packed her suitcases and moved out, never to return.

Bobby couldn't have been happier.

The following spring, he jumped into his truck and chased a supercell across the plains of Oklahoma. The thunderstorm pelted his vehicle with a barrage of hail, which cracked his windshield and sent his adrenaline pumping, before unleashing a violent category F4 tornado that cut a swath of destruction three miles long and one-quarter of a mile wide. Luckily, the twister had touched down in a mostly uninhabited area, so most of the damage it caused was limited to uprooted trees, splintered fences, and knocked-over telephone poles.

Bobby turned off the main highway and onto a dusty county road in an attempt to follow the storm as it moved to the northeast. About a mile down the road, an old, two-story farmhouse came into view. It appeared to have taken a direct hit from the angry, whirling winds of the tornado. As Bobby drove closer to it, he could see that most of the roof had been ripped away and the south side of the structure had collapsed inward. Strewn around what was left of the building were piles of splintered boards, the remnants of smashed furniture, chunks of plaster, and twisted pieces of metal. Clinging to mutilated tree branches were pink clumps of rain-soaked fiberglass insulation that waved in the steamy breeze like soggy cotton candy.

Bobby turned his battered truck into the long gravel driveway, turned off the ignition, and snuffed out his cigarette in the ashtray. "Christ Almighty!" he said out loud to himself as he surveyed the devastation that lay before him. It looked even worse up close than it did from the road. The aftermath of the storm was so horrific, he knew his chances of finding anyone alive inside the destroyed farmhouse were slim to none. But being the Good Samaritan that he was, he felt it was his duty to check for any survivors and render his assistance if help was needed. He climbed out of his vehicle with his military grade LED flashlight in hand and proceeded to the farmhouse, taking great care not to trip over any bits of rubble or step on any downed electrical wires.

"Hello?" he called out in a loud voice. "Is anyone in there?" Can you hear me? Hello?" He waited a moment, listening for a reply or for any other sound from within the storm-ravaged building or from underneath the debris that surrounded it, but he heard nothing. He walked around to the rear of the house, carefully navigating through the wreckage, and once again shouted, "Hello? Is there anybody inside? Hello?"

This time, something that sounded like a faint voice answered him. It was so wispy and muffled that Bobby couldn't be sure at first if what he was hearing was a small child crying, a kitten meowing, or just a rush of wind through mangled trees and missing fence posts. He listened harder and realized it was the voice of a woman. She sounded terrified. "Help me!" she yelled. "I'm trapped! Please help me!"

Bobby instinctively sprang into rescue mode. "Hang tight! I'm gonna call for help and get you out of there as soon as I can!" he shouted, pulling his cell phone from his pocket. There was no signal. *Damn it*, he thought. *The tornado must've wiped out the cell tower.* He shoved the useless device back into his pocket and proceeded to climb over the debris, inadvertently slicing open the side of his forearm on something sharp. He was so focused on the mission at hand that he neither felt any pain nor noticed the blood drizzling from the gash. As he quickly made his way towards the rear entrance of the house, he saw that the tornado had ripped the back door from its hinges. The woman's cries for help grew louder as he got nearer.

He was now inside the farmhouse—or, rather, what remained of it. The interior was in as bad of shape as the exterior, if that were at all possible. He surmised from the toppled Hoosier cabinet that was blocking his path, and broken pieces of crockery covering the floor like an apocalyptic mosaic, that he was in the kitchen. A loud cracking noise suddenly came from overhead, prompting Bobby to pause and look up. A wave of panic washed over him. The sagging ceiling beams looked as though they might collapse on him at any moment. He knew he had to act fast.

"Where are you?" he called out.

"I'm in the cellar!" the woman replied. "Help me!"

"I'm coming to get you! Everything's gonna be all right, ma'am," he reassured her. "Is there anybody else down there with you?"

"No. Just me. Please hurry!" she cried. "I can smell gas!"

Bobby felt his stomach tighten. "Just try to stay calm, and I'll have you out of that cellar before you know it!"

He trudged through the debris until he reached the Hoosier cabinet. Before he could move it out of the way, his ears detected the weak and agonized moan of a man. A chill traversed his spine when he realized that someone was pinned underneath. Summoning every ounce of his strength, he grabbed one end of the heavy cabinet and lifted it off the crushed man, freeing him.

"Sweet Jesus," Bobby said, under his breath, as he stared at the bashed-in head of a heavyset man in denim overalls. His face was blanched to a deadly pallor, and rills of blood trickled from his ears and nostrils. Bobby knelt down beside him. "I've got to get you to a hospital, mister."

Bobby didn't relish the thought of dragging the injured man outside and running the risk of injuring him further. But, given the circumstances, he felt he had no other option. It was imperative that he move him to safety.

Once again, the woman in the cellar shrieked for help.

The man on the kitchen floor suddenly reached out a bloodied arm that was tattooed with an image of Christ wearing a crown of thorns. He clamped his clammy fingers around Bobby's wrist. "Don't go…into…the cellar," he gurgled before he gasped and went limp, his vacant eyes staring upward.

Bobby put his ear to the man's chest and listened for a heartbeat but was unable to detect one. Writing him off as dead, he proceeded to clear away the debris blocking his path and followed the sound of the woman's voice until he was able to locate the door leading to the cellar. But, to his dismay, he found that it was either locked or jammed and would not budge. Using a front kick, he drove the heel of his foot into the door just below the doorknob. On the third try, he was able to break down the door.

"Help me!" cried the woman. "Get me out of here!"

As Bobby rushed down the rickety wooden stairs into the underground darkness, his nose encountered the rotten-egg smell of gas odorant. Shining his flashlight into the cellar, Bobby was stunned by what he saw. Standing in the corner with her arms straight up and both wrists handcuffed to an overhead water pipe was a young woman. Bobby estimated her age to be somewhere between late-teens to mid-twenties. She was naked and shivering.

"Oh, my, God," rolled off of Bobby's tongue. Never before in all his years of storm chasing had he ever encountered anything as bizarre as this.

"Thank goodness you've come!" the woman wept, tears streaming down her pallid face. "I thought I was going to die in this horrible cellar."

"What the hell is going on here?" Bobby inquired. "Who did this to you? The man with the religious tattoo?"

"Yes!" cried the woman. "He's insane! He's had me chained down here for weeks, maybe months. I don't know how long it's been. It feels like an eternity! Oh, I'm so afraid. And hungry. Help me, please! He keeps the key to the handcuffs on a key chain in the back pocket of his pants. Hurry, please!"

"Now don't you worry, ma'am. You're safe now," Bobby said. "There's no need for you to be afraid. That man can't hurt you any more. He's dead."

The enslaved woman began to sob with joy. Strands of her long brunette hair clung to her cheeks, which were moist with tears. A feeble smile manifested on her parched and nearly colorless lips. "Oh, thank God!" she exclaimed with exuberance in her voice. "My prayers have finally been answered!"

"I'm gonna go up to the kitchen now and get those keys, but I'll be right back. I promise."

Bobby turned to start for the stairs and was aghast to find the man with the bashed-in head stumbling like a drunkard towards him. In his hand was a camouflage-handled buck knife.

The woman shrieked, "Watch out! He's got a knife! He'll kill you!"

"What the hell are you doing down here? I told you not to go into the cellar!" the man shouted at Bobby. His voice was like gravel and filled with rage. "Get the hell away from that woman! You hear me, boy? She don't belong to you!"

Bobby took a step back. "What kind of sick, deranged bastard are you?" he growled. "I'm not leaving this house without her!"

"I don't want to have to take your life, but I'll gut you like a pig before I let you release her into the world!" the man shouted insanely. "Don't you understand? I'm doin' the Lord's work."

With his adrenaline pumping, Bobby swung his heavy flashlight at the man's face, striking him hard between the eyes. He dropped the knife and plummeted to the dirt floor, landing on his back. Filled with rage, Bobby swung the flashlight again and again, hacking flesh and shattering bones, until the man's face resembled regurgitated steak tartare. He wasn't sure if the lunatic was dead or unconscious, but that was of no concern to him at this point. All he could think about was freeing the woman and safely getting her out of the tornado-ravaged farmhouse as quickly as possible. He wiped the sweat away from his brow and then rolled the bashed man onto his beer belly. The key chain was in his back pocket, just as the woman had said.

Bobby pulled it out and hurried back to her.

"I'm gonna get you out of here," he declared. "Don't you worry."

With his hands shaking nervously, he attempted to unlock the handcuffs, but the first key didn't work. He tried the next one, but that didn't work either. Nor did the next one.

"Hurry!" the woman pleaded, as the house creaked and groaned ominously.

At last, Bobby found the right key. The handcuffs popped open and fell to the floor with a clank.

"I'm free!" the woman rejoiced. "Free at last!" She entwined her arms around Bobby and squeezed him tight. Her embrace was cold and chilled him to the bone.

"Come on, let's get you out of here," Bobby said, fearful that the buckling building was going to collapse at any moment.

"Your arm," the woman whispered into Bobby's ear, "It's bleeding."

"Don't worry about me," Bobby replied. "I'll be all right. But we really should get out of here. This structure is unstable and…"

"It's been such a long time since I've had a drink," the woman interrupted. "And your blood smells delicious."

Bobby suddenly felt something sharp sink deep into his throat, and he cried out in pain. His mind reeled with confusion, and a wave of dizziness surged through his head as the woman, who had now transformed into a blood-sucking beast, siphoned his crimson juices from the two puncture wounds she had created with her deadly fangs. He tried to free himself from her grasp, but could not escape. It seemed the more she fed, the stronger she grew.

As the farmhouse began to crumble around him, Bobby could feel his life slipping away. He fished the cigarette lighter from his pocket and flicked it, welcoming the merciful peace that the ensuing ball of fire granted him.

MARCY'S DIARY

Dust particles danced like ghost-orbs in the shaft of late afternoon light that crept through the tiny window in the gable. The long-dead corpse of a housefly, drained of its juices, dangled from the time-ravaged remains of a spider's web that clung from the top corner of the frame near a semi-circular crack in the pane. A creak cried out from a dusty floorboard and then the rusty metal hinges of a cobweb-enshrined trunk groaned as the lid lifted up, releasing a pungent perfume of mustiness, and revealing its hidden treasures that had, for years, reposed in a shroud of darkness.

"Oh wow!" Janice Lemort cried with excitement. Her hazel-green eyes, which were ghoulishly made-up with thick, black eyeliner and dark purple eyeshadow, grew wide with astonishment. "There's an old diary inside this trunk! I bet it's *her* diary!"

Brimming with equal parts curiosity and trepidation, Janice's younger sister, Marlayna, cautiously peered into the trunk. She then let out a bit of a gasp. "Do you really think it's Marcy's diary?" she asked, a slight tremble in her voice. "The girl who used to live in this house?"

"Yes," Janice replied with glee. As she bent down to retrieve the diary, some of her long hair, which she'd dyed raven-black with startling streaks of bright red, fell in front of her blanched face. She brushed the strands away with her hand as she returned her torso to an upright position, taking care not to accidentally hook one of her fingertips on the stainless-steel ring that dangled from her pierced septum. "Marcy," she continued, "the psycho girl who chopped up her family with an axe while they slept. After she did it, she hanged herself from a beam right here in this very attic. It's amazing that this diary's been hidden away up here all these years!"

"Oh Janice, I wish you'd put that book back in the trunk and lock it," Marlayna pleaded. Her voice sounded distressed. "I don't like it one bit. It's evil. I can feel it. Just the sight of it is making my skin crawl."

Janice slowly ran her fingertips across the faux-leather cover of the diary, which was almost as black as the nail polish that darkened her long fingernails.

"Most of the people in this town keep pretty tight-lipped about the axe murders, even though they happened over twenty years ago," she said. "But there's this one girl in my math class, her name is Carla Bennett, and she told me the gory truth about what occurred in this house. Her uncle was one of the detectives on this case. He told her that all the walls and ceilings were completely red with splattered blood, and there were bits and pieces of human body parts lying all over the place! Chopped-off hands and feet… eyeballs… intestines…"

"Oh, my God!" Marlayna exclaimed, wrinkling up her face in repulsion. "That's totally disgusting! I think I'm going to throw up." She paused for a few moments. "Do you suppose our parents know what happened here?"

"I'm pretty sure they do," Janice replied as she opened

the diary and began browsing through its yellowed pages. "I mean, there's a law in this state that says people have to disclose that kind of stuff when they sell you a house. 'Stigmatized properties' I believe they're called. It's no wonder our parents got this place for so cheap."

"Well, I wish they had bought a different house in a different town," lamented Marlayna as a faint look of disquiet flickered in her eyes. "Cheap or not, I don't like this place at all. Something about it doesn't feel right. Do you know what I mean? Sometimes, at night when I'm alone in my room, I feel like something's watching me."

"Oh, stop being such a paranoid little mouse," Janice scolded her sister. "I think it's pretty awesome if you ask me. I mean, seriously, not every girl can honestly boast that she lives in a bonafide crime scene. Plus, the rumor going around school is that our house is haunted. And not haunted by just any old run-of-the-mill ghost, but by the spirit of the deranged axe murderess herself! I found that out from Carla Bennett too. What do you think of that, Marlayna?"

"I think you and your goth friends are a sick bunch of weirdos," Marlayna blurted out, shaking her head from side to side. "I'm going back downstairs. I've had enough of this attic and all this talk about Marcy."

Janice snickered, "You're so pathetic. Afraid of an old diary. Afraid of ghost stories. You're even afraid of your own shadow."

"No, I'm not!" Marlayna snapped, her tone of indignation clearly a source of amusement for her grinning sister. "It's too hot and stuffy up here, that's all. And besides, I don't even believe in ghosts."

"You do so," Janice calmly contradicted, her eyes glued to the pages of the journal. "Hey! Check this out, Marlayna! The last entry in Marcy's diary is dated August 2nd, 1997, and says: 'I must bid you farewell, dear diary, as this will be my final entry. You've been my only friend and confidante for the past seven months, and I will miss you more than these mere words could ever express. I feel like I've finally awakened from a long dream that had my mind trapped like a helpless insect in the web of some gigantic spider. Tonight was the night I've waited sixteen years for. The deed is done and I'm free at last. There's no turning back from it now. The lambs have been slaughtered in the most brutal way. I feel no remorse, guilt, or shame for bringing death to those who cursed me with life. I know I should probably feel something…anything. But I don't. Emotions are reserved for those with a soul. And I don't have a soul.'"

Janice suddenly generated a wild-eyed look. "Oh my God, Marlayna!" she exclaimed, excitedly. "There's even a bloody smudge mark at the bottom of the page! Take a look!" She held up the open diary for her sister to see.

A sudden gust of wind conjured forth a ghostly wail as it rattled the windowpanes like some frightful invisible entity desperate to find its way inside the attic. The shadows in the corners seemed to grow a bit darker, and an icy tingle slithered along Marlayna's spine.

"I'm out of here," she abruptly declared, as Janice cracked an amused smile. Goosebumps were beginning to spring up on the young girl's forearms and it felt as though some of the honey-blonde hairs at the back of her neck were standing on end.

Wasting no time, Marlayna dashed to the door, and then scurried down the creaky wooden stairs that lead from the dark and musty confines of the attic to the sun-lit second floor. Within a matter of seconds, she was gone from sight.

Unable to contain her laughter any longer, Janice's black-painted lips parted slightly, and she let out an impish giggle. She placed the diary back into the trunk and shut the lid.

"Good night, dear diary," she whispered to the book, grinning.

That night, Marlayna restlessly tossed and turned in her

bed. She opened her eyes and glanced over at the eerie green glow of the digital clock that sat upon her nightstand, along with a dancing ballerina music box. Three o'clock. She shut her eyes once more and began counting backwards from one thousand in her head. She had read somewhere that it was an effective technique for inducing sleep.

She had reached 969 when a sharp, shrill cry came from Janice's bedroom, which was directly across the hall from hers. Without hesitation, Marlayna sprung up out of her bed and rushed to her sister's room to check on her.

"Janice! Are you all right?" Marlayna asked, switching on the light.

Janice was sitting up in her bed. Her face was clearly marked by a look of fright. "She was here! She was in my bedroom!"

"Who was?" Marlayna asked with curiosity.

"Marcy," Janice replied. "She was standing right over there at the foot of my bed. She had an axe in one hand and she was covered in blood!"

"There's nobody in this room but you and me," Marlayna insisted, looking around the bedroom. "And there's no blood on the floor, or anywhere for that matter. You were just having a bad dream because of that horrible diary up in the attic."

"No!" Janice protested. "It wasn't a dream, Marlayna. It was real. I don't care if you believe me or not, but Marcy really was here. And she even spoke to me."

"She spoke to you? What did she say?"

"Oh, my God," Janice whimpered, burying her face in her hands. "I don't even want to repeat the words. They're too horrible."

"Tell me, Janice!" Marlayna demanded. "What did she say to you?"

Janice went silent for a minute before replying to her sister. "She told me... that it's my destiny to kill everyone in this house, the same way she did. She said it has to be carried out because the dark entity that dwells within the shadows of this house demands a sacrifice to nourish it!"

The palms of Marlayna's hands started to perspire and her mouth went dry. "Janice," she began, her voice fraught with worry. "Stop it. You're frightening me with that kind of talk. Marcy's dead. She committed suicide over twenty years ago. And the dark entity doesn't exist. It was just a nightmare. It wasn't real."

There suddenly came the sound of something moving in the hallway, and then, to the horror of both sisters, the knob on the bedroom door began to turn. As the door slowly creaked open, Marlayna gasped and Janice shouted out, "Go away! Leave us alone!"

The door swung completely open, and a feeling of relief instantly washed away Marlayna's mounting terror when she saw her parents enter the room.

"What's all this racket about?" Mr. Lemort inquired. His voice vibrated with anger. "Do you girls realize it's after three in the damn morning? I have to be up for work in less than three hours."

"We heard screaming," Mrs. Lemort stated, an expression of concern covering her fatigued face. "Is everything all right?"

"We're fine, Mom," Marlayna replied. "Janice just had a really bad nightmare, that's all. I heard her scream and came in to see if she was okay."

"I'm sorry," Janice apologized. "I didn't mean to wake everyone up."

"You look like you just saw a ghost," Mrs. Lemort said to Janice. She walked over to the bed and placed the back of her right hand upon her daughter's forehead to check for a fever. "Look at your face, honey. It's so pale. Are you sure you're all right?"

"Yes," Janice answered, a trace of annoyance in her tone. "I'm okay now. Really. I am. Everybody, just go back to bed."

As her parents exited the bedroom, her father ordered, "Get to sleep, you two. You both have school in the morning."

* * *

In her classes at school that day, Marlayna found it difficult to concentrate on her studies. The teachers' words were but mere mumblings from some far-off galaxy that possessed neither meaning nor importance. All she could think about was Marcy and the infamous axe murders. The dreaded image of the young murderess' diary haunted her brain, as did her sister's macabre dream that shattered the stillness of the early morning hours.

Could it have been more than just a nightmare? Marlayna pondered, as she gazed out the classroom window at nothing in particular. *Was it possible for Marcy's restless spirit to roam the earth, and did she have her sights set on possessing Janice? Could she actually manipulate Janice against her will to do her evil bidding?*

Marlayna's questions left her hungering for answers. The more she thought about Marcy and the diary, the stronger her uneasiness grew. She felt overcome by a feeling of helplessness and debated with herself whether or not she should inform her parents.

"Are we having a pleasant daydream, Miss Lemort?" thundered a sarcastic voice that startled her back to reality.

"I'm sorry, Mr. Krueger," Marlayna apologized, her cheeks turning red from embarrassment as giggles and whispering voices spread like a contagion through the classroom. She could feel the eyes of her fellow students burning into her and wished she could make herself disappear.

"Not as sorry as you *will* be when report card time comes around," replied the teacher with an air of haughtiness. "If you fail this class, you'll never make the cut for college. I suggest you look sharp, young lady."

"Yes, Mr. Krueger," Marlayna answered meekly, while lowering her head as if in shame.

The teacher sneered at the girl and then shook his head in disgust before making his way back to the front of the classroom and resuming his lecture. Every so often, he would shift his glance back to Marlayna and flash her a look of disapproval.

That afternoon, while walking home from school, Marlayna's ears detected an unfamiliar female voice softly calling out her name. She stopped and quickly turned around to look, but found no one there. She was all by herself. A feeling of panic rose up inside of her and she began to run. It wasn't until she reached the long flagstone path leading to the front door of her house that she paused to catch her breath. She looked to make sure no one was behind her and then, feeling relieved, continued on her way.

However, no sooner had she resumed her walking, a strong gust of wind blew a yellowed and slightly crumpled page from a newspaper in front of her. Burning with curiosity, she crouched down and picked it up. It was dated the third of August, 1997. As she un-crumpled the sheet of paper to read it, the bold words of an unnerving headline came into view: FAMILY OF 3 BRUTALLY AXED TO DEATH: KILLER COMMITS SUICIDE. Below it was a black and white photo of an all too familiar looking house—*her* house.

Marlayna gasped. She was suddenly overcome by a sensation of light-headedness and let go of the newspaper. As soon as it landed on the ground, another gust of wind picked it up and carried it off. Marlayna's eyes were then drawn to a figure moving behind one of the upstairs windows of the house. Gazing up, she could make out the face of a teenage girl. Pale. Expressionless. It stared down at her from Janice's bedroom with dark and cadaverous eyes.

Marlayna rushed into the house and found her mother in the kitchen preparing supper. She asked if Janice had a friend over and was told that her sister had not yet returned home from school. Marlayna then bolted up the stairs and, with adrenaline pumping in her veins, opened the door to Janice's bedroom and timidly stepped inside, panting. There was no sign of the girl she had seen at the window. And then the sound of a wire hanger falling on the floor emanated from the bedroom closet. Marlayna's heart was now racing with fear. She cautiously approached the closet, placed her hand upon the knob, and slowly turned it. She then yanked the door open and looked inside, only to find her sister's mostly black clothes hanging from a wooden rod. As she shut the door, she happened to look down. The sight of a wire hanger on the floor of the closet sent a shiver running down her spine.

During supper, Mrs. Lemort complained more than once that Marlayna had barely touched her food. She also made it no secret that she found her daughter's strange behavior to be rather worrisome. Janice, on the other hand, was oddly ravenous.

* * *

It was shortly after midnight when Marlayna awoke with a start. She popped open her eyes and gasped in horror at the sight of a raised axe blade illuminated by the light of the full moon pouring in from her bedroom window. For a moment, she thought she was dreaming, but soon realized that she was awake. Wide awake. She opened her mouth to scream.

"Shhh," she heard Janice whisper. "Don't scream. It's only me."

Marlayna sprang up in bed, beads of cold sweat forming on her brow. "What are you doing in my room?" she asked. "And where the hell did you get that axe?"

"It was hidden under one of the floorboards in the attic," Janice answered. Her voice was oddly monotonal and devoid of any emotion. "Marcy came to me again tonight and lead me to it. She told me it was the same axe that she used to chop up her parents and younger brother with. If you look closely at the blade, you can see traces of dried blood on it." She pointed to the tool's cutting head, and a morbid grin crept across her ashen face. "Look, Marlayna."

An icy chill of fear gripped Marlayna, causing her to shiver. "If this is some kind of practical joke," she contended, "it really isn't very funny."

"I wish it were a joke," Janice stated, her eyes fixed upon her sister's, glazed and unblinking like those of a cadaver. "But I'm afraid this is totally serious. Marcy explained it all to me, and now I know what I'm required to do. Don't you understand? I have no choice but to do it… for Marcy… and the demon that dwells within the shadows."

"Janice! Stop it!" cried Marlayna. "I can't tell if you're playing with my mind or if you've gone insane. All I know is that you're terrifying me right now! Put that axe down, please, for God's sake!"

"I'm sorry, Marlayna. It's too late for God."

Janice turned and ran from the bedroom, disappearing into the darkness that infused the hallway. A deathly silence fell over the house and lasted for a dozen seconds that seemed like an agonizing eternity. And then the screaming began. It was blood-curdling and so loud that it nearly drowned out the sound of the axe blade plunging into meat, again and again. The blows were relentless and filled with uncontrollable rage. The sound of a lamp crashing to the floor commingled with the hellish chorus of screams and desperate cries for help. It was then followed by a fit of maniacal laughter that dripped with evil like foam from the mouth of a rabid beast.

Marlayna immediately threw the covers aside and

jumped out of bed, her heart pounding with rampant fear. Barefooted, she ran down the hallway in her babydoll nightgown of pink chiffon, screaming for her parents. As she drew closer to the master bedroom, where her mother and father slept, the laughter and horrendous chopping sounds grew louder. And as she opened the door, her nostrils were assailed by the sickening, metallic smell of blood. Her head swam and her stomach churned as her eyes drank in the nightmarish sight of her crazed, blood-splattered sister brutally hacking her parents into pieces with Marcy's death-dealing axe.

Her parents' king-size bedspread of white, tufted chenille was soaked with so much blood that it appeared to be completely red. Splatters of gore clung to the light blue damask wallpaper and the ceiling like hideous pinwheels, and stomach-turning chunks of chopped flesh, like pieces of rare steak, lay about the room, oozing their juices.

"Oh, my God!" Marlayna cried out, her eyes wide with disbelief, her mouth gaping with unbridled horror. "Janice, what have you done?" Her body began to shake violently, and tears welled up and then streamed down her cheeks, as the gory sight of her parent's hacked-up remains burned into her eyes like a glimpse into Hell.

Janice's insane laughter suddenly ceased, and she slowly turned her head in Marlayna's direction, making eye contact. "There is no Janice anymore," she growled in a gravelly, demonic-sounding voice. "There's only Marcy." She then raised the blood-smeared axe blade and, with frothy slime dripping from her lips, snarled, "It's your turn to die!"

Horrified, Marlayna let out an ear-piercing scream and ran for her life, her murderous sister in close pursuit. Halfway down the stairs, Marlayna lost her footing and tumbled the remainder of the way down until her battered body came to rest in a twisted heap on the hard parquet floor of the foyer. She could hear her sister's footsteps drawing closer, and knew if she didn't act quickly, she would be the next to die.

Ignoring the pain inflicted by the fall, Marlayna picked herself up from the floor and, at lightning speed, fled from her house of bloody horror into the crisp black night. She darted across the street to the old Queen Anne-style house where her teacher, Mr. Krueger, and his wife resided. She banged furiously upon their front door with her fists, all the while screaming, "Help me! Mr. Krueger! Help me!"

Moments later, the front porch light came on and Marlayna heard the sound of locks being unlocked. The door opened a crack and Mr. Krueger cautiously peered out, looking a bit groggy from just having been woken from his sleep.

"Marlayna?" he asked, sounding startled, as he was unaccustomed to finding one of his students at his front door in the middle of the night. "It's half past midnight. What on earth are you doing here at this ungodly hour?"

Marlayna's eyes were filled with tears and her body trembled uncontrollably. "Please!" she begged, her voice filled with desperation. "Let me in before she gets me too!"

"Before *who* gets you?" Mr. Krueger inquired, poking his head out the door and looking around. "There's nobody out there. You need to calm down, young lady. Are you high on drugs or something?"

"No! You must believe me, Mr. Krueger!" Marlayna pleaded. "My parents… they're both dead! She killed them! She used the axe like Marcy did! Oh, God! She's going to kill me too! It's all happening, just like in the diary!"

The baffled teacher opened the door wider and, with his hand, motioned for the terrified girl to come inside. He watched as she rushed into the house, and then he promptly shut the door and re-locked it.

"Who's at the door, Marshall?" a sleepy-eyed Mrs. Krueger called down from the top of the stairs. She craned her neck to get a look. "What's all the commotion down there?"

Mr. Krueger shouted up to his wife, "It's Marlayna Lemort from across the street. I'm not exactly sure of what's going on. The girl's hysterical. She said something about her parents being murdered. You'd better phone the police, Lorraine!"

"Oh, dear!" gasped Mrs. Krueger, and she scurried back to the master bedroom to make the call.

At that moment, the sharp and heavy blade of the axe split the wood of the Krueger's front door and Marlayna let out a terror-filled scream. She watched as her sister chopped her way through the door and then turned the axe on Mr. Krueger. The first blow struck his chest with a thud and blood spurted into the air like a bright red geyser. A second blow sliced across his abdomen and his intestines spilled out onto the floor. The axe then hacked off his head and limbs, and transformed the front parlor into a grisly scene of blood-soaked carnage and nightmarish gore.

In an effort to escape from the murderous rampage, Marlayna inadvertently stepped on one of Mr. Krueger's dislodged eyeballs and lost her balance. She fell forward and her forehead banged against the shelf of an antique whatnot that displayed Mrs. Krueger's extensive collection of vintage ceramic cats from around the world. Upon impact, she saw "stars" and then promptly blacked out.

* * *

The glaring light from an overhead incandescent bulb assaulted Marlayna's eyes as she slowly raised her eyelids. Her mind reeled with confusion upon finding herself sitting at a wooden table in the center of a tiny room. A pair of stainless-steel handcuffs restrained her wrists. In front of her, on top of the table, sat a tape recorder. Sitting directly across from her was a strange man, who had a five-o'-clock shadow and appeared to be in his mid-to-late fifties. Draped over one side of his wrinkled pinstripe dress shirt was a brown leather shoulder holster, which contained a gun.

"Where am I?" Marlayna asked, looking around at her unfamiliar surroundings. "Why am I in handcuffs? Who are you?"

"I'm the detective and I ask the questions here," replied the man. His voice was harsh and carried a trace of a Boston accent. "Perhaps, now that you've had your little nap, you'd care to explain to me your motive for doing it. What possessed you to murder all those people?"

"What are you talking about?" Marlayna cried. "I didn't murder anybody! My sister, Janice, is the one who killed them! She's possessed!"

"Possessed?" asked the detective, as he stared intently into the eyes of the agitated girl. "As in possessed by the Devil or a demon?"

"She was possessed by the spirit of a girl named Marcy," Marlayna explained, aware that her story probably sounded incredible to her interrogator, but hopeful, nevertheless, that he would believe her.

"Marcy," the detective echoed flatly. The tone of his voice was a clear indication to Marlayna that he was incredulous. He continued to stare at her without blinking.

"Over twenty years ago, Marcy and her family lived in the same house that my family and I recently moved into," Marlayna explained. "She went berserk one night and killed her entire family there with an axe. Janice discovered Marcy's diary in an old trunk up in the attic and it talks all about the murders and why she did it."

"Is this the diary you're referring to?" the detective inquired, tossing a small book with a black cover onto the table. He watched as the girl took it in her shackled hands and then, after a moment, flung it back onto the table as though it were on fire and had scorched her fingers.

"Yes," Marlayna answered, sobbing. "That's Marcy's diary. It's giving off an evil energy that's even stronger now than it was before. Can't you feel it?"

"Miss Lemort," began the detective, sounding annoyed, "I've lived in this town for almost sixty years, and I can assure you that, prior to the events of last night, no murders ever took place in the house that your family moved into. I've known all the families that have lived there and none of them had a daughter named Marcy. So, how's about you stop with the bullshit and start telling me the truth?"

"But I *am* telling you the truth!" Marlayna insisted, her voice growing excited. "A girl named Marcy *did* live there! And she *did* murder her family in that house! A girl in one of Janice's classes even told her about it, and her uncle was one of the detectives on the case. Plus, Marcy's confession, in her own handwriting, is inside that diary. There's the proof. Read it for yourself!"

"I *have* read it," replied the detective. "It contains only one entry, which our handwriting analysis expert confirmed was written by your sister, Janice." He picked up the diary, opened it, and read the entry out loud. "Dear Diary, I'm sorry to start you off on such a negative note, but I don't know who else to talk to about this. I know diaries are for writing down your thoughts and feelings, so here goes. I'm really worried about my little sister Marlayna. She's been acting weirder and weirder with each day that goes by, and seems to be totally obsessed with Marcy, even though I admitted to her that I made her up for a joke, along with a ridiculous axe murder story. She told me she's been having nightmares about Marcy and claimed that Marcy appeared in her room last night and demanded that she get an axe and slaughter everyone in the house while they sleep! I could hardly believe my ears when she told me that! Talk about creepy! I tried warning Mom and Dad that Marlayna was going off the deep end and maybe needs to get professional help. But, as usual, they never take anything I say very seriously. They just laughed it off, saying she has an overactive imagination and I shouldn't worry. But how can

I not worry? She's my little sister and I feel extremely guilty for whatever it is that's happening to her mind. I wish now that I had never invented that stupid story about Marcy. But you and I both know that wishes can't undo the damage that's been done."

"No!" shrieked Marlayna. "That's impossible! Those are all lies! Horrible lies! Janice read to me the entry that Marcy made in the diary. And then Marcy's ghost appeared in Janice's room that night and instructed *her* to kill everyone in the house with an axe, just like Marcy did over twenty years ago. Why don't you believe me? I'm telling you the truth! Where's Janice? She's the one who did it. You need to be questioning her, not me!"

For the first time since the interrogation session began, the detective cracked a slight grin. "Stop playing games with me, Miss Lemort. I think we both know that *that* isn't possible, now, don't we?"

"Isn't possible?" Marlayna questioned, echoing the detective's words. Her confusion increased. "I'm afraid I don't understand. What are you talking about?"

"I'm talking about the fact that you brutally axed your sister to death, along with your parents and the Kruegers. We found your sister's decapitated head inside your bedroom closet when we searched the house. It was hanging from a coat hook by its nose ring."

With tears streaming down her cheeks, Marlayna let out a scream and jumped up from her chair. "That can't be! Janice was the one who committed the murders with Marcy's axe! I saw her do it! I'm not a murderer! I'm innocent!"

The detective stood up and pounded his right fist on the tabletop, angrily. "We have audio of Lorraine Krueger's 911 call to report that you broke into her house and were attacking her husband with an axe. We also found your fingerprints all over the murder weapon, Miss Lemort!" he shouted. "In fact, they were the *only* fingerprints on it! How do you explain all that?"

Marlayna let out a loud gasp of horror as the detective's words sent a chill down her spine and rattled her to the core. A cold sweat beaded up on her forehead and her breathing rapidly increased until she was hyperventilating. The room suddenly felt as though it was spinning and Marlayna grabbed onto the table with both of her hands in an effort to steady herself. Everything around her grew blurry, and then she fainted.

Hours later, while making her rounds, a female corrections officer was aghast to discover Marlayna Lemort's lifeless body hanging in her jail cell above a sickening puddle of bodily fluids. A clear plastic bag covered her head, and wrapped tightly around her neck was an improvised noose fashioned from a bed-sheet. The dead girl's face was hideously bloated and bluish-gray in color, and her tongue, like a swollen purple serpent, protruded from her bloodstained, gaping mouth.

On the last page of Marcy's diary, which sat in a cardboard box in an evidence room at the police station next door, a new entry mysteriously appeared. It was scribbled in Marlayna's handwriting, and read:

"Dear Diary, You've been my trusted friend and confidante for some time; however, this will be my final entry. The nightmare that has spun its web around me has only one means of escape, and that is death. I have come to realize that, and I accept it wholeheartedly. I'm even looking forward to it. Before I go, I wish I could tell you why I felt compelled to murder all those people, but I honestly don't know. It's as much a mystery to me as to everyone else. I used to fear an imaginary monster under my bed when I was little, but the fear I feel now for the all-too-real monster that I've become is far greater. It must be stopped, or it will go on killing. Besides, how could I ever live with myself, knowing that I deliberately and brutally snuffed out the lives of the people I loved the most? Their screams continue to ring in my head. The look in their eyes just before I swung the axe blade at them continues to haunt me. Oh diary, I wish I could tell them all how sorry I am for what I did and how much I love them! But I know it's too late for that. Please forgive me for the horrors I've committed and for what I'm about to do. With a heavy heart, I bid you good-bye. Forever yours, Marcy"

TALL, DARK AND RANCID

The spicy aroma of apple-cinnamon permeated the inside of Lenore Finch's house as she made her daily rounds with her eight-ounce can of air freshener. It mingled with the other sweet fragrances unleashed by the numerous scented candles and jars of potpourri positioned throughout the residence. The smell produced an overwhelming, almost intoxicating, perfume that hung heavy in the air.

She paused in front of the hall mirror and gazed at her reflection. *Howard loved when I wore my hair up like this,* she thought. *He always said it reminded him of Audrey Hepburn.* Fighting a twinge of sadness, she did a careful inspection of her lipstick and eye make-up to make sure nothing was smudged. She wanted to look her best for the man who was coming to call on her. His name was Terry Robards, and he lived in the next town over. She had never met him in person before but had heard a slew of wonderful things about him from her best friend, Carole, who had arranged the blind date. According to Carole, he was "very charming, for a pharmacist," and could be a tad on the shy side at first.

Lenore checked her wristwatch for the time. In less than an hour, she would be on her first date since the untimely death of her husband from sudden cardiac arrest. She headed downstairs to the kitchen to make herself a drink, hoping a gin and tonic would help to calm the butterflies in her stomach. *Nothing must go wrong tonight*, she told herself as she pulled open the door to the well-stocked liquor cabinet. *Everything has to be perfect.* But no sooner had she wrapped her fingers around a bottle of Beefeater than the chiming of the doorbell echoed melodiously throughout the house, startling her out of her thoughts.

She looked down again at her wristwatch. *It couldn't be Terry*, she thought. *I'm not expecting him to arrive this soon.* She shut the cabinet door and headed to the foyer. The doorbell rang again, and the butterflies in her stomach fluttered wildly. She took a deep breath to steady her nerves and then opened the door.

Outside on the stoop stood a denim-clad man holding a single red rose. He was tall and dark-haired, just as Carole had described him over the phone. And, despite his eyes being obscured by a pair of dark aviator sunglasses, he appeared to be much younger than Lenore had expected. Not that that was a bad thing in her book by any means.

Behind him, the early-November sky, the color of granite tombstones, formed a bleak backdrop. Windborne leaves, their brilliant autumn colors now faded, swirled around his snakeskin cowboy boots like dancing rats. Spots of raindrops began to speckle the flagstone pathway leading from the front door to the street, where, oddly, no vehicle was parked.

"Hello. Are you Terry?" Lenore asked the stranger. "Terry Robards?" Goosebumps were beginning to spring up on her exposed arms as she stood in the open doorway, giving her ivory skin the less-than-alluring appearance of a plucked goose. As she attempted to rub them away, she wondered if the chill that hung heavy in the air was to blame, or was it her date night jitters, a feeling she hadn't experienced since her very first date with Howard, decades ago.

The man responded to Lenore's query with a nod of his head and extended the rose to her. He remained cloaked in silence as if waiting for her to make the next move. A muscle flinched in his cheek, causing one side of his bushy mustache to twitch.

Lenore remembered Carole mentioning Terry's shyness. Truth be told, she found it a rather endearing quality. However, the shaggy walrus mustache drooping over her date's upper lip was an entirely different matter. No heads up had been given on that particular attribute, which she found less than appealing. Dearly departed Howard had always kept his face clean-shaven. Facial hair would never do. Lenore made a mental note to recharge his old electric shaver to use later.

Hoping that her date wouldn't notice her goosebumps, she reached out to accept the rose. As she held it below her nose and inhaled its fragrance, the man took her other hand in his rough, manly paw and raised it to his mouth. He then gazed into her eyes through his tinted lenses and placed a kiss upon the back of her hand, which seemed to make his breathing quicken. Lenore found his reaction a trifle odd, but flattering, nonetheless. She couldn't remember the last time a gentleman had kissed her hand.

"I'm Lenore," she said, smiling as she introduced herself. "It's a pleasure to finally meet you, Terry. Carole's told me so much about you—all good, I might add." A nervous giggle escaped her lips. "Do come in and make yourself comfortable."

She ushered him inside her home and led him into a dark-paneled parlor bathed in the dim glow of a Spanish wrought iron chandelier dangling above. She paused to poke the fire in her stone fireplace back to life. She then looked up at her reflection in the large baroque mirror that hung over a mantel flanked by intricately carved gargoyles with the most menacing of faces. Relieved to find her hair and make-up still in place, she proceeded to place the red rose into a cut-crystal bud vase that sat on the mantel next to an Edwardian clock. She offered her guest a drink, which he declined with a shake of his head. *Damn it*, she thought. *A teetotaler.* She motioned for him to sit down next to her on a tufted, leather Chesterfield of oxblood red, which he did.

A low growl of thunder sounded off in the darkening distance as the man sat down and removed his sunglasses. He smiled as his eyes connected with Lenore's, and she smiled back at him. Despite the overgrown mustache, he wasn't a bad looking fellow, albeit not nearly as handsome as Howard.

Dear, dead Howard. On his deathbed, just before his untimely demise, he had told his distraught wife that he didn't wish for her to spend the rest of her life a lonely widow. He said it was—her *duty*—to find someone new after he died. She wondered if he would approve of her choice.

"Nice place you have here," he commented, his eyes scanning the room. Their gaze locked upon a large mahogany curio cabinet. It was brimming with grotesque statues of horned anthropomorphic creatures, nightmarish death masks, and bizarre primitive fetishes. His nose wrinkled in bewilderment as he stared at the macabre menagerie.

"I can tell by the expression on your face that you possess an appreciation for fine art," Lenore commented. "My husband, I mean my *late* husband, had a passion for... the unusual. He collected these little oddities during his many travels abroad. He was particularly fond of occult artifacts from Africa and the Middle East."

The man shifted his gaze back to Lenore. "You don't say." He offered up another smile. "Occult artifacts…that's different. Some people might even call it weird. But, hey, everybody collects something, right? Some people collect antiques, some collect trophies. Either way, it's the thrill of the hunt that makes collecting all worthwhile."

Lenore nodded her head. "Truer words were never spoken." Her eyes suddenly brightened. "The artifacts in that curio are just a small part of the collection. There's more upstairs. Much more. And some very special pieces that I think you might find interesting. I'd be happy to show you if-"

Before she could finish her sentence, the ringing of the old, black rotary telephone in the other room interrupted her. *Damn it! Someone's got bad timing.* Rising from the sofa, she politely excused herself and hurried to the den to answer the phone, which sat atop an antique writing desk.

"Hello?" she said into the mouthpiece, trying her utmost not to sound irritated.

"Hi," said a man's voice. "Is this Lenore?"

"Yes. Who is this?" Lenore enquired. She didn't recognize the voice in her ear.

"It's Terry. Terry Robards."

Terry Robards? "Is this some sort of a joke?"

"No joke. But I do have some bad news. I'm afraid I'm having a bit of trouble with the old Caddy. Can't seem to get her started. So, it's looking like I won't be able to keep our date tonight."

Horror and disbelief pummeled Lenore like a brutal fist, rendering her stunned, almost to the point of speechlessness. "Terry?" she squeaked.

"I can't begin to tell you how truly sorry I am, Lenore. You have no idea how much I was looking forward to meeting you. I even had something very special planned. If you're not busy tomorrow evening, perhaps we can reschedule our date for then?"

A shiver descended upon Lenore's spine. Her hands turned to ice, and she felt the phone slipping from her grasp. "Oh, no…"

At that moment, a startling boom of thunder vibrated the house. The connection crackled and then the line went dead with a buzz. As she returned the handset to the cradle, her thoughts quickly flashed to the stranger she had left in the parlor. *If he isn't Terry, then who the hell is he?* She felt a shiver of dread run through her body and thought it best to arm herself with a weapon of some sort in the event that his intentions were unsavory. Her mind recalled Howard's old bronze ritual dagger with the dragon-shaped handle—a souvenir he had brought home from a Tibetan excursion many decades ago. He always kept it in the top drawer of the desk, and frequently used it as a letter open, right up until the day that he departed this world. She pulled the drawer towards her and took the dagger in her right hand, the metallic dragon leaving its impression in her palm as she tightened her grip on it.

Concealing the dagger behind her back, she returned to the parlor to confront the imposter, only to find him nowhere in sight.

"Terry?" she called out, even though she now knew that wasn't his true name.

Her call was answered only by dead silence, save for the ticking of the clock on the fireplace mantel.

Lenore exited the parlor and cautiously made her way down the hall to the foyer, where she found the front door standing wide open. Dead leaves tumbled across the checkerboard marble floor, as a bone-chilling gust of wind came sweeping in with a ghostly moan, making the flames of Lenore's scented candles flicker wildly. Above, the tinkling prisms of a glittering chandelier stirred in the rush of air like tiny skeletons performing a danse macabre.

Lenore peered from the doorway as another gust of wind stormed in, prickling her exposed flesh. Outside, monstrous clouds of mordant black were amassing. Her eyes scanned the front area of her house as the bare branches of trees waved at her like scolding fingers. But there was no trace of the mysterious man. Surmising that he took flight after overhearing her conversation with the real Terry, Lenore let out a sigh of relief. She shut the door and locked it securely. *Weirdo*, she thought.

She returned to the parlor, plucked the red rose from the vase, and tossed it onto the crackling logs in the stone fireplace. Its petals curled and shriveled, and it emitted what sounded like a tiny whimper as the flames consumed its beauty.

Lenore headed into the kitchen for a broom and dustpan with which to clean up the leaves in the foyer. She laid the dagger upon the kitchen table, next to a can of air freshener—one of many that she kept throughout the house, ready for employment in the event that any foul odor should rear its ugly head.

She let out a scream as the door of the utility closet suddenly burst open and the man in the snakeskin boots lunged at her, his teeth bared, his eyes wild. Within seconds, she found his rough, meaty hands clamped around her throat, stopping her breath. A wave of horror swept over her. She could scarcely believe what was happening. It was like a horrible dream. She dug her fingernails into his wrists, drawing small rivulets of blood. She kicked and struggled to pull his hands away from her neck, but to no avail. His strength overpowered her.

"Women are the most beautiful," the man grunted, "when death dances in their eyes."

Lenore's ears were ringing and she felt a small trickle of blood emanate from one of her ear canals. She began to feel lightheaded and detached from her body. She knew if she blacked out that would mean certain death at the hands of her assailant. As long as she clung to consciousness, she had a fighting chance to save her life. Mustering every ounce of her remaining strength, she drove her knee up into the man's groin as hard as she could. It had no effect. Refusing to give up, she rammed her knee into his testicles again, and again, and again until he finally released his death grip on her throat and doubled over, howling in pain.

A rush of oxygen filled Lenore's deprived lungs. Gasping, she turned to flee from the kitchen, but her escape was thwarted when the man seized her by the hair and slammed her into the kitchen table, toppling the can of air freshener, which rolled off the table and onto the floor with a loud clunk.

"You let the devil into your house when you invited me in!" he yelled.

Without hesitation, Lenore grabbed the dagger from the table. Once again, the bronze dragon imprinted its ancient image into the palm of her hand. A struggle ensued and the blade bit into the man's upper arm. Blood blossomed like a dark red rose, staining the lacerated sleeve of his denim shirt.

"You rotten whore!" he snarled as he caught Lenore by the wrist and wrestled the dagger away from her. He backhanded her across the face, a monstrous grin twisting his lips. The force of the blow sent her crashing onto the cold, tiled floor. Her head swam in a daze.

When her fog cleared and her eyes could focus again, Lenore found the man kneeling over her, holding Howard's dagger against her bruised throat. She felt death was imminent and wondered if she would actually see her life flash before her eyes as she drew her final breath. Or was that simply an old wives' tale?

"Look what you did to my arm!" the man yelled. His warm breath was like an ill breeze violating Lenore's face. His tone became mocking. "That's no way for you to behave on our first date, Lenore." He shook his head, indicating his disapproval. "No way at all." He grinned, but then his face became somber. "And we were having such a fun time too…before you stabbed me."

"Who are you, and why are you doing this?" Lenore sobbed, tears glistening in her eyes, black trails of eyeliner and mascara running down the sides of her face. "What is it that you want from me? Money? Is that what you want? My husband left me with lots of money. We can go to the bank in the morning, and I'll withdraw all of it and give it to you. I promise. Please, just don't kill me!"

"Shut up! Shut up! Shut up!" the man bellowed with rage. He pressed the blade of the dagger harder against Lenore's trembling throat. "I didn't come here for your filthy money! Do I look like a goddamn robber to you? Or some kind of Skid Row loser?" Madness gleamed in his dark eyes. "Answer me, or I'll slit your throat right now!"

A cold sweat was forming on Lenore's forehead. "No, no, of course not," she nervously tried to assure him, hoping to diffuse his sudden swell of anger. "I'm sorry. I didn't mean to offend you. I don't think you're a bad person. But you're hurting me. Please. Put down the dagger. You don't have to do this. I can help you if you let me."

"You must think you're something pretty special, don't you? Well, you aren't!" the man growled through a spray of spittle. "You're no different than all the others I've hunted and gutted. You're nothing but a meat trophy!" His breathing became heavy as he slithered a finger lightly across the contours of Lenore's face. His voice softened. "I can smell your fear, Lenore. It smells, oh, so sweet," he whispered into her ear.

Wincing, Lenore turned away in a feeble attempt to escape his touch. Her eyes spied the fallen can of air freshener on the floor. It was within arm's reach.

"It makes me hungry," he continued, his arousal increasing. "It makes me want to rip you apart and devour you. And I will. I'm going to do things that you've never, in your worst nightmares, imagined." His breathing became frenzied. His head tilted back, and his eyes rolled up as if in rapture.

Seizing her opportunity, Lenore grabbed the can of air freshener, and before the man could react, she blasted his eyes with a blinding burst of the aerosol. He pulled the dagger away from her throat and instinctively covered his eyes with his hands in a fruitless attempt to suppress the burning sensation that assaulted them. Lenore struck the side of his head with the can. The blow was hard enough to put a dent in the metal. With one sudden, hard shove, she pushed his body off of hers and ran from the kitchen as fast as she could.

Cursing all women of the world, the man staggered in a besotted fashion to the kitchen sink and proceeded to splash copious amounts of cold water into his bleary, burning eyes. When enough of the chemical irritant had been flushed out, enabling a return of vision, he picked up the bloodstained dagger and set out to find Lenore…and to finish her off.

With stealthy footsteps, he moved through the house like an animal hunting prey. He searched the first floor in its entirety, and then made his way upstairs to the bedrooms, looking in closets, behind chairs and under beds.

There was only one bedroom remaining in which to look. It was at the end of the hall, hidden behind a white six-panel door. The man licked his lips in anticipation of the orgy of slaughter he was planning for his victim. As he crept towards the room, he deliberately scraped the point of the dagger along the wall. It produced an ominous sound, like the tearing of flesh, as it ripped a long gash in the floral wallpaper.

He turned the knob and gave the door a shove. It swung open with a slight creak. Without warning, the malodorous smell of something musty came rushing into his nostrils. Ignoring the odor, he stepped inside, dagger poised to strike.

It was a capacious, high-ceilinged room, decorated, like

much of the rest of the house, with dark antique furniture. A massive canopy bed, draped on all sides in heavy scarlet linens, stood at one side of the room, facing a pair of tall French doors leading to a small balcony overlooking the front of the property. Large oil paintings depicting fiendish-looking, winged creatures that were not of this world adorned the brocade walls, giving the room a weird vibe. But even weirder were the two open coffins sitting side-by-side on the floor in the center of the room.

"What the hell?" the killer muttered to himself as he slowly advanced toward the coffins. The nearer he drew to them, the more phenomenal in its foulness the musty odor became.

He found one coffin to be empty, but the other was occupied. Inside it lay what appeared to be the mummified remains of a man dressed in formal attire, a black bow tie around its desiccated neck. The skin on the corpse's gaunt face clung like a hideous leather mask over its skull, and its ears, nose and eyelids were a blackish color. Hanging loosely on its withered ring finger was a gold band set with a large black onyx, the stone engraved with mysterious symbols—runes or perhaps hieroglyphs. It looked to be a relic from a time long past.

He slowly laid the dagger at the edge of the coffin and stared at the ring for several moments, as if mesmerized. Then he tugged it from the mummified man's digit and slid it onto the fourth finger of his left hand. It was a perfect fit.

As his eyes remained transfixed on the ring, Lenore emerged from her hiding spot behind one of the floor-length drapery panels flanking the French doors. In her right hand, she held a gun with a silencer on the end of its barrel. She raised it and aimed it at her assailant's heart, which she concluded was as black as the depths of Hades.

"I see you've met my husband," she remarked. "Unlike you, Howard is a *true* gentleman." With her gun still pointed at the man who intended to murder her, she turned to the musty corpse in the coffin and spoke to it as if it were still alive. "Howard, sweetie, I hope you can hear me. Tonight is the night, just as I promised. This man here is going to be your new vessel. I do hope you approve of him."

The man snapped out of his trance. "New vessel? What the hell is that supposed to mean?"

"It means I'm going to help you, just like I said I would. You're a sick man, a rabid animal, but I'm going to fix all that. I'm going to give you a brand-new lease on life. I know it's hard for you to believe, but I swear it's true. I have the knowledge…the ability to do that."

"What the hell are you babbling about?"

Lenore smiled. "Let me enlighten you. You see, I'm going to perform a soul transfer, right here in this very room. It's an ancient ritual. Extremely powerful. It will enable Howard's soul to take possession of your physical body, essentially rebirthing him. And you'll be…"

"Like two peas in a pod?" he interrupted, flippantly.

"Not exactly," Lenore explained. "You see, all workings of black magic require a sacrifice of some sort as payment to the old gods—the dark ones who have roamed the earth for eons before the birth of Christ. That malignant thing within you that passes for a soul will be offered up to them in accordance with the ancient laws of sacrifice. They will devour it, and then, that part of you will simply cease to exist. But there's no reason for you to worry. It'll be quick and painless, unlike the torture you like to put your female victims through. Now, kindly get into the empty coffin."

Lenore could tell by the man's roar of laughter that he discredited her words.

"You can't be serious, lady," the man snickered. "No hocus pocus or ancient gods are going to bring that stiff over there back to life. If you actually believe you can resurrect the dead by transferring souls or whatever, you belong in a nut house."

Lenore grinned with amusement. "Do I? If you ask me, I'd say that was the pot, or the *crack*pot in your case, calling the kettle black. Now, do as I tell you and get into that damn coffin before I lose what little patience I have left."

The man began to inch his way towards Lenore. "You aren't going to shoot me. You don't have the guts to pull that trigger. You and I both know that." He wrinkled up his nose. "All that blood and guts everywhere…"

Lenore cocked the gun and shouted, "I'll shoot you if I have to! I swear it! Don't make me do it. I prefer not to put holes in Howard's body-to-be."

The man stopped in his tracks and threw his hands up in the air. "Okay, okay. Take it easy, Lenore. I'll play your whacked-out little game…for now." He took a step back, turned and stepped into the coffin. He stared blankly at Lenore, his hands still raised. "Now what?"

"Now lie down," Lenore instructed. "Do it!"

The man did as he was told. Lenore walked over to the coffin, reached into her pocket with her free hand and extracted a handful of strange black powder, which she blew into his face as though she were blowing him a kiss. He began coughing furiously. His eyeballs rolled up into his head, and soon, an acrid, black fluid began dribbling from his nostrils and the corners of his mouth. Lenore slammed the lid shut and locked it to prevent the man from escaping before the somniferous properties of the powder took their full effect.

The sound of her captive's fists pounding frantically against the inside of the burial container that enveloped his body was a sweet melody to Lenore's ears. It brought a smile to her lips and inspired within her a sense of euphoria.

And then the melody ceased and there was only silence, save for the low moaning of the wind about the velvet-draped windows.

"It won't be long now, sweetie," she whispered to her husband's corpse. "Soon, very soon, we will be together again."

After giving the room another blast of apple-cinnamon and drawing the drapes on the French doors, Lenore began preparing for the long-awaited ritual that she believed would reunite her with Howard. She dabbed her forehead with a drop of perfumed anointing oil she'd obtained from an occult apothecary shop. Its aroma was heavy and almost intoxicating. She then cloaked herself in a black ritual robe edged with mystical gold symbols. She drew a large magic circle on the floor around the two coffins, marking each of the four cardinal direction points with black pillar candles. Her heart thumped with excitement as she opened a black, leather-bound grimoire and began reciting an evocation written in an ancient tongue. The words from her book of magic spells reverberated on her lips, waking the old gods from their deep, dark slumber.

Lightning set the sky ablaze, followed by a peal of thunder that rattled the heavens. The French doors blew open and the velvet drapes danced wildly in the wind that howled through the room like a pack of wolves—or, as Howard was fond of saying, a choir of sinners.

* * *

Having completed the final step of the ritual, Lenore closed the grimoire and set it upon her ornately carved dresser, next to the gun. Butterflies were aflutter again in the pit of her stomach as she eagerly unlocked the coffin containing the body that now served as the living vessel for Howard's disembodied soul.

"Wake up, Howard," she cooed. "The ritual is over. It's time for you live again!"

She waited for a response but received none. Not even the faintest sign of revival. After a few restive moments, she tried once again to rouse Howard's soul from its sleep. But still the vessel's eyes remained shut, his mouth wide open, frozen in a silent scream. He didn't appear to be breathing, which prompted Lenore to press her ear to his chest and listen for a heartbeat.

There was none.

She grabbed one of the hands that had tried to brutally strangle the life from her earlier. It had a waxen pallor and felt like a chunk of refrigerated meat. She screamed, "Howard! I implore you to wake up! Take possession of this man's body now, before it's too late! It's your new vessel!"

Then she took notice of the onyx ring. She attempted to slide it from the man's lifeless finger but was unable to budge it more than a fraction of an inch. The finger was swollen and refused to give up its talismanic treasure. Determined to retrieve the ring and return it to its rightful place on her husband's hand, even if it meant resorting to the use of gardening shears to sever the finger, she wiggled and twisted and yanked it until, at last, she was able to pull it off.

"I don't know what went wrong," she lamented, as she slid the ring back onto Howard's finger. "I followed the ritual to a tee. I don't understand why it didn't…"

She lapsed into speechlessness as she observed in wonderment Howard's hollow chest suddenly rise and fall as he heaved in a breath and released it. A morsel of dust spilled from his nostrils. It was an unearthly sight, but one that set Lenore's heart reeling. After all this time, her beloved was at last returning from beyond the grave, albeit not in the intended body.

"The magic worked!" Lenore cheered. "And just as I was beginning to lose all hope. Howard, sweetie…can you hear me? It's Lenore. Rise and shine. Your sleep of death is over!"

Lenore's delight quickly turned into horror as Howard's cadaverous eyelids unfolded before her, revealing two spider-infested holes where his eyes should have been. To her shock, he suddenly sprang up. His horrendous hands, with greenish skin stretched tight like parchment over its bones, latched onto her wrists like a pair of vise grips. A terror-filled scream rose from her lungs as he attempted to pull her into the coffin with him. Struggling to free herself from the corpse's clutches, she found it possessed great strength despite its wizened state. Howard's decayed mouth opened and the voice that resounded was not that of Howard, but rather of the killer in cowboy boots, whose body lay exanimate in the other coffin, ripe with the smell of death.

"You twisted witch!" he bellowed with a puff of musty dust. "You put me in the body of your dead husband! I should have slit your stinkin' throat when I had the chance!"

Lenore belted out another scream and wrested herself free. She ran for the gun on the dresser, her heart pounding wildly in her chest. She wondered if a bullet would suffice to kill something that was already dead… something that, by all laws of nature, was not even supposed to exist. She tripped over one of the black pillar candles and fell face-first to the hardwood parquet floor. As she scrambled to her feet, she saw that the corpse had climbed out of its coffin and was stumbling toward her. She made it to the dresser and took the gun in her hand, took aim at the thing that was once her husband, and pulled the trigger.

The gun jammed.

She pulled the trigger a second time.

Again, the gun jammed.

The advancing monstrosity was but inches away from being within arm's reach of Lenore. She threw the inoperative gun at it. It struck the corpse in the chest but did not faze it. She lifted the heavy grimoire from the top of the dresser with both her hands, and with a grunt, swung the book with all her might at the side of the corpse's head. It made impact with a loud thud that made Howard's teeth rattle. The head tore away from its neck and sailed across the room, striking one of the demonic paintings on the wall and sending it crashing to the floor. From the stump of its neck, hundreds of tiny spiders emerged. But even sans head, Howard's possessed corpse remained animated.

Its hands were wrapping around Lenore's throat when she rammed the grimoire into the corpse's chest, sending it staggering backwards. She gave it a furious shove with her foot, causing it to topple back into the confines of its coffin. Wasting no time, she retrieved Howard's head and tossed it into the coffin as well. *This isn't exactly what I had planned for the evening*, she thought as she secured the lid.

Riddled with exhaustion and shaken to the core, Lenore changed out of her ritual attire and cleaned herself up. Afterwards, she settled down in her Rococo style tufted chair, where she soothed her frazzled nerves with a much-needed gin and tonic and pondered the strange events of the day. She scolded herself for letting that deranged man into her home. How could she have been so careless? After several close brushes with death, she felt fortunate to still be alive, although crushed by the failure of the ritual. What could have gone wrong? She was sure she'd followed all the instructions outlined in the grimoire…and then she realized Howard's onyx ring was on the other man's finger during the ritual.

His wearing of the ring must have somehow affected the ritual, transferring the wrong soul into the wrong body, she surmised. *I'll have to make sure nothing like that happens next time.*

The chiming of the doorbell derailed her train of thought.

Who on earth could be at the door? she wondered. An unsettling thought caused a wave of dread to rise inside her, and she sprung from her comfortable chair. *Could it be that someone—perhaps a neighbor or some passerby—heard screaming coming from the house and phoned the police?*

She opened the French doors and, with a sense of foreboding, stepped out onto the small, windswept balcony, which afforded her a view of the front door below. Looking down, she observed a well-dressed man standing on the stoop. He was tall with dark, wavy hair. In one hand he held a flat, white box tied with a red bow, in the other a bouquet of purple dahlias. He turned and began walking towards an older model Cadillac parked on the street in front of the house.

"Hello!" Lenore called down to the man. He turned and looked up at her. "Can I help you?"

A smile appeared on his face. "Hello there!" he replied, as he started back for the house. "I'm Terry Robards. And you must be the lovely Lenore."

Lenore nodded her head. After everything she had just been through, she wasn't sure if his words were truthful.

"I finally got the Caddy to turn over," he explained, pointing at the car. "She can be a bit temperamental at times. Anyway, I tried calling you to tell you I was coming, but the phone lines were down. I hope it's not too late for us to have our date…if you haven't had a change of heart, that is."

Lenore began to tingle with excitement. *A second chance to perform the soul transfer*, she thought. *This time, I'll make sure nothing goes wrong.*

"No change of heart," she gleefully assured Terry. "Give me a minute or two and I'll be right down."

He smiled and nodded his head.

Lenore quickly checked her hair and make-up in the mirror, then took a long fashion scarf from one of the drawers in the ornate dresser and wrapped it around her neck to conceal the bruises. She also made sure to refill her pocket with the black sleeping powder in case she couldn't make Terry pass out with alcohol or a roofie. As she headed out of the bedroom, a banging sounded from the inside of Howard's coffin. His decapitated corpse was trying to get out.

Ignoring the noise, Lenore hurried down the stairs, spritzing the air with more apple-cinnamon scented spray as she went. She hoped it would mask the musty odor of her mummified husband, as well as the death stench of the other man, who needed to be dragged down to the cellar, dismembered with Howard's power tools, and shoveled into the incinerator. But that was a task that needed to wait until morning. This night was reserved for something far more important.

Lenore turned on the stereo in an effort to drown out the banging before opening the front door and greeting her date. His brown eyes twinkled at her. His face was clean-shaven and blessed with handsome features, although not as handsome as Howard, of course. His cheeks took on a rosy blush as he presented Lenore with heart-shaped chocolates and flowers. *Carole was right about him. He is very charming...for a pharmacist.*

"I hope you like chocolates," he said in a bashful manner. "I hope you like dahlias too. I would have brought you a dozen red roses, but I didn't want you to think I was the Red Rose Killer."

"The Red Rose Killer?"

"You haven't heard? He's a modern-day Jack the Ripper who likes to butcher women. His last victim was a retired schoolteacher from the next town over. I'll spare you all the gory details of the murders, but this psycho likes to leave behind a red rose dipped in blood at his crime scenes. The cops haven't caught him yet, so you need to keep your doors and windows locked and be very careful who you let into your home."

A chill ran through Lenore's body. "How horrible!" she remarked, as another ripple of goosebumps began to break out across her arms. "There certainly are a lot of sick people running around loose in this world."

Terry nodded his head in agreement, and then Lenore

led him into the dark-paneled parlor and offered him a drink.

"I'll have whatever you're drinking," he said, politely.

"Okay then. Two gin and tonics coming right up! Just as soon as I find a vase for these beautiful flowers."

The banging was growing louder. No longer could the music conceal it.

Terry gave Lenore a puzzled look. "What's that noise?"

Lenore's mind raced to find an answer—one that would sound convincing. "That? Oh, it's nothing to worry about. Just a loose shutter on one of the upstairs windows. It bangs like that every time the wind blows. One of these days I'll have to get a handyman to fix it."

"I'd be more than happy to take a look at it sometime tomorrow, if you have a tall ladder," Terry offered. "I might be a pharmacist by trade, but I've been known to be pretty handy around the house."

The banging came to an abrupt stop and the house went eerily silent.

Lenore thanked Terry, and then with bouquet in hand, headed to the kitchen for a vase and two glasses of gin and tonic, one of which would be spiked with a pulverized sleeping tablet. Halfway down the hall, she hesitated. *Was that a creak on the stairs?* She listened for a few moments, barely breathing, her heart in her throat. The noise did not repeat. Dismissing it as her imagination or the wind blowing outside, she continued on her way.

She had just placed the dahlias in a hand-painted, ceramic vase and was filling it with cold water from the kitchen tap when she suddenly felt a pricking sensation, like the jab of a hypodermic needle, in her buttocks. Before she could comprehend what was happening, she lapsed into unconsciousness and slumped to the floor, where she lay surrounded by purple dahlias and pieces of the broken vase.

When Lenore regained consciousness, she found herself in a candlelit basement, her body attired in a wedding gown of white lace and strapped securely to a gurney. She struggled to free herself but could do little more than wiggle her fingers and toes and turn her head a bit in either direction. A rancid smell of rotting meat permeated her olfactory senses, and she soon realized its source was the putrefying body of a dead woman that was sitting upright in a chair beside her.

Both eyes of the corpse were black and blue, and its forehead appeared to be split right across, practically from one ear to the other. The head was missing patches of hair from its scalp, and slivers of ivory-colored bone peeked through spots on the discolored arms and legs where the flesh had rotted off. Flies and gnats buzzed about the lifeless horror that had, at one time, been a living, breathing woman. From one of the nostrils of its broken nose, a wriggling maggot came forth, and dropped into its lap.

Lenore heard the sound of approaching footsteps. She didn't know if someone was coming to rescue or to murder her. She felt trapped in a nightmare. Nothing made sense. Her anxiety intensified as the footsteps grew louder. She prayed it wasn't the Red Rose Killer. And then Terry appeared in her field of vision.

"Terry!" Lenore cried out. "Thank God it's you! Where are we? Why am I strapped to this gurney?"

"Shhh. There's no need for you to panic," Terry answered. He gently caressed Lenore's cheek with the back of his fingers and offered her a comforting smile. "You're okay now, and everything will be all right. I promise."

"Why is there a dead woman sitting in that chair? Did you…did you kill her?"

A slight smile pulled at Terry's lips, and he looked upon the corpse with a loving gaze.

"That's my wife, Katherine…or, rather, what's left of her. She was killed in a car accident just over a month ago. A drunk driver t-boned her at an intersection downtown. She died instantly." He turned back to Lenore. "I've kept her down here in our basement because I can't bear to let her go."

It was then that Lenore's eyes glimpsed the black leather-bound book in Terry's hand, and she began to realize her fate. Struggling harder against the leather straps pinning her down, she beseeched the widowed man to free her, promising him the moon in exchange for her release. But her tear-filled pleading proved to be in vain. She begged him not to hurt her.

"I have no intention of harming you, Lenore." Terry began lighting black candles and placing them at the four quarters of a circle inscribed on the floor. "You're the perfect vessel for Katherine's soul." He opened the black book and started reciting an evocation written in an ancient tongue.

Lenore's scream was muted by the deafening rumble of thunder that shook the very foundation of the house as the old gods once again awakened from their deep, dark slumber.

THE STORM RIDER

For three days and three nights, the rain fell with a vengeance. Riverside Parkway was closed due to flooding, and Reginald Madden was forced to follow a detour, which ultimately deposited his maroon Lincoln Continental sedan onto Twisted Oaks Road – a lonely and desolate stretch of unlit roadway that snaked around the outskirts of town.

He vehemently disliked traveling this particular thoroughfare; for the past twelve months he had avoided it at all costs. But, on this storm-filled night, he had no choice but to take it, even though it made him cringe. He continued down Twisted Oaks, driving in and out of ghostly patches of fog that swallowed him up and spit him out; and then, without warning, something darted in front of the vehicle. He swerved in an attempt to avoid hitting whatever it was.

Thump.

Thump.

He jammed his foot onto the brake pedal and his body lurched forward. His chest made impact with the steering wheel as the tires screeched to a halt.

"Son of a bitch!" he yelled.

Wasting no time, he unbuckled his seatbelt. With his black umbrella in hand, he got out to inspect the front of the car for any damage. To his relief, there were no dents. He then took a quick look around, expecting to find a dead or dying animal – or something far worse. However, there was no sign of any road kill.

Madden started back to his car when a dazzling flash of lightning lit up the scenery around him. And it was then, when the fury of nature had transformed nighttime into daylight for one brief moment, he came to notice her at the side of the road, near a hedgerow rising up from a blanket of white mist. She stood there, poised like a statue, motionless, watching him.

He thought it odd that a woman should be standing alone in the proverbial middle-of-nowhere, and in the throes of a raging thunderstorm. Should he be daring and inquire if she was in need of help? Or should he play it safe and simply leave without getting involved? He studied her for a few moments, while weighing his options. Another flash of lightning illuminated her face enough for him to determine that she was young – probably in her early or middle twenties.

His mind suddenly reeled back to the mysterious thing that had run out in front of his car and the ensuing thumping sounds. Dread enshrouded him. Could he have accidentally run over a dog belonging to the woman at the side of the road? If he had, where did it go?

"Hey there!" he shouted to her. "Is everything all right? Do you need some help?"

A chilling wind whipped up as he waited for the woman to reply, but the constant swishing of the windshield wiper blades and the incessant pitter-patter of raindrops beating against the taut nylon of his umbrella were the only sounds that broke the silence.

Reginald Madden was not a man who advocated the

practice of hitchhiking; he had never before picked up a hitchhiker, and was proud of the fact. He had always lectured people on the dangers of doing it. But for some queer reason that was unclear to him, he felt it was necessary to offer a ride to this particular stranger. Perhaps it was merely the unrelenting storm that compelled him. Or perhaps it was something far darker than the clouds looming above.

"Can I give you a lift into town?" He was astonished by the words spilling out of his mouth and could scarcely believe they were his, despite hearing them uttered in his own voice. "I'm heading in that direction, and I could sure use the company."

The woman still did not answer; Madden began to ponder her strange silence. Could she be deaf? Did she not speak English? Was she mad, perhaps? Strung out on drugs? Whatever the reason was, he no longer cared. He was tired of standing in the cold rain and growing anxious to return to his car and be on his way.

"Suit yourself," he sighed, feeling annoyed and relieved at the same time as he proceeded to get back into his waiting vehicle. However, no sooner had he gotten in and shut the door, the woman made her way over to his car, opened the passenger door, and climbed inside without so much as a single word.

"I'm glad you decided to take me up on my offer," Madden stated, dishonestly, as he put the car into drive, an artificial smile stretching his mustached-draped lips. "This is certainly no night for a lovely young woman to be roaming around, with the storm and all."

There was nothing 'lovely' about the woman to speak of. Her beady eyes of black possessed an almost rodent-like quality about them. Her hair, black and stringy and oozing with rainwater, dangled in front of her lumpy, colorless face like a wet, dirty string-mop veiling a blob of dough. She stared straight ahead at the dashboard, her face void of expression.

"So," Madden began, "if you don't mind me asking, what *were* you doing out in the storm? Did your car break down? Are you in some kind of trouble?"

The passenger maintained her stony silence.

Fed up with being ignored, Madden snarked. "You're not a very talkative person, are you? Cat got your tongue?"

At that moment, a trickle of blood issued from the woman nose, and then blood began to ooze from the inner corners of her vacant eyes. Within seconds, her eyes rolled up into her head; her body went limp as a rag doll, and her head slumped back. She began breathing rapidly, gasping for air.

"Oh my God!" Madden was seized with alarm. He could feel the hairs on his arms standing on end as his eyes frantically shifted from his passenger, to the road, and back again. "What the hell is going on? Are you freaking out on drugs or something?"

The woman let out an agonized groan, which rapidly developed into a loud and frightful growl, and her body launched into a cluster of violent spasms. A red wave of frothy blood washed over her lips and ran down her chin, contrasting the stark pallor of her skin in an appalling way.

"Jesus Christ almighty!" Madden bellowed, horrified. "You're bleeding all over the place! This is great. Just *fucking* great!"

His stomach quivered with nausea, and he turned his attention back to his driving. He was now regretting his decision to break his longstanding personal rule against picking up hitchhikers. He had always told himself that they were more trouble than they were worth, and tonight's events were proving him right. The urge then came upon him to stop the car and let the woman out. After all, she wasn't his responsibility, he told himself. She was little more than a stray animal, and probably a junkie, or perhaps even a carrier of some horrible disease. He felt if she were going to die, it was better that she does it on the side of the road in the storm instead of inside his precious Lincoln Continental and ruin the full leather interior.

A dense mass of fog appeared and then something again darted in front of Reginald Madden's vehicle; he swerved to the right to keep from hitting whatever it was. The rear of the car hydroplaned across the slick pavement for a second, and then there came an all-too-familiar sound...

Thump.

Thump.

This time, he did not stop to take a look; he continued down the road, increasing his speed at the very instant the fog dissipated. He again glanced over at his passenger. She was no longer growling or convulsing. To his surprise, she was sitting quietly and staring out at the road ahead with an eerie calmness, as if nothing had happened. He studied her face, startled to find that all traces of the blood had mysteriously vanished. Confusion ripped into his mind like the sharp claws of a cat upon a scratching post. *What the hell just happened? Did I simply imagine her bleeding? Perhaps,* he reasoned with himself, *I was far more tired than I realized.*

He took a deep breath in an effort to reinstate his composure. He cleared his throat. "Are you," he began, cautiously, "all right?"

The woman slowly turned her head and stared at him. Within the abyss of her eyes, a glaring hatred, like a seed, sprouted. She remained steadfast in her silence; her muteness was beginning to unnerve the man behind the steering wheel. He cleared his throat once again, feigned a meager smile, and attempted to carry on in a normal fashion in spite of the uncomfortable silent treatment he was receiving.

"Believe it or not, you're the first hitchhiker I've ever picked up. I normally don't give rides to strangers, you know. It's too risky – especially nowadays with nuts running around loose everywhere. If that dog, or whatever it was, hadn't run in front of my car, I would have never stopped. I wouldn't have even seen you standing there in the dark, in the storm. You're lucky that I did. Who knows what sort of creep might have picked you up if I hadn't come along? You know, a young woman like you really shouldn't be out at night, all by herself, thumbing rides from strangers. Don't you know it's dangerous? You could get hurt – or worse."

"You mean like that woman you killed in that hit-and-run accident last year?" the woman asked, while staring out the rain-blurred window at the passing scenery. Her voice was marred by hoarseness, and possessed an acrid quality.

Madden was somewhat startled to hear the woman finally speak, and stunned by her unexpected question. It rendered him momentarily speechless. His fingers tightened their grip on the steering wheel and his knuckles began to turn white. Once the initial shock passed, he regained his voice.

"What? Is this some kind of joke? I've never been involved in any hit-and-run accident! What the hell would make you accuse me of something like that?" he demanded; his tone was defensive and coupled with indignation. "Well? You'd better start explaining because I don't have any idea what you're talking about!"

"Don't you?"

Madden huffed. "Like I already told you: No! I don't!" He hurled a look of anger in his passenger's direction, and then added, "And I don't appreciate being accused of a crime. You've got some gall, lady. You don't even know me!"

"Oh, but I *do* know you. I know you all too well, Mister Reginald Madden. I've waited so long for this night… for this storm."

A crooked bolt of lightning split open the sky, followed by a booming crash of thunder. The rain now seemed to be falling with greater intensity – ferocity, if you will. The windshield wipers, even set to their quickest speed, could scarcely keep up with the barrage of pummeling water droplets.

"How do you know my name?" Madden inquired, coolly: his tone of anger overridden by curiosity and suspicion. "We've never met before. Just who the hell are you? What kind of twisted game are you playing?"

"A game with *my* rules."

"Don't talk to me in goddamn riddles," Madden snapped, an angry tone once again in his voice. "What, exactly, do you want from me?"

The woman threw her head back, gently, and replied with amused laughter. "What I want is for you to play this little game that I devised especially for you. I want to watch you squirm. I want to watch you suffer. I want to revel in the anguish that darkens your soulless eyes when this game concludes and the long-awaited moment arrives for you to pay in full."

"I see. So, it's money you're after, is it?" Anger bubbled and coursed through his veins like a lava flow. "Very well. You have me at a disadvantage, so I'll indulge you in your little game of blackmail. Let's cut to the chase. How much do you want?"

The woman did not offer a reply. She stared out the window, which only served to enrage Madden further.

"Well, come on then! I haven't got all night to play this goddamn game of yours! I'm keen to get this whole matter settled. Now, tell me. What's your price for silence?"

"You'll find out."

"What the hell is that supposed to mean? I've already told you I'm willing to meet your price, whatever it is. But don't take me for a fool. I'm warning you."

Several silent minutes, which felt more like hours to him, passed by. He slowed the car and then turned off onto a bumpy gravel road leading to a derelict textile mill that looked to be abandoned for decades. A flash of lightning transformed the ruins into an imposing and ominous silhouette. He proceeded to the rear of the mill, which overlooked a dark and turbulent river reaching flood stage, and stopped the car. It seemed the perfect place to dispose of a body.

"End of the line," he announced.

He flipped down his sun visor, revealing a pistol tucked into an elastic holster. Without hesitation, he took hold of the loaded firearm, cocked it, and pointed it at the woman in the seat next to him; she exhibited a blank expression. Madden's lips curled into a grin. He was back in control.

"Your little game has grown boring, so I'm changing the rules. We're going to play the rest of it by my rules now. *Capisce?* Now, be a good girl and get out of the car."

The woman obediently did as she was instructed without protest. Madden then exited the vehicle and approached her, clutching his umbrella in his left hand and the gun in his other. He aimed it at her chest. Another flash of lightning illuminated the night sky, and was followed by a long rumble of thunder. The rain was stinging Madden's hand; but, the feeling of having power over life and death was exhilarating to him, almost intoxicating.

"This is where we say goodbye. But, before we part company, I want you to explain to me how you know so much about that… incident."

"Because," the woman began in her hoarse voice, "that hitchhiker you killed in cold blood during the hit-and-run… was me."

Madden snorted. "You're as crazy as you are stupid. I don't know how you really obtained your dirt about me, but you know far too much for your own good, and for mine. You could easily destroy me, along with my business and my family. And I can't let that happen, now, can I?"

He took a quick look around to ensure they were alone, and then squeezed the trigger of the pistol. The bullet exited the barrel and passed through the woman's body, leaving no wound. He fired a second shot, which yielded the same result. Madden's jaw dropped in disbelief.

"You can't kill me twice," she gloated with a grin before bursting into a fit of maniacal laughter. She tossed her head back and wailed and howled, her laughter growing so raucous that tears were streaming from her eyes. "You can't kill me twice!"

Her words were like swords that impaled the very fibers of Reginald Madden's being.

Horror-stricken and confused, he watched as the woman, like a mirage, gradually faded away into nothingness; only the sound of her laughter remained. The loud revving of an eight-cylinder engine vibrated his eardrums, and he spun around to behold the sight of his Lincoln Continental barreling towards him at a lightning-fast speed. It would be the last thing his eyes would ever see.

Thump.
Thump

A MATTER OF TASTE

"**A**nd in local news, more human remains have been found in a Port Devlin sewage treatment plant for the third time in less than a week. Authorities report that two feet and a thumb were found Friday morning at the same facility where a man's leg and pelvis were found on Tuesday. Last week, a suitcase containing partially eaten female breasts and other body parts was found in a wooded area by hikers, and the week before that, a Chinese food takeout box containing an ear and a spleen was found in a trash bin by a dumpster diver. Police suspect foul play was involved and are investigating. Anyone with information is asked to contact the sheriff's office or the Crime Stoppers twenty-four-hour hotline. All calls will be kept confidential. Now, back to the soothing sounds of classical music…"

Roberta Pickering, a woman of impeccable taste and breeding, shook her head in disgust. *What is this world coming to,* she asked herself before turning her thoughts to more important matters, namely the unpacking and putting away of her Chateau Baccarat wine goblets. Being the *bon vivant* that she was, she'd never dream of sipping her Romanie-Conti from anything less exquisite than imported French glasses costing $150 apiece.

Being married to a retired hepatologist with a fat Louis Vuitton wallet, she could have easily afforded to pay the men from the moving company to unpack all of her boxes, but she preferred doing the job herself rather than trust her treasures in the grimy, careless hands of modern-day Neanderthals.

As she was placing the last of her crystal goblets on the top shelf of her tall Chippendale display cabinet, the loud growling of a stomach and the nauseating stench of halitosis prompted her to turn around. She gasped as terror sliced through her corpulent body like the claws of a beast, causing her to drop the goblet onto the herringbone parquet floor of the dining room. Her mouth opened wide and from it burst forth a shrill scream. It was loud enough to drown out both the classical music from the radio and the sound of lead crystal exploding into an array of expensive fragments.

To Roberta's horror, standing not more than five feet from the stepladder upon which she stood was a strange and unsavory couple that, for all intents and purposes, appeared to have crawled out of a garbage dumpster.

Intruders!

The man, a disheveled ogre with an acne-scarred face and slick-backed hair resembling a drowned rat, stared at her with deranged eyes. His shirtless upper body was a crazy quilt of nefarious tattoos with a large Grim Reaper dominating the front of his torso. A black spider web design covered both elbows, while lurid portraits of infamous serial killers dotted the landscape of his arms.

Sensing her fear and disgust, he twisted his cold sore encrusted mouth into a menacing grin revealing two frightful rows of yellowish-brown teeth, which, for a reason beyond Roberta's comprehension, had been filed into sharp points. With his lips parted, the smell of halitosis intensified in the room and assaulted Roberta's delicate senses. She struggled to keep the puke from rising in her throat.

The woman at his side, a musty little scarecrow with heavily tattooed arms and bleached hair hacked into a messy mullet, giggled like an overgrown urchin. Her excessively twitching eyes were rimmed with copious amounts of smudged black eyeliner, giving them the appearance of a rabid raccoon. Clad in a long, tattered tank top, ripped fishnet stockings and mud-caked Doc Martens boots, she looked every bit like a middle-aged reject from a punk rock concert.

"Didn't mean to scare you, honey," she said, smacking a wad of bubblegum like a cow chewing its cud. Her husky smoker's voice resonated with a twang that, to Roberta's ears, was simply lacerating. "We saw you just moved in and figured we'd mosey on over an' welcome ya'll to the neighborhood. You know that little ol' red house behind your backyard? That's our love shack."

The color drained from Roberta's face. She was shocked to learn that any living creature, apart from vermin, would call that dilapidated, paint-peeling shack their home. Peeking out from a cluster of oaks and sugar maples abutting the rear of her new property like some leprous, inbred thing, it was a hideous eyesore—a blight upon its surroundings. Roberta had made her husband Gordon promise to have a contractor erect a high wall to block the offending view, as well as to keep out "all those horrid little animals" that she so detested. Just the thought of wildlife evacuating their bowels on her manicured lawn made her shudder with revulsion.

"I'm Raelene Borza and this here's my ol' man, Earl," the blinking woman continued, gesturing toward her husband with her thumb. "Some folks call him Gator, on account of his teeth, but ya'll can call him anything ya want. Jus' don't call him late fer dinner."

Earl emitted a grunting noise that Roberta guessed was

a laugh. With his eyes transfixed on her ample breasts, he began to run the tip of his tongue along his lips and a bit of drool glistened at the corner of his mouth.

Roberta grimaced and felt her skin crawling.

Raelene giggled. "Don't you pay no mind to big Earl there, Miss Roberta. He's just a horny old hound dog with an eye for big purty ladies."

Roberta felt goosebumps populating her arms. "How did you know my name?" she inquired, eyeing her uninvited guests with suspicion. "And how did you...*people*...get in my house?"

"With a key, of course," Raelene giggled, amused by the sudden expression of panic that flashed across Roberta's face.

"You...have a key to my house?" Roberta hurried down from the stepladder and held out her hand, palm up. "I'll take that key if you don't mind."

Raelene's giggling abruptly ceased and her face went serious. "But I do mind. Earl and me came here with the very best of intentions, we did. But now you're givin' me the feeling like you don't trust us or something. Or maybe you think you're better than us lowlife crackers, Miss high-and-mighty in your Estee Lauder lipstick."

Grinning like an amused gibbon, Earl let out one of his laugh-grunts.

"I asked you, politely, to hand over that key," Roberta reiterated. She was fighting to maintain her composure; however, her voice revealed a tone of irritation. "Now, I would appreciate it if you-"

Raelene slowly turned her head from side to side. "Now, Roberta, don't you go and be like that. It ain't very neighborly of you. And you don't wanna be un-neighborly now, do you?"

"The key!" Roberta shouted, no longer able to contain her outrage.

At that moment, Gordon Pickering limped his way into

the dining room, leaning on a sterling silver handled walking stick. He was well past middle age with graying temples framing his bespectacled, yet kindly, face. And like his wife, he was encumbered with corpulence.

"Is everything all right?" he asked, his voice unruffled. "I thought I heard someone scream."

"Oh Gordon!" Roberta cried out with relief as she ran to her husband's side. "Thank heavens you're here! These people," she pointed to Earl and Raelene, "they're from that red hovel behind our property. Did you know they have a key to our house? And they're refusing to relinquish it! Do something!"

The smile reappeared on Raelene's face as she cast her blinking eyes on Roberta's rotund spouse. "Your wife spooks real easy," she stated, nodding her head in Roberta's direction.

"Yeah, real easy," Earl echoed Raelene's words, twining them with a menacing tone. He still had not shifted his gaze from Roberta, who was, at this point, visibly shaken by his unceasing and peculiar stare.

Raelene proceeded to introduce herself and her 'old man' to Gordon and explained that they came over to welcome him and his wife to the neighborhood.

"It's a pleasure to make your acquaintance," Gordon chirped. His double chin quivered as he cordially extended his hand to the grotty couple despite his wife's glare of disapproval. If her looks could kill, he surely would have been pushing up daisies on the spot. "A pleasure indeed! I'm Doctor Gordon Pickering, but please feel at ease to call me Gordon."

"We ain't never had no doctor for a neighbor before," said Raelene. "I feel like this is our lucky day. You a veternarian or somethin'?"

"Actually," Gordon began, his face wearing a rather amused expression, "I'm a hepatologist—that's a liver specialist, in case you were wondering. But I'm retired now; happily retired, I might add. I haven't practiced medicine in years, at least not in the conventional sense."

"Well, all's I can say is retirement sure seems to agree with you," Raelene cooed flirtatiously. "But I bet you miss havin' all them young, sexy nurses around you, all ready, willing and able to do what you tell them." Her voice suddenly took on a mocking tone. "Yes, doctor. Right away, doctor! Anything you want, doctor!"

Gordon cleared his throat. "Ah, yes, well…" Sensing his wife's growing irritation, he decided it best to change the subject, and fast. "Borza—now that's a name one doesn't hear very often. Polish?"

"Hungarian," Earl replied before letting out a foul-smelling belch, which caused Roberta to turn her head away in disgust. Never before in her life had she encountered a couple as uncouth as Earl and Raelene. Everything about them made her cringe.

Not to be outdone by her spouse's indecorum, Raelene winked one of her raccoon eyes at Gordon. "Tell me, doc, are you and your ol' lady swingers?" she enquired, trying to make her raspy voice sound as alluring as possible.

The room fell uncomfortably silent for a few moments, the only sound being the vexatious smacking of Raelene's gum.

Roberta's eyes widened in disbelief. Her insides churned with revulsion. "Certainly not!" she angrily fired back, recoiling with indignation at the offensive suggestion. "I'll have you know that Gordon and I are respectful members of society! We would never lower our standings in the community by indulging in such sordid activities! Now if you don't hand over that key to our house, you'll leave us with no other option than to call the police!"

Dropping the key into Roberta's upturned palm, Raelene snickered, "Take it easy, girl. Here's your old key. I was just havin' a bit of neighborly fun with you, that's all. There ain't no crime in that." She turned to Gordon. "Now ain't that right, doc?" Turning back to Roberta, she grumbled under her breath, "It's not like we don't have other ones."

"You have a delightful sense of humor," Gordon observed, much to his wife's dismay. "As we used to say in the hospital: laughter is the best medicine…unless you have fecal impaction, in which case an enema would be more effective."

Raelene tossed her head back and let out a loud cackle that elicited a grimace from Roberta. "You're a real cut up, doc. I bet you left all your patients in stitches. Get it, stitches?"

Gordon smiled while Roberta rolled her eyes, unamused by Raelene's pathetic pun.

"You know what?" Raelene continued. "How 'bout you and your ol' lady come on over to our place tonight, after supper, of course. We can chew the fat and get to know each other better over a couple of brewskies and…"

"We don't drink… *brewskies*," Roberta interrupted, her nose high in the air. "And neither do we chew fat. Really, do we look like a couple of Eskimos to you?" But before she could utter another word, Gordon stunned her by accepting Raelene's invitation. Her stomach did a flip-flop as she heard him announce, "My wife and I will be over at eight o'clock sharp. You can count on us to be there."

A look of impish glee spread across Raelene's face like a rash and Earl's demented grin widened, resembling that of a shark. Slack-jawed, Roberta glowered at Gordon, who seemed oblivious to his wife's obvious distress.

"I just know we're all gonna have us a real fun time," Raelene said, as the music on the radio was interrupted by a breaking news bulletin reporting the gruesome discovery of yet another body part in the local area. "And you're just gonna love Earl's taxidermy collection."

"Taxidermy?" Roberta sounded repulsed.

"Yeah. Earl likes to play with dead things," Raelene

explained with disturbing delight. "Ain't that right, Earl?"

Still grinning, Earl nodded his head and then licked his lips as if the very thought of it aroused a feeling of hunger within him. "Eight o'clock," the toothy brute grunted as he and Raelene made their way to the back door. His parting words, "We'll be waiting for you," sounded more ominous than welcoming.

"Don't worry, honey," Raelene said over her shoulder to Roberta in a dubious attempt to calm her neighbor's frazzled nerves. "We ain't gonna hang you from a meat hook in the basement, then cut you up like a frog in a high school science class. Unless that's the kind of thing you're into."

And with that being said, the Borzas left the Pickering house, laughing.

A huge wave of relief surged through Roberta as her jiggling frame rushed to lock the door behind them. But, no sooner had she secured it, her short-lived relief gave way to burning anger.

"Have you taken leave of your senses, Gordon!" she shrieked. "I can't believe you actually expect me to spend the evening at that run-down house of those horrible people, those… those moral defectives! Have you completely lost your mind?"

"Now, Roberta, there's no need for expostulation."

"No need for expostulation?" A sickened look appeared on Roberta's face. "Those people turn my stomach, in case you hadn't noticed. I swear there's something creepy, something—*abnormal*—about those two. Call it woman's intuition, if you like, but I get the feeling that they're somehow connected to all these body parts popping up in the area."

"Don't be silly, dear. Earl and Raelene, they're just…well, uncultured."

"Uncultured you say? Why, they're the epitome of riffraff! They're mangy mongrels! Vermin!" Her expression quickly transformed into one of petulance. "What on earth ever possessed you to accept their invitation? Are you trying to send me to an early grave, Gordon? Really, I can't understand how you weren't thoroughly appalled by their appearance and behavior. They wouldn't know good taste if it caught rabies and bit their faces off!"

"I was simply being neighborly," Gordon explained, before injecting into his wife's bejeweled ears one of his mini-lectures on the sad state of social affairs. "The problem with the world today is that everyone keeps to themselves. No one bothers to get to know their neighbors anymore like they did back in the good old days. Everyone's either too busy or too scared to even stop and say hello. Now, I'll admit the Borzas aren't quite the champagne and caviar crowd we left behind in New York, but I'm sure…"

"That Raelene has *got* to be the most repulsive woman this side of the Mississippi," Roberta cut in. "Those rags she tries to pass off as clothes and all that hideous black stuff smeared around her eyes. And that trailer trash hairdo, which I'm every bit sure was crawling with lice, looked like a large rodent gnawed the top of it. That woman is a walking social disease." Roberta's eyes blazed. "And did you see the way that repulsive thing she calls a husband kept gawking at my breasts and licking his lips the entire time? Talk about drooling perverts. I wouldn't be one bit surprised if he turned out to be a psychotic serial killer with corpses hanging from meat hooks in his cellar!"

Gordon shook his head and chuckled. "You're allowing your imagination to run wild again, Roberta. You watch too many of those true crime documentaries on television. They have you suspecting everyone of murder."

"That may be so, but I still think those Borzas are abnormal," Roberta reiterated as she began sweeping up the pieces of her shattered wine goblet. "I really don't feel comfortable going over to their filthy little dump to 'chew the fat' with them as they so nauseatingly put it. You know I don't respond well to squalor, Gordon."

"I'm well aware of that, dear," Gordon said. He gently took his wife's hand in his and offered up a loving look. "But it's not right for us to judge others. Remember, it says in the Bible that we must love our neighbors. And our enemies, too. And to paraphrase the late, great Oscar Wilde: not everyone is good, but there's *always* something good to be found inside of everyone. Remember that little old lady who lived in the park—Mrs. Sniffen—the one who sent you into a fit of rage because she wore white shoes after Labor Day?"

Roberta nodded her head as her mind called up an image of the homeless, gray-haired spinster in her frumpy frock and moth-eaten winter coat.

"You must admit, dear, she turned out to be such a sweet thing despite her faux pas. And did you not grow to love her after I convinced you to have her over for Thanksgiving dinner?"

Roberta smiled. "Now that you mention it, she *was* delightful."

"Savor the memory, dear. Savor the memory."

As she basked in the recollection, a serene look came over Roberta's face and the pupils of her eyes twinkled in their blue irises like the stars in heaven. "You're absolutely right, as usual, dear. I'm sure, despite their distasteful outer appearances, the Borzas are very good people—deep down inside. You know, honey, I'm actually kind of looking forward to this evening now." She gave her husband a peck on the cheek. "I'd better start getting to work on the canapés."

Gordon nodded his head, approvingly.

Roberta finished up her sweeping and then merrily set about assembling the ingredients for her hors d'oeuvres. As she worked her culinary magic, she began to hum a happy tune, oblivious to the dark clouds gathering ominously outside the kitchen windows like witches at a Black Mass.

* * *

Roberta gazed down at the Ballon Bleu de Cartier watch on her wrist. It was eight-thirty. The better part of the past half hour had been spent on a rickety, stained sofa in the fetidness of the Borzas' tastelessly decorated habitation, watching them scarfing down the canapés. She took great pains to hide her disgust as her horrendous hosts stuffed their gullets, their gobbling accentuated by a soundtrack of gluttonous grunts and smacking lips. The last time she had witnessed such a blatant disregard for table manners was during feeding time at the zoo. She turned to look at Gordon, who was sitting next to her, smoking his pipe in silence, and wondered if his stomach, like hers, was twisted with revulsion.

Outside, the wind was fierce; one might even say raging with unrelenting fury. The sudden banging of a tree branch against a filthy windowpane made Roberta jump like a startled cat, the sight of which aroused a giggle from Raelene.

After consuming the last of the canapés, Earl wiped his mouth on the back of his inked arm and once again demonstrated his talent for boisterous belching.

"So…" Gordon began, in an attempt to engage in polite conversation, "What line of work are you in, Earl?"

"Exterminating," Earl replied.

Gordon took a puff on his pipe. "Ah, pest control. It must be quite a satisfying job."

"Earl's one of them independent contractors," Raelene added. "Killin' things is what he's best suited for." Her eyes suddenly glazed over and she said, as if in a trance, "Did ya'll know that the large intestine is like five feet long while the small intestine is two or three times as long? Ain't that a hoot?"

An icy chill shot up Roberta's spine.

"Yes, I knew that," Gordon answered. "And it is most definitely a hoot."

An awkward and slow-as-molasses minute passed before Roberta spoke. "Isn't that just horrifying, all those disgusting body parts turning up all over the neighborhood?" She stared into Earl's eyes, accusingly. "It's obviously the work of some deranged thrill killer."

Gordon placed his hand on Roberta's knee. "One of my wife's many obsessions…" he paused to clear his throat. "I mean *hobbies*, is watching true crime documentaries. She fancies herself to be quite the amateur forensics expert."

"The twisted mind of a serial killer is fascinating, yet somewhat predictable," Roberta continued. "The more people they murder, the more emboldened they become, believing themselves to be untouchable. And that's when they become careless and make a mistake. You see, their overconfidence often proves to be their undoing."

Raelene laughed. "That might be true for some, but there's plenty that don't never get caught. There's a whole bunch of killings that ain't never been solved, and ain't never will neither. The way I see it, if a body's dumb enough to get themselves murdered, then they got what they deserved."

"A most illuminating theory," Gordon remarked before turning to Roberta. "Wouldn't you say, dear?"

"Yes, most illuminating," she agreed.

"Well now, since ya'll brought up the subject of hobbies," Raelene grinned, "Earl and me wanna show you ours. It's in the cellar. Come on, we'll take you down there."

Roberta wrinkled up her nose. "Thank you, however, I'd rather not. I've never found taxidermy to be a tasteful practice."

Gordon gave his wife a subtle nudge with his elbow and

flashed her a frown. "Be polite," he whispered into her ear. "We mustn't offend our neighbors, dear. Remember how Mrs. Sniffen turned out."

Roberta looked at her husband with pleading eyes. "I know, Gordon, but I just can't. My stomach is way too delicate. I'll just wait here while you go."

At that moment, Earl produced a loaded gun, which he had kept hidden between the grubby cushions of his chair. He pointed it at Gordon and Roberta. "You're both goin' down to the cellar if you know what's good for you," he ordered, baring his unsightly, sharpened teeth. "Now get your fat asses movin' unless you wanna eat some lead right here in the livin' room!"

"Earl ain't joshin'," Raelene cautioned. "You'd best do what he tells ya."

"Well, I *never*!" Roberta exclaimed in her most indignant tone.

Gordon gently squeezed his wife's trembling hand. "Let's not panic, dear. I think we should do as the man says."

"I'd listen to your ol' man if I was you," Raelene advised. "Now, hurry it up, you two! Earl gets real mean when he gets impatient."

With Earl's gun aimed at their backs, Roberta and Gordon followed Raelene down a set of creaking wooden stairs leading to the basement. As they descended, the ghastly stench of rotting flesh assaulted their nostrils. It grew stronger with each step they took. Roberta covered her nose and mouth with her hand to keep from barfing.

Upon reaching the basement, Raelene announced with pride, "Welcome to Raelene and Earl's Odditorium."

"*Earl* and Raelene's Odditorium," Earl corrected.

Roberta gasped as her eyes were met by the shocking sight of dozens of human taxidermy mounts, each one assembled from various body parts stitched together into freakish forms and posed in a variety of different ways.

As if inspired by the gaffs of old carnival sideshows and dusty dime museums, there were multi-headed monstrosities, Frankenstein-ish grotesqueries that combined both male and female pieces, and nightmarish creations that were part human and part animal. There was even a psychotic version of P.T. Barnum's infamous Fiji mermaid consisting of a stuffed and mummified lady's torso flawlessly stitched to the back half of a Beluga sturgeon. Arranged in a row on a shelf near a gore-smeared autopsy table were the decapitated heads of women and men, all with their mouths sewn shut, and some with their eyeballs surgically removed. Bloodstained bone saws and meat cleavers decorated the grimy walls and, above this real-life chamber of horrors, a pair of ominous meat hooks dangled from a beam, foreshadowing the unspeakable atrocities about to unfold.

"I hate to say I told you so," Roberta said to Gordon, "but at the risk of sounding crass in front of the neighbors, I feel compelled to say I told you so."

"As always, your intuition was right on the money," Gordon admitted.

"Shut up!" Earl boomed, waving his gun from side to side. "Which one of you whales want to be the first to die?"

"I vote for the snooty bitch." Raelene pointed to Roberta, who was now clinging tightly to Gordon's arm like a terrified child. "I hate snooty bitches! Now the doc, on the other hand, I kinda like him. He's got a good sense of humor, so I say we kill him last."

"Hear that, doc?" Earl laughed. "You're gonna have the pleasure of watching your ol' lady get gutted like a hog. Soo-weee!" An alarmed look suddenly swept across his unshaven face and he began to teeter like a drunkard. "Raelene, get them zip ties and…"

Earl began to cough and gasp for air. Frothy drool foamed down his chin onto his chest. His eyes bugged out, giving his reddening face the appearance of a large insect.

He dropped his gun and then collapsed to the floor, his body shaking like an epileptic in sharp spasms, his teeth chattering and the color of his face changing from red to blue.

"Earl!" screamed Raelene as she dropped the zip ties and rushed to her soon-to-be-a-cadaver husband. But all she could do was watch, horror-stricken, as he thrashed about and spilled his bodily fluids onto the basement floor. "You're a doctor! Do something!" she screamed at Gordon. "I think he's dying!"

"I wholeheartedly concur with your assessment," Gordon remarked in a composed and doctorly fashion. "He most definitely is dying."

Raelene grabbed the gun from the floor and pointed the barrel at the Pickerings. "Looks like I'll have to finish what Earl started!" she growled, her eyes wild like those of a rabid dog. "Get ready to die, bitches!"

She was about to squeeze the trigger when an intense cramp seized her gut, causing her to double over in excruciating pain. Her heartbeat became erratic and a strange tingling sensation overcame her toes and fingers, causing her to lose her grip on the gun. It landed on the floor with a dull clank.

"I feel… so sick… what's… happening?" Raelene coughed out her words, frothy drool beginning to appear at the corners of her mouth. Her body was now twitching like a ghastly jumping jack and her face convulsed with terror. "Those canapés," she gasped, "you spiked them… with… something... you bitch!" Her eyes were now starting to bug out like Earl's. "What the hell… did you… put in them?"

"*Really*, Raelene," Roberta said, sounding flabbergasted. "I couldn't *possibly* divulge a secret family recipe! It's a matter of tradition, a matter of taste."

Gordon wrapped his arm around his wife's shoulder and both stood in silence and observed as the crazed taxidermists drooled and spasmed and gasped their final breaths. It was by no means a pretty sight to watch, yet an enthralling one nonetheless. Their deathwatch continued for several minutes before Earl's leg jerked as if kicking an invisible bucket and the rising and falling of his chest subsided. A short while later Raelene followed suit.

Springing into doctor mode, Gordon crouched down and palpated Earl's carotid artery and then Raelene's. Unable to detect a pulse in either, he pronounced them dead with a detached nonchalance.

Looking down at the Borzas' lifeless bodies, Roberta made the sign of the cross and eulogized, "Quiet neighbors make the best neighbors."

"Amen," said Gordon.

* * *

Rays of morning sunlight spilled through the windows of the Pickering house, filling each room with a mellow, golden glow. In the kitchen, clad in one of her designer muumuus, Roberta hummed a happy tune as she stood before the stove and stirred a large stew pot filled with meat and vegetables.

Still wearing his silk pajamas and bedroom slippers, Gordon sat at the kitchen table, spreading pâté on a Ritz cracker. "I think our little get-together with the neighbors last night was just the thing we both needed," he declared. "And, I must add, those canapés of yours were a real knockout!"

"Thank you, honey," Roberta said. "They always are, if I do say so myself."

Gordon let out a little chuckle. "And to think, you were so worried about the Borzas. That Raelene turned out to be quite a sweet girl, even sweeter than our dear old Mrs. Sniffen—and *she* was well aged! And what a good heart that Earl had. He wasn't nearly as tough as he appeared on the outside."

"Thank goodness for meat tenderizer," Roberta remarked. "It makes all the difference!" She glanced out the window facing the backyard. In the distance the smoldering timbers and pile of charred bricks that were once the abode of the Borzas brought a gleam to her eye. "What a glorious morning it is! And the view from this window is so much better today."

Gordon sunk his teeth into the pâté-covered cracker and immediately shut his eyes, pausing to savor the lusciousness. "This pâté of yours is out of this world!" he exclaimed. He gobbled up the rest of the cracker with gusto.

Roberta began to blush. "That's quite a compliment coming from a liver specialist!"

"Who would have ever imagined that crackers on a cracker could be so delectable?"

"Raelene was right," Roberta laughed. "You *are* a cut up!"

"It's all in how you hold the scalpel, dear," Gordon replied. Licking his lips in anticipation of flavor, he spread some pâté on another cracker. "I'm a lucky man to have a magnificent cook like you for a wife. I mean, who else but a culinary maven like yourself would have ever thought to make a Hungarian goulash using actual Hungarians?"

Roberta beamed with pride. She sprinkled some more paprika into the pot on the stovetop, gave it another stir and then took a taste. Her eyes lit up. "Mmmm. I was so wrong about the Borzas having no taste." She spooned a bit more goulash into her mouth and her taste buds danced with heavenly delight. "They're actually *quite* tasty!"

ONE FOOT IN THE GRAVE

D ark clouds had been gathering since sunrise, slowly blotting out the sky and draping the uniformed rows of grave markers with shadows. A biting wind transformed a scatter of dead leaves into a swirling mass that spiraled into a dance of death before falling back to the earth to wait for another gust to send them airborne. It was only the second day of November – All Souls' Day – but the merciless chill of winter was already in the air.

A light drizzle began to descend from the heavens like weeping tears, darkening the mournful marble figures of religious icons and innocent lambs that stood in silent vigil over the final resting places of the dead. As the drops landed upon their heads and rolled down their cheeks, they gave the solemn stone faces the eerie appearance of crying.

Jerome Crippen paused for a moment to open his black, five-hundred-dollar, Maglia Francesco umbrella to shield himself from the rain. He then continued on his way until he arrived at the grave of his dearly departed wife, Laura. He had nearly forgotten where her grave was located. He had only been to it once, and that was on the day of her burial. He stood as still as the statuary around him and stared down at the small bronze grave marker before him, which bore his wife's name, along with the dates of her birth and death, the image of a cross, and the Biblical quote: WHITHER THOU GOEST, I WILL GO. He recalled that it was also raining on the day her body was laid to rest, and felt strangely amused by the coincidence of it.

Laura Crippen had died exactly one year ago on this day, leaving Jerome an enormously wealthy widower, thanks to a hefty life insurance policy that he had taken out on her several years prior to her passing. According to her death certificate, the cause of death was cardiac arrest. Despite her demise occurring at such a young age, nobody questioned the certifying physician's opinion, for Laura was known to possess an enlarged heart resulting from years of untreated high blood pressure.

Jerome took a quick look around to determine if anyone else was in the cemetery with him. Confident that he was the sole person there – at least, the sole *living* person – he cracked a bit of a crooked grin.

"Wake up, Laura," he said softly, almost in a singing voice, to the bronze grave marker. "It's Jerome, your loving husband. It's been one whole year now since you've been gone. Time sure flies, doesn't it, my dear? Do forgive me for not coming to visit you sooner, but you see, I've been rather busy enjoying that money your insurance policy paid out to me. I'm sure you'll be pleased to hear that you left me well provided for. In fact…" he paused to snicker, "I've been living like a king and enjoying the finest of cars, clothes, restaurants and women. Mmmm, especially the women!"

Another gust of wind swept through the cemetery and a miniature tornado of brown leaves that had dropped from the branches of some nearby tress during the previous month sailed past Jerome's Italian leather shoes. The rain felt like it had suddenly grown colder, almost icy to the touch, and was now falling harder than before, giving off a loud pitter-patter as it struck the grave marker.

"It's a bit amusing, don't you think," Jerome continued, "that you always told me I could never do anything right. Not even poison a rat. Yet, I succeeded in poisoning you, Laura, and I did it quite well and got away with it, if you don't mind me touting my own horn. Nobody suspected a thing. With that bad ticker of yours, they all knew you had one foot in the grave."

Jerome chuckled to himself as his mind rewound to that fateful day when, after months of careful plotting and indecision, he finally mustered up enough courage and greed to see his plan through and spike the whiskey sour drink of his unsuspecting wife with a tincture of aconite root. During his researching of poisons, he had read online that a fatal dose of this plant, which is also known as wolf's bane, results in paralysis of the heart or respiratory center, with the only post mortem signs being those of asphyxia. It sounded to him like the ideal, and least messy, way to dispose of one's unwanted spouse.

Jerome remembered, with what only can be described as a fiendish fondness, the agonized expressions on his dying wife's face as the poisoning process inched her closer to death's door, and him closer to a world of freedom made sweeter by a half-million-dollar death benefit payout. Laura had initially complained of a bad headache, followed by unpleasant bouts of nausea and diarrhea. In time, her mouth and face began to tingle and then grow numb, as did her arms and legs. A fiery sensation burned deep within her abdomen, causing her to double up in pain. Confused and sweating profusely, she struggled desperately to get a breath of air as her husband nonchalantly observed from the comfort of a tufted chair in the corner of their master bedroom, while leisurely savoring a glass of imported cognac.

And then, nearly three hours from the time that Laura had unwittingly ingested the cleverly disguised poison, she let out one last loud and horrible gasp and her painful ordeal finally reached its deadly conclusion. Her body lay cold and still upon the heavy damask comforter of black and gold that draped the queen-size bed. Her pink peignoir was brown and sodden with vomit, and her lifeless eyes wide open and staring accusingly at her murderer.

A rumble of thunder sounded in the distance and Jerome looked up at the sky. It had formed into an ominous patchwork of gray, dark green and black, illuminated by random flashes of lightning.

"Well, my dear," Jerome sighed as he returned his gaze to his deceased wife's grave marker. "I believe the time has come for me to bid you farewell. Go back to sleep now, Laura."

He turned and started to walk away. But then, for some unexplainable reason, an odd urge overcame him. He stopped and bent down to snatch up a rain-soaked wreath from a nearby burial plot. He then made his way back to Laura's grave with the wreath in his hand and tossed it onto the grassy ground that covered her remains. After blowing her a mocking kiss, he uttered, "I'll see you around."

Suddenly, with a loud explosive boom, a jagged bolt of blinding lightning struck Laura's bronze marker and shook the ground. It instantly knocked Jerome off his feet and the costly umbrella from out of his hand. He flew backwards and landed on his backside atop the wet and sticky ground that had been turned to sludge by the rain. His dropped umbrella was lifted up by a howling gust of wind and carried off before he could grab onto its curved cherry wood handle.

"Damn it!" he cursed.

As he struggled to free himself from the grip of the earthy-smelling muck, the unthinkable happened.

Like a scene from out of a horror film, or perhaps from

the darkest of nightmares, the ground in front of Laura's grave marker began to tremble until a small fissure appeared, and from out of it emerged the foul and rotting limb of a woman. Its purplish hand turned in Jerome's direction and slowly opened like a blossoming nightshade.

Paralyzed by abysmal horror, Jerome recognized the gold rings on one of the corpse's fingers. They were Laura's bridal set. He felt a scream rise up in his numb throat. But before it could exit his mouth, Laura's bony, claw-like hand wrapped itself around his right ankle and began dragging him toward her grave.

Jerome's scream finally found its way out, but was drowned out by another deafening crash of thunder. He fought desperately to free himself from the dead woman's powerful clutch, but her supernatural-infused strength won out.

The corpse had pulled Jerome's leg calf-deep into the grave when, all at once, he felt the terrifying sensation of teeth chewing on his ankle. Deeper and deeper into his bone they gnawed. The pain was unbearable and unlike anything he had ever experienced. He continued to struggle, and he bellowed out a series of hair-raising man-shrieks that reverberated in all directions, ricocheting off of tombstones and statues and the walls of mausoleums. The pain was tantamount to the most horrendous of torture and Jerome found himself drifting in and out of consciousness until the agony was mercifully supplanted by a numbness that raced up the entire length of his leg.

At last, he was able to free himself from the hellish hole that had swallowed him alive. He yanked his limb from the muddy grave, only to discover that his right foot was gone. It had been completely chewed off and a gory hemorrhage was pouring out from the ragged stump at the bottom of his partially devoured leg.

His mind reeled from the horrendous sight and his thoughts swirled inside his brain like the dead leaves whipping in the wind around him. Soon, his vision blurred and faded to black. His body violently convulsed. The rapid-fire beating of his heart ceased and Jerome Crippen lay lifeless at the foot of Laura's grave, his blood staining the wet blades of dormant grass a ruddy color that not even the November rain could wash away.

DISCONNECTED

Aleister Liddell, a middle-aged cell phone junkie, had been creeping down Main Street, as usual, his head bent and his eyes transfixed on the screen of his so-called 'smart phone,' all but oblivious to the real world around him. No matter where he went, or what he was doing, he carried it in the palm of his right hand. He never left his home without it for fear that the world might come to an end if he did. The thought of being without it struck terror deep within his heart. He couldn't imagine life without it. His cell phone had become an extension of his hand, his identity, his being. And, in return, he had become a slave to it. Drivers angrily honked their car horns at him as he crossed the street against the light, like a mindless zombie in a trance, looking only at the screen of his cell phone, nearly causing traffic accidents. It wasn't until he felt the solid ground beneath his feet suddenly vanish and his body plummeting like a rock down a deep, dark hole that he tore his eyes away from the device in his hand.

Faster and faster he plunged, twisting and turning, his

arms flailing, his free hand unable to grasp onto anything to stop his fall. Confusion raced through his mind. Panic lashed at his guts. He let out a primal scream. As he descended deeper into the abyss, darkness gobbled up the bright rays of the autumnal sun illuminating the world above, and the warmth of the day turned mausoleum cold. He wondered if he would ever stop falling. And then he crashed into the bottom of the hole with a loud thud, the impact knocking the wind from his lungs and sending him into unconsciousness.

When he regained his senses, he found himself encased in nebulous darkness, lying limp like a broken doll on a bed of damp earth and putrid animal droppings, his left leg seized by a searing pain that caused him to cry out. Exploring with his hand, he could feel his splintered shinbone poking through his skin and blood seeping copiously from the laceration. It almost didn't feel real. But then nothing was feeling very real anymore. It all seemed like a dream…a very bad dream. His dazed mind wondered if he had died and gone to Hell.

"Help!" he yelled as loudly as he could, his voice echoing in the gloom. "I need help! Can anybody hear me?"

There came no reply—not that he was expecting one at this depth, in whatever godforsaken place he had ended up in. His mind began to race. How far down into the earth had he fallen? And how would he manage to get out? Climbing straight up—especially with his leg in its present condition—was clearly not an option. Was he destined to meet his demise in this unseeable pit? Would his remains ever be discovered? His thoughts then turned to his wife, Jenine. He wondered if he would ever see her again. If he died down there, how long would it take before she met someone new and remarried? He tried to chase the disturbing thoughts away, but they nagged at him, just as the excruciation ate at his leg, bringing tears to his eyes.

Jenine harbored a strong dislike for most forms of

modern technology, and often cited her husband's cell phone obsession as a major source of vexation. On more than one occasion, she pleaded with her obstinate spouse to seek professional help for his addiction to his mobile device, only to be met by his stout resistance, which habitually manifested itself in outbursts of scorn or outright disregard.

As Aleister pushed himself up into a sitting position, his wife's words echoed inside his pounding head, *"That damn cell phone of yours will be the death of you yet!"* For a brief moment, he wondered if Jenine had been right all along. But then the sudden realization that his cell phone—his best friend and lifeline to the outside world—was no longer in his grasp sent a tsunami of panic that surged from his belly and gnawed its way through his limbs. Cold beads of perspiration formed like midnight dew along his brow. His mouth went dry and his pulse raced. He began to hyperventilate. *My phone! Where's my phone?* Aleister could feel a full-blown panic attack working its way to the surface as he groped desperately in the pitch-blackness for his lost cell phone.

At last he located the device, and breathed a sigh of relief. *Now I can call for help*, he thought. *I'll be rescued!* Praying that his cell phone was still in operating condition, he pressed the power button and waited with bated breath. The LCD screen, despite now bearing a jagged crack from the fall, came to life, its greenish glow offering him a glimmer of hope. But that glimmer proved to be short-lived when it displayed two words that were both chilling and final: No Signal.

Aleister felt the bottom drop out of his increasingly fragile sanity. "Nooooo!" he screamed at the useless device in his hand, feeling the panic returning to smother him. The pain in his leg was growing worse, and he knew he had no choice but to fight against it and try to find a way out of the dark hole…or else succumb to it. He activated the cell phone's flashlight function and shined the beam around.

The light revealed that the pit he was in was quite cavernous. Jagged blades of white stalagmites and stalactites jutted menacingly from the floor and the ceiling like vicious fangs waiting to tear into flesh. A large aperture in one of the rocky walls appeared to be the entrance to a tunnel, reigniting Aleister's extinguished glimmer of hope. Perhaps the tunnel would lead him out of this subterranean hellhole.

Howling with intense pain, he began dragging his crippled body in the direction of the aperture, but stopped when his flashlight unveiled a strange and startling sight. Cell phones—hundreds, perhaps even thousands—littered the floor of the pit. They included all brands and models, newer ones mixed with older ones, many with cracked screens like his, and some that were broken into bits. Aleister gasped with surprise upon the realization that he wasn't the only cell phone junkie who had plummeted down the hole in the ground. There were others. Perhaps he wasn't alone down there. Once again, he called out for help, but still there came no reply. And then he heard someone, or something, moving about in the tunnel.

"Hello?" he shouted. "Is anybody in there? My leg is injured and I need help! Hello?"

He waited a few moments for a reply that never came before continuing to drag himself through the wasteland of broken cell phones until he arrived at the mouth of the tunnel. He shined the flashlight inside and immediately felt his blood run cold. The tunnel, which he had hoped would be a passageway to freedom, was actually a ghastly catacomb in which the skeletal remains of multitudes of human bodies were being stored. Appalling piles of bones and grinning skulls were everywhere, and Aleister surmised that they belonged to the unfortunate owners of the cell phones he had seen. Was this to be his fate? The thought made him cringe.

Again, he heard the sound of something moving about, and then his eyes fell upon a sight so terrifying that it made even an atheist like him cry out, "Holy Mother of God!" He could scarcely believe what he was seeing. Within that dank depository of the dead, like something straight out of a nightmare, was a monstrous, black hare, standing as large as a Shire draught horse and gnawing on a human femur. Its blood-red eyes zeroed in on him, and its ravenous mouth gaped wide, revealing two rows of fangs resembling pointed spearheads. Its malodorous breath, like a wind blowing hot from the bowels of Hell, assailed Aleister's nostrils and sickened his insides as the creature let out an ungodly screech for sustenance. It dropped the femur on the ground and lunged at him. Within a matter of seconds, it succeeded in ripping his throat out with its razor-sharp claws, changing his screams into the sickening sound of gurgling gore before plunging its teeth into his convulsing, blood-spurting body and devouring him alive…

"A monstrous, man-eating hare? Ugh. What a load of rubbish," Clarence Hornbuckle grumbled to himself, as he closed the Word document and hit the delete button on his computer's keyboard. The gray-haired man shook his head in disgust at the story he had just read. "These Indie horror writers and some of the weird crapola their warped minds whip up."

He removed his reading glasses, closed his strained eyes and massaged the bridge of his nose for a few moments before looking up at the clock on the wall above his desk. It was nearly five o'clock. His lips curled into a hint of a smile. It was his first and only smile of the day. After putting in a long eight hours at the publishing house, reading and rejecting all those terrible short story submissions, he was anxious to escape the confines of his drab, little office and head home to a good book and a snifter of warm cognac.

Hornbuckle shut down his computer, taking pleasure in the sound of the hard drive whirring to a stop. He rose from his chair and stretched his arms above his head to loosen his cramped muscles before heading for the door. But no sooner had he switched off the overhead light and was about to walk out of the office than he heard a low hum and noticed a flickering glow emanating from the monitor of his computer. The machine had re-booted itself.

Dammit! he cursed.

Letting out his breath with a harried huff, he made his way back to his desk to once again turn off the computer. He was dumbfounded to find the deleted story about the man-eating hare displayed on the monitor. *What the devil?* He hit the delete button, but the computer failed to respond. He tried again, but still the story remained on the screen, as if to taunt him. Mumbling a few profanities under his breath, he attempted to turn off the computer by pressing the power switch, but the machine was defiant and refused to shut down.

Determined to deactivate the obstinate computer, one way or another, the perturbed editor unplugged its power cord from the wall outlet next to his desk, only to discover the machine still running, its monitor glowing brighter than before.

"What in the Sam Hill… This is impossible!" A look of incomprehension filled Hornbuckle's eyes and he yelled at the computer as if it could hear and understand him. "I pulled out your damn plug!"

All at once, the computer began to tremble and then shake violently as though being rocked by a powerful seismic event. An ear-piercing screech blared from the speakers, causing Hornbuckle to cover his ears with his hands in an effort to block out the deafening sound. A strange and putrid smell permeated the office. And then the glowing screen burst apart with an explosive sound as the huge foreleg of a monstrous, black hare lunged from the monitor and ripped out the screaming man's throat with its razor-sharp claws.

Later that evening, when Delfina the Puerto Rican cleaning lady made her rounds, she was so horrified by what she saw, she dropped her cleaning supplies and dashed from the building screaming for the *policia*. There on the floor in the drab, little office of the editor lay a broken computer monitor next to the rather unfortunate Clarence Hornbuckle, or rather what remained of him—a pair of mangled reading glasses and an appalling pile of gnawed bones with a grinning skull.

AILUROPHOBIA

Ailurophobia – "An abnormal fear of cats."
Webster's New World College Dictionary, Fifth Edition

A storm was forming that sweltering day when Officer Rodriguez arrived at the white-clapboard house across the street from the derelict textile mill with the boarded-up windows and graffiti-covered brick walls. With the exception of the alarming amount of rubbish that had swallowed most of the tiny front yard, and the great army of feral cats that could be seen patrolling in the overgrown garden whose flowers had long been strangled by weeds, the house was not at all unlike the other sad sagging structures that stood side-by-side along the street.

Rodriguez had been dispatched to the residence after more than one neighbor had complained of a "gut-wrenching" odor emanating from the house, which from a first impression appeared to be abandoned and unoccupied, save for the scores of mange-covered felines that peered out in silence from dark gaps in the rain-dampened clutter and watched with suspicious green eyes from paint-peeling window sills and along the edge of the roof. They emitted low rumbling growls and serpentine hissing sounds as he approached the house. *Their* house.

The neighbors were right about the overpowering stench and the officer had to restrain himself from vomiting as he climbed the rickety steps of the front porch. He knocked on the wooden door, which was partially blocked by the piles of old furniture, rusted trunks, and broken plastic crates filled with an assortment of useless junk and garbage. He waited a few moments and then pounded on the door with his fist while calling out in a loud voice, "Hello? Is there anyone home?" The door was not locked and the force of his fist upon it caused the door to swing open. The putrid stench was stronger now and nearly overpowered his senses.

He switched on his flashlight and slowly and cautiously stepped foot inside the foul darkness within. Nearly gagging from the smell of ammonia and decomposing garbage, he once again inquired if anyone was in the house and identified himself as police officer Rodriguez. He waited a few moments, listening for a reply of any kind or even perhaps a faint cry for help, but he was answered only by silence.

Like the yard and the front porch, the interior of the house was cluttered with what appeared to be decades' worth of odd accumulations, some stacked so high that they came close to touching the cracked plaster ceilings. The beam of the flashlight also revealed huge piles of feces, which covered almost every inch of the floors like a horrific carpet.

Rodriguez proceeded deeper into the depths of the house with a sick feeling beginning to gnaw at his stomach. He made his way through the mountains of old magazines, outdated telephone directories and bundles of yellowed newspapers, nearly knocking over a tower of boxes overflowing with clutter, and arrived at a closed door at the far end of what had probably been at one time a hallway. The stench grew even stronger now and he could hear the sound of someone or something moving about on the other side of the door. He drew his Glock semi-automatic pistol and again called out but no reply was forthcoming. The sound of thunder rumbled outside as he pushed open the door with his booted foot and aimed the beam of his flashlight into the dark room.

Rodriguez was far from being a rookie cop. He was a seasoned veteran who had devoted over twenty years of his life to the police force and had seen more than his share of blood and tears in the proverbial urban jungle – not only from his numerous years on the job but also from his growing up in the mean streets of the same unforgiving hellhole of a city that he now was paid to patrol. He had always considered himself to be tough and unshakable. He had seen scores of victims of accident, murders, and suicides, and he wasn't squeamish at the sight of blood. He had always prided himself on being conditioned to respond to a variety of situations and be under complete emotional control while doing so. He never once fathomed there could be an event so disturbing, a sight so horrifying, that it could unnerve a man such as himself – a man who once believed that he possessed nerves of steel. But now a cold sweat had overtaken him and his heart was pounding.

On the filthy bloodstained floor before him lay the owner of the house – or rather what was left of her. She was an elderly woman who had long ago lost her husband and, at some point, her sanity as well. She had lived in the house by herself for many years with little or no human contact, hoarding junk and living in squalor and loneliness with only feral cats to keep her company. She had recently died and the dozen or so cats that had been trapped in the closed room with her were feeding on the last scraps of flesh from her decomposing corpse, their eyes glowing eerily in the beam of the flashlight.

Driven mad with hunger, the cats all at once turned from the body of their dead mistress and lunged at Rodriguez, hooking their sharp claws into the dark blue material of his uniform and biting him with fangs that had now acquired a taste for human flesh.

The horrified police office began firing his gun at his feline attackers and using his flashlight as a club to smash in some of the cats' skulls. His mind was reeling and he lost his footing and fell onto the widow's maggot-infested remains. The cats continued to pounce upon him and sink their little razor-like teeth into his arms and legs, growling and screeching as they tore into his flesh. He managed to return to his feet and continued shooting and frantically clubbing to save his life. He fired shot after shot, and even after the last cat lay dead on the floor and the smell of gun smoke and singed fur joined the toxic stench of death, garbage, feces, and urine, he continued shooting until the magazine of his gun was empty, and clubbing at the air with his flashlight until the batteries died and he was swallowed up by the foul darkness. He then stumbled out of the house in a daze, and as a jagged bolt of lightning streaked angrily across the storming sky above the textile mill across the street, he regurgitated the coffee and doughnuts he had consumed for lunch.

* * *

"Anastasia, don't stand there daydreaming all day!" growled the balding man standing on the front porch of the old white-clapboard house. "Hurry up with your stuff before it starts to rain. Goddamn it, Anastasia!"

The golden-haired girl snapped out of her trance-like state and gasped slightly. With quickness she shifted her gaze from the strange eyes that she was sure had been staring at her from behind the cracked windowpane to the hulking form of her father standing on the dilapidated front porch. His tattooed arms were crossed and upon his face was worn a certain expression of annoyance and brewing anger, which the young girl had grown all too familiar with.

"I'm hurrying, Daddy," she replied, almost apologetically, in a timid, thirteen-year-old voice. As she neared the porch an uneasy feeling that unseen eyes were watching her grew within her and the inside of her head began to buzz in a peculiar manner. She stopped and closed her eyes for a few moments, making a silent wish for it to stop.

"Anastasia!" her father belted out in a gruff voice that was pungent with the stench of whiskey. "I mean it, young lady! Get your ass in here right now with that box of your junk or I swear to God I'll take off this belt and give you another good beating! Is that what you want?"

Anastasia Waverly opened her eyes and then quickly and obediently brought the cardboard box holding her collection of beloved teddy bears and other stuffed toy animals into the house and into her new bedroom. As she placed the box upon the old calico quilt that was draped over her bed, the buzzing in her head seemed to intensify, now mingled with bits and pieces of faint and distorted voices.

Doing her best to ignore the mounting noises within her head, she returned outside to retrieve the remainder of her possessions from the rented moving van without uttering a single word. Since her bittersweet homecoming, Anastasia had feared the return of the voices; however, this time she would not tell her father for she knew he would only send her back to that place where wire-covered windows dissected the afternoon sunlight into disjointed rays, and the dark hours were held together by the repetition of white shoes echoing dreamily down endless corridors of dismal gray.

Anastasia picked up a carton containing her desk lamp, some books, a small radio, and an old wooden picture frame that held an even older photo of her dark-haired mother, who had died in a tragic automobile accident on Anastasia's ninth birthday. While on the way to the zoo, a cat had darted out in front of the family car, which her father was driving. He swerved to avoid hitting the animal and lost control of the vehicle. The sounds of crunching metal and breaking glass filled Anastasia's ears as the car collided with a tree, killing her mother instantly. It wasn't long after that when the faceless voices began whispering things to her. At first, she was convinced that her mother was speaking to her from beyond the grave, but then gradually other voices joined in and the constant distortion within her head became so severe that she had to be taken out of school and sent away to "that place."

Nearly a year had passed since the local newspaper ran the sensationalized headline: *POLICE OFFICER SHOOTS MAN-EATING CATS IN HOARDER'S HOUSE OF HORRORS*. Anastasia's father, John, kept a copy of the grisly newspaper story in his toolbox, but made it a point to keep the horrific history of the house a well-kept secret from his daughter in order to spare her any emotional disconcertion. A middle-aged building contractor who was sometimes employed and sometimes sober, he had purchased the house for a ridiculously low price at a real estate auction. His winning bid had been made with the intention of fixing up the house while living in it with his daughter and then re-selling it for a decent profit.

While Anastasia remained unaware of the past horrors connected to her new home, she nevertheless sensed there was something not quite right about the place and felt no fondness for it whatsoever. In fact, she thoroughly despised it. She found the physical condition of the building quite appalling and not at all like the pretty yellow house in which she and her parents lived happily before the accident that claimed her mother's life. The ugliness contained within the dreary interior of this new house seemed to mirror the ugliness she saw in her father's eyes ever since that bleak November afternoon when her mother's casket was lowered into the ground and a bitter cold rain fell like tears weeping from the heavens above.

The first nine days in the new house passed without incident, and then, on a Saturday evening when Anastasia was in her bedroom reading Edgar Allan Poe's, *The Black Cat*, and listening to the radio, the first taste of evil came to call. A chill that was as icy as death's grip slowly seeped into the room, drawing the girl's attention away from her book and causing hundreds of tiny goose pimples to rise up on the flesh of her arms. Her body began to shiver and she struggled to keep her teeth from chattering. The music that was playing on the radio began to crackle with static and fade away until the only sounds that emanated from the speaker were strange hissings and growls.

Anastasia closed her book and placed it on top of her nightstand table. She then turned the knob on her radio to locate another station, but no matter where on the dial she stopped, the sounds continued. She switched the radio off; however, not only did the hissing and the growling continue, they intensified, building up and pounding inside her head like waves crashing angrily upon the shore until her brain felt that it was being shredded into small pieces, and nausea twisted her insides. And then, something out in the hallway that had taken the form of a small dark shadow ran past the door of the girl's bedroom without producing any sound.

Filled with enough curiosity to kill a cat, Anastasia rushed out into the hallway where she glimpsed the tail end of the shadow-thing disappear through the crack of a slightly ajar door at the end of the hallway. At that very moment, the intense cold and the near-deafening noises inside her head came to a sudden end. Warmth and silence returned. She crept down the corridor until she reached the room into which the strange shadow-thing had run. She slowly pushed against the heavy, paint-peeling door, which coughed out a few stuttering creaks as it opened to reveal a room of murky darkness.

Leaving the light of the hallway behind, Anastasia cautiously entered the room and ventured deeper into the thick mass of darkness that engulfed her. She fumbled around inside of it until her hand located the hanging chain of the light fixture on the ceiling. She pulled down on it. With a click, the bulbs lit up the room and revealed the thing that lay on the floor just inches from her feet. Her heart began to pound wildly and she stared at the thing with a mixture of horror and disbelief.

It was a wretched monstrosity of something that had once been human. Its face had been entirely eaten away, leaving only a grinning skull framed by a matted tangle of hair and dried clots of blood. What little flesh remained on its limbs and torso was greenish in color and in an advanced state of putrefaction.

Anastasia stared down at the thing. She wasn't sure if what she was seeing was real or not, so she squeezed her eyes shut several times in an attempt to make it go away. But the gruesome sight in front of her remained in place. And then a disembodied voice, like wind through dead trees in winter's bleakness, began to murmur, "Come to me, Anastasia. Stay with me, for always."

Anastasia covered her ears with her hands, but she was unable to block out the voice.

"Come to me Anastasia. Don't be afraid. Come."

And then the thing on the floor began to slowly rise up into a sitting position and it turned its head to gaze upon the trembling girl with its horrible dead eyes.

Overcome by terror, Anastasia let out a scream that echoed throughout the house and took off running as fast as her feet could carry her. She dashed down the hallway, past her bedroom where the music was once again playing on the radio, and into the small grimy kitchen, where her father sat, drinking from a half-empty bottle of whiskey.

"What the hell is going on?" John Waverly yelled, slamming his bottle down upon the table. He grabbed his hysterical daughter by her arm, stopping her in her tracks. She screamed and struggled to break free from his grip, but he held on to her tightly. "Goddamn it, Anastasia!" he growled. "What in hell's name is wrong with you?"

"I saw it! I saw it!" Anastasia screamed, pointing to the hallway with her finger. "The thing in the room at the end of the hall!"

"What thing?" he asked, shaking his head. "What the hell are you talking about, girl?"

"It was on the floor!" Anastasia cried out. Tears were drenching her cheeks. "It was dead! But it was alive too! I saw it! It's in there! Oh, Daddy! Don't let it get me! Please!"

Anastasia's father grew annoyed. "Calm down and stop all this crazy babbling of yours!" he barked. "There's nothing in that back room. You're starting to see things that aren't there again. I had a feeling you should have stayed in that place, Anastasia. Bringing you home was a bad idea."

"No Daddy!" cried Anastasia. "This time it was real. I know it was! You have to believe me!"

"All right then, you show me this whatever-it-is that you think you saw in there," John Waverly grumbled as he dragged the terrified girl from the kitchen and down the entire length of the hall. She shrieked and struggled to break free from his grip, but he held on to her arm tightly, his strength being no match for hers. When they reached the room at the end of the hallway, he pushed the door open with his foot and shoved her inside. "Look!" his voice boomed as he pointed around the room with his hand. "There's not a goddamn thing in here except a stain on the floor that I have to sand out and that old box of junk over there that you were supposed to have hauled out to the alley for me yesterday. I can't even count on you to do something as simple as that. You're as useless as you are screwed up in that head of yours!"

The tears began to well up in Anastasia's eyes as emotions of hurt and anger clawed violently at her insides. "I hate this house and I hate you!" Anastasia blurted out at her father as she fled to the sanctuary of her bedroom. She slammed the door shut and then balled herself up in the corner and sobbed uncontrollably for almost an hour until drowsiness overcame her and she drifted off to sleep. The calm of her slumber, however, was soon bedeviled by a bizarre and disturbing nightmare of a skeletal hand bursting forth from the dirt of a grave to grab her ankle and pull her underground. It was the same dream that haunted every one of her sleeps since the automobile accident that claimed her mother's life.

Morning brought with it a dismal sky of gray. A sunny day had been forecasted by the television weatherman the night before; however, it seemed to Anastasia that the rays of the sun all too often refused to shine down upon this grimy part of the city. The gloom matched her mood as she fulfilled her promise to her father and dragged the heavy cardboard box of junk across the overgrowth of the back yard to the alley. She shut and locked the squeaky wooden gate that cried out for oil, and was trudging her way back to the house when she caught sight of something out of the corner of her eye. She turned her head and spotted a cat scurrying along the top of the cinderblock wall that separated the backyard from the filthy graffiti-covered alley. Its long hair was as white as snow and contrasted with the dark red and brown bricks of the old buildings that back dropped it.

The cat paused for a moment and stared into Anastasia's eyes before leaping from the top of the wall and disappearing into the lofty blades of un-mowed grass and stinging nettles.

"Here kitty, kitty!" Anastasia called out as she searched through the high weeds of the back yard for the illusive feline. She suddenly felt a firm hand clamp down on her shoulder, which caused her to quickly spin around with a gasp. A cold chill surged through her body as her eyes beheld the sight of a black-haired man towering above her. He wore a slashed and bloodstained blue uniform like that of a police officer, and Anastasia could see that his face and hands were covered with scratches and teeth marks, and one of his eyes was nothing more than a hollow socket out of which squirming white maggots began to drop.

"Anastasia," he whispered in a monstrous voice. "They're waiting inside the walls."

Anastasia began to hyperventilate and stood frozen with fear for several moments, which felt like an eternity, before breaking free from the spell that held her captive. She let out a loud high-pitched scream and took off running back to the house. To her horror, she found that the back door would not open.

The man began to run towards her.

Anastasia frantically jiggled the knob and pulled on it again and again to open the door, but it failed to budge. The maggot-eyed man was getting closer and closer by the second.

The door became unstuck and Anastasia dashed inside the house. She quickly shut the door and locked it, and then peered out the window into the backyard. The man was nowhere to be seen. It was as if he had simply vanished into thin air. Anastasia began to wonder if she had actually seen him or had he merely been an imaginary vision? And then she again felt a firm hand clamp down on her shoulder. She let out a cry of terror, and then sighed with relief when she realized that the man standing behind her was only her father.

"Did you get rid of that box of junk?" he asked.

Anastasia fought to regain her composure. She didn't want to tell him about the man in the back yard for she knew he wouldn't believe her. "Yes, Daddy," she replied. "I put it in the alley like you asked me to."

"It's about time," grumbled her father as he started to walk away. "I'm going down to the cellar to get some work done and I don't want you bothering me."

"Yes, Daddy," said Anastasia, looking down at the floor. "I won't bother you."

After her father left the room, she hurried back to the window and pulled aside the curtain to look out. She found the maggot-eyed man waiting for her with his face pressed against the windowpane. He grinned and a maggot dropped from his parted lips. Anastasia squeezed her eyes shut and told herself that he really wasn't there. When she re-opened her eyes, he was gone.

Downstairs in the musty confines of the cellar, John Waverly was cutting wooden baseboards with his power miter saw when he was suddenly overcome by the peculiar sensation of eyes upon his back. He turned his head to look but found no one there. He shook his head and set up another piece of wood to be cut. He was hardly a man who believed in the existence of such things as ghosts. However, shortly after moving into the old widow's house where she was devoured by her own cats, he had begun to notice cold drafts and peculiar odors that would suddenly manifest and then mysteriously vanish without explanation. There were also several times that he heard scratching sounds emanating from empty rooms, but they would always cease abruptly the moment he'd enter the room and turn on the light. He figured there were probably mice inside the walls.

Once again the sensation of being watched washed over him, raising the hairs on his arms and the back of his neck. It was far stronger this time and filled him with a sense of uneasiness. He made an effort to ignore it and carry on with his work. However a loud creak coming from the stairs compelled him to stop what he was doing and look over his shoulder. The unexpected sight of his daughter standing directly behind him with a wild gleam in her eyes unnerved him. He gasped and then exhaled a sigh of exasperation.

"Goddamn it, Anastasia!" he yelled. "Don't creep up on me like that! I thought I told you not to bother me while I was busy working."

"Daddy, may I please have a cat?" the girl asked, smiling sweetly and trying to sound as polite as possible. Her eyes expressed a wistful look. "Please? Please?"

"No! You may not have a cat, please, please," her father replied, imitating her in a whining nasally voice. "Now leave me the hell alone so I can get back to my work." A look of disgust contorted his sweaty unshaven face.

"Please, Daddy," Anastasia pleaded. "I promise I'll feed the cat and clean up after him and I'll never…"

"What part of 'no' don't you understand?" growled her father. "If I've told you once, I've told you a thousand times, no goddamn cats!"

"Oh please, Daddy, please! Why can't I have a cat?" Anastasia asked.

"You know damn well why not."

"No, I don't," said Anastasia with dejection. "I don't understand one little bit."

Her father bellowed with anger, "I hate cats! They're all filthy little bastards, good for nothing! I'd shoot every last one of them if I ever got the chance." Before his daughter could interject another plea, he snarled, "If it wasn't for some son of a bitch cat your mother would still be alive and maybe, just maybe, you wouldn't be the way you are."

The words were venomous and jagged and burned in Anastasia's ears until she was unable to contain her tears. "Why are you always so mean to me?" she cried. "Sometimes I wish you were the one who was dead instead of my mother!"

"You ungrateful little bitch!" her father bellowed as the back of his calloused hand slapped Anastasia across the face with such force that the girl flew backwards and landed against a bundle of baseboards leaning against a sawdust-covered workbench. He then ordered her to her room and threatened her with an even harder slap if she failed to obey him. With the palm of her hand pressed against her stinging reddening cheek, she ran up the basement stairs sobbing as the sound of the power miter saw resumed.

Anastasia dashed into her bedroom, slammed the door shut behind her, and then flung herself onto her bed. She curled herself up into a fetal position and sobbed until her teary eyes filled with redness and were stinging. Suddenly she envisioned the walls and the ceiling of the room splattered with copious amounts of blood and bits and pieces of human tissue. Red droplets oozed from the cracked plaster above and splashed upon her face and body. She wrapped her arms around her pillow and hugged it while at the same time shutting her eyes and praying for the blood to disappear. And then there came the sound of a whispering voice, and Anastasia squeezed her pillow harder and gently chanted under her breath, "Go away, go away, go away..."

The whispering was barely audible at first, but Anastasia could tell that it was the voice of a woman. She ceased her chanting and wondered if perhaps her mother was trying to return to her from beyond the grave, but as the voice grew a bit louder, it didn't sound like her mother at all. It was a much older voice and one that she had never heard before. Anastasia was unsure if the whispering she was hearing was real or just inside her head, but she listened intently, trying her hardest to decipher what it was saying to her. It gradually grew more audible and instructed her to go to the window. She was frightened to do so at first, but then gathered up her courage and crept to the window and slowly pulled back the curtain.

To Anastasia's surprise and delight, she discovered a small black kitten waiting for her on the outside ledge of the window. It looked at her with eyes that were as green as jade and emitted a tiny meow. Without hesitation, the girl lifted up the sash and picked up the kitten. She bestowed a kiss upon it and rubbed her left cheek against its silky fur.

"You heard my request, and you came to me," Anastasia said to the kitten. She spoke in a low whisper to prevent her father from overhearing her. She knew all too well if he found out she had brought a kitten into the house, he would be furious. "You're such a beautiful little thing and I know you can understand every word I'm saying to you. I'm going to name you... Avenger."

Anastasia returned to her bed and gingerly placed the kitten upon her pillow. She then laid down on her side with her face next to it and, as she lovingly stroked its fur of pitch, she noticed that the room had returned itself to normal and the bloody gore that had covered the walls and ceiling just a short while ago was now gone without a trace.

The minutes stretched into hours and Anastasia remained in her bedroom, petting and playing with her new furry companion. She ventured out to the kitchen when the coast was clear to gather up some food and a saucer of milk, which she sneaked back to her bedroom and gave to the kitten.

At the supper table that evening, not a single word was spoken between father and daughter. They both ate their meals in silence, avoiding eye contact with each other. The ticking of the clock upon the kitchen wall seemed to intensify inside Anastasia's ears until it was pounding like the thunderous heartbeat of some great monster poised to strike its prey.

After supper, John Waverly headed off to the living room with his bottle of whiskey in hand and switched on the television to a pro-wrestling match. Anastasia washed the dishes as quickly as possible and then returned to the sanctum of her bedroom, where Avenger greeted her with a loving purr.

"I love you, " she said to the kitten as she cuddled it in her arms like a baby. "I won't let anybody ever hurt you. I promise."

She then placed Avenger on the pillow next to her face and stroked its shiny black fur. The gentle purring it resounded sounded like music to Anastasia. The sound made her temporarily take her mind off the cruelty of her father, who was in the other room slowly getting himself intoxicated, and the dreadful run-down house that he had brought her to. The purring continued on and on like a tiny vibrating motor, lulling Anastasia to sleep.

Shortly after the clock chimed the first quarter of the midnight hour, Anastasia awoke in the darkness from her usual nightmare. Her body was drenched in a cold sweat and her heart was pounding. She reached underneath her pillow for her flashlight, turned it on, and was relieved to find Avenger still on her pillow, fast asleep. Just then, one of the floorboards in her bedroom emitted a creak and Anastasia could make out the silhouette of something moving in the cloak of blackness that had draped her room. She turned the flashlight in the direction of the sound and felt an unparalleled horror race through her body like an icy chill when the hazy beam of the light illuminated the faceless and partially eaten cadaver from the room at the end of the hall. It was now in her bedroom, standing at the side of her bed. It whispered, "Anastasia, come with me."

Anastasia began to moan as if in pain as the hideous thing extended its rotting limb and then its bony hand clamped around her slender wrist. She accidentally dropped the flashlight, which returned the room to total darkness, and began screaming while trying to free herself from the dead thing's cold and horrible grasp.

"Leave me alone!" Anastasia screamed. "Let go of me! I don't want to be dead like you!"

She heard her father bellow from the living room, "What the hell is going on in there?" She then heard footsteps coming down the hallway. They grew louder as they approached her bedroom door. And then, all at once, the dreadful dead thing that had been holding onto her wrist disappeared.

"Anastasia!" her father yelled from the other side of her door. "Who are you talking to in there?"

"It was just a bad dream, Daddy," Anastasia called out as she hurried to hide Avenger underneath her calico quilt. "Everything's okay now."

The bedroom door flew open and John Waverly staggered in and switched on the light. His whiskey bottle, which was almost empty now, was still in his hand. He gazed around the room and then stared at his daughter with his drooping bloodshot eyes. "What's going on in here?" he asked, slurring some of his words.

"Nothing," Anastasia replied, trying her best to appear unruffled. With one hand, she held on to the kitten, which was struggling to emerge from the confines of the heavy coverlet. "It was just another one of those nightmares, that's all."

The inebriated man took a swig of whiskey from the bottle and then wiped the wetness from his lips with the back of his shirtsleeve. "I was gonna tell you in the morning, but I might as well say it now. I made a decision where you're concerned," he stated bluntly. "You haven't been acting right since you come back home, and I just can't take any more of it, you hear me? It was a mistake for them to let you out... a big mistake! Those goddamn shrinks should have kept you locked up... in that place."

Anastasia felt her body begin to tremble. "What are you saying, Daddy?"

The man took another swig from his bottle. "I'm saying that you need to go back to the sanitarium. Maybe they can do something for you. I sure the hell can't!"

"But, Daddy," cried Anastasia with tears welling up in her eyes. However, before she could utter another word, her father interjected.

"Don't 'but Daddy' me," he snapped. "It's not going to work this time, Anastasia. I've made up my mind about it. You're going back whether you like it or not, and that's all there is to it."

Silence fell over the room for a moment and then Avenger let out a succession of tiny meows from underneath the quilt. Anastasia's face went pale as her father's reddened with anger.

"Did I just hear a goddamn cat in this room?" he growled.

Anastasia quickly shook her head from side to side with a look of fear in her eyes.

"Don't you lie to me, young lady! I told you I won't have a goddamn cat in this house and I meant it. Now where is the little bastard? You'd better tell me!"

Avenger let out another round of panic-stricken meows, and John Waverly rushed over to his daughter's bed and yanked down the covers, revealing the tiny black kitten. His daughter shrieked out a long cry of "no!" as he snatched up the kitten by the scruff of its neck and gazed upon it with a look of contempt.

"I knew it!" he shouted. "Well, I'm going to put an end to this crap right now!"

"What are you going to do to my kitten?" asked Anastasia, tearfully. "Don't hurt him, Daddy. Please! He hasn't done anything bad to you."

"I'm going to do to this furry little sack of shit what I should have done to you when you were born," her father replied as he staggered from the bedroom with the kitten in one hand and his beloved bottle of whiskey in the other.

Anastasia leapt out of bed and followed her father down the hallway and into the bathroom. He placed the bottle on top of the toilet tank and then, with his free hand, lifted up the hard plastic lid of pink. He proceeded to drop the helpless kitten into the toilet bowl, and it immediately cried out and hissed and thrashed about in a desperate attempt to escape from the cold water. Anastasia let out a horror-stricken scream as she witnessed her father crouch down and, with both of his hands, hold the struggling kitten under the water in an attempt to drown it.

"Don't you dare hurt him!" she screamed; her eyes growing wild and glazed over. "You're nothing but a monster! Let him live! I'm warning you!"

She picked up the whiskey bottle and swung it at the back of her father's head with all her might. It produced a loud thud as it made impact, and with a dazed look in his eyes, the intoxicated man lurched forward, releasing his grip on the fighting feline, and crashed into the toilet before landing on his side on the black and white honeycomb of the hexagon ceramic tiles that covered the bathroom floor. Avenger sprung from the toilet bowl with a splash of water and then took off running until he was out of sight. Some of the droplets hit Anastasia's face and mingled with her tears.

"Avenger!" Anastasia called out as she took off to search for the terrified kitten, but she was stopped dead in her tracks by the sight of the door at the end of the hallway beginning to open. She squeezed her eyes shut as tightly as possible. "If this is a dream," she said, "please, God, let me wake up. Don't let me die."

"You rotten little bitch!" a groggy and inhumane voice barked from behind her.

Anastasia turned around to find her father standing there, tottering, with his brown leather belt in his hand. The top part of his shirt was soaked with blood.

"It's time I taught you a good lesson," he growled in an ominous tone. "One you'll never ever forget!"

The teenage girl cried out in pain as the leather strap stung her and caused bright red lash marks to welt up on her flesh. The whipping sent her crumpling to the floor of the hallway. She attempted to shield her face with her arms as blow after blow from the belt was delivered to her with drunken rage.

By this time, the door at the end of the hallway stood wide open and from the blackness behind it emerged dozens of small dark creatures made of shadow. They moved with great speed down the dimly lit passageway and then took on the form of large cats – some black, some white, some tan. There were cats with tiger-like stripes, some with calico markings. There were shorthaired cats, longhaired cats, ginger tabbies, Persians, Siamese, and tuxedo cats. They emitted howls and screeches that were as terrifying as they were ear-piercing as they pounced upon John Waverly, ripping at his skin with their razor-like claws and sinking their sharp teeth into his flesh. He dropped his belt and fell to the floor, waving his arms and screaming, "Anastasia! For the love of God, help me!"

The demon cats were unrelenting and continued slashing and biting until the screaming and struggling of their victim ceased and he lay lifeless in a pool of his own blood. They then began to feast upon his corpse, ripping his flesh from his bones with their little fangs and devouring him, piece by piece, with ravenous appetites.

Avenger reappeared and lapped up some of the blood that was spreading across the floor of the hallway. After it had its fill, the kitten licked its chops with its little pink tongue, and then jumped into Anastasia's lap, purring softly.

Anastasia smiled and stroked the kitten's silky black fur as her father's blood inched closer to where she sat. "Good kitty," she said, enraptured.

BAD HAIR DAY

A tingle of adrenaline coursed through Gloria's wiry body as she plucked the wig from the fiberglass mannequin head with the disturbingly elongated neck and skillfully shoved it into her faux alligator tote bag without anyone seeing her do it. Her heart thumped with excitement as she casually strolled past Harriet DeGroot, the sour-faced sales clerk perched behind her cash register like a she-gargoyle. Gloria flashed the woman a phony smile before exiting the vintage clothing shop on Bradmore Street with her stolen prize. A feeling of accomplishment caused a wicked grin to tug at the corners of her mouth, out of which escaped a little giggle of delight.

Gloria had long prided herself on being what she considered "an expert shoplifter," stealing whatever small items she could fit into a purse or pocket, and boasting an impressive track record of never having been caught. She began crooking things while in elementary school; by the time she entered high school, her frequent five-finger discounts graduated to full-blown kleptomania.

Unlike some unfortunates who must resort to stealing

in order to survive in this dog-eat-dog world, Gloria did not need to steal, but rather she *loved* to steal. The illegal act of taking something from a store without paying for it provided her with an incomparable thrill. However, by the time she arrived home a short while later, the rush had dissipated.

She was paused on the front stoop of her townhouse, fishing through the tote bag for her keys, when she heard a nasal voice call out her name. She knew who the voice belonged to without having to turn and look. It was Melvin Finkel, her trash-picking transvestite neighbor from next door. As usual, he was accompanied by his incessantly-yapping companion, an epileptic Pomeranian he called the Goddess Jennifer.

"Today is a very special day," Melvin announced, his voice grating on Gloria's nerves like fingernails scraping down a chalkboard. "It's the Goddess Jennifer's birthday! She just turned three!" He beamed like a proud parent. "Isn't that just sublime?"

"Spectacular," Gloria replied without enthusiasm, still searching for her keys.

"I'm throwing a little soirée for her, tonight at seven. She just *adores* parties, you know. You *will* come, won't you?"

A birthday party for a dog? Gloria had to fight hard to keep from rolling her eyes. The very idea was ludicrous—the most ridiculous thing she had ever heard. Truth be told, she couldn't stand the mangy little fleabag, and she wasn't overly fond of its owner either. Her mind raced for an excuse to decline the invitation.

"That's so sweet of you to invite me," she began. "Unfortunately…"

"You simply *must* come," Melvin insisted. "The Goddess Jennifer and I won't take 'no' for an answer!" He picked up the tiny yapping beast and cradled it in his arms. "Isn't that right, sweetie-kins?" he said to the dog in a nausea-inducing baby-talk voice. "Daddy's little princess."

Gloria reluctantly agreed to come to the party, despite the fact that she had fantasized more than once of poisoning the guest of honor.

At last she located her keys and escaped posthaste into her townhouse, quickly shutting the door behind her while her neighbor rambled on about the dog's "wonderful" birthday pedicure. Gloria wasted no time retrieving the wig from her tote bag and depositing the hairy thing on top of her vanity table. With her nose wrinkled, she wondered what on earth possessed her to take that particular wig. It was downright ugly. In fact, she was quite sure it was one of the ugliest things that had ever made its way inside her tote bag, which she had also stolen. With its ratty streaks of black and white human hair, it had the looks and all the charm of a skunk's amputated tail.

Emitting a sigh, Gloria knew that her ill-gotten acquisition, like the hundreds of other useless things she had pinched from stores over the years, would soon be relegated to a box or garbage bag in the musty-smelling storage room down in the basement and forgotten about.

With the thrill of the steal now behind her, Gloria poured herself a glass of wine to celebrate and then retreated to her favorite corner of her couch. She slowly sank into a mire of boredom. When her wine glass was empty, she went back to her vanity table and took another gander at the wig. Laughing to herself, she pinned her flowing blonde hair on top of her head and, just for a lark, put on the wig.

I guess I could always wear this hideous thing for Halloween, she thought as she gazed at her reflection in the mirror. Youth's vernal charms had begun to fade from her features, allowing the wig to give her face an almost witch-like appearance.

And then, just for an instant, her image in the mirror somehow changed. Her familiar reflection was no longer that of hers. The face now looking back at her belonged to someone, or some*thing*, else… something with dark hollows for eyes that seemed to radiate with evil. Something that wasn't quite human.

Startled, Gloria sucked a short gasp of air into her lungs and blinked her eyes. The mysterious face in the mirror suddenly vanished, and, much to her relief, her own reflection once again stared back at her from the glass.

As she reached for the wig to take it off, her scalp suddenly began to tingle in a most peculiar fashion; it was as if an electric current were flowing into the top of her head. And then she felt the mesh of the wig cap start to tighten like a boa constrictor preparing to squeeze the life from its prey. She grabbed the wig and tried her utmost to yank it from her head. However, she discovered, much to her horror, it would not come off.

In her panic-stricken struggle with the wig, she inadvertently knocked her tufted vanity chair to the floor and then tripped over it while attempting to flee the townhouse for help. Landing with a painful thud that brought stars to her eyes, she writhed about on the floor for one terror-filled minute that felt like a lifetime before unconsciousness submerged her brain into the blackness of merciful oblivion.

When she finally came to, Gloria found herself on an unfamiliar street dotted with large, stately homes boasting meticulously manicured lawns and circular driveways filled with expensive cars. With her mind wrapped in a dream-like haze, she had no inkling of where she was, how she arrived there, or to where her feet were carrying her. They seemed to have a will of their own.

The street dead-ended at a cul-de-sac dominated by an imposing English Tudor style house set back behind high hedges and a gated driveway. Gloria watched in amazement, as her finger seemed to know the right gate code to punch in to unlock the gate. It slid open and she followed the long, Italian cypress-lined driveway to the rear of the house. The back door was equipped with a keypad door lock, to which Gloria somehow also knew the security code. She punched it in and pulled down on the polished brass lever. Seconds later, she was inside the mansion.

Confusion flooded her brain. Why did she come here, and how did she know the security codes? She could find no explanation for any of it. She had never stepped foot in this house before, let alone this part of town.

Her footsteps echoed eerily as she ascended a carved marble staircase leading to an oak-paneled hall decorated with swords and oil paintings from another century. At the far end of the hall, nestled behind an intricately carved arched door, was a cavernous study filled with towering antique bookshelves contrasted by modern, black leather swivel chairs sporting chrome legs. In front of a trio of leaded lattice windows stood a desk, upon which sat a Tiffany "Venetian" desk lamp from the early twentieth century and a curious bronze paperweight in the shape of a charging boar.

Gloria sat down at the desk and gazed out the windows as she waited, unsure of who or what exactly she was waiting for. The view they afforded her was one of a garden of blue anemones adorned with a white octagon gazebo with a two-tiered pagoda style roof.

The flowers and paperweight reminded her of the story of the goddess Aphrodite and her mortal lover, Adonis. According to the ancient myth, Adonis died in Aphrodite's arms after being gored by a wild boar during a hunting trip. His blood mingled with the weeping goddess' tears and gave rise to the anemone.

Except for the faint ticking of a clock, the house stood shrouded in silence. Time seemed to stand still and Gloria began to wonder if she might actually be dreaming all of this. She felt oddly detached from herself, swept away in a torrent of unreality. It was something she had never in her life experienced and it rendered her fearful.

Suddenly there came the sound of heavy footsteps from out in the hall. Each step grew a little louder as they drew closer. They came to an abrupt stop outside the door to the study, which then began to slowly swing open. Despite the warm rays of morning sunlight streaming into the windows, an icy chill, like a breath of death, seemed to breathe upon the room.

"Marisol?" came a man's voice from behind Gloria. "It can't be. You're…"

"Dead?" Gloria completed his sentence. "Is that the word you were searching for, Jason? Dead?" Her confusion multiplied itself. She had no idea why she said what she did, or how she knew the man's name. The voice that came from her mouth sounded like hers, but the words were somebody else's. "I believe a more appropriate word would be, murdered," she added.

She swiveled her chair to face him.

Jason was standing in the doorway of the room, his arms crossed. A neatly trimmed beard and a dark blue, three-piece Italian suit gave him a rather dapper appearance. His dark eyes met Gloria's and he snarled, angrily, "Who the hell are you?"

"Have you forgotten me already?" Gloria whined with mock sadness. "That hurts my feelings, Jason. It truly does. But I haven't forgotten you."

A scowl came over Jason's face. "Look lady, I don't know who you are or what kind of sick joke you're trying to play here. But this bullshit's gone far enough. I'm ending this, right now!" He took a step back into the hall and turned his head toward the staircase. "Marguerite!" he thundered. "Phone the police! There's an intruder in the house!"

"It's Thursday—Marguerite's day off. Remember?" Gloria announced, matter-of-factly. She then made a 'tsk-tsk' sound with her tongue and shook her head. "You seem to be forgetting a lot of things today."

"Fine. I'll just call the police myself."

Gloria let out a taunting laugh. "Go ahead, Jason. Call them. I'm sure they'd be all too interested to know where you hid my body after you strangled me with that exquisite Christian Lacroix tie I gave you for your birthday…the same tie you're wearing right now, as a matter of fact. Isn't that just precious?"

Jason's mouth dropped open but no words were forthcoming.

"Do you want to hear something else that's precious? Do you, Jason? Well, I'll tell you. You see, I wasn't quite dead when you tossed that last shovelful of dirt over me." Gloria once again laughed as the color began to drain away from Jason's face, only this time her laughter was louder and maniacal, and chilled her to the very marrow of her bones. "I was still alive… just barely, mind you, but still alive. Did you know that, Jason? Did you know that when you buried my body in the backyard, you buried me alive? It's true. You never could do a job right—especially in the bedroom."

Jason's eyes narrowed with contempt, which brought a strange feeling of elation to Gloria. But still he remained silent.

"But be my guest and call the police," she continued, winding down her harangue. "I'll even dial the number for you. And after they dig up the flagstone floor under that lovely gazebo you had built over my grave, guess who'll be trading in those handsome Italian threads for an orange jumpsuit?"

Jason slowly advanced into the room, the pallor of his face now reddening with ire. He shut the door behind him and pressed the button on the knob to lock it. As he slowly made his way toward the chair where Gloria sat, he undid his tie and yanked it from around his neck.

"That was quite a performance," he said, sounding almost complimentary. "For a moment there you almost had me convinced that Marisol's ghost had come back from the dead. *Almost.* I don't know who you are, but if you think you can blackmail me…"

"Go ahead, Jason. Do it!" Gloria cackled. She swiveled the chair so that her back was once again facing him. "You can't kill me twice!"

In an instant, Jason was behind the chair and had his tie wrapped around Gloria's neck, choking her.

"Don't worry, bitch," he growled with teeth clenched. An angry vein pulsated in his perspiring temple. "I'll do the job right this time!"

He pulled tighter and the silky material of the tie bit into Gloria's flesh.

Gasping for air, she reached into her tote bag and extracted a large and ominous-looking hypodermic syringe. She hadn't the faintest idea how it came to be in her bag. However, she knew, almost instinctively, that it was filled with ten milliliters of a chemical drain opener containing liquid lye and sodium hypochlorite. Without hesitation, she plunged the needle into her assailant's wrist, injecting the entire of its deadly contents into his bloodstream.

Jason let out a horrendous yowl as the caustic mixture raced through his veins. He released his grip on the tie and doubled over in serious agony. Within seconds he was rolling about on the floor, his eyes bulging from their sockets and pinkish foam bubbling from his mouth like a rabid animal. Now, *he* was the one gasping for a breath.

Gloria nonchalantly rose from her chair and stood over Jason's dying body, gloating. She couldn't help but to notice that his bladder had released a torrent of urine, which soaked not only his pants, but also the plush, white carpeting upon which he lay. A slowly spreading puddle of salmon-pink slime—some of it streaked with bright red gore—had formed on the floor around his twitching head.

"Marguerite's going to have her job cut out for her when she returns tomorrow morning," Gloria remarked as she fluffed up her wig with her fingers. "Hopefully she can get all those nasty stains of yours out of the carpet."

After awhile, Jason's struggle to breathe finally came to an end. His convulsions ceased and the pink lava flow from his mouth abated and then stopped all together. His once-handsome face was now contorted in a ghastly rictus and had turned a frightful shade of blue.

Satisfied that the man on the floor was dead as the proverbial doornail, Gloria departed the mansion, but not before swiping the bronze boar paperweight from the top of the desk and depositing it into her tote bag. It was an ugly little thing, but Gloria was unable to prevent herself from taking it. Once a thief, always a thief. That was the motto by which she lived.

And so began Gloria's glorious murder spree.

The high that it gave her that fateful day was most exhilarating. You might even say electrifying. She had never before experienced a rush of pleasure so deliciously intense. It was even more intoxicating to her senses than the act of shoplifting some useless trinket from a store. No longer could she imagine living a life without murder. She craved more.

Her next victim—a panhandling street mime in whiteface—met his untimely end when the wigged-out thrill killer shoved him in front of a speeding bookmobile en route to an emergency book club meeting. Gloria tingled with delight and squealed with glee as the tires of the vehicle ran over his body with two loud thumps and then sped away. He died as he lived—without saying a word.

Feeling quite pleased with herself, she proceeded down a nearby alley until she came across a raggedy old man sleeping inside a large cardboard box, a half-empty bottle of cheap whiskey by his side. Giggling, Gloria picked up the bottle and bashed it into the drunk's head. Upon impact, his skull made a loud cracking noise as it split open. Blood spilled out, turning the weed patch of matted gray hair on top of his head the color of beetroot wine. His drooping eyelids flew open, revealing a pair of bloodshot eyes, yellow with jaundice from the progression of alcoholic liver disease. They were fixed on Gloria as if entranced.

Gloria was in seventh heaven. However, she wasn't finished with the old man just yet. Humming a happy melody, she doused his twitching body with the whiskey until the bottle was as empty as her soul. With the toss of a single lit match, she set him ablaze, stepped back and admired her handiwork. A foul-smelling, black smoke filled the alley as the flames licked at the derelict's body, charring his flesh and boiling his eyes in their sockets.

The remainder of the afternoon was spent killing as many people as possible—men, women, even children—it didn't matter much to Gloria. Each kill supplied her with an indescribable rush, each rush greater than the rush before. By five o'clock she had snuffed out so many lives she was no longer able to keep count. It was a beautiful day for murder.

After beating the minister of the local church to death with his own Bible and nailing his body to the cross in the chancel, Gloria was feeling terribly ravenous. She had worked up quite an appetite from all the physical activity of the day and decided to head home for a bite to eat. While her stomach was growling, her mind was busy plotting new methods to put people to death. She could incapacitate her victim with a date rape drug and then saw his body in half like Simon the Zealot. She could capture a longhaired woman and then choke the life out of her with her own braids. If she happened to be feeling old school, there was always scaphism—an ancient and barbaric method of execution whereby the condemned is drenched with a mixture of milk and honey and left to be devoured by creeping things like insects and other vermin. There was suffocation by cow manure, impalement by beach umbrella, rectal explosives, even a poison toothpick like the one that did in Agathocles of Syracuse in 289 BC. The possibilities were endless.

So many fun and creative ways to kill, she thought with a smile on her face, *and so very little time.*

As Gloria strolled past the vintage clothing boutique on Bradmore Street, Harriet DeGroot peered out the shop's plate glass window at her. A wild look filled her eyes and within a matter of seconds she had sailed out the front door of the boutique and was shrieking, "Wig thief! Wig thief!" on the top of her lungs. The long, bony index finger of her right hand pointed accusingly at Gloria. "Somebody stop that woman! She's a filthy shoplifter!"

To Gloria's dismay, passersby were beginning to stop and stare. Some even went as far as to pull out their cell phones and record the drama unfolding on the sidewalk. Mortified, Gloria tried to diffuse the sales clerk's rage with an apology and an offer to pay for the wig. However, after her credit card was declined, the irate DeGroot cut it in half with a pair of scissors and handed it back to Gloria in a huff, threatening to phone the police and have her arrested.

Horrified by the prospect of going to jail, Gloria's immediate instinct was to run from the boutique as fast as her feet could carry her. But then a strange urge took root inside of her, and with an expeditious wave of her arm, she slashed the sales clerk's throat with the sharp end of the cut credit card. Blood immediately gushed out of the gash and the woman screamed out a four-letter word, clutching at her throat in an effort to quell the bleeding and alleviate the pain.

Gloria's hand then dipped into her tote bag and pulled out the bronze boar. With a battle cry of "Eat bronze, bitch!" she promptly bludgeoned DeGroot to death with the heavy paperweight. When she was through, the woman's sourpuss resembled bloody chunks of raw hamburger meat with stark white bits and pieces of bone poking out here and there.

After washing the splattered gore from her face and hands, Gloria left the bloodstained boutique and hurried back to her townhouse. She popped a frozen TV dinner into the oven and plopped herself down in front of the television to unwind with a glass of wine. Just as her favorite crime drama was beginning, it was interrupted by a special news bulletin:

"Police in Haroldsville are investigating a rash of gruesome homicides that began earlier today and have left at least twenty-five people dead," reported the stone-faced news anchor with the laughable bowtie. "Police Chief Dunning has advised terrified residents to remain in their homes and keep their doors and windows locked until the killer, or killers, have been apprehended. As yet police have no motive for the vicious attacks and no arrests have been made. However, several eyewitnesses have reported seeing a suspicious-looking woman in a black and white streaked wig in the area at the time of the murders."

Suddenly, a face appeared on the TV screen and Gloria nearly choked on her wine.

The face was hers.

"A passerby filming an altercation in front of a second-hand clothing store on Bradmore Street captured this image on her cell phone of a woman fitting the description of the one wanted for questioning in connection with today's grisly citywide slayings," the news anchor continued. "Police are asking the public for their help in identifying this person of interest. Anyone with information about this woman and/or the murders is asked to call the police department's violent crime tip line at…"

Gloria turned off the television and, feeling on the verge of hyperventilation, sprinted to her vanity table, where she fixed her eyes upon her reflection in the mirror. Her scalp was now beginning to tingle under the wig like before, and once again she felt herself slowly falling under its malignant spell. She knew she had to resist. She fought against the surging urge to massacre the masses, and she fought hard. It wasn't easy. Not by any means. The power of the wig was not only evil, but also quite formidable. Gloria instinctively realized that she needed to destroy the wig… before it destroyed her. She frantically pulled at it with all her might, but her efforts to remove it proved to be an exercise in futility.

"Damn you!" she screamed, knowing all too well that it was only a matter of moments before the wig would take full possession of her body and her mind. Gloria was determined not to let that happen.

Desperate times call for desperate measures.

Gloria grabbed a purple can of Aqua Net Extra Super Hold hairspray and applied a copious amount of the flammable hairstyling product to the wig. She then struck a match and a huge fireball instantly engulfed her head. Gloria let out a blood-chilling scream that could be heard as far away as the townhouse next door, causing Melvin's dog to break into a fit of barking. The flaming wig released its deadly grip and leapt to the floor as if it were alive.

With tears stinging her eyes, the un-possessed serial killer rushed to the kitchen sink and began running cold water over her smoldering head in an effort to cool the searing pain. A short time later, when she mustered up enough courage to look at herself in the mirror, she felt sickened by what she saw. Not only had the combusting hairspray singed off every bit of her gorgeous blonde hair, leaving her completely bald, but her scalp was blackened and riddled with huge, watery blisters. She then looked down at the wig lying on the floor. To her bewilderment, it appeared to be fully intact and unscathed by the fire. Not one of its streaky strands showed even the slightest bit of scorching.

Gloria felt uneasy about going near the wig. It was not to be trusted. However, she wanted it out of her home and out of her life—and the sooner the better. She grabbed a broom from the utility closet and cautiously swept the wig into a dustpan, keeping a watchful eye on the malevolent clump of hair the whole time. Keeping it at arm's length, she promptly deposited it inside the aluminum trashcan outside her back door. "Good riddance," she mumbled to herself as she slammed the lid shut, relieved that her terrifying ordeal was at last over.

Sleep did not come easy for her that night. Even the softest of pillows hurt her burnt head. It seemed impossible to find a comfortable position. She tossed and turned, her mind plagued with mental images of all the people she had brought death to. But eventually exhaustion overcame her and sleep mercifully ensnared her in its net of dreams. But, as luck would have it, her peaceful slumber was not to last for very long.

"You dirty bitch!" screamed a high-pitched nasal voice that yanked Gloria out of a pleasant dream of shoplifting in Bloomingdale's. She awoke with a start, momentarily disoriented. She felt something strange wrapped around her neck and then, as the sleep cleared her eyes, she saw there was a man in her bedroom. She realized Melvin was standing over her, his beloved Pomeranian by his side. His face was coated with layers of garish make-up and he had on a blue chiffon evening dress. Around his neck was a string of pearls and atop his head was the wig Gloria had thrown out.

"Melvin?" she asked, confused.

Gloria suddenly felt the thing around her neck tighten and realized it was a dog leash.

"I'm Mel-*vee*-na!" the wild-eyed transvestite shrieked in a falsetto voice, causing the dog beside him to bark, excitedly. "And I look better in a dress than you could ever hope to. Bitch!"

Gloria tried to move but found her wrists and ankles were bound tightly to the bed. Fear raced through her body. Her heart pounded like jungle drums in her chest. With desperation in her voice she begged her next-door neighbor to untie her and let her go, but her words fell on deaf ears.

"How *dare* you stand us up! You promised you would come but you didn't. I suppose you think you're better than us; too high and mighty to have the decency to call. Well, your lack of manners upset the Goddess Jennifer so badly she had a seizure! You ruined her birthday party, you bitch! You rotten, evil bitch!"

"Melvin, I mean Melvina, please don't hurt me," Gloria pleaded. "I'm so sorry. Really I am! I promise I'll make it up to you and your dog. I've had an accident. My head…"

"Lies! Lies! Lies!" Melvin screamed, pulling harder on the leash, which burned a red mark into Gloria's neck. "How should we punish this conniving woman for her wrongdoings?" he asked the dog, which set off a barrage of yapping. He turned back to Gloria and issued a deranged smile. "The Goddess Jennifer says the punishment for you is… death!"

Singing *Happy Birthday* to his tail-wagging dog, he proceeded to tighten the leash around Gloria's neck, blocking the flow of air to her lungs. The minutes passed like dripping molasses and eventually her struggling lost steam and her body went limp. A bluish tint, the color of blue anemones in the springtime, embellished her face. Her bulging, lifeless eyes were fixed in a death stare at the wig on her executioner's head.

Melvin basked in the splendor of his dastardly deed. The high that it dispersed throughout his entire being was most exhilarating. You might even say electrifying. It was even more intoxicating to him than the feel of a Chanel little black dress caressing his manly flesh. He craved more.

And so began Melvin Finkel's glorious murder spree.

THE TAPHOPHILE

I am a taphophile, and have been for many years. Perhaps you've heard of the word before… perhaps not. At any rate, it literally means "a person with a fondness for, or is attracted to, graves, tombs, and/or funerals." As a taphophile, one of my passions is visiting old cemeteries to photograph the tombstones, mausoleums, and funerary statues. I realize there are some who would regard my unusual interest as a rather morbid pastime. But that's only because they don't see the *beauté de la mort* – the beauty of death – through the same eyes as mine.

It was in the early springtime, on the kind of day when little islands of melting snow cling to the awakening hills, and winter's slowly dying breath lingers stubbornly in the air, that the cemetery known as Primrose Hill called out to me. As I was parking my van on a patch of level ground, alongside the gravel-covered road that wound its way past the graves of corpses from another century, a news bulletin came over the radio, reporting that a search was underway for yet another local area woman who had gone missing. There had been so many over the past few months, I lost count. I switched off the ignition and set off on foot with my digital camera in hand.

With the exception of the occasional cawing of an unseen crow and the crunching sound my boot heels made as I walked upon the loose aggregation of crushed stones, the place was blanketed in a peaceful silence. There appeared not to be another soul around, which was fine by me since I'm hardly what you'd call a 'people person.' Solitude is one of the things that I cherish dearly, yet one of the things I never seem to get enough of.

For a small-town cemetery, Primrose Hill was fairly large and bordered on three sides by the wilds of a sprawling forest preserve. Its oldest section dated back to the mid-nineteenth century and was dotted with weathered gravestones into which were engraved poetic epitaphs. Mausoleums with Gothic, Grecian and Art Nouveau architectural details sprung up from the hillsides, and larger-than-life statues – some with missing hands, and others, entire arms – stood like motionless sentinels with perpetually mourning faces.

After about fifteen minutes of walking about and snapping pictures, I came upon a small mausoleum situated alongside the main road. My eyes were instantly drawn to its ironwork doors, which featured an elaborate Egyptian-themed design. Unlike the chained and padlocked doors of all the other mausoleums I had seen and photographed, these were unlocked and stood invitingly ajar. My taphophile heart jumped for joy!

I had photographed many mausoleums in the past, but never their interiors. The unlocked doors of this one were beckoning me to enter, and I was unable to resist the temptation. The unexpected and rare opportunity to photograph one from the inside was too good not to take advantage of.

I took a quick look around to ensure that no one was watching, and then began to ascend the mausoleum's slab-like steps that lead up to its entrance. But just as I reached the top, the crunching sound of tires on the gravel road stopped me in my tracks. *Damn it!* I cursed to myself, dreading that it was the cemetery's caretaker in his rickety, white Ford pickup truck, for I'd had a few unpleasant run-ins with him in the past. A cantankerous old louse whose mouth bore a slight droop from a long-ago stroke, he had made it quite clear that his feelings for "morbid weirdos" like me were anything but amicable. All I needed was for him to accuse me of breaking into a mausoleum and call the police, which I had little doubt he would do, given the opportunity.

The vehicle turned out to be a black, late model Corvette, and I exhaled a sigh of relief. As it slowly crept past me, the driver – a dark-haired man in his mid-to-late thirties – turned his head in my direction and flashed me an overtly flirtatious smile. I found it to be a rather odd thing, considering he had an attractive, blonde-haired woman sitting right next to him. She stared straight ahead at the road, avoiding eye contact.

After the car disappeared from sight, I took a peek through the open doors of the mausoleum and then ventured inside with camera in hand. Curiously, the air within the mausoleum was noticeably colder than the air outside. The walls at each side contained several crypts, and on the back wall a colorful stained-glass window depicting a winged hourglass encircled by a wreath of lilies radiated in the sunlight.

I had taken at least a dozen pictures when, all of a sudden, a bone-chilling gust scattered some dead leaves across the marble floor. I was sure I heard, within the moaning of the wind, a faint and ghostly voice telling me to go home. I chuckled at my over-active imagination and then proceeded to snap a few more photos, including some "selfies." With my curiosity satisfied, I exited the mausoleum, shutting the doors behind me. I then continued strolling through Primrose Hill, stopping periodically to capture with my camera a particularly interesting gravestone or the haunting beauty of a weeping stone cherub.

I was photographing vistas from the top of a pine-covered hill at the other end of the cemetery, when my ears were suddenly filled with loud rock and roll music. I instinctively turned my head in the direction from which the sound came and observed the same black Corvette that had passed by me earlier pull over to the side of the road at the bottom of the hill. It sat there for several minutes with its engine running and radio blaring before the door on the passenger's side flew open and the blonde-haired woman bolted from the vehicle, screaming wildly on the top of her lungs. The driver's door swung open and the dark-haired man jumped from the car and took off after the fleeing woman. He quickly caught up to her, and then, to my absolute horror, I watched him place what appeared to be a long, white extension cord around her neck and began violently choking her with it. She struggled for a bit, kicking and clawing at her assailant, and finally collapsed upon the ground. The man stuffed the cord into the front pocket of his jacket and then started dragging the woman's limp body into the nearby woods.

I could scarcely believe what my eyes had just witnessed. It was surreal, to say the least! Terror assaulted me, like a monstrous bird flapping its wings within the confines of my chest, throwing my heartbeat into disarray. My palms broke out in a cold sweat. My blood pressure shot up, and I could feel an increase in muscle tension as my fight-or-flight response kicked in.

Terrified, I took off running as fast as I could, my feet stumbling over grave markers and tree roots that protruded from the earth like gnarled fingers. All I could think about was getting out of Primrose Hill as fast as possible and notifying the police. I scolded myself for not getting the license plate number of the Corvette, even though I was too far away to make it out clearly. And then I regretted not heeding the warning of the ghostly voice in the mausoleum. I was convinced beyond the shadow of a doubt that it was portentous in its nature. *Oh, why didn't I listen to it and leave when I had the chance?* I grilled myself.

I had been running for quite some time and felt as if I were going in circles. I then realized I had managed to get myself lost. I paused to catch my breath and collect my thoughts by a granite sarcophagus guarded by a large metallic angel whose copper alloys had oxidized to blue-green. My lungs felt as though they were on fire and a cold sweat beaded up on my forehead. I ordered my trembling body to calm down, and tried to convince myself that everything would be all right; I would surely find my way back to my van, sooner or later. I gazed around and was relieved to see no sign of the Corvette. I took a deep breath and then once again broke into a run.

The road eventually forked and I had to choose whether to go left or to go right. A gut feeling – call it 'woman's intuition' if you like – prompted me to go right, so I did. The scenery began to look familiar, which imparted a slight sense of comfort to me. I then spotted the mausoleum with the unlocked doors just up the road and knew I was heading in the right direction.

"Yes!" I shouted with a temporary burst of glee. I could feel a smile form on my lips despite the dread and panic raging deep within me.

I began to run faster and, within a few minutes, my parked van came into view. Nothing could have been a more welcome sight at that moment! I suddenly felt overwhelmed by a flood of emotions, and tears welled up in my eyes.

I unlocked the door to my van, rushed to get in, and then quickly locked the door. With my hand shaking, I inserted the key into the ignition and turned it. Like a scene out of some godforsaken horror movie, the van wouldn't start. *This can't be happening.* "God damn it!" I screamed at the instrument panel.

I tried to start it again, but the engine still refused to turn over. And then I spied the black Corvette ominously approaching. A wave of dread washed over me. The car pulled up alongside of me and the driver got out and casually walked up to my door. I instantly recognized him as the man who had strangled the blonde. He rapped on my rolled-up window with his knuckles and asked if I were in need of any help. *Maybe he doesn't know that I saw what he did to that girl*, I said to myself, trying to calm the terror that was rising up from the pit of my stomach. I turned to him and forced a smile upon my lips. "I'm fine, thank you," I lied, trying my utmost not to sound as though I had just witnessed a cold-blooded murder. "I'm just waiting for my husband." I gazed down at the watch on my wrist and then turned back to the man who was peering at me through the window. "He should be showing up any minute now."

"Oh, you don't say?" he asked me. The tone of his voice told me he didn't believe my story. (I guess I never was very good at telling fibs.) A frightful scowl contorted the muscles of his face. His watery blue eyes glared at mine, filling me with uneasiness. They were cold and empty eyes, like those of a predatory animal... and he was stalking his prey.

I nodded my head, straining my face to maintain the smile. Panic was clawing at my insides, but I had to keep a calm exterior. If I exhibited even the slightest sign of fear, he would surely know that I had witnessed his unspeakable crime.

He turned and began to walk back to the Corvette. I exhaled a sigh of relief. However, it proved to be premature, as he stopped after taking a few steps and then returned to my window. His face was now aglow with an eerie, feigned smile, as though he had slipped on a friendly-looking mask to gain my trust while he had his back to me.

"You wouldn't, by any chance, be lying through your teeth to me, would you?" he inquired.

"No," I lied through my teeth. "Of course not. I have no reason to do that."

The smile on his face dissolved back into a snarl. His eyes turned menacing. "Women are always lying! It's what they do best!" he yelled. "You're no different from the others." He then burst into an obscenity-laden rant about 'whores' and 'prick-teasers' and all the 'stuck-up bitches that thought their pussies were made of gold.'

"My husband is going to be arriving any second now!" I reiterated, hoping it would prompt the man to leave. But it soon became apparent that he had no such intention.

He went over to his car, opened the door on the passenger side, and retrieved something from the glove compartment. To my horror, he then returned to the spot where I was parked. His right hand was wrapped tightly around the handle of a black, steel, expandable baton. I blared my horn, but it didn't faze him in the least. With his teeth clenched, he swung the baton against my window, taking out a small chip of glass. I frantically pumped the gas pedal and tried the ignition key again and again, but the van stubbornly refused to start. There came another swing of the baton and a crack resembling a spider's web fanned out with a loud thud. Shielding my face with the back of my hand, I let out a scream, and then another swing of the baton completely shattered the window, showering me with pieces of broken glass. I scrambled across to the passenger seat as he pulled up on the lock and opened my door. Like a wild animal, he lunged at me, but I managed to open the passenger door in the nick of time and fled from the van into the adjoining woods.

Branches and prickly weeds scratched at my face and body as I ran like a doe from a hunter. The forest grew denser and darker, and I felt like a small, helpless creature being swallowed alive by some giant monster with a voracious appetite.

I don't know for how long I had been running. It felt like an eternity. My leg muscles were on fire with pain, my stomach was cramping up, and my pounding heart felt ready to burst. The terror-stricken little voice in my head told me I had to keep moving, but my fatigued body demanded a rest. I paused for a brief bit to catch my breath, all the while keeping my ears alert to the sound of the killer's approaching footsteps. But all I heard was a loud droning coming from beyond a fern-guarded outcropping of low rocks. I don't know why, but I felt strangely compelled to follow the sound, as if my will was no longer my own.

The buzzing grew louder as I climbed over the ferns and rocks, until, all at once, it became intense, filling my ears with the rapid beating of a thousand swarming wings. Gazing down, my eyes were met by the sickening sight of six dead bodies. The maggot-infested carcasses all appeared to be female and were arranged in disturbingly obscene poses. Some were partially clothed, while others were completely nude. All had been grotesquely mutilated. Hordes of flies and bees and other winged insects crawled upon them, feasting on their remains, while others circled in the air above them. The eyes of one of the fresher-looking corpses were being pecked at and consumed by a trio of contentious crows.

My brain reeled and my stomach churned. I turned away and vomited onto a carpet of moss and fallen branches. The spell was broken and once again I sprinted as if my feet had suddenly sprouted wings.

Through a thicket of trees, I could make out the shape of a building in the near distance. I ran towards it. However, as I drew nearer to the structure and realized that it was nothing more than the derelict ruins of an old chapel that had long ago been abandoned and boarded-up, my short-lived spark of optimism extinguished like a burning wick in a rain storm.

Part of the wall at the rear of the chapel had crumbled away over the years, leaving a small opening at the bottom that was partially obscured by a clump of dead, thorny briars and brambles. It appeared to be large enough for me to squeeze my body through it, so I decided to venture inside and hide from the killer that was pursuing me. And then a thought ran through my mind. *Perhaps I'd get lucky and find something within the building that I could arm myself with should he discover my whereabouts.* Using a thick stick as a primitive tool to keep the thorny branches at bay, I crouched down in front of the opening and then crawled through it on my hands and knees, taking care not to damage my camera. My back, on the other hand, did not make it through unscathed. A jagged piece of stone protruding like a stalactite from the upper part of the hole ripped through the material of my jacket, slicing open my flesh from between my shoulder blades down to the small of my back. I clenched my teeth and forced the pain out of my mind, daring not to make a sound in case the killer was within earshot.

I was now inside the chapel, which was lit by hazy rays of sunlight that beamed through random holes where the rotting roof had fallen away. I stood up and, with my hands, dusted off the dirt and webs from my clothes. I gazed around at my surroundings, keeping my eyes peeled for anything with potential as a weapon for self-defense. The floor was buried under years of dirt, bits of broken plaster, and splintered wood. Filthy wooden pews, some broken, were strewn about, and a rust-encrusted, wrought iron chandelier that had fallen victim to a crumbling ceiling and gravity, sat idly on the ground, enshrouded by long-forsaken spider webs, thick with dust.

I made my way across the rubble to the altar, hoping to find some heavy brass candlesticks that could be used to bash a man's skull in, but there were none to be found. Upon the altar were nothing but a dusty taper candle and an equally dusty box containing a single wooden match. Looking around, my eyes caught sight of a large, round object on the floor, which I estimated to be roughly six inches in diameter. Using my foot, I cleared

away the debris around it and discovered it was the iron pull ring of a trap door in the floor. I grabbed onto it and lifted up the door. Ten stone steps leading down to what appeared to be an ancient crypt came into view. At the bottom, a large rat scurried by and vanished into a veil of shadows.

My instincts were strongly advising me not to go down there. But rats or no rats, I felt I was really left with no other alternative. In the likely event that the killer came looking for me in the chapel, the underground chamber afforded me the best, and only, hiding spot. It was my one and only chance to survive.

I struck the match against the side of the altar. No flame... not even a spark. On the fourth try, its sulfur head ignited and I lit the candle in preparation for my descent into whatever hell awaited me below. I began to climb down the steps, shutting the trap door over my head. The dim glow of the candle's flame cast flickering shadows upon the walls of stone below, and gave the room the ambiance of a medieval dungeon. The crypt itself was long and narrow, abundant with cobwebs, and deathly silent except for the slow and steady sound of dripping water. On the cobblestone floor, in the center of the dank, subterranean chamber, sat six dust-covered, wooden coffins. They were rather plain in appearance and looked to be extremely old.

On any other given day, I would not have hesitated to raise their lids and capture some postmortem shots with my camera. However, I couldn't risk the sound of squeaking coffin hinges giving away my hiding spot in case the killer was lurking nearby.

The flame on my candle suddenly sputtered and then met its demise, and I was swallowed up by the immediate ensuing darkness. I stood motionless. Waiting. Listening.

Drip...

Drip...

Drip...

And then the sound of something scratching at wood came from somewhere in the black void that surrounded me like a sea of pitch. It stopped for a few moments and then continued; only this time it was louder than before. My thoughts flashed back to the not-so-small rat I had seen dart by earlier and I felt a panic attack brewing. My fear of rats started in childhood after watching the 1970's film, *Willard*, and far outweighed my other phobias, which were spiders and heights. I listened with dread in my heart as the sounds of tiny claws intensified. Soon, they were joined by other scratching noises coming from different locations around me in the dark. I envisioned myself surrounded by an army of hideous, gigantic rats. I struggled furiously to restrain myself from freaking out.

Suddenly, I felt something sharp, like long fingernails, pierce the flesh of my right upper arm. The pain was searing and caused me to scream and drop my camera. It hit the stone floor with a crash and the impact activated the flash and the fingernails immediately withdrew from my arm. The bright light that momentarily illuminated the confines of the crypt unveiled a terrifying scene that seemed too nightmarish to be real. Yet it *was* real.

Standing around me were half a dozen corpses in varying states of decomposition. Rotting faces, some more skull than flesh, gazed upon me hungrily from all directions. To my ultimate horror, these things that should have been dead and lying still in their graves were alive as if by some power most unholy.

The light from the flash died away after a second and

the inky blackness once again consumed the crypt. I could hear the horrible breathing noises emitted by those undead things, followed by the sounds of their dragging feet moving closer to the spot where I stood, paralyzed from head to toe with fear. My blood instantly turned to ice in my veins. I let out another scream that was loud enough to wake up the dead; however, it was quite

evident that they already were. I turned to flee, but my escape from the crypt was impeded by the long fingernails of other hellish hands that dug into my flesh like razor-sharp talons. My screams ricocheted off the damp walls of stone and echoed throughout the crypt and the chapel above as I struggled to free myself.

At last I managed to break away from the living dead things, which were now emitting high-pitched shrieking noises that were as horrible sounding as they were inhuman. Rushing towards the steps that lead out of this chamber of horror, I knocked one or two of the foul creatures onto the ground. The sound of their brittle bones cracking and their skulls shattering assaulted my ears. It was like a sound straight out of a nightmare… a sound that will never leave my memory for as long as I continue to live.

Running as quickly as humanly possible, I made it half the way up the stairs before tripping. I fell facedown, twisting my left ankle and banging up my knees and forearms in the process. Patches of my skin had been shredded by the rough texture of the stones, and from my stinging wounds my blood dribbled out, exciting those abominable things that I could hear getting closer. My heart was thumping furiously in my chest. I thought at any

given moment it might burst and that would be the end of me. A quick death would certainly be preferable to being devoured alive by these decaying things that, by all accounts, should have been dead; yet, in defiance of the laws of the natural world, were not.

All at once, I felt a skeletal hand wrap its bony fingers

around my injured ankle and attempt to drag me back down into the crypt. A surge of panic-driven adrenaline provided me with the strength needed to kick myself free from the monstrous grip. Ignoring the pain from my injuries, I picked myself up and made a mad dash the rest of the way up the stairs and out of the ruins of the abandoned chapel.

My ankle was rapidly swelling up and the pain was growing in its intensity. However, I dared not stop to rest. I had to keep running, no matter how great the pain. Through the leafless branches of tangled trees and shrubs, I could see glimpses of the winding road up ahead. I then heard the sound of tires rolling over loose gravel and could make out a vehicle. It was the white Ford pickup truck belonging to the cemetery's caretaker. *Oh, thank God*, I thought, and then almost chuckled out loud. Never in my wildest dreams would I have thought the day would come when I'd be pleased to see that man. But that day was today. As I continued to run towards the road, I began to shout for help and wave my arms wildly, hoping that he would hear my voice or see me and stop.

And then, I felt something slip around my neck, stopping me in my tracks and cutting off my supply of air. Without seeing it, and even before clutching at it in an attempt to rip it away from my throat, I knew right away it was the killer's garrote. As I fought tooth and nail to regain my freedom, as well as my breath, I could see, through the branches, the white pickup truck drive past and disappear around the bend. My hope for being rescued vanished right along with it.

"You didn't really think you were going to get away from me that easily, did you, bitch?" came a man's raspy voice from behind me. It was void of humanity and filled with a cruelness that ran deep. "Stop struggling and just accept your fate," he demanded. "Don't you understand? You have to die. I can't leave any witnesses."

I was certain that my demise was but minutes away and

I became panic-stricken. However, with my throat being crushed, I was unable to scream or even plead for my life. A frightful gurgling noise was all I could manage. My heart was pounding. My vision was getting blurry. I could scarcely believe what was happening to me. It had to be a bad dream. It just *had* to be.

I had always heard that it was a common thing for death to be preceded by the flashing of one's life before their eyes. However, the only thing I could see in my mind's eye was the horrifying image of my strangled corpse decomposing in the woods, alongside the dead bodies of the madman's other victims.

Confusion and dizziness were now setting in and I found that I was rapidly losing the strength to struggle. My arms were going limp. The cord around my neck tightened and its fibers cut deeper into my flesh. I could feel my face puffing up and I somehow sensed it was turning a shade of beet red or perhaps even purple. I then heard my assailant's voice taunting me with his twisted plan to rape my corpse.

I wasn't a religious person; but, at this point, I found myself praying inside my head to God, or to anyone else who would listen, to stop my agony. I just wanted my inevitable death to be swift and mercifully bring this living nightmare to an end. I suddenly began to slip into a drowsy, almost dream-like, state and my panic melted away into a strange peacefulness. I knew my death was rapidly approaching.

My body was starting to slump to the ground when I heard the man behind me wailing out loud like a demon. He released the cord from my neck and I landed on the wet leaves that carpeted the floor of the woodland. I immediately gasped to refill my lungs with air and then coughed and panted like an overheated dog. My head was pounding with pain that was far worse than any migraine headache I had ever experienced and it hurt like hell to swallow. But there were no words to describe how wonderful it felt to still be alive.

Just before I descended into unconsciousness, my eyes beheld the horrific sight of the six undead creatures from the chapel's crypt savagely ripping the head and limbs from the killer's torso. His blood sprayed in the air in every direction, and some of the splatter, still warm to the touch, landed in my hair and on my face. His wailing ceased and the creatures began to feed on his bloodied body parts.

When I came to, I found myself sitting on the glass-covered front seat of my van. My dented camera was sitting on the seat beside me, and there was no sign of the black Corvette. Confusion flooded my brain. *How did I get back to my van?* I wondered. *Was it all just a horrible dream?* Nothing made any sense. I examined my throat in the rear-view mirror. It was badly bruised, and a dark red mark left by the extension cord confirmed the reality of my nightmarish ordeal.

With curiosity eating away at me, I picked up my camera and switched it on. I was pleasantly surprised to find it still in working condition after having been dropped on a cobblestone floor. I set it to playback mode and scrolled through all the pictures until the last one taken was displayed on the LCD screen. It was a tilted, low-angle shot of an empty crypt.

OF BLACK BUTTERFLIES SHE DREAMT

Whiter than calla lilies, the soft satin of Marie's gown billowed like clouds around her; the whispering jasmine breeze from the window caressed her flaxen hair like a secret lover, and of black butterflies she dreamt.

In slow motion, she glided across a sun-drenched meadow, her naked feet barely touching the ground. Arriving at a hilltop, she laid her body down upon a blanket of dewy grass blades and nodding wildflowers; the azure-blue canopy of sky above flooded her eyes with its expanse. And then, within her field of vision, there arrived a butterfly with majestic wings the color of midnight. It circled her in its dance of silent grace before it lit down upon her forehead. And then there came another black butterfly, which circled her as the other one had done, and then landed on her hand. Soon, there were more – dozens, hundreds, thousands; the winged insects covered every inch of her body and face, pinning her helplessly to the ground, obscuring the azure-blue from her eyes. Parting her lips to scream, her mouth became an open invitation, and scores of butterflies fluttered into it until no space remained, silencing her, choking her. In the back of her mind, she heard, like water droplets echoing in a dark cave, the choppy voice of the punk-haired Chinese woman from her psychiatrist's waiting room. "Black butterflies," the stranger explained in a whisper, "are the harbingers of death. Very bad omen." Marie's ivory flesh suddenly felt pricked as if by millions of tiny needles. She could feel a million tiny droplets of her blood being siphoned into a million tiny proboscises, simultaneously. She came to realize, with ultimate horror, that the black butterflies were slowly devouring her alive.

Marie awoke with a start. Her heart was rapidly beating; her face was dampened by sweat turned cold by the night breeze from the open window. She instinctively reached across the bed, groping in the darkness to procure the comforting warmth of her husband's body; however, cold and empty space next to her was all she could feel.

She spoke his name, softly, almost inaudibly, "Cliff. Where are you? Cliff."

She waited, swathed in shadows, for his familiar voice to emerge from out of the darkness and whisper to her, "I'm here, Marie. You needn't be afraid. I'll never ever leave you." Minutes passed, slowly at first, then grew agonizingly long. The darkness of the bedroom remained voiceless. Marie felt alone, abandoned. She then recalled the dream, her mind's eye playing and replaying the scenes, mercilessly. The disembodied words of the Chinese woman haunted her memory like a ghost unable to rest in its grave.

Shuffling noises, accompanied by several thumps and creaks, sounded from across the room. Marie turned her head in the direction from which they emanated. She was unable to make out who, or what, was moving about in the darkness.

"Cliff?" she called out in a slightly louder voice than

before. "I need you."

The door to the master bath creaked part way open and brightness spilled out into the bedroom and into Marie's eyes, causing her to squint until she adjusted to the light. From the bed, she was afforded a partial view inside the adjoining bathroom. To her ultimate horror, the white tiled walls surrounding the bathtub, as well as the tub itself, were splattered with copious amounts of blood. A tall, longhaired man, whose face she was unable to recognize, hummed softly to himself as he diligently wiped up the red splashes and drips with one of the embroidered face towels, which he periodically rinsed and wrung out in the sink.

Oh dear God, Marie thought. *He's murdered Cliff!*

Sickened by the prospect that her husband was dead, and fearing for her own life, she gingerly slipped from the bed, crept across the bedroom in a stealthy manner, and quietly hid herself inside the closet, keeping a constant watch through the slanted louvers on the door. Her heartbeat pounded like a bass drum in her ears as adrenaline pumped through her body like liquid fire.

Time stood still, suspended in fear. Marie's mind floated with a heightened sense of awareness. And then, from out of a realm of obscurity, there came the sensation of fingers, frigid like dead meat, curling around her wrist. A chill sliced through her like a blade on a quest for blood, and she struggled to stifle the scream that was pushing its way up her throat and into her mouth. The unseen fingers closed around her wrist all the tighter, dominating the warmth of her flesh with their horrible lifeless cold, crushing her to the bone. Marie shut her eyes and winced with pain.

You aren't real, she denounced, inside her head. *Go away. You don't belong here.*

The fingers withdrew to the shadows. The pain ceased. The warmth returned. Marie re-opened her eyes and resumed her vigil. The minutes multiplied.

Upon completion of his gruesome task, the man with the long hair switched off the bathroom light, and a veil of blackness once again fell over the bedroom. He paused for a moment or two, as if listening for any stirrings of life; Marie tried not to breathe, fearful he would hear her. He let out a cough and then exited the room; Marie allowed her breath to creep back into her lungs. She waited and listened, and when the diminishing footsteps could no longer be heard, she emerged from her sheltering space and crept through the lampblack darkness, careful not to make a sound. She located the bedside table and the telephone that was perched atop it. She picked up the receiver and dialed 911.

"The number you are trying to reach is no longer in service," the recorded voice of a woman stated. It was cold, monotonal, almost scolding. "Please hang up and try your call again." There was a click, followed by a succession of loud, rapid beeping sounds. Marie followed the recording's instructions, only to again reach a disconnected number. She hung up, stunned. Her panic level was increasing by the second.

The house was heavy with a deathly stillness and filled with shadows as Marie cautiously made her way along the empty hallway and down the stairs to the kitchen, where she armed herself with the chef's knife she kept in a cutlery drawer. Creeping on tiptoes, she proceeded from the kitchen into the dining room, and then into the living room. From atop the painted mantel of the fireplace, eyes stared at her from framed family photographs.

Oh, how she yearned for the power to will her body into the sanctuary of those smiling images, forever frozen in time. In a photograph, she would remain safe, always blissful. She would never again know pain or fear or sorrow. Dreams of black butterflies would never be able to find her. She sighed with sadness at the impossibility. Words that she once read in a book, in a time long ago and far away, floated into her head like wispy midsummer clouds. *Photographs can steal your soul.*

The spell of her wandering mind was abruptly shattered by the sound of a car's engine starting up. She followed the sound, like a moth to a flame. She slowly cracked open the door leading to the attached garage and peered inside, unprepared for the sight of what was waiting for her.

The trunk of Cliff's car was open, and the tall, longhaired man who had scrubbed the blood from the master bath was loading black plastic trash bags into it. From the bottom corner of one of the bags, there came a scarlet seepage of blood that left a heart-shaped puddle on the concrete floor of the garage.

Marie cringed as she watched, and realized. *Oh, dear God! Cliff's body parts are inside those bags!* Her lips trembled. Her legs felt weak, as if any moment she might collapse. A sick feeling gnawed at her stomach like a rat and she fought hard to overcome the urge to vomit.

Tighter and tighter, her fingers squeezed around the handle of the knife, as an animalistic desire to kill surged through her body. She imagined plunging its stainless steel blade deep into the killer's back, cracking bones, slicing through muscle, severing arteries, and puncturing vital organs. The mental images filled her with glee. She hungered to avenge Cliff's murder and the unspeakable acts done to his lifeless body. She took in a deep breath and advised herself to act with patience, to strike only when the opportunity afforded itself to her. The timing of the kill had to be just right. Nothing less than perfection would do.

The door on the driver's side of the car swung open, and to Marie's relief, her husband, who was very much alive, emerged. Tears of joy instantly welled up in her eyes, and the urge to run to Cliff for comfort twisted her stomach into knots. She felt compelled to scream out her undying love to him, and she ached for him to hold her and make her nightmare vanish. And then her eyes shifted to the bloodstained shirt he was wearing, and her blood turned to ice in her veins. He strolled to the rear of the vehicle and helped the other man load the rest of the bags into the trunk.

The longhaired man glanced over at him and chuckled. "You'd better change that shirt before we go, just in case." His voice, which bore a trace of a California surfer accent, was friendly sounding and had a youthful quality to it. It wasn't at all like the voice of a monster that Marie had expected.

"Don't worry, Jason," Cliff reassured. "I will."

The man, who Marie now knew was named Jason, gave Cliff a wink. He tossed another black bag into the trunk. "You know, Cliff, I never thought you were really serious about carrying out our plan. I know we talked about it for almost two years, but I never believed this night would actually become a reality."

"Well, it's a little late to start having second thoughts."

"I'm not," Jason replied, shaking his head, gently. "And there's no regrets either," he added. The corners of his mouth curled up into a smile. "Hey, haven't I always been your ride-or-die buddy? I'm with you all the way on this, Cliff. You know I'd do anything for you. Anything just to be with you."

The two men embraced in the way that lovers entwine around each other. And as their lips met in a tender kiss, the seam of one of the overstuffed trash bags split open and out rolled a decapitated head. Its face was gruesomely contorted, and, despite the dark coagulated blood that matted its hair and clung to most of its face like a mask of gore, Marie was able to make out the features. It was a face that she instantly recognized. It was hers.

This isn't real. This isn't real, Marie chanted to herself, hoping the nightmarish scene in the garage would retreat into the shadows like the hand in the closet. But, to her dismay, it remained steadfast in its horror.

She slowly shut the door to the garage. In a daze, she

staggered into the living room, vertigo spinning its web around her like a spider. The stench of car exhaust, plastic bags and death continued to assault her nostrils. Reality disconnected itself from her, and all pain and fear and sorrow crystallized into a numbness that reminded her of the unchanging faces in the picture frames. She returned to the kitchen and placed the knife upon the gray granite countertop. She would no longer be in need of it.

Floating in a haze, she managed to make her way back up to her bedroom. She once again picked up the receiver of the phone; this time she dialed her psychiatrist's number. After what seemed like a million rings, the answering service picked up.

"Please," Marie begged, "let me speak to Doctor Wexler. This is Marie Gravelle. I must talk to the doctor. Please! This is an urgent matter!"

"Hello?" A hint of irritation crept into the switchboard operator's voice. "I said, 'you've reached the answering service for Doctor Wexler.' Is there anybody on the line?"

"This is Marie Gravelle!" Marie shouted into the phone. "I need to talk to the doctor right away! Something horrible is happening to me again! Can you hear me? This is an emergency! A matter of life and death!"

"Hello? Is anyone there?"

Before another word could erupt from Marie's paling lips, there came the sound of a click, followed by a dial tone that buzzed in her ear like the eerie drone of a bee in flight. In slow motion, she returned the receiver to its cradle, a sinking feeling overcoming her. Staring blankly, she turned away from the phone and her feet carried her, zombie-like, into the master bath, where the stinging smell of chlorine bleach still lingered in the air.

She reached for the medicine chest containing her pills, but froze. She expected to hear herself scream, and knew that she should have, but silence gripped her vocal chords. Her mind struggled to make sense of what was happening.

Ever so gently, she placed the palm of her right hand against the mirrored door of the medicine chest. She could feel it, cool and solid; it was really there, and not a dream. What choice did she have but to accept the inevitable? She had gazed into the glass, but no reflection of her had gazed back. The only thing the mirror showed was the white tiled wall behind her. Marie's mind slowly filled with clouds.

She stumbled back to the bedroom, without her pills, and lay down upon the bed to stare up at the ceiling. She didn't know what else to do. Soon, she found herself surrounded by dewy grass blades and nodding wildflowers. Above her, the white ceiling became a sky of azure-blue. She felt Cliff's body lying next to her; his breath danced inside her ear, warm like the whispering jasmine breeze. Slowly, he opened the front of her satin gown, whiter than calla lilies, and gently caressed her naked breasts. His fingertips circled her rose-colored nipples, and Marie shut her eyes. *I'd do anything for you. Anything just to be with you.*

Something warm and sticky glazed her bosom. With her eyes still shut, she imagined it to be honey, golden like the tresses of her hair, sweet like the taste left upon her lips after a tender kiss. Not wanting to, she opened her eyes and gazed down at her breasts. They were smeared with bloodied handprints, as was her gown. She turned her head to look at Cliff, but he was no longer next to her. She was alone in the sun-drenched meadow, except for the single black butterfly perched above her heart.

HOLY SHIT!

Some men collect comic books and baseball cards; others collect postage stamps and coins. A man of means might collect classic European automobiles, big game trophies, fine art, or other items possessing great value. Louis IX, commonly known as Saint Louis, collected saints' relics and built temples for them. Napoleon Bonaparte collected countries.

Malcolm Thorndike, a man of vast wealth and questionable taste, also possessed a passion for collecting, although his was a peculiar one, to say the least. By the time he had reached the age of thirty, he had invested (some would say squandered) a large chunk of his sizable inheritance amassing an impressive and one-of-a-kind collection of rare stools from around the world. Not the kind of stools one would sit on, but rather the kind discharged from one's bowels after food has been digested.

Within his spacious Fifth Avenue mansion overlooking the wilds of Central Park, locked bookcases and lighted curio cabinets lined the walls of every room, their spotless shelves overflowing with the turds of celebrities, saints and sinners, as well as the dung of exotic animals and royalty—all proudly on display under clear glass domes that were polished three times a week by Malcolm's faithful Japanese houseboy, Motoshi. Smaller, albeit equally prized, specimens were housed in shadow boxes that dominated the stairwell and halls like exhibits in a SoHo art gallery. And in the center of the mansion's opulent and capacious paneled parlor, directly beneath a monstrous chandelier with hundreds of red crystals like drops of frozen blood, a fossilized pterodactyl dropping that set Malcolm's bank account back nearly five thousand dollars graced the top of an antique Chippendale desk. It pulled double duty as a paperweight and conversation-starter.

An icy drizzle blurred the windowpanes as, one by one, the guests arrived at the feces-filled mansion and gathered in the parlor like six of the seven deadly sins. There were R.J. Solomon—Chairman and Chief Executive of a multinational luxury goods conglomerate; Cromwell Mortimer—a British petrol-industrialist and founder of a major oil company; Giselle Delacroix—French socialite and heiress to one of the world's largest cosmetic companies; Gunther Vogel—German billionaire businessman and owner of an international pharmaceutical empire; billionaire shipping magnate, Jules Christos; and filthy rich (and filthy-minded) televangelist, Skyler Raines.

They were, without question, half a dozen of the world's wealthiest individuals. They had the best that money could afford—luxurious homes, luxurious cars, luxurious yachts, and the finest of everything. Yet, despite their extravagances and exorbitant toys, they still felt dissatisfied with their lives. However, their wealth and dissatisfaction were not the only things this group had in common: they each shared a burning desire for immortality… and were willing to pay any price to obtain it.

A low rumble of thunder echoed in the distance as the

guests waited in jittery silence for their host to make his entrance. A cloud of shallow-breathed anticipation hung thick and heavy in the air. Giselle Delacroix lit one of her stubby French cigarettes, crossed her legs and eyed the German and the televangelist as the two men strolled about the room like art connoisseurs examining the unusual exhibits. Cromwell Mortimer, growing restless, cleared his throat and began tapping his fingertips on the arms of his chair. The others sat motionless, staring out into nothingness.

Lightning streaked past the rain-obscured window, dispatching a sharp finger stabbing toward the earth. Another rumble of thunder, louder than the previous one, growled overhead as if to herald the arrival of slow and rhythmic footsteps that echoed out in the hallway. They grew louder as they drew closer to the parlor.

A massive, carved oak pocket door slid open with an oil-thirsting squeak and Malcolm Thorndike stepped into the room. Motoshi immediately followed, wheeling a serving cart upon which rested a small, ornate tray of sterling silver and an ancient alabaster jar, which was sealed with a wooden plug covered in decaying black wax.

Malcolm took a quick gaze around the room. Satisfied to find all his guests present, he flashed a smile of rehearsed cordiality and greeted them. "Welcome! Welcome to my humble abode. I'm delighted that you've all chosen to accept my invitation!" He quickly turned and thanked his servant. "That will be all for now, Motoshi. I'll summon you when we're ready."

The Japanese houseboy bowed and departed the room.

No sooner had the squeaking pocket door slid shut, Malcolm popped the stopper from the alabaster jar and tilted it on its side until a shiny black log of petrified poop slid out of the ancient vessel and onto the ornate tray. A silvery-white aura faintly shimmered around the turd.

"Behold!" he trumpeted like an overacting thespian.

"This is my latest acquisition! The crown jewel of my collection!"

Gunther Vogel wrinkled his bulbous nose in disgust and his upper lip curled upward to reveal a row of tobacco-stained teeth. "I did not travel all the way to the United States from Germany to look at a turd on a silver platter!" he remarked, his voice smoldering. "I came because I was told you had uncovered the secret of immortality!"

"An elixir that renders death obsolete, I believe," Jules Christos added.

R.J. Solomon cleared his throat. "A ten-million-dollar elixir to be exact. That's what we've all come here for." He turned to Malcolm. "Time is money, Thorndike, so let us get down to the business at hand. I have a plane to catch at ten."

"I wholeheartedly agree," said the televangelist, his high-pitched voice tinged with a southern accent. "Enough of this talk about turds."

"Ah, but the turd you see before you on this silver platter is no ordinary turd," the collector replied with a gleam in his eyes. "That I can assure you!" He gazed down lovingly at the excrement. "This is a turd so special, so venerated, so *sacred*, that it was kept under lock and key at the Vatican for centuries." Malcolm paused, grinned from ear to ear, and then continued. "Friends and colleagues, feast your soon-to-be-immortal eyes upon the holy shit of none other than the Son of God himself!"

A mixture of startled gasps and chortles filled the parlor.

"After Jesus died on the cross for our sins, he, to put it bluntly, shit himself—something a lot of dead people do as the muscles in their body relax. Mary Magdalene, who attended the crucifixion, gathered up the crap of Christ after the Roman guards had departed Golgotha and stored it in this alabaster jar."

Lightning illuminated the window and another rumble

of thunder sounded as the guests exchanged hushed whispers among themselves.

"My friends," Malcolm continued as the thunder and whispers died away, "I have promised each and every one of you everlasting life, and everlasting life is what you will have… tonight! I have gone to great lengths and expense to acquire this divine stool, for this is the stool of immortality! According to a lost scripture tucked away in the vaults of the Vatican, a life eternal—not in heaven, but right here on earth—is guaranteed to all who partake of the Christ turd!"

"This is blasphemy!" Skyler Raines declared, clutching the diamond-encrusted gold cross he wore around his neck. "But tell me more."

"Hold on a minute. Are you telling us we have to *eat* it?" Jules Christos asked, squinting his eyes in apparent puzzlement. His voice clearly rang with anxiety, which he seemed to make no effort to conceal.

Malcolm grinned, amused by the expression of alarm raging on the shipping magnate's face, and nodded his head. "Relax, Jules, old boy. A turd of antiquity possesses neither an unpleasant odor, nor taste."

"I'm not going to inquire as to how you've come to know that," the Greek man stated. "I will simply take your word for it."

Malcolm chuckled at his guest's remark and then explained to everyone, "Just one pinch of powdered Christ turd added to a goblet of wine will make you immune from the clutches of death. Or, if you prefer, you can snort a line of it like nose candy. The choice is up to you."

Giselle sensuously drew on her cigarette and exhaled the smoke ever so slowly before breaking her silence. Her lips, which matched the color of the Chateau Margaux in her crystal wine glass, parted, and in an impassive voice laden with a French accent, she inquired of her host, "Malcolm, darling, these things you tell us are, how do you say," she paused to find the right word in English, "extraordinary! But how can we be sure that the legend of this holy relic is rooted in fact, or even that it's safe for us to ingest it? After all, it doesn't appear that anyone has ever put it to the test."

Before Malcolm could string together the words to form a reply, the voice of an intruder bellowed from the pocket door that had slid open when no one was watching. It was a gruff-sounding voice, allocating dread and blazing with fury. It was a voice clad with familiarity.

"Everybody put your hands in the air! Now!" the intruder growled, his gaze darting around the room, his trigger finger ready to dispense death. "I want to see those goddamn hands!"

Without the necessity of turning around to look, Malcolm instantly knew the intruder's identity: It was a man by the name of John Butler—a master jewel thief to whom he had paid what one would call "a small fortune" for services rendered... services that included stealing the Christ turd from the Vatican and the killing of several Swiss Guards in the process. Malcolm had no delusions about the thief's motives. He knew he had come to rob him of the holy shit.

Giselle threw her head back in a defiant gesture, and the diamonds in her gold earrings caught the light of the massive, red chandelier above. "You have your nerve!" she blasted Butler, her painted lips curled in an insolent sneer. "Just what is the meaning of this *vulgarité*?"

"Shut your trap, lady, and get your hands up in the air like I told you!" the gunman shot back, the level of anger rising in his voice. He waved his gun recklessly in front of the woman's high-cheekboned face. "Do it, if you know what's good for you."

Giselle reluctantly did as ordered, all the while grumbling something in French.

Appeased by the woman's compliance, Butler turned his eyes to the other guests, whose faces reflected varying degrees of shock and dismay. Pointing his gun at random targets, he barked out more instructions. "Don't anybody try to be hero. I won't hesitate to blow a hole through your head if you so much as move a finger." His right eye began to twitch. "Just do as you're told, and nobody gets hurt. Got it?"

Heads nervously nodded in unison.

"Hello Butler." Malcolm said, flatly, his voice devoid of its usual good cheer. "So, we meet again, as they say in the movies."

"Hello shit collector," Butler replied, aiming his gun at Malcolm's chest.

"What do you want?" Malcolm inquired. "More money?"

Butler smiled, contemptuously. "You're a screwball, but you're not a stupid man, Thorndike. You know exactly what I want, and you know I won't hesitate to kill you and everyone else in this house to get it. Now, hand over that Christ turd!"

Malcolm placed his hand protectively over the stool on the silver tray. "For what possible reason could you want my Christ turd?"

"The Vatican hired me, of all people, to retrieve their precious turd. They had no idea I was the one who stole it in the first place!" A laugh escaped Butler's mouth. "They're paying me almost as much as you paid me to steal it. But when I found out its true value and *why* they wanted it back so desperately…"

"You decided it would be more advantageous for you to double-cross them," Malcolm said, finishing Butler's sentence.

"You're nothing but a blasphemer!" shouted the televangelist. His cheeks were flushed with rage and a pulsating, blue vein that traveled from the edge of his left eyebrow to his hairline made itself prominent. "There's a special place in hell for sinners like you!"

"Not if I become immortal," Butler snapped back.

"Thou shalt not steal!" Raines blurted out. His words did little but to arouse a look of amusement from the thief's face. "God shall judge and punish accordingly those who willfully break any of his Ten Commandments! You need to repent, my son. Let me save you."

Outraged by the T.V. preacher's blatant hypocrisy, Butler flew into a rage. "Shut up, you sanctimonious sleazeball! If God is going to give anyone a one-way ticket to hell, it'll be con artists like you who fill the heads of your weak-minded followers with lies and false hopes so you can milk their bank accounts in the name of religion!" He then pivoted and waved his gun before the trembling host. "The turd, Mister Thorndike… "

Unbeknown to John Butler, Motoshi had stealthily crept up behind him during his tirade, a heavy cast iron wok clenched tightly in his hands. Being the ever-loyal servant that he was, he raised the bowl-shaped frying pan above his head and then struck it against the back of Butler's head with all his might. The blow produced a loud cracking sound. Butler's eyes rolled up into his head, becoming ghost-white orbs. His body lurched forward in response to the impact, and he involuntarily squeezed the trigger of his gun. A shot rang out and a bullet darted across the room, ripping open a ragged gash in the throat of the Reverend Skyler Raines, before shattering one of the glass domes and imbedding itself in the oak paneling behind him.

Dropping her wine glass, Giselle erupted with a scream as Butler collapsed onto the floor before her feet, and the horrified preacher frantically clawed at his blood-spurting throat. From his bleeding mouth came a sickening gurgling sound in place of words. Raines began to stagger as though intoxicated and then fell forward into the antique Chippendale desk, knocking over the fossilized pterodactyl dropping. His legs gave out from underneath him and he sank to the floor, still clawing and gurgling.

Stricken with panic, Malcolm's guests leapt from their seats and bolted in the direction of the open pocket door. But, before they could escape from the feces-filled room and its metallic stench of blood, Malcolm blocked the exit, waving the holy shit in the air.

"My friends, please, you have no reason to panic!" he shouted, his eyes wild as the storm raging outside the mansion. "I implore you all to return to your seats! There's no need for anyone to leave. I have this situation well under control, as each and every one of you will soon bear witness to!"

The eyes of his rattled guests followed him as he calmly made his way over to the profusely bleeding televangelist and then grew wide with shock when he proceeded to insert the turd into the bullet hole in the man's throat. Within a matter of seconds, there emanated a loud sizzling sound from the wound, not unlike the hissing of bacon in a hot frying pan. He gently withdrew the turd from the wound and the river of blood that had turned Raine's white shirt the same color as the red leather interior of his brand new Rolls Royce Wraith ceased to flow. The room resonated with gasps of disbelief as all traces of red spillage mysteriously vanished and the ragged gash just as mysteriously mended itself. Malcolm then helped Raines to his feet.

The stunned televangelist brought his ring-adorned hand up to his throat and placed it over the spot where the bullet hole had been just moments ago. He then checked his hand for blood. There was none. Finding the wound completely healed and his neck as good as new, a look of astonishment spread over his face like an oil lick.

"It's a miracle! I've been healed!" he marveled. "Praise be to the divine turd of our Lord and Savior, Jesus Christ!"

Malcolm smiled at him and then turned to face the others. "Behold the miraculous powers of the Christ turd!" he exclaimed, holding the hallowed fecal matter high in the air for each of his astonished guests to feast their eyes upon.

The words that flowed from his lips ignited a blaze of cheers and applause from everyone in the room, with the exception, of course, being John Butler, who lay facedown on the floor, the graying hair at the back of his bashed-in head matted with dark and foul-smelling blood that was now congealing and mixed with bits of his shattered skull.

"If any of you had entertained even the slightest doubt about its life-giving power," he continued, "the spectacle you all just witnessed, here in this very room, with your very own eyes, should be more than enough to lay those doubts to rest."

The hand-clapping horde rose, almost in unison, from their seats, bestowing upon their host a standing ovation. Like an actor on a stage, Malcolm took a bow before his adoring audience.

"Who's ready for eternal life?" he asked, coyly.

The six immortality-craving guests immediately responded to his question by extracting bundles of cold, hard cash from purse and pockets and eagerly depositing them into his open hands, which he had cupped to receive them.

After stuffing his pockets to their brims with the money, he returned the turd to its alabaster jar and replaced the wooden plug. He then motioned for Motoshi with his hand and told him to take the turd to the kitchen and "prepare it," following to a tee the detailed instructions he had written down for him. However, before he could pass the jar to the young, obedient houseboy, he suddenly experienced the powerful grip of a hand around the ankle of his right leg, stopping him dead in his tracks. He instinctively looked down and saw that the hand belonged to Butler, who was, to his surprise, still alive. He attempted to kick his captured leg free, but was unable to do so. And then the sensation of sharp teeth sinking themselves deep into the tender flesh of his right calf muscle burned him to the core with excruciating pain. He lost his balance and fell to the blood-slicked floor, alongside John Butler, howling in agony.

The French woman let out another scream, springing from her seat and darting to the other side of the room in a fruitless attempt to find a spot where she might feel safer.

The unrelenting pain was bringing tears to Malcolm's eyes. He smashed the alabaster jar against Butler's forehead, again and again, until the Christ turd flew from the centuries-old vessel and landed on the floor. But still his assailant refused to release him from the death grip of his fingers and teeth, which now were stained red with Malcolm's still-warm blood. Fighting against his pain, he wrapped his fingers around the rock-hard turd, and with one mighty blow, plunged it into Butler's right eye, bloodying the gelatinous orb and bringing forth the spew of its milky-white contents like a geyser erupting into the air.

"If thine right eye offends thee, pluck it out and cast it from thee, so sayeth the Gospel of Matthew!" shouted the wild-eyed televangelist like a cheerleader at a sporting event. "For it is profitable for thee that one of my members should perish, and not that my whole body should be cast into hell!"

Butler shrieked, releasing his teeth from Malcolm's blood-drenched leg. In turn, Malcolm dislodged the turd from Butler's annihilated eyeball. Small, sticky blobs of stomach-churning matter clung to the fecal matter like chunks of red Jell-o. Butler covered what was left of his right eye with his hand, as if the action could bring relief of the savage pain and somehow restore his mashed eyeball to its former state.

Malcolm's mind was now racing with adrenaline-fueled madness. He jammed the turd into Butler's other eye and twisted it back and forth until the decimated orb spilled its gooey contents like a punctured, cream-filled, white-chocolate Easter egg. A sudden awareness that the wailing and thrashing of the man had stopped washed over him and his mania all at once subsided. He was sure that Butler was dead; comforted by the realization that a turd possessing the power to bring life could also bring death.

He withdrew the gore-covered turd and stumbled to return to his feet, despite the gnawing pain in his leg. He wasn't worried about his blood loss or risk of infection. He was confident that, after his partaking of the Christ turd, his physical wounds would immediately depart as the blessing of eternal life flowed through him. Looking down at John Butler, he was astonished, yet strangely satisfied, to observe the man's gore-filled eye sockets squirming with hundreds, if not thousands, of fat, little maggots. The legless fly larvae ate and ate, rapidly multiplying in their numbers, and feasted upon the eyeless corpse until a dark crimson puddle was all that was left of it. The puddle and the maggots slowly disappeared from sight until not a single trace of John Butler remained.

"Another miracle!" Malcolm exclaimed, his heart returning to a normal pace.

The preacher brought his palms together in prayer and raised his eyes to the ceiling. "We thank Thee, O Lord, for the gift of Thine divine defecation. Amen!"

A choir of "Amen" came from the others in the room.

Motoshi wrinkled his nose, unable to conceal his disgust, as he took the turd from his employer, placed it upon the ornate silver tray, and with it in hand, disappeared through the pocket door. Nearly half an hour passed before he returned to the parlor with the silver tray. Upon it now sat a decanter of expensive red wine, seven sterling silver goblets, and an eighteenth-century snuffbox, decorated with the Coat of Arms of the Thorndike family and filled with the pulverized remains of the coveted Christ turd. He emptied the powder from the snuffbox into the decanter and swished it around a few times, then poured some into each of the seven goblets.

One by one, Thorndike's guests reservedly took a

goblet from the tray and stared, in silence, at the wine within its metallic confines. It was clear to Malcolm that they were all waiting for him to drink his portion first. He was unsure if it was due to politeness or cowardice, but nevertheless, he raised his goblet, offered up a toast to everlasting life, and then downed the wine. He licked the fragrant liquid that moistened his lips and smiled.

His guests followed his suit, each anxious to feel the blessing of immortality flow through their systems. With death no longer an encumbrance, they would be free to amass even greater wealth, even rule the world if they so desired. Nothing and nobody could ever stand in their ways again. They would be indestructible. Their collective euphoria overpowered any apprehension that dwelled within their hearts.

After an hour filled with idle chatter and the smoking of tobacco products, Malcolm's guests were growing agitated, waiting for something, anything, to happen. They had all expected a sign of something miraculous, an ineffable mystical experience, the phenomenon of religious ecstasy, or an epiphany. At this point, they would have even settled for a buzz, but they felt nothing. They were just as empty as they were before coming to the Thorndike Mansion. Some were entertaining doubts about Malcolm's immortality claims and began to feel they had been swindled out of their money.

"I think I speak for everyone in this room when I say we've waited long enough for a sign that a change in the status of our mortality has taken place," Mortimer Cromwell announced. He was normally a man of very few words; however, his rising anger was propelling his comments. "It's quite obvious to me that the Christ turd didn't possess the powers that you claimed it did."

The other guests agreed with him.

Cromwell then demanded that Malcolm return his money, and the others joined in, expressing their demands for a full refund.

"Everybody, please calm down," Malcolm begged, dreading the thought of parting with all that money that was weighing down his pockets like bricks. "These things require time to take effect," he said, hoping to stall for some time. "I think we should all wait and see what happens in twenty-four hours, or maybe give it three days—the time it took for Jesus' resurrection."

The raging anger burning in his guests' eyes scared him, but not enough to hand over the money. Visions of being torn limb from limb invaded his mind's eye. He contemplated how to make his escape.

Giselle retrieved Butler's gun from the floor near her chair and pointed it at Malcolm, aiming for between his eyes. "My money back, please, or I swear you'll be the first to have your immortality tested."

Malcolm panicked at the sight of the gun, but he tried to remain cool and collected. "Giselle, dear, please put down the gun. Don't do anything you'll regret later."

"I never regret killing men who steal my money," she replied.

"Motoshi!" Malcolm yelled, the sound of fear in his voice increasing. "Come here at once!"

Moments later, the Japanese houseboy entered the parlor through the pocket door. "Yes, Mister Thorndike?"

"Motoshi, did you prepare the Christ turd exactly the way I showed you?"

The servant nodded his head.

"And you performed the ritual of immortality without leaving anything out?"

Motoshi again nodded.

"I don't understand what could have gone wrong!" Malcolm's face was growing paler by the second.

"Say your prayers, Malcolm!" Giselle ordered, her finger anxious to pull the trigger.

With their voices rising up like an angry mob, the others

began to shout for Giselle to fill their host with lead. As far as they were all concerned, he had fallen from grace and punishment by death was in order.

Malcolm fell to his knees, tears glistening in his terror-filled eyes, and begged, "Please, don't kill me. I don't want to die. All I ask for is a little bit of time."

"I'm afraid you're time has run out," Cromwell Mortimer observed.

The chant calling for Malcolm's murder grew in its intensity, prompting him to cover his ears with his hands. It rang throughout the mansion and was loud enough to drown out the sounds of the storm outside.

A deafening thunderclap suddenly shook the mansion like an earthquake as a hole ripped open in the ceiling of the parlor, and from it, a swirling column of blinding white light beamed down, illuminating the entire room. Cracks, like crooked lightning bolts, zigzagged down the walls, sending mirrors and artwork and turds on display crashing to the floor. Above, the chandelier swayed back and forth like a gibbeted man in a gale, its prisms of crystal tinkling. Doors banged with violent force as if trying to break free from their frames. Windows rattled and sprung cracks across their panes. Objects took flight from their places atop shelves and glossy table surfaces, as if thrown by invisible hands, pelting Malcolm and his screaming guests.

It was then that the venerated turd, which had, eons ago, made its way out of the holy bowels of the Son of God, rose out of Motoshi's pocket and floated across the room. Upon witnessing this, Malcolm realized that his manservant had double-crossed him, pretending to prepare the Christ turd in the prescribed manner, while intending to keep the holy relic for himself. Anger swam through his veins like piranhas. However, before he could do or say anything, the turd began to slowly rise up within the beam of white light.

"No!" Malcolm bellowed angrily, as he made a lunge for the ascending chunk of fecal matter. "That turd belongs to me, God damn it!"

A searing heat instantly engulfed his hands as he thrust them into the column of white light to grab his levitating prized turd before it could gain momentum on what he assumed was its heaven-bound journey. He cried out in agony as his flesh sizzled and peeled away from the bone. Unable to endure the blistering pain, he quickly withdrew his hands from the light, only to find two charred and smoldering stumps where his hands should have been.

Horror laced with adrenaline ripped at his gut. Choking on the greasy smoke escaping from his new stumps, Malcolm staggered on his heels like a drunkard after a nightlong drinking binge. He dropped to his knees, spasmed from shock, and then collapsed facedown on the floor. He prayed for God to deliver him unto the merciful hands of death; however, the god he prayed to was a cruel, bloodthirsty god, and had other plans for Malcolm and his guests.

All at once, they experienced a peculiar, warm tingling feeling racing through them, beginning at the tops of their heads and terminating at the tips of their big toes. They thought they could hear the trumpets of angels in between the claps of thunder. It aroused confusion, mixed with a strange elation, within their souls. They all knew something monumental was about to happen to them. They knew not what, but could feel it in their bones.

Motoshi watched, almost mesmerized, as the people in the room began to spin around like whirling dervishes. Faster and faster, they spun until their legs could no longer support them, and, simultaneously, they plummeted to the floor, soaked from sweat, and lost in the intoxication of rapture.

But then something most horrible and quite unexpected occurred. Their skin began to take on a black, shiny appearance, and they could feel every one of their bones cracking and their internal organs painfully rearranging.

Screams of unholy terror burst forth from their gaping mouths, which were now foaming with white froth like the mouths belonging to rabid beasts. Their bodies took on a round shape, formed a hard, protective cover, and began to shrink in size until they were no larger than two and a half inches. From their new bodies, six insect-like legs sprouted, followed by a pair of flying wings. From their heads a pair of horns emerged.

To their ultimate horror, they had physically transformed into dung beetles, and instinctively knew they were doomed to wander the earth, for all eternity, eating shit.

Motoshi, ever the efficient houseboy, swept the insects into a dustpan and deposited each one of them into the alabaster jar that had once belonged to Mary Magdalene. He sealed the top of the jar with the waxy wooden stopper and placed it on top of the antique Chippendale table, next to the pterodactyl dropping.

"Enjoy your immortality," he said, cheerfully, before turning off the light and locking the pocket door behind him.

THE BOY UNDER THE BED

The hysterical scream of a child echoed through the cobweb-shrouded corridor of the derelict castle. The flames of the torches on the stony walls flickered, and then a second scream, louder than the first, sounded. There soon came another scream, followed by yet another one.

A gargantuan humanoid beast, awakened by the screams, darted down the corridor in the direction of the child's bedroom, his razor-sharp talons scraping along the wall. Scales covered his body in armored plates, and dark green dreadlocks, like thick ropes of seaweed, hung from the back of his elongated head.

The moment he opened the door of the bedroom, the screaming stopped.

The beast's lips, black and slimy like a pair of eels, peeled back to reveal a row of needle-like teeth that were as dreadful as they were sharp. His reptilian eyes zeroed in on the terrified child in the bed for several seconds, and then he spoke.

"Damn it, Gruelian! It's the middle of the day and you

should be sleeping! What's the meaning of all this screaming? Did you have another pleasant dream?"

The child sat up and shook his head from side to side. Tears were flowing from all three of his eyes, staining the dark green scales on his cheeks.

"No, Father. It wasn't a dream. There's something underneath my bed. Something too horrible for words! Its face is pale like a lifeless squid and splattered with brown dots, and the fur growing out of the top of its head is fiery red!"

The father beast crossed his arms and shook his head with disgust. "Oh, here we go again! I suppose the next thing you're going to tell me is that you saw the little boy that lives under your bed?"

The curved horns protruding from the sides of Gruelian's head like a steer drooped a bit as he nodded, fear of his father's wrath merging with his fear of the boy under his bed.

"We've been through all of this before. How many times do I have to tell you, Gruelian, there's no such thing as little boys? Humans don't exist. They're nothing but a figment of your overactive imagination."

"But I didn't imagine it," the distraught monster-child protested. "The boy... it really does exist. I've heard it moving around and I've seen it, too, with my own three eyes. If you take a look under my bed, Father, you'll see it for yourself!"

"This is utterly ridiculous!" the father beast growled before taking a quick peek under his son's bed in the hope of calming his fears. "There, are you happy now? I looked, like you asked me to, and I didn't see a thing. There's no little boy living under your bed."

"It must have ran into the closet when it heard your footsteps approaching," Gruelian reasoned. "Please, Father, take a look in the closet. I'm sure it's hiding in there."

The father beast's eyes glowed an angry red and a small

flame shot out from one of his flaring nostrils. "No! I've had enough of your nonsense for one day! When I was your age, son, I was already breathing fire and terrorizing dwarfs. It's high time for you to start acting your age and not your hoof size!"

Gruelian sniffled and wiped the tears away from his trio of eyes. "I'm sorry, Father."

The father beast grunted in disgust and started for the bedroom door; but, before exiting the room, he stopped and turned to look at his teary-eyed disappointment of a son. "You know, Gruelian, if this abnormal behavior of yours keeps up, you'll leave your mother and me with no choice but to send you to a child psychiatrist. Do you understand me? Now, stop all of this boy nonsense and go back to sleep!"

A sinking feeling began in the pit of Gruelian's stomach as he watched his peevish parent exit the bedroom, shutting the door behind him. With resignation, he lay back down, pulled his fleece blanket up to his pointed chin, and listened to his father's footsteps recede down the corridor until they vanished away into grim silence. He shut his eyes and attempted to go back to sleep as his father had ordered him. But just as he was starting to drift off into slumber, he was startled awake by a creaking sound. He opened his eyes and turned his head in the direction of the noise, horrified by what he saw.

The door of his bedroom closet was slowly opening.

Paralyzed by fear, Gruelian watched as a ginger-haired, freckle-faced boy of about nine years of age emerged from the closet and proceeded toward his bed. His heart pounded a frenetic pace as the boy drew closer, and his fangs began to chatter. He pulled the blanket up over his head and shut his eyes, tightly.

"Go away!" Gruelian's voice rang out with dread. "You aren't real."

"Oh, yes I am," the boy replied with a slight air of

indignation, his fists on his hips.

Gruelian was utterly astonished. He could scarcely believe what his pointed ears had just heard. He lowered his blanket and gawked at the boy standing at his bedside.

"You can speak?" he asked.

The boy chuckled with amusement. "Of course I can speak, you silly monster."

"But… but… you're a human! How are you able to speak?"

The boy rolled his eyes, which were the color of a hangman's gibbet. "All humans can speak. We're the ones who invented language. Don't you know anything?"

Gruelian shook his head. "I don't believe you. Humans can't be trusted to tell the truth. And besides, they don't exist… and that includes you. You're nothing but a figment of my overactive imagination. My father told me so."

The boy let out another chuckle. "Is that a fact? Well, I've got some news for you, monster. Your father is wrong. He's either not telling you the truth, or he doesn't know what he's talking about."

Gruelian's three eyes widened with fear, and the horns at each side of his head quivered with trepidation. "Shhh! Don't let my father hear you say that! He doesn't like to be contradicted."

A smug expression came over the boy's face. "I'm not afraid of your father."

"Well, you should be," Gruelian warned. "My father is the fiercest fire-breathing monster in all the land!"

The boy reached behind his back, and to Gruelian's horror, brandished a large silver dagger that had been concealed in a leather sheath attached to the back of his belt. His eyes twinkled with impishness that soon turned menacing. "And I'm Marcus the Brave—the fiercest monster-slayer in all the land!"

"M-m-monster slayer?" Gruelian nervously stuttered, his panic-stricken heart beating a mile a minute.

"That's right," the boy replied, proudly. "I've killed all kinds of monsters with my trusty dagger, then I mount their ugly heads on my bedroom wall as trophies. They don't stand a chance against me!"

"But why?" Gruelian asked, confused. "Why would you want to kill innocent monsters who've done no harm to you?"

The boy rolled his eyes in response to the young monster's naïveté. "Because killing things is what humans like to do. It makes us superior." He pressed the blade of his dagger against Gruelian's twitching throat. "Now hold still so I can make a clean cut."

The terrified monster shut his eyes, and in a desperate attempt to make the little boy disappear, began chanting, "You aren't real. You aren't real. You aren't real."

He suddenly felt an intense burning sensation as the sharp metal began to slice through his flesh. He grabbed the boy's wrist with his claw-like hand in an attempt to pull the blade away, and bellowed out a ghastly scream that echoed throughout the castle.

At that moment, Marcus awoke to find himself in his own bed. Groggily, he sat up and rubbed the sleep from his eyes. A sinking feeling of disappointment engulfed him upon the realization that his monster slaying mission was nothing more than a vivid dream.

But it couldn't have been a dream, he thought. *It was too real.*

His ears suddenly detected the sound of footsteps rushing down the hall toward his bedroom. The door swung open and the light clicked on.

In the doorway, clad in a pink quilted housecoat and even pinker fuzzy slippers, stood Marcus' mother—a slightly plump, thirty-something woman with flaming red hair wrapped around pink plastic curlers. Her round face bore a worried look as she peered into the bedroom.

"I heard a loud scream come from your room," she

announced, her tone one of motherly concern. "Are you all right?"

"I'm fine, Mom," Marcus replied. "It wasn't me who screamed. It must have been that monster that lives under my bed."

The boy's mother crossed her arms and flashed her son a look of disapproval. "Here we go again. If I've told you once, I've told you a thousand times, there's no monster living under your bed! Monsters aren't real. They exist only in your imagination."

"But, Mom…"

"Don't 'but Mom' me. I don't want to hear any more talk about monsters under beds, and I don't want you watching any more of those silly monster movies on T.V. with your older brother. They always end up giving you bad dreams."

"But I'm telling you, the monster under my bed is real!" Marcus insisted, his eyes begging to be believed. "It's not something that I dreamed. It really *is* there! I'm not making it up. You have to believe me, Mom! If you take a look underneath my bed, you'll see it for yourself!"

Heaving a weary sigh, the boy's mother shook her head and then started out of the room. She paused for a moment and turned back to her son.

"It's the middle of the night, Marcus. I have to get up early in the morning for work, and you have school. Now, stop all of this damned monster nonsense and go back to sleep!"

With that being said, she switched off the light and left the room, shutting the door behind her. Her footsteps echoed down the hall until they faded away and an ominous silence enveloped the house.

Marcus shut his eyes, determined to return to the dream and finish slaying the monster in the castle. But the sound of a creaking floorboard prompted him to open his eyes and sit up. From the relative safety of his bed, he nervously glanced around the room. There were no monsters in sight, and no monster heads mounted on the walls. However, a metallic object on the floor, illuminated by the moonlight that crept like silent cat paws through the window, caught his eye. A rush of adrenaline surged through his body when he recognized what the object was: It was the monster-slaying dagger from his dream.

He felt compelled to climb out of bed and retrieve the weapon. His hands begged to hold it as they had done in his dream and to feel its power over life and death.

With his eyes on his prize, he swung his legs over the side of his bed. But just as the bottoms of his feet were about to touch the floor, a claw-like hand, covered completely in scales of dark green, shot up from the shadows beneath the bed and wrapped itself tightly around one of Marcus' ankles. Before the young monster slayer could emit a cry for help, the monstrous hand pulled him from the mattress and his body landed on the floor with a thud. The blood in his veins turned as cold as ice.

With all the strength a young lad of his age could muster, he struggled against the hand that held him captive, at the same time stretching his arm as far as it would go in the direction of the dagger, which sat just inches away from his fingertips.

A second claw-like hand reached out from its hiding spot and wrapped itself around the boy's other ankle. Marcus felt himself being reeled in like a fish. He opened his mouth to cry out that he was the fiercest monster slayer in all the land, but before his words could form, he disappeared into the darkness underneath the bed, never to be seen again.

MAUSOLEUM 13

The rusted hinges of the iron cemetery gate screamed out like a bird of prey in the night as Bradley Bishop pushed the gate open just wide enough for his girlfriend, Carly, and himself to slip through into the cemetery. From somewhere off in the distance, the eerie baying of a dog rose up and was carried away on the wind like an omen of something dreadful to come. The howling was like that of some diabolical beast, tormented and soulless, that was doomed for all eternity to roam the earth on death-cold nights such as this one.

"Hurry up, Carly," Bradley barked with impatience in his voice. "It's going to be midnight in less than twenty minutes. Must you always be so slow?"

"I'm coming," Carly answered as she squeezed through the crack of the gate and stepped inside the desolate cemetery. "Don't be so impatient, Brad. Remember, patience is a virtue." She pulled the collar of her jacket up around her ears to shield them from the bite of a chilling December gust. Apprehension was beginning to tie a dark knot inside her stomach as snow flurries danced and swirled, ghost-like, in the air. The tiny frozen flakes landed upon her nose and cheeks, and immediately melted.

"Honestly, Brad, I don't know why I let you talk me into doing this," Carly grumbled, looking from left to right to make sure no one else was around. "I really think we should turn around and head back before someone catches us in here. It's against the law to wander around in graveyards after sundown. And besides, this is a crappy way to spend a Christmas Eve."

Bradley rubbed the palms of his hands together in an effort to warm them. "Admit it, Carly. You're afraid that the legend might be true."

Carly rolled her eyes. "Don't be ridiculous. The legend of mausoleum thirteen was invented a long time ago by a bunch of superstitious fools. I don't believe in that silly old wives' tale."

"You don't believe that if you knock thirteen times on the mausoleum's doors at midnight on Christmas Eve, the specter of death will answer?" Bradley asked.

"Of course not." Carly shook her head. "And I don't believe that he'll whisper in your ear the name of the next person destined to lie in the graveyard."

Bradley smirked. "Well, I guess tonight you and I will find out if that silly old wives' tale is true or not. That is, unless you're too scared to go through with it."

"I'm not scared," Carly retorted. "But I *am* freezing to death. So let's hurry up and get this over with."

The two teenagers trekked through the old cemetery past macabre statues of weeping angels, white bronze obelisks, and row upon row of crooked and weathered gravestones marking the burial spots of long-forgotten names from centuries past. Another chilly blast of wind nipped at their faces, flushing their cheeks. The bright ribbons of a Christmas wreath that hung on a dead child's tombstone fluttered in the wind like red flags.

And then a small gothic-styled building of gray stone

with double doors of Art Nouveau ironwork came into view. It bore no family name, as did the other mausoleums; only the number thirteen, which was engraved into a curved stone block above its arched entrance. Built sometime back in the late nineteenth century, the structure had become a local mystery and the subject of strange legends. Nobody in town, not even the oldest residents, knew for sure who had built the mausoleum, or whose bodies were entombed within its walls. Some people believed it was haunted, while some claimed it housed the body of a high priest who led a devil-worshipping cult.

Bradley looked down at the ticking watch upon his wrist to check the time. It was now ten minutes before the hour of midnight, and a light snow was beginning to fall, turning the bare branches of the trees and the tops of the tombstones a ghostly shade of white.

"It's almost time," he said as he climbed up the four stone steps leading to the front of the mausoleum. "I hope you aren't going to chicken out on me."

Carly reluctantly joined her boyfriend, continuously looking over her shoulders to ensure that no one was following them. "This is crazy, Brad. I can't believe we're actually doing this. I could be home right now, snuggled up in my nice warm bed, instead of standing out here in the cold in front of..."

"Shhh." Bradley held his pointed index finger in front of his mouth and nose. He then whispered, "I think I hear footsteps."

Carly's face went pale and she quickly spun around to see if anyone was coming. Her body tensed up, and she appeared ready to make a run for it

"Oh, never mind," Bradley teased with a stupid grin on his face. Carly's reaction amused him. "It was probably just some headless ghost wandering around looking for its head." As a finishing touch, he made a moaning ghost sound.

Carly's body relaxed. She crossed her arms over her chest. "You jackass," she muttered, her eyes throwing daggers at her giggling boyfriend. "You nearly gave me a heart attack. Don't ever scare me like that again."

Bradley loved teasing Carly and getting a rise out of her. He began doing it back in elementary school, where he first met her. It was his boyish way of expressing affection for the girl he liked, even though there were times when his playfulness genuinely annoyed her. Like tonight. He again gazed down at his wristwatch and announced that it would be midnight in less than one minute. He then began counting down the seconds. At the stroke of twelve, as a church bell echoed in the distance to signal the start of Midnight Mass, he pounded thirteen times upon one of the iron doors with his fist.

The echoing thuds of fist against metal rumbled like booms of thunder, bringing an uneasy look to Carly's face. She nervously looked around as if worried that the noise would attract the attention of the cemetery's caretaker, who lived in an old cottage across the road.

"Hey! Specter of death!" Bradley called out. "Are you in there? We want to know, who's going to be the next one pushing up daisies in this graveyard of yours? Will it be Carly? Come on and tell us. We're *dying* to find out."

Carly sighed and rolled her eyes again. "That's not funny, Brad. Can we go now?"

"You have to be patient, Carly" Bradley whispered into her ear. "Like you always tell me, patience is a virtue." Ignoring his girlfriend's pronounced frown, he turned back to the iron doors and rephrased his question. "Tell me, Death, who's the next one to die?"

The wind in the graveyard seemed to turn a little colder, and then a strange voice that possessed an unearthly quality to it whispered from within the darkness beyond the doors of mausoleum thirteen, "Bradley Bishop is next."

Carly went rigid. An expression of terror swept across

her face, and her mouth dropped open. She turned to look at her boyfriend, whose face was cloaked by a look of shock. And then, much to her horror, the doors began to creak and squeak and slowly open up.

Carly let out a scream that bounced off the mausoleum's walls and echoed against the silence of the cemetery. Without hesitation, she took off running like the proverbial bat out of hell. Within a matter of seconds, she was out of Bradley's sight, leaving behind only a trail of footprints in the thin dusting of freshly fallen snow that clung to the ground.

The mausoleum doors opened wide, revealing Bradley's best friend and fellow practical joker, Fletcher. The two young men looked at each other and then burst into uncontrollable laughter.

"You should have seen the look on Carly's face before she screamed loud enough to wake the dead!" Bradley laughed, tears streaming down his cheeks. "I thought her baby blues were going to pop right out of her head when she heard you whisper my name! Oh man, that was too funny! But, Fletch, you were supposed to have said *her* name, not mine."

Fletcher stopped laughing and a serious look came over his face. "That wasn't me, Brad," he explained. "I thought *you* were the one who whispered it."

Bradley smiled. "Yeah, right. You can't bullshit a bullshitter, dude. Like I don't know it was you. We've only had this joke planned out for like what… the last two months?"

"But I swear it, bro," Fletcher insisted. "It wasn't me. And if it wasn't you, then I don't know who the hell it was."

Bradley was beginning to feel annoyance with his buddy's insistence that he wasn't the ghostly whisperer when he knew for a fact that he was. He stepped inside the mausoleum and walked past Fletcher, who stood, looking dumbfounded. With his hand on his forehead like a visor and a sardonic expression on his face, Bradley roamed around in the small space, pretending to search for a third person.

"You know what, Fletch?" he said sarcastically, "I've looked high and low and I don't see anyone else inside this mausoleum besides you and me. Unless it's the Invisible Man."

The sudden sound of stone grinding against stone echoed within the walls of the mausoleum and Bradley and Fletcher turned their heads in the direction from which it came. All at once, the heavy lid of the burial chamber located at the rear of the mausoleum beneath a small stained-glass window slid open. And then, like a bad dream, *it* appeared.

Hideous. Vile. Reeking of absolute evil. It was a thing of inhuman form and unearthly origin; nightmarish in its appearance and ravenous after its long sleep in the blackness of the crypt. Its yellowish, snakelike eyes fixed themselves upon Bradley's, and then the thin, blackened lips of its vertical gash of mouth pulled apart to reveal the horrific rows of glistening, tapering fangs that protruded from the upper and lower sections of its great oral cavity. They resembled grotesque stalactites and stalagmites inside a cave dripping with foul and venomous slime.

Stunned by disbelief and too horrified to speak, Bradley and Fletcher stared at the beast, unable to take their eyes off of it. They watched as it rose up higher from the crypt, darkening them with its shadow as the top of its octopus-like head nearly touched the ceiling of the mausoleum. And then, without warning, it lashed out a long tentacle with talon-like claws on the end that hooked deeply into the flesh of Bradley's throat, causing blood to shoot out through his mouth and nose. Within a split second, the creature reeled in its convulsing human prey and returned to the darkness of the crypt to feast upon its long-awaited meal. Its victim's screams echoed through the stone structure but were soon muted by the heavy lid that slid back into place, resealing itself.

Fletcher let out a blood-curdling cry of terror and ran from the mausoleum in a cold sweat as the ghostly voice whispered his name on the cold wind, over and over and over. He tripped on the four stone steps and landed face down in a pile of lifeless leaves that were the color of dried blood.

When the bright sun of Christmas morning burned away the gloomy shadows of the night before and the baying of the distant hound was replaced by the sound of wintry stillness, the gray-haired caretaker arrived for work right on time. While making his rounds through the snow-shrouded cemetery, he discovered Fletcher wandering aimlessly around mausoleum thirteen, babbling to himself incoherently.

His eyes were hollows of madness.

THE LURID TALE OF TRUMPELTHINSKIN

Once upon a time, in a strange and faraway land, a beautiful, golden-haired daughter was born to a miller and his wife who were so poor they couldn't afford to name her. She grew into a fair young maiden, endowed with a busty figure that was pleasing to the eye of all the randy male peasants of the village—except, of course, for those who fancied a hung knight instead. The cantankerous fishwives of men with a wandering eye for the maiden began to spread vicious rumors that her radiant beauty was the result of sorcery.

One fateful day, whilst in the woods gathering herbs to treat her father's flatulence, the miller's daughter was seized by the king's royal guards and taken to the castle on the cliff, where she was locked away in a straw-filled tower room with only a rickety, old spinning wheel and a few scurrying mice to keep her company. The mentally unstable king, whose delusional thinking led him to believe that dried stalks of grain could be spun into gold, told her, "I shall reward you, beautiful sorceress, by making you queen if you succeed in spinning all the straw in this room into gold. But you must accomplish this task before the rising of the sun."

"But, your Majesty, I'm no sorceress," the girl explained. "I'm merely the daughter of a poor miller. I know not how to spin straw into gold!"

The king gave her a sneer. "You have until the rising of the sun," he recapitulated, his voice growing irritable. "Now set to work, girl, and if by the first rays of dawn you have not spun this straw into gold, you shall taste a cruel death at the hands of the royal executioner!"

He then left the room and bolted the door from the outside so the miller's daughter could not escape. She looked around at the many piles of straw on the floor and then sat at the spinning wheel and wept. She wondered which method of execution would be used to take her life: Would it be the gallows? Impalement? Beheading? Would she be burned alive at the stake? Perhaps the wheel would bring about her untimely demise. Or maybe she'd be drawn and quartered by four of the king's horses. Each possibility filled her with an equal amount of dread. "Oh, whatever am I to do?" she bemoaned to herself as tears escaped from her eyes and rolled down her rosy cheeks.

"Greetings and salutations!" a strange voice rang out from behind her.

Startled, the miller's daughter turned around and immediately let out a shriek of horror. There, before her long-lashed eyes of sky blue, stood a grotesque little creature possessing a peculiar orange complexion. His hands were disproportionately tiny like a tyrannosaurus rex, and frizzy strings of hair, the color not unlike a Russian prostitute's urine, draped his head in a bad comb-over.

"Who, or what, are you?" the shocked girl asked the repugnant beast in wonderment of his ability to enter the room in spite of the door being secured with a bolt.

"My name is Trumpelthinskin," he replied. "Donald J.

Trumpelthinskin to be exact. Why do you weep like a sad willow? Tell me what troubles you."

Exerting all efforts to regain her composure, she replied to the creature, whose name she found to be as foul as his face, "I am a prisoner in this tower, and unless I spin all this straw into gold before sunrise, the king will have me executed." Tears once again welled up in her eyes and she sniffled. "I weep for I have not the power to accomplish such a fantastical task. Therefore, I am destined to die."

"Never fear, my fair maiden. Gold is my forte! I can turn anything into gold, in a bigly way—even the straw that's in this room!" the creature boasted. "There's not a finer gold-maker in all the land than I. Believe me."

A faint glimmer of hope danced in the eyes of the miller's daughter. "If you were to turn all this straw into gold for me, you would save me from a fate most dreadful!"

"I'm an expert at the art of the deal. Before I save your life, I am desirous to know what it is you will give me in return?"

"I'm afraid I'm but a poor girl with nothing of any value to offer you. What is it that you would want?"

Trumpelthinskin rubbed his tiny orange hands together and a fetid string of slimy saliva drooled from the corner of his mouth. "I want to move on you like a bitch and grab you by the pussy! I also want you to give me your firstborn child."

A sharp gasp exited the girl's mouth. Taken aback by Trumpelthinskin's loathsomeness, she thought, *Never in the whole of my life have I ever encountered a creature so vile.* She sighed. "Those are such lurid requests, sir. But, alas, what choice do I have?"

Not wholeheartedly believing the creature's incredible claims, the miller-maid nodded her head in agreement, and Trumpelthinskin took her place at the spinning wheel. The imp-creature grinned and winked at her. "Straw into gold, straw into gold, let my magic spell unfold," he chanted in a low voice as he whirled the wheel. Within the blink of an eye, and much to the girl's absolute astonishment, every bit of straw in the room was miraculously changed into shining bricks of pure gold!

"I can scarcely believe what my eyes are telling me!" she exclaimed, delighted beyond measure at the sight of the piles of gold that surrounded her. "My heart rejoices for my life will be spared!"

"Behold, miller-maid. There are enough bricks of gold here to build a wall." Trumpelthinskin's bright orange tongue slid out of his mouth and he licked his putrid lips that were puckered like an inflamed anus. "And now it's time for my payment!"

The girl's stomach reeled with nausea, and her nose wrinkled up in disgust. "Keep your filthy paws away from me, you horrid little shit-gibbon! Don't touch me! I'm virginal!"

"A deal is a deal!" the creature hissed as he lunged at her, hiking her tattered cotton skirt up with one of his grubby little hands, while grabbing for her lady parts with the other. "No wench says 'no' to a stable genius who makes gold!"

The miller's daughter let out a scream.

Trumpelthinskin roared with haughty laughter as he continued grabbing her genitalia, feeling entitled to do so. Suddenly, to his surprise, the miller-maid's labia parted like a gaping jaw, and his hand was sucked deep into her vagina by a mysterious powerful vacuum. He tried with all his might to free his hand but found he was unable to retrieve it. And then, to his ultimate horror, multiple rows of razor-sharp teeth appeared inside the birth canal and clamped down upon him, slashing his flesh into jagged shreds. He howled with pain most intense as the man-eating orifice chewed his hand into a blood-gushing stump, and then sucked his arm inside, where it met the same horrible fate as his hand. He cried out for mercy, but the vagina had no intention of granting him any. The suction continued to pull him in, and the teeth continued to rip and tear until every last inch of his body had been devoured.

The miller's daughter sighed with contentment and then let out a little burp.

Morning arrived like a cat on creeping paws, bringing with it a sun as golden as the stacks of magically spun bricks that filled the room at the top of the castle's tower. Footsteps echoed on the stone stairwell outside, rousing the nameless girl from her slumber. The door was unbolted and swung open. The king stepped foot inside the room; his eyes immediately lit up, enthralled by the impressive sight of the gold before him. He excitedly rushed over to one of the stacks and picked up a gold brick.

"It's pure gold!" he cried with exhilaration as he examined it, closely. "You've spun all the straw that was in this room into gold! I'm very pleased, and as such, I will spare your life."

The miller's daughter breathed a sigh of relief and curtsied. "Thank you, your Majesty. If I may be so bold as to ask, do you still seek to marry me and make me queen?"

"No," replied the king as he returned the gold brick to the top of its stack. "After seeing all this gold, I've changed my mind. I've decided that you are to remain locked inside this room and continue spinning straw into gold for me with your sorcery." He turned for the door. "I will have the footman bring up more bundles of straw at once!"

With his back to the girl, he didn't see the golden brick gripped in her hands. She raised it above her head and then, with a crushing force, came down with it upon the back of the king's noggin. A loud crackling sound rang out as his skull shattered. He let out a groan, and like a drunkard having partaken of too much drink, began to stagger about in a daze. And then the gold brick came down upon his head, again and again. Blood, scraps of scalp, and mangled chunks of brain matter flew in all directions.

The king then fell to the floor with a thump, his body void of life. His arms and legs twitched with postmortem spasms as a crimson puddle spread out around his battered head, and then he became as still as a stone. A warm dribble of royal pee moistened the floor under his crotch as his involuntary functions shut down and his muscles spontaneously relaxed.

The miller-maid exchanged the gory murder weapon for several non-bloody golden bricks and then, taking care not to slip on the blood, fled from the castle as swiftly as the wind. She returned to her parents' mill, and now wealthy with gold, the three of them lived the rest of their lives happily ever after.

SINISTER CONSEQUENCES

His appearance was a mystery, if not a complete impossibility. There was no humanly way he could have gotten in, assuming that he was, in fact, human. The door to the windowless death row cell was locked tight and carefully guarded by a night duty officer.

On one side of the tiny room, across from a stainless-steel toilet, Veronica "Ronnie" Rippengale (dubbed "Ronnie the Ripper Gal" by the press) tossed and turned on a thin plastic mattress atop a steel bed. Being one of the fifty or so women on death rows across the United States, she hadn't had one restful night since her arrival at the prison nearly eighteen years ago. But on this particular night, her sleep was more restless than ever before.

Garbed in a suit of black, the man—or whatever he was—strolled over to the bedside of the sleeping woman, his feet making no sound on the cold, gray floor, his body casting no shadow. He leaned forward and whispered into her ear, "Wake up, Ronnie." His words flowed off his lips like liquid velvet. "I've come to make a deal with you."

Ronnie awoke from her troubled sleep and sat up. Her

forehead was dotted with droplets of cold sweat. "Is it time?" she asked, her voice sounding fragile. Dread clung to her question like drops of morning dew.

The man presented her with a smile. His eyes were dark like a starless sky in the dead of winter. "It is time for you to make a choice regarding your life," he replied.

"A choice regarding my life?" Ronnie asked, confused and rubbing the sleep from her bloodshot eyes. "My execution is in the morning. I'm a dead woman in just a matter of time."

"Six hours, six minutes, and six seconds to be exact," said the man.

Ronnie was puzzled. She had never seen this man before but yet something about him seemed familiar. She couldn't quite figure him out. "Who are you?" she asked, pulling her state-issued sheet up to her collarbone in order to cover her chest. "How did you get past the guards and inside my cell?"

"I think you know who I am, Ronnie. You've always known me, and I've always known you. I was there when you murdered your husband for the insurance money, hacked his body into little pieces, and buried them in the flower garden behind the house. I must say I was quite proud of the way in which you plotted the crime and carried it out. And you almost got away with it too. Such a pity that you didn't. I was really rooting for you."

"Are you…are you Death?" Ronnie asked, cowering with fear.

The man chuckled and shook his head, no.

Ronnie let out a little gasp. "The Devil?"

"Oh, my dear, you flatter me." the man replied. "But no. I'm not the Devil either."

"Then who are you?"

"My true name is unpronounceable in your tongue, so you may call me Charlie, if you like. I'm your personal demon, at your service."

"My personal demon?" Ronnie sounded astonished. "I wasn't aware that I had one."

"Of course. Everybody has one," the demon replied. "Demons are assigned to each and every human at the moment of their birth. Just as angels are. But they aren't nearly as influential, or as fun, as we can be."

Ronnie shook her head in disbelief. "I must be dreaming. This can't be real. You're nothing but a figment of my imagination."

The demon gave a small laugh and then assured Ronnie that she was very much awake and that he was quite real. "My good woman, as I've told you before," he reiterated, "I've come to offer you a choice. Life in another place and time, or death in the gas chamber. The choice is up to you, Ronnie. What do you have to lose?"

Ronnie pondered the demon's offer for a few moments and then nodded her head in agreement. "All right, Charlie. If what you've said to me is true, then naturally I'll choose the first option: life in another place and time. Anything's better than a room filled with hydrogen cyanide. And the farther away from here, the better."

"It's really a no-brainer!" the demon winked at Ronnie.

She eyed him with suspicion. "Okay. There has to be some kind of catch. There's a catch to everything," she asserted. "So tell me, what do I have to do to seal the deal?"

"Just sign your name, in blood, of course, in the Master's Black Book, and the exchange will be made." From out of thin air, a large book with a black leather-bound cover materialized in the demon's hand; a long silver pin appeared in the other.

"The exchange?" Ronnie asked. She felt a trifle puzzled.

"Life in another place and time in exchange for your soul," the demon answered. "Now, don't look so alarmed. You're a smart woman, so you must be aware that the murder you committed has already guaranteed your soul eternal damnation. So you have nothing really to lose by engaging in this friendly little transaction." And with that being said, he smiled once again. He appeared quite confident that Ronnie's fear of death and desire to live would persuade her to give him what he had come for. "My time grows short, Veronica, or do you prefer Ronnie the Ripper Gal? Now, do we have a deal or not?"

The very idea of selling her soul to the Devil filled Ronnie with an uneasy feeling. But the demon did have a good point, she told herself, and like he had said, she really had nothing to lose at this point. His offer was her only chance of escaping the frightening fate that awaited her in the prison's gas chamber.

"Okay. It's a deal," she said, nodding her head.

The demon handed Ronnie the silver pin and then held the book open for her to sign. She shut her eyes and pricked the tip of her left thumb with the sharp end of the pin. The stinging sensation that ensued caused her to let out a small gasp. She opened her eyes and squeezed out a droplet of blood from the tiny puncture wound, dipped the tip of the pin into it, and then used it like a fountain pen to scrawl her name in the infernal book.

All at once there came a thunderous rumbling sound from somewhere deep within the earth and then Ronnie felt as if she had awakened from a long dream. She found herself alone and in a strange room that smelled like the inside of a barn. The cobble-stoned floor beneath her feet was strewn with straw and in the corner was a small bed made from bundles of straw tied together. Above the bed, a tiny rectangular window was letting in the first rays of morning sunlight.

Curious as to where she was, Ronnie climbed onto the bed and peered out the window to take a look. To her amazement, she saw a small village of Colonial-styled houses and unpaved roads upon which hordes of people dressed in what appeared to be seventeenth century attire walked and men on horses pulling carts rode. Oddly, they were all traveling in the same direction and within a short matter of time had gathered in the village square, chattering and laughing.

As Ronnie watched the size of the crowd swell from a few dozen to several hundred, she began to laugh out loud. "I tricked the demon and his master!" she said out loud, feeling quite proud of her cunning. "I'm in another place and time now. I haven't taken anyone's life. There's been no murder of my husband, which means I've not committed a sin. I'm an innocent woman now, so my soul is safe from eternal damnation. My name won't even appear in the Devil's book until hundreds of years from now! I beat him and that demon of his at their own game! I'm free!"

The sudden rattling of metal keys popped Ronnie's musing like a balloon. Her mind immediately surged with fear that this new place and time she had been transported to was nothing but a dream and at any moment she would open her eyes to find herself back in her prison cell with the priest and warden ready to escort her to the gas chamber.

The seconds seemed to drag into hours as the door was being unlocked from the other side. And then it slowly opened. To Ronnie's horror, there stood her husband, dressed in odd attire. He wore a full-sleeved blouse, over which was a waistcoat and a doublet. Below that was a pair of breeches fastened at each of his knees with a garter. The lower half of his legs were covered by cotton stockings and high-topped boots with turnovers, and upon his head he wore a large felt hat with a wide brim. He stared her in the eyes.

"William!" she screamed in disbelief as she backed up from him, fearfully. "Oh my God! You're alive!"

The man stood in silence for a few moments before speaking. "Beggin' your pardon, Miss, but thou must have me confused with someone else. Me name's Elias, not William. And I should hope to be alive!"

Ronnie carefully studied the contours of the man's face. The resemblance to her dead husband was uncanny. She breathed a sigh of relief and then asked him, "Could you please tell me where I am and what is today's date?"

The man gave her a queer look and then replied with a grin. "Why, surely thou must know. In the jail of Salem Village is thee, on the twenty-second morn of September in the year of our Lord, sixteen hundred and ninety-two... the day thou hangs on Gallows Hill for the crime of consorting with the Devil!"

The color drained from Ronnie's face, leaving her white as the moon that brings lunacy to men, and she filled the room with a scream of hopeless despair. Her knees buckled underneath her, and she sank to the straw-covered floor. She cried out Charlie's name. "You tricked me, you evil, rotten, lying bastard! You Goddamned scum of Hell!"

Elias burst into a fit of laughter, and from his mouth came the voice of the demon. "Oh, my dear, you flatter me."

THE CRIMSON MANSION

It had been less than a week since Vanessa Fellowe's arrival at Grimrose Mansion, and already she had been asked…no, *ordered*, to leave. The request came directly from one Professor Myles Greyson, the man who had hired her, along with several others, to journey to this remote part of New England and assist him with research for a book on ghosts and hauntings that he and his assistant were writing. The research included an ongoing paranormal investigation, led by Greyson, in a house that he had leased for the term of six months—a house with a most evil reputation. Greyson had chosen Vanessa after learning she was gifted with psychokinesis—the rare psychic ability to move physical objects without physical interaction.

Marauding storm clouds had turned the heavens into a palette of gray and black, and wind-driven rain had darkened the stone walls of Grimrose Mansion on the day Vanessa arrived. From the moment she first laid eyes upon it, she knew, somewhere deep inside her tormented brain, that the cathedral-like, Neo-Gothic structure that stood before her like a monstrous behemoth of ribbed vaults and pointed arches harbored something dark, something ravenous. It seemed to be watching her every move, like a spider waiting to ensnare a helpless butterfly in its web. Staring up at the building's stained-glass rose window and lofty towers that speared the autumnal sky, she could feel it exuding a malevolent energy—a festering evil that she knew had always lived within its walls, and would continue to do so until it was destroyed. It frightened her, revolted her even. Yet, for reasons unknown, even to her, she felt drawn to the decaying mansion like the proverbial moth to a flame. Fighting against her instincts to flee, she cursed the warning voices inside her head.

A standoffish servant with all the charm of a slop basin lead Vanessa up a seemingly endless flight of creaking stairs to her quarters located in the south tower. The room was decorated in period furniture that was as aged as the house itself, and upon entering, Vanessa's heightened senses were assaulted by the heavy mustiness of century-old wallpaper and decomposing fabrics that hung in the air like a warning not to disturb.

While unpacking her suitcase, Vanessa paused for a moment to gaze at her reflection in an ornate mirror affixed to the wall above the dresser. The discolored glass showed her the face of a woman with fading youth and unfulfilled dreams.

She looked away and continued unpacking. When she again looked at the mirror, she was shaken to the core. Her reflection was now one of a rotting corpse, each of its hollow eye sockets a mass of writhing maggots. It expanded its foul mouth and whispered in a voice that sounded like a gibbet creaking in the wind, "Hell is empty. All the devils are here."

Suppressing a scream, Vanessa shut her eyes as tightly as she could. *Go away. You aren't real. You aren't real.*

Time felt suspended. Silence devoured the room. There came not even the ticking of the mantel clock or the beating of Vanessa's heart. The odor of decomposing flesh invaded her nostrils.

But I am real.

Vanessa squeezed her eyelids even tighter. *Leave me alone.* What had been mere minutes passed by like eons until the ticking of the mantel clock and the steady sound of her heart beating melted away the silence. She slowly raised her eyelids and looked into the mirror. The reflection of her face stared back at her. *Go away, Vanessa. You aren't real.*

Later that day, she had been introduced to the other members of the research group. They consisted of Professor Myles Greyson, a respected member of a university faculty with an interest in paranormal research; his assistant, Glenn Merrick, a psychic whose preferred method of communication with the spirit world was automatic writing; Colin Reese, an EVP expert with a duffle bag stuffed with a plethora of electronic ghost-detecting devices; and a Romani spiritualist-medium who went only by the name of Starlina.

Professor Greyson was exactly as Vanessa had pictured him in her mind during her drive up from New York. He was a well-dressed man of average height and build, graying at the temples, and sporting a neatly trimmed black beard, which she felt gave him an air of distinction. Piercing blue eyes twinkled from behind the lenses of his Ivy League tortoiseshell reading glasses, and when he removed his pipe from his mouth to speak, his voice was melodic and carried a hint of a slightly nasal, upper class Boston accent. He was quite knowledgeable on the subject of the mansion and its malignant history, and most eager to document the paranormal activity that was said to take place within it.

Built just prior to the American Civil War by a wealthy recluse named Thaddeus Grimrose, the mansion that bore his namesake harbored a fascinating albeit dark past filled with murders, suicides, Satanic rituals, insanity, demonic possession, and even cannibalism.

Thaddeus' first wife, Cordelia, had been brutally murdered in her bedroom in the south tower—the room in which Vanessa now slept. A horrified chambermaid discovered her satin-draped body shackled to the richly carved posts of her canopy bed, decapitated; her head, like her murderer, was never to be found.

The second Mrs. Grimrose, whose name was Adeline, committed suicide by drinking tea made with oleander leaves after her son, Zachary, perished at the age of twenty-one in a most peculiar manner: he was torn apart by a pack of wild dogs on the grounds of the estate. His body, or to be more accurate, the bits and pieces of his gnawed and scattered remains were discovered the following morning by his young fiancée, Eliza Colby. According to an unsubstantiated local rumor, the grisly sight of her betrothed caused her to descend into a state of madness from which she never recovered. Two years later, on what would have been the anniversary of her wedding to Zachary, she succumbed to what was said to be "malignant catatonic complications of melancholia."

Sometime in the late 1920s, the once-grand mansion of the seemingly cursed Grimrose family was turned into a lunatic asylum—a hellhole where inhumane experiments and torture in the name of psychiatric progress were routinely carried out on the patients, leaving many of them disfigured, crippled or dead. The cruelty continued on, unabated, until All Hallows' Eve in 1935, when the inmates of the asylum, donned in grotesque, makeshift masks, attacked the doctors and nurses, brutally slaughtering them all in an orgy of carnage and gore, earning the house its sinister nickname "The Crimson Mansion."

Believing it a place where the dead refused to stay dead, the locals gossiped in hushed voices about the house, and most avoided the place at all cost. The most superstitious among them regarded it the devil's playground. The handful of townspeople brave enough to work as hired help at the mansion always left before the sun would sink low behind the rolling New England hills, ushering in the night and all unholy things that dwell within shadows.

That night, in the darkness of the tower, as a gentle rain fell against the velvet-covered windows and cobwebbed cherubs looked down in silence from high corners, Vanessa tossed and turned in her bed, troubled by a Tarot reading Starlina had given her in the dining room after dinner.

"We choose the cards we are meant to see," the Gypsy explained, "and you chose The Devil, The Lightning-Struck Tower, and Death. These cards, they warn of great danger that will befall you. You must take care to protect yourself against the evil forces at work in this house."

After the not-so-pleasant reading, Starlina surprised Vanessa with a kiss on the lips before leaving the room. Vanessa had never kissed another woman before, with the exception of her mother when she lay dead in her casket. How well she remembered those lips—those cold, parched, ancient lips that, in life, never had a kind word to say to her. Starlina's lips were nothing like those. Hers were warm and soft and tasted like sweet cherries.

When Vanessa finally surrendered herself to sleep, she was plagued by nightmares unlike any she had ever experienced—nightmares of things too hellish for words. She was awakened in the dead of night by the touch of something that felt like fingers upon her arm, something that exuded the unsettling frigidity of corpse flesh. She sprang from her tormented sleep, beads of chilled sweat clinging to her brow, and switched on the antique banquet lamp on the bedside table, illuminating the room with artificial light and chasing away the unseen fingers.

The mustiness that had hung heavy in the room earlier was now gone, replaced by a sweet fragrance that had manifested without warning or explanation. Vanessa found it a curious aroma, but one that was not entirely unpleasant, somewhat like funeral bouquets, or her mother's floral-scented perfume that she wore to church each Sunday.

The temperature around her began to plummet as her eyes scanned the room for an intruder; and although she found no one to be there, she was able to sense the presence of something at the foot of her bed. Her ears detected the faint, nearly inaudible, sound of breathing, which came not from her, but from some unseen thing not far away. She felt the eyes of a stranger watching her, and it raised goosebumps along her arms.

Who are you, she asked, inside her mind.

No reply, verbal or telepathic, was forthcoming.

She felt her heart thumping within her chest, and then, to her horror, a large shadow, like that of a man, appeared on the wall next to the fireplace. She stared at it for quite some time, waiting for it to vanish or to make a movement, but it did neither. Curiosity began to chip away at her fear. When she could restrain herself no longer, she threw off her bedcovers, and without thinking to slide her bare feet into slippers, made her way over to the shadow, taking slow and careful steps across the moldering tapestry-like rug that covered the floor. The closer she came to the shadow, the colder the room grew, and the louder the sound of breathing became.

She looked down at her hand. As though someone else were controlling it, it was reaching out to touch the anomaly. *No! Don't do it!* She felt evil swarming around her. She could smell it, taste it. It was almost intoxicating. She wanted to pull back her hand, to cry out in a voice loud enough to wake the others, to make what was happening to her stop. But no screams, no cries for help, would make it past her trembling lips. The only thing she could do was watch, like a helpless bystander, as her hand, operating independently from her protesting brain, made its dreaded contact with the thing on the wall.

All at once, a sensation not unlike that of a searing

electric current shot through the sum of Vanessa's body, knocking her to the floor, a noise like the screams of a thousand maniacs pounding within her head.

Unable at this point to distinguish reality from nightmares, Vanessa found herself running through the mansion, down hazy, dimly-lit hallways, past open rooms where the insane in their blood-splattered hospital gowns greeted her with deranged smiles as they stabbed and sliced into the jittering flesh of their screaming victims with kitchen knives and a variety of sharp surgical tools. She saw crazed men and women sawing limbs from torsos, plucking eyeballs from their sockets, and gutting human carcasses like fishes. Some were creating childish drawings upon the walls with the blood on their fingertips, while others were feasting like starving savages on the mutilated remains of those who had been their doctors and nurses.

From out of one of the rooms, a blood-drenched man with his tongue cut from his mouth came staggering, begging God for mercy as gurgling blood bubbled from his lips. He was quickly taken down by the mental patients, who wasted no time gouging out his eyes before performing an impromptu lobotomy on him with the shaft of an ice pick.

Rivers of blood flowed through the halls of the mansion, their slickness causing Vanessa to slip and fall, twisting her ankle. On her hands and knees, she crawled through the gore, past scene after scene of mad butchery until she reached the end of the hall where a life-size portrait of Thaddeus Grimrose hung upon the wall. She stared up at it.

Rivulets of bright red blood began to trickle from the portrait's sardonic grin, and then from its nostrils and eyes. At the same time, Vanessa felt her own blood seeping from her mouth, nose and eyes, and she let out a horror-stricken scream before fading into a black abyss of unconsciousness.

Vanessa awoke in what felt like a drunken stupor, the sound of unfamiliar voices in her ears. Some were speaking her name in a solicitous manner; others seemed to be asking all sorts of questions that made no sense to her. The voices seemed to be coming at her from every direction, diving in and out of her ears and fluttering about her head like gossamer moths. As her senses came into focus, she realized she was lying on the floor at the end of the hallway, where the stern face of Thaddeus Grimrose stared down at her from crackled paint on an old linen canvas. There was not a drop of blood anywhere. Standing in a circle around her were Professor Greyson, Colin Reese, Glenn Merrick, and Starlina. Vanessa noticed they were all dressed in their nightclothes.

"What happened?" she asked. "How did I get here?"

"You must have been walking in your sleep," the professor offered.

"We heard screaming," Starlina added.

"Yes. It woke me right out of a nice dream I was having," Colin complained. "I'm sure I'll have dark circles under my eyes in the morning."

Glenn asked Vanessa if she were all right as he and the professor helped her to her feet.

"I think so." Embarrassment crept up her neck and inched its way across her cheeks, heating them a deep, rosy hue. "I just had the worst nightmare ever. I'm so sorry for waking everyone up. I feel like such an idiot."

"Are you prone to episodes of sleepwalking?" the professor asked.

Vanessa shook her head. "No. This is the first time it's ever happened to me."

"Most people who walk in their sleep are completely unaware that they're doing it and have no recollection of it when they wake up," Professor Greyson stated. "Studies have linked some cases of sleepwalking, or somnambulism as it's known by its proper name, to stress. An oppressive atmosphere such as the one in this house can make anyone feel stressed out. Are you sure you're all right, Vanessa?"

"I'm fine. Really. You all can go back to bed now."

Starlina offered Vanessa a smile before heading back to her own bedroom. "If you get scared, for whatever reason, you can spend the rest of the night with me. I'll leave my door unlocked."

"Be careful," the professor warned in a half-joking manner. "You might invite things that are best left uninvited."

During the remainder of her stay in Grimrose Mansion, Vanessa experienced no further bouts of sleepwalking; however, disturbing nightmares continued to plague her sleep and grew more disturbing with each passing night. She attributed them to the mansion's gruesome history, or to the strange paranormal phenomena that infested the house. On one occasion, threatening and obscene words had mysteriously appeared on the door of her bedroom and then vanished. There came rapping on walls and furniture by unseen hands; spectral faces manifesting themselves in the crackling flames of the fireplace; objects moving about on their own accord; disembodied footsteps, shadows, whispers, whimpers and laughter. All these things began to take their toll on Vanessa's already fragile mind. She started to exhibit peculiar behavior, staring for hours at Thaddeus Grimrose's portrait, sudden and unprovoked emotional outbursts, and strange utterings in unknown tongues.

The others noticed the changes in her and began to worry that she was taking leave of her sanity. It was almost as if the unseen malevolent entities in the house were slowly taking possession of her thoughts, and possibly her soul. During a séance held the previous night, she had slipped into a trance-like state and began speaking in reverse, in a man's voice. With a dagger that mysteriously manifested on the table, she attempted to stab Professor

Greyson in the heart before being restrained by Colin and Glenn, and then she slipped into a temporary state of unconsciousness. After that incident, it was unanimously decided that she should be sent home at once.

Morning had now arrived and pockets of white mist drifted ghost-like across the hills that stood behind Grimrose Mansion, giving them an ethereal beauty. Mourning doves cooed in the oleanders as if in drowsy contemplation. With her reluctantly packed suitcase resting on the ground beside her, Vanessa stood next to her car, arms crossed, gazing up at the circular stone towers of the mansion. From one of the windows something wispy resembling a face peered out, but as soon as Vanessa's eyes focused on it, it was gone. She shut her eyes and felt herself becoming as one with the house as a cold gust of wind rushed past her, causing her braided bun to come undone. Her head fell back as if in a swoon. The cooing grew louder.

"Vanessa! Vanessa!" Glenn yelled, breaking Vanessa's trance. "Snap out of it already!" The furrow between his eyes reflected his annoyance with her. "I've been calling to you for the past five minutes! What's the matter with you? Didn't you hear me?"

"I was just listening to the cooing of the doves," Vanessa said. "It seems to have a mesmerizing effect."

"Filthy, little disease carriers," Glenn commented, turning his head in the direction of the oleanders. "Did you know that the Algonquian Indian tribes consider it a bad omen to hear a dove cooing? They believe it means someone is soon going to die. Oh, I'm sorry. I didn't mean to upset you with that. Pay it no mind. It's nothing but superstitious rubbish!"

A look of desperation came over Vanessa's face. "Glenn, please, don't send me away," she begged. "I don't know what came over me last night. It must have been the excitement of the séance. I have no other explanation for it."

"It doesn't matter," Glenn replied. "There's really no need for you to explain."

"I apologized to Professor Greyson, more than once, but he won't even look me in the eyes. You're my friend, right? Perhaps if you spoke to him, you could convince him to let me stay and help with the research. I know he'd listen to you."

"Vanessa…" Glenn slowly turned his head in disapproval.

"I swear on a stack of bibles nothing like that will ever happen again," Vanessa continued on, her voice sounding more desperate with each word that passed from her lips. "You must believe me, Glenn. All I'm asking for is a second chance." Vanessa's tone suddenly grew irate. "Oh, stop shaking your head! What do I need to do? Get down on my knees and beg for forgiveness? Is that what you're waiting for? Is that what you want from me?"

"Calm down, Vanessa! What I want is for you to get into the car so we can get going. It's a long drive back to New York, and I would like to get you to your destination before nightfall. It's easy to get lost on these country roads at night."

"But Glenn…"

"No buts. Look, Vanessa," Glenn said in a firm voice, the last shred of his patience dwindling away, "We've been through all of this, and more than once. You know that Greyson, as well as the rest of us, think it's best for you to leave Grimrose Mansion—and the sooner the better for your sake."

"But I'm fine now," Vanessa argued. "Can't you see that?"

"I can see that you're on the verge of a nervous breakdown. Everyone here can see that, except for you. That's why Greyson asked me to accompany you back home, to make sure you're all right. Your mind…well, let's just say the atmosphere here is enough to push anyone over the edge."

With anger rushing through her veins, Vanessa climbed into her car and took her place in the driver's seat. She slammed the door shut and started up the engine as Glenn walked around to the passenger side and opened the door. He stopped before getting in and began to fish around in his pockets.

"Hang on," he said, "I left my cell phone in the house. I'll be right back." He shut the door and started back towards the house.

Vanessa looked up into the rearview mirror, which reflected the terrifying image of Grimrose Mansion staring back at her like a hungry predator lying in wait. She could see Professor Greyson standing in front of the mansion's towering front door with its hideous gargoyle-like carvings, his smelly pipe between his lips, looking smug as always. By his side stood the know-it-all Colin Reese with his nose held high in the air. And not far away was beautiful Starlina wrapped in a black crocheted shawl, shivering in the cold, her raven hair billowing in the wind.

They're all standing around, waiting for me to drive away from here. But I have no intention of driving away. I have just as much right to be here as they do. Look at them. I know they all think I've gone insane. Vanessa howled with wild laughter. *I'll show them just how insane I really am!*

Glenn was halfway to the house when Vanessa grabbed the shifter and threw the car into reverse. She floored the accelerator pedal, aiming the car at Glenn, and closed her eyes in rapture as she ran him over. There came a loud thud and she could feel the car crush his bones. She opened her eyes and smiled. She then threw the car into drive and ran him over again while Professor Greyson and the others looked on in horror and screamed. She shifted back into reverse and ran over Glenn's battered and now-lifeless body once more before stopping the car and exiting the vehicle, exhilarated. When she observed the blood seeping out of the young man's mangled corpse, it delighted her to no end.

Professor Greyson ran towards the blood-spattered car. No longer was he wearing his smug expression. His face was now pale and frantic. "Vanessa!" he cried out. "My God, what have you done?"

"That woman is out of her mind!" Colin Reese, who was trailing close behind him, chimed in. "I told you, Greyson. You should have sent her away the very first night like I suggested! She showed every sign of being mentally unbalanced. But, as usual, you didn't listen to me. You never listen to me, or to anyone else for that matter! Now look what's happened. A man is dead! You're partly to blame for this, I say!"

"For the love of God, man, will you shut the hell up!" Professor Greyson exploded with rage. "Go back to the house and notify the authorities that there's been…an accident. I'll stay here with Vanessa and wait for them to arrive. Well, don't just stand there. Do it!"

With a huff, Colin turned around and began to make his way back to the house.

Professor Greyson glanced down at the grisly mess that was once Glenn Merrick and gave it a sickened grimace. He quickly turned away, shifting his eyes to Vanessa, who was sporting a proud grin. She seemed quite pleased with her handiwork. "As much as I hate to admit it, Reese is absolutely right. I should have sent you home at the very first sign of your instability. If it hadn't been for the research…" All at once a horror-stricken look overcame his face. "Oh, good lord, the research, my book! Do you realize, Vanessa, if the press catches wind of this little stunt of yours, my book has little to no chance of ever being published? My upstanding reputation, my academic career, my years of dedicated research into the paranormal, will all be ruined in the blink of an eye! And need I remind you, I come from a respectable New England family, and a scandal such as this…"

His rant was interrupted by a loud, animalistic snarl that issued forth from Vanessa's mouth. His eyes grew wide and his jaw dropped in disbelief as he observed Vanessa raising her outstretched arms to the sky, the irises of her eyes glowing a bright red like burning embers. A long rumble of thunder vibrated the ground beneath his feet. The heavens above darkened as if overtaken by a swarm of locusts, and then a barrage of tiny pebbles began falling from out of the sky, some pelting the top of his head. He instinctively tried to shield himself using his arms.

"Bloody hell!" he exclaimed with glee in his voice. "This is better than a genuine cold spot! I must document this phenomenon at once for the Society of Psychical Research! I can't wait to see the looks on the faces of my colleagues in the academic world."

Colin Reese let out a yelp as pebbles began falling on him as well. He made a mad dash for the house, but tripped and landed facedown on the driveway. Starlina stood in front of the doorway and watched. Oddly, none of the pebbles fell upon her.

Another rumble of thunder shook the ground and the mysterious pebbles turned to large, jagged rocks that beat down upon the two men with an unbridled fury so great they were rendered punch drunk.

"Vanessa! Make it stop!" Professor Greyson clamored as he staggered forward to seek shelter in her car. Blood gushed from his battered head and ran down his face in scarlet torrents. A loud cracking sound filled the air as a rock broke the bridge of his nose, causing even more blood to gush. "You must restrain your telekinetic powers! This is exactly the sort of thing that led to the extinction of the Montusi bushmen!"

Dazed, he fell to his knees and attempted to crawl underneath the bloodied car, but the falling rocks knocked him into unconsciousness and then split his head wide open, exposing his illustrious brain and turning it into a substance resembling chopped liver.

No sooner had Greyson and Reese breathed their last breaths, than the deadly hail of rocks came to an end. Vanessa's eyes returned to their normal color, and she gazed upon the lifeless bodies smitten by her wrath. Blowflies had already flocked to the corpses and were busy feasting. A smile of satisfaction imprinted itself upon Vanessa's face.

Grimrose Mansion stood against the autumn-tinged hills like a massive stone sentinel guarding its darkness within. It seemed to be alive and watching. Vanessa shut her eyes and thought she could hear it calling her name. Her head began to swim with a strange intoxication until the shrill of Starlina's scream broke the spell of the house, plunging Vanessa's mind back into reality.

"Murderer!" Starlina hurled at her, the depths of her dark eyes bathed in terror and revulsion. "You witch! Stay away from me! You're evil!" She darted to the front door and disappeared inside the house.

Go after her, a voice inside Vanessa's head commanded. *You cannot let her live. The Gypsy will destroy you.* All at once, an axe materialized in Vanessa's hand. *Kill her!*

"Starlina!" Vanessa called out, as she sprinted into the mansion, on the hunt for her human prey. She searched room after room, but no trace of Starlina was to be found.

She eventually made her way up to the attic, where the honeyed perfume of century-old wooden rafters and planks barged into her nostrils, and sticky cobwebs blanketed in gray dust shrouded her face like a hellish bridal veil before her hand quickly brushed them away. Sporadic flashes of lightning illuminated a tall arched window leading to a small balcony located at one of the gable ends as Vanessa wound her way through a dusty maze of castoff furniture and old trunks and boxes filled with long-forgotten relics of the past.

Again, she called out to the elusive Gypsy girl, receiving only a vexing silence, followed by a low rumble of thunder, in place of a reply. "I know you're in here, Starlina," she announced, almost singing her words. She tightened her grip on the axe handle. "You can't hide from me forever, sweetheart. I'll find you sooner or later." Almost in a whisper, she added, "The house will see to that"

At that instant, there came a creak of a floorboard, and Vanessa turned her head in the direction of the sound just as something ran past her in the dim haze. The figure moved with such swiftness that Vanessa's murder-filled eyes were unable to determine who, or what, it was. Nevertheless, her gut instinct convinced her it was Starlina, and she ran after it in close pursuit, her axe poised to strike, until it escaped out the door to the attic steps and seemingly vanished into the ether. Vanessa stood in the doorway, staring down at the empty stairwell, trying to make sense of the situation.

And then she heard the footsteps.

They came from somewhere down below. They were heavy but irregular, and it soon became apparent to Vanessa that they belonged to more than one pair of feet. Several, she estimated. Their sounds grew louder as they slowly ascended the stairs, drawing closer with each step. The sweet and dusty smells of the attic became supplanted by the pungent, stomach-turning stench of decomposing flesh as the source of the footsteps became apparent.

Frozen by disbelief as much as fear, Vanessa could no longer tell if what her eyes were showing her was real or not. All she could do was watch, terror-struck, as the reanimated remains of Professor Greyson, Colin Reese and Glenn Merrick climbed the stairs, dragging their feet, leaving behind them a trail of blood mixed with mud. Vanessa told herself that she was in a dream. She had no other explanation for how the battered, rotting bodies of these men could be dead and yet alive at the same time. Her brain was unable to register such horror.

"Vanessa…" the Professor called out, his voice little more than a whisper. "We've come for you. Soon, you'll be one of us, the undead."

"No!" Vanessa screamed. "You're dead! You're all dead! I killed you myself. You aren't real!"

She shut her eyes and tried willing herself to wake up. But then she felt something cold wrap around her wrist. She opened her eyes and a scream rose from her lungs. The Professor's putrefying hand had a tight grip on her, and from the tips of its fingers, long fingernails, purplish-black and jagged, had sprouted. Vanessa yanked herself free and swung the axe into the side of the corpse's neck, but to no benefit. The three living corpses now surrounded her. Screaming, Vanessa swung her axe at them and broke through the circle, retreating back into the attic. She slammed the door shut and upon realizing it was not equipped with a lock, she proceeded to push a large, heavy trunk in front of it to block it.

The corpses pounded their fists upon the door and scratched at it with their claws, prompting Vanessa to cover her ears with her hands in an attempt to block out the noise. Their determination to get in was relentless, and Vanessa felt, at any moment, she would go mad. The pounding and scratching continued, unabated, for quite some time until at last they breached the barrier and were inside the attic. Colin stood guard at the door as Professor Greyson and Glenn advanced towards Vanessa, trapping her in the gable end of the attic.

"Vanessa," they called in their whispery, cadaverous voices. "Vanessa…"

Another flash of lightning lit up the arched window, and Vanessa remembered the balcony. It seemed her only means of escape. Perhaps there was a nearby trellis or downspout she could climb down, or maybe the rooftop of another part of the building she could jump onto. There was only one way to find out. She attempted to open the window but it was jammed. And the undead creatures were getting closer. Their claws seemed to have grown even longer, and their foul-smelling mouths now sprouted long, fang-like teeth. Vanessa swung the head of the axe at the window, smashing the glass, and climbed out onto the balcony, where the wind whipped her hair and a cold sheet of rain stung her face and arms. Her last shred of hope quickly dissolved upon the realization that there was no trellis, no downspout, and no rooftop to save her. She leaned over the railing of the balcony and looked down. A leap from that height would mean certain death.

Vanessa turned around to see Greyson and Glenn climbing through the window onto the balcony. The voice inside her head told her that the only way to stop them was to chop off their heads. She raised the blade of her axe, but before she could swing it, a blinding bolt of lightning shot down from the heavens with an eardrum-rupturing sound, striking Vanessa's axe. Within thirty milliseconds, the jolt coursed through her body, stopping her heart and causing her hair and clothing to burst into flames. She toppled over the railing and landed facedown on the side of the driveway, her scorched body broken and lifeless.

The following morning, a white van driven by Glenn Merrick pulled into the driveway leading up to Grimrose Mansion. From his place in the front passenger seat, Professor Myles Greyson shouted for his assistant to stop the vehicle. He opened the door and rushed over to examine Vanessa's smoldering corpse. Glenn got out and joined him, followed by Colin Reese and Starlina, who had been sitting in the back seat.

"Good heavens!" Professor Greyson exclaimed, "This body has been burned from head to toe. I've never seen anything quite like it."

Starlina let out a gasp and turned her face away. "How horrible! Is she dead?"

"Dead as a door nail," Glenn replied before gazing up at the house. "I don't see any traces of a fire. I wonder what the hell happened here?"

"I have no idea," the Professor replied. "It's the most curious thing."

"Who could it be?" Colin wondered aloud. "One of the hired help, do you suppose?"

"I have a feeling it's Vanessa Fellowes," Starlina offered, caressing a small black pouch she called a *putsi*, which she wore on a leather cord around her neck. It contained a holed stone that served as an amulet to protect against dark forces.

The Professor shook his head. "That's highly unlikely, Starlina. Miss Fellowes isn't scheduled to arrive until tomorrow." He turned to his assistant. "We'll need to contact the authorities straight away."

Glenn pulled out his cell phone, but was unable to get a signal. "I'll call from inside the house."

"No!" Starlina cried out. "You mustn't go in there. No one must ever go in there. The burnt body…it's a bad omen. We should turn around and leave at once."

The Professor placed his hand on Starlina's arm as if to comfort her. "I respect your beliefs and your fears," he said. "But I assure you, my dear, there's nothing to be afraid of. Whatever happened to that poor soul over there was simply a freak accident, and nothing more. I'm quite sure of that. We're perfectly safe here. No one has ever been physically harmed by the spirits of the dead."

Starlina gazed up at the mansion and felt it was somehow watching her every move, knowing her every thought. Mourning doves cooed in the oleanders, and a sudden chill wafted around her, bringing a shiver to her spine. And then a faint voice on the breeze whispered in her ear, "Hell is empty. All the devils are here."

JUDY'S TURN TO DIE

There are some things in this world that can neither be forgiven nor forgotten. Betrayal is one of them.

Judy Richter had been my best friend since elementary school. We were like sisters. Inseparable. We shared a bond that kept us connected for many years, through good times and through bad. A bond that was unbreakable, that is until Johnny Hornsby came into the picture.

You see, Johnny was the love of my life. He was good looking, sweet-talking, and a real boss dancer. No one could do the twist, the stomp, or even the mashed potato as good as Johnny. I gave him my teenage heart, along with my virginity, in the back of his Ford Woodie station wagon, where he kept his surfboard. He told me how much he loved me. He even promised to marry me. And, despite all the warnings from my girlfriends that he was no good, I truly believed he was sincere.

No girl should have to die at her Sweet Sixteen party. But I did, back in 1963, surrounded by faceless silhouettes and pink and white balloons, as Bobby Vinton's voice crooned from the speakers of my record player, "bluer than velvet were her eyes." Don't misunderstand me. It's not the death of my physical body that I'm speaking of, although that would have been preferable. It wasn't even a spiritual death. It was something far worse than that: it was the death of my innocence.

Johnny and I had just finished dancing to The Contours' hit record, *Do You Love Me*. He told me all that dancing worked up a thirst, so I went over to the punch table to get us each a cup of punch. When I returned, Johnny was gone. I looked everywhere for him but he was nowhere to be found. I felt so confused. Where had he gone? Was he all right? He had never ditched me at a party before.

Later on, just as Bobby Vinton's *Blue Velvet* began to play, I saw Johnny waltz through the door with my best friend Judy Richter by his side. He had his arm wrapped around her the way he used to wrap it around me. Judy flashed me the meanest smile I had ever seen, and I was mortified when I saw she was wearing Johnny's ring! They strolled past me like a king and a queen as if I weren't there and began doing a slow drag to the music. Soon they were kissing with such passion that I thought for sure they were going to make out right there on the dance floor.

I suddenly felt everyone's eyes on me, and I heard them whispering and laughing behind my back. I felt so humiliated, so heartbroken. I just wanted to curl up and die. I tried to pretend that it didn't bother me, and I told myself, *that's the way boys are*. However, the tears staining my lilac embroidered, chiffon party dress betrayed me, as did my lover and my best friend.

How could they do that to me? How could they be so cruel? It was all too much to take. And then something strange happened to me. I felt something inside my brain snap like a rubber band. My tears of sadness became tears of rage. I felt like making a scene—and I did! I opened my mouth and screamed. And once I started, I couldn't stop. I went ape and threw the punch bowl on the floor. It broke, sending pieces of glass and fruit punch all over the place. I picked up the glass cups and, one by one, hurled them at my guests. One hit Danny Bleecker in the face, breaking his brand-new Buddy Holly glasses. Another bounced off of Betty Valentino's bouffant and hit Mary Lou Kaminski in the forehead, knocking her unconscious. When I ran out of glasses to throw, I pushed the table over and let out a savage growl. Nobody was whispering or laughing at me anymore. They were all screaming and running for the door, some slipping on the wet floor. It was sublime! I continued to rampage until two men strapped me to a gurney and took me away in an ambulance.

Hey, you would snap too if it happened to you.

Nine months later, Johnny Junior was born, out of wedlock, with protruding ears, bulging eyes and a condition known as facial palsy, which left him unable to laugh or smile, or express any facial movement whatsoever. He was taken away from me after I gave birth to him, and was raised by strangers until we reunited, years later. It infuriated me to learn that these people had horribly abused my son. But it warmed my heart to read in the newspaper that their dismembered bodies had been found in garbage bags along the Massachusetts Turnpike. The killers were never caught.

The day I returned to my hometown with my son, now a fully-grown man, we moved into the white clapboard rooming house on Main Street, run by old Franklin Jasper and his wheelchair-bound wife, Essie. Neither of them wanted to rent to us; they had their reasons—all of them cruel. But, with the help of Johnny Junior, I managed to persuade them.

After settling in to our new home, the first thing I did was to get in touch with my old friend-turned-nemesis Judy Richter, who now went by the name Judith Hornsby. I phoned her at the real estate agency where she worked. Using an assumed name and under the pretense of selling a house, I arranged for her to meet me at the Jasper place. The appointment was set for two o'clock that afternoon, and she was right on time, eager to earn her five percent commission, just as she was all too eager to steal my fiancé so many years ago.

"Hello. I'm Judith Hornsby, from the real estate agency," she announced, a phony smile plastered across her carefully made-up face. She extended her right hand to shake mine while her left one clutched the handle of an expensive-looking leather briefcase, no doubt filled with contracts and forms and other paperwork pertaining to her sales trade.

Restraining my urge to do her bodily harm, I shook her hand in as cordial a manner as I could bring myself to muster and returned the smile. Unlike hers, mine was genuine. I had waited nearly a lifetime for this glorious day, planning for it, rehearsing it over and over again in my mind, dreaming about it until it became an all-consuming obsession gnawing at my sanity like a disease-carrying sewer rat. I invited her inside and shut the door behind her, taking care to secure the deadbolt lock.

"Are you having a party?" she inquired as she gazed around at the pink and white balloons decorating the room.

Still smiling, I nodded my head. "Today's my birthday."

Seeming a bit surprised, she wished me a happy birthday, and then her eyes shifted to my lilac embroidered, chiffon party dress. It was obvious that she was trying hard to hold back her laughter. "Oh my, what a cute dress," she commented in a polite but condescending voice. Her compliments had always been as fake as her eyelashes. "I haven't seen anything like that since the early sixties. It's so…so *retro*."

"I do hope you'll stay for my party, Judy. You don't

mind me calling you Judy, do you?" I asked. Before she could answer me, I added, "There's birthday cake with candles, party favors, and records to dance to. It'll be dreamy. Just like in the old days."

I could tell by the expression on Judy's face that she was feeling uncomfortable. She began to squirm a little bit, and that pleased me.

"Uh, thank you, that's very kind of you," she replied, choosing her words with great care. "But I'm afraid I have a three o'clock appointment over in Marshfield and I'm a bit pressed for time. I'm sure you understand. Now, as far as putting this house on the market, I'll need to speak to the Jaspers, since the property is in both their names."

"Of course," I nodded. "Follow me and I'll take you to them. Old Frankie boy and Essie are waiting for you in the dining room."

"You know, I can't quite put my finger on it, but there's something about you that seems awfully familiar," she remarked. "Maybe it's your eyes, or your voice. I'm not quite sure. Have we ever met before?"

"I don't think so," I lied, enjoying my little game of cat and mouse far too much to reveal my true identity to her before the start of the party. "I'm sure I would have remembered if we had."

"It's just the weirdest thing," Judy continued, unable at this point to focus on anything other than my face. "You really do remind me of someone—a girl I knew a long time ago."

"You're mistaken," I said as I opened the dining room door and ushered her in. "I've never seen you before in my life."

Seated at opposite ends of the table, under a festive canopy of pink and white balloons and plastic streamers, sat the Jaspers, the top of their heads crowned with glittery paper hats, while multi-colored party blowers dangled from their grayish lips. In the center of the table, next to a large and very sharp meat cleaver, sat a cake frosted with white icing and pink writing that read: Happy Birthday Leslie. The orange glow from the cake's sixteen candles cast shadows across the mannequin-like faces of the old couple.

A look of horror suddenly raced across Judy's face. "Oh, my God!" she shrieked. "You're Leslie! I thought you looked familiar! But, but, how? I mean, I thought you were…"

"Committed to a state mental hospital?" I completed her stuttering sentence for her. "Yes, it's true. I was. But I'm all better now. See? Just as good as new. That's why they let me out. I've waited so long to see you again. What's the matter, Judy? Your face has gone all pale."

"Just what the hell is going on here?" my nemesis demanded to know. "Is this supposed to be some kind of a joke?" She called out to the Jaspers, but they didn't answer. Nor did they move or blink an eye. Silly Judy, she couldn't tell they were corpses until she ran over to them and tried to shake them awake. They slumped down in their chairs. "Jesus Christ! They're dead! Did you kill them, Leslie?"

"No," I replied in my most sarcastic-sounding voice, "they accidentally stuck their heads in a plastic bag and tied a belt around their necks until they suffocated. Don't be so stupid. Of course, I killed them!"

Judy's eyes grew wide with horror. "You're insane! They should have never let you out of that institution! I'm calling the police!"

She reached into the pocket of her blazer and extracted a cell phone, which I promptly swatted from her hand. Before she was able to retrieve it from the floor I stomped it with my foot, smashing it into pieces.

"You bitch!" she screamed. "You crazy bitch! That was a two-thousand-dollar cell phone! I'll see that you pay for that if it's the last thing I do! I'm out of here!"

I could tell Judy was about to make a run for it, so I grabbed the meat cleaver from the table and blocked the door. "Leaving so soon? I wouldn't hear of it!" I yelled. "Don't you know it's rude to leave a birthday party early? Don't be rude, Judy. Have some cake. I baked it just for you."

Judy's face turned ugly. She told me to "get screwed" and to shove my cake. She hurled vulgar derogatory names at me and demanded that I get out of her way so she could leave. Her rudeness was truly appalling, her conduct most unladylike. And I told her so. She took a swing at me with her expensive leather briefcase and missed. I took a swing at her with my meat cleaver and sliced off a small chunk of flesh from her upper arm. A gush of blood rushed out of the wound. The sound of her scream was pleasing to my ears.

I pressed the cleaver firmly against her throat and ordered her to take her place at the dining room table. With tears streaming down her terrified face, she nodded and obeyed my command. So far, this was turning out to be a very good day!

I cut a big wedge of cake and placed it in front of her on a paper plate. "Have some cake," I said.

She shook her head in defiance.

I pushed the cake closer to her. "I said, have some cake!"

"I don't want any cake," she bawled. "I just want to go home."

"Dammit, Judy!" I was beginning to lose my patience with this one. "I told you to eat the damn cake! What's the matter? Are you afraid I put rat poison in it? Maybe some razor blades? Crushed glass? Eat it, you ungrateful, back-stabbing slut!"

Judy picked up her fork, but instead of sticking it into her slice of cake like a normal person, she stabbed it into my arm and then leaped out of her chair, running straight for the door.

My adrenaline was pumping so hard I was beyond feeling any pain. I lunged at her, knocking her to the floor.

I rolled her over and began bitch-slapping her mascara-streaked cheeks. It was an exhilarating feeling for me, even though she made me break a couple fingernails. After my hand tired, I pulled her up by her hair, and shoved her back into her chair. I then proceeded to bind her hands and ankles together with balloon string and plastic streamers before yanking the gold band from her finger.

"What are you doing, you heartless bitch?" she cried. "That's my wedding ring!"

"Johnny was mine, and you stole him away from me," I hissed. "That ring was meant for me! It belongs on my finger, not yours."

"Is that what this is all about?" Judy asked, as I slid the ring onto my finger and admired it. "That's ancient history, Leslie. It was decades ago! So Johnny chose me over you. Get over it, bitch. Besides, the man is dead and buried now. Let him rest in peace!"

I glared into Judy's eyes. "I have one question for you: why did you betray me like that? You were my very best friend in the whole world, and I trusted you."

Judy let out a venomous laugh. "It's about time you knew the cold, hard truth, Leslie. I was never your best friend. In fact, I've always hated your guts! Yes, that's right, Leslie. I hated you. And still do. The very sight of you literally turns my stomach, and always has."

Judy's words stabbed me in the heart like a dagger.

"You were chunky and ugly, and still are," she continued. "None of the kids at school, including me, could stand to be around you. We all laughed at you behind your back. So did the teachers. Here's a newsflash: I only let you hang around me because my mother made me. She felt sorry for you. All the while I was secretly wishing you'd drop dead! You don't know how glad I was when I heard they locked you in a padded cell in that mental hospital. And I prayed that you'd grow old and die in there so I'd never have to lay my eyes on your ugly face again."

Judy's eyelids were swollen and her face had turned an exquisite shade of black and blue. It was quite becoming on her. But I felt she needed a little something extra to complete her look. I placed the palms of my hands firmly upon the back of her head and shoved her face down into the birthday cake, despite it being covered with lit candles. She screamed into the frosting and hot wax.

"Yes, Judy. You were always the pretty one," I conceded. "And now I've made you even prettier!"

I called out to Johnny Junior, who was hiding in the kitchen, to bring out my birthday surprise. Moments later, he entered the dining room, pushing Essie Jasper's wheelchair with the disinterred body of my beloved Johnny sitting in it. He was mostly skeletal, his bones held together by the remains of leathery connective tissue and rotting clothing. But in my eyes, he was as handsome as ever. And this time he was all mine. "Surprise, Judy! Johnny's come back to me!"

She let out a piercing scream, like I knew she would. It was so loud it made my ears ring. I thought for sure she'd shatter the lenses of old Frankie boy's glasses like an Italian opera singer shattering a crystal wine goblet when their voice matches the resonant frequency of the glass, but she didn't. Instead, Essie Jasper's glass eye popped out of its socket and landed on the dining room table, where it spun around like a Hanukkah dreidel before rolling off the edge and onto the floor. I was delighted!

"Oh, sweet Jesus! What have you done?" Judy wanted to know, after she finally cooled it with the god-awful screaming.

"I invited Johnny to my party," I replied. "And, as you can plainly see, he accepted my invitation."

"You demented lunatic!" she screeched. "Everybody always said you were nuts, but this is beyond insanity! What sort of twisted fiend goes to the cemetery and digs up a dead man to bring to a party? I swear to God you're going to rot in hell for this!"

"Don't be such a twat, Judy," I said as I placed a Bobby Darin record on the turntable. "You're just jealous." I turned to my beloved Johnny. "I've saved the last dance for you, my darling." I wrapped my arms around him and lifted him out of the wheelchair. Despite not having much meat left on his bones, he still had some weight to him. He smelled like decay and damp earth, just the way a man should. The aroma was like a weird aphrodisiac, and I felt my lady-parts start to quiver. As our bodies swayed to the music, magic filled the air and I was sixteen again, transported back in time. It was ever so beautiful… until Judy had to go and spoil it all by breaking free from her restraints and smashing a chair over my back. There just seemed to be no end to her rudeness. Johnny and I crashed to the floor, his skeletal remains coming apart. It was now my turn to let out a scream. Johnny Junior grabbed my ex-best friend and threw her against the wall with such force that the back of her head put a delightful dent in the plaster. I beamed with pride, as any mother would.

Judy started back up with the screaming and tried to come at me again. Johnny Junior locked her in a reverse bear hug, allowing me to pick up poor Johnny's now detached humerus and beat her in the head with it until she slipped into unconsciousness, giving my ears a rest.

We strapped her into the old lady's wheelchair and gagged her mouth so she wouldn't disturb the neighbors with her silly screams. And then we waited until nightfall. Under the dark cover of a starless sky, Johnny Junior wheeled her down Main Street and over to the cemetery on Dorsey Road, while I followed close behind, carrying our shovels and a lantern. The caretaker of the cemetery had locked the gates at sundown, but I didn't fret. I simply picked the padlock using a little trick I had learned from a fellow inmate at the hospital. It worked like a charm! The hinges creaked as we swung the gates open.

By the light of the lantern, we made our way up a meandering lane, past a dozen or so rows of tombstones and a fancy mausoleum filled with snooty stiffs from our town's only millionaire family. It didn't take us long before we arrived at Johnny's gravesite. It was just as we had left it the night before with a huge pile of excavated dirt alongside it. We wheeled Judy to the foot of the open grave. I undid her straps and Johnny Junior tilted the wheelchair forward, depositing Judy into the murky pit. She landed with a thud like a sack of potatoes.

She came to just as Johnny Junior and I had started filling in the hole with shovelfuls of dirt. She squirmed about the rocks and roots like a giant earthworm, which was amusing to watch. And then, to my dismay, the gag came loose from her mouth. She suddenly turned religious and cried out, "Oh God! Help! Help! Save me!"

"Keep you voice down, Judy. You'll wake the dead," I laughed. "Besides, God has better things to do than waste His time on the likes of you."

"Why are you doing this to me?" she cried. "Why?"

Judy never was very bright.

I paused my shoveling for a moment and let out a sigh before enlightening her. "You want to know why? I'll tell you why. Because… it's my party, and I'll kill if I want to!"

I tossed in another scoop of dirt and smiled, content in the knowledge that Judy Hornsby—no, Judy the Ratfink Realtor Richter—would never sell another house. And it was just as well since the housing market had already hit rock bottom… just like Judy.

ACKNOWLEDGEMENTS

Grateful acknowledgement is given to the following publications in which many of the short stories in this collection originally appeared.

"The Absinthe Bottle" was first published in *Madame Gray's Poe-Pourri of Terror*, Austin, Texas: HellBound Books Publishing LLC, October 15, 2022.

"Ailurophobia" was first published in *Dig Two Graves: An Anthology Volume II,* Death's Head Press, July 9, 2019.

"Bad Hair Day" was first published in *Madame Gray's Creep Show,* Austin, Texas: HellBound Books Publishing LLC, October 26, 2020.

"Beauty *is* the Beast" was first published in *Demons, Devils and Denizens of Hell: Volume 2,* Austin, Texas: HellBound Books Publishing LLC, October 2017. It was reprinted in *Mixed Bag of Horror: Volume 1,* Austin, Texas: HellBound Books Publishing LLC, January 29, 2019.

"The Boy Under the Bed" was first published in *Monsters, Monsters, Monsters, Monsters*, Austin, Texas: HellBound Books Publishing LLC, December 13, 2021.

"The Crimson Mansion" was first published in *Schlock! Webzine:* August 2023.

"Disconnected" was first published in *Schlock! Webzine: Vol. 17 Issue 2*, September 2022.

"Don't go into the Cellar" was first published in *Jitter Press: Issue 7,* Prolific Press, October 12, 2018.

"Dust to Dust" was first published in *Coffin Bell Journal: Volume 2, Issue 4,* October 2019.

"The Green-Eyed Monster" was first published in *EconoClash Review: Volume 1,* February 2018.

"Holy Shit!" was first published in *Blood and Blasphemy*. Austin, Texas: HellBound Books Publishing LLC, December 6, 2019.

"Judy's Turn to Die" was first published in *The Chamber Magazine*, April 7, 2023.

"The Lurid Tale of Trumpelthinskin" was first published in *Trump Fiction: ECR Special Edition,* October 2018.

"The Maddening Cry" was first published in *Phantoms,* Creative James Media, September 10, 2021.

"Marcy's Diary" was first published in *Bloody Good Horror,* Austin, Texas: HellBound Books Publishing LLC, December 13, 2021.

"A Matter of Taste" was first published in *Madame Gray's Vault of Gore,* Austin, Texas: HellBound Books Publishing LLC, November 11, 2021.

"Mausoleum 13" was first published in *Deadman's Tome Cthulhu Christmas Special: Other Lovecraftian Yuletide Tales,* December 2017. It was reprinted in *Jitter Press: Issue 7,* Prolific Press, October 2018.

"Of Black Butterflies She Dreamt" was first published in *Stuff of Nightmares Anthology,* Blood Moon Rising, September 2019.

"One Foot in the Grave" was first published in *Outstanding Outpost Stories,* December 2017.

"Reindeer Games" was first published in *Night Picnic: Volume 3, Issue 1,* February 2020. It was reprinted in *Merry Evilmas,* Creative James Media, October 29, 2021.

"The Storm Rider" was first published in *Graveyard Girls,* Austin, Texas: HellBound Books Publishing LLC, June 13, 2018.

"Tall, Dark and Rancid" was first published in *Camp Slasher Lake: Volume 1*, Fedowar Press LLC, September 28, 2022.

"The Taphophile" was first published in *The Toilet Zone: Number Two*, Austin, Texas: HellBound Books Publishing LLC, December 18, 2020.

"Vow of Obedience" was first published in *The Toilet Zone: The Royal Flush*, Austin, Texas: HellBound Books

Publishing LLC, March 12, 2022.

ABOUT THE AUTHOR

Gerri R. Gray (also known as Madame Gray) is an American novelist, editor, poet, and short story writer in the horror and bizarro genres. She is the author of ten published books, including her popular debut novel, *The Amnesia Girl* (HellBound Books).

Her work has appeared in numerous anthologies and literary journals. A part-time antique dealer and former B&B proprietor, Gerri lives in upstate New York in an historic and decidedly haunted nineteenth-century house with her husband and a bevy of spirits.

When she isn't busy creating strange worlds filled with even stranger characters, she can often be found rummaging through antique shops, exploring haunted places, dabbling in the occult or traipsing through old cemeteries with her camera in hand.

Facebook:
www.facebook.com/AuthorGerriGray
Goodreads:
www.goodreads.com/author/show/17311761.Gerri_R_Gray

Other titles from HellBound Books

Madam Gray's Poe-Pourri of Terror

A haunting collection of twenty-three terror-filled tales that pay loving homage to - and capture the very essence of - Edgar Allan Poe.

So, prepare yourself for blood-chilling nightmares as murder, madness, and the supernatural are masterfully blended together to create a delectably wicked potpourri of the macabre.

Featuring 23 exemplary stories of horror from:

R. C. Mulhare, Scot Carpenter, Stephen A. Roddewig, Gerardo Serrano R., Greg Patrick, Drew Nicks, J. Rocky Colavito, Bernardo Villela, James Musgrave, Carlton Herzog, Barbara Jacobson, Guy Riessen, Jane Nightshade, Floyd Mcmillan, Jr., Jeanette Gibson, Bill Camp, J Louis Messina, N.D. Coley, Brett Knepper, Josh Poole, Jameson Grey, and the inimitable Gerri R. Gray

Madam Gray's Vault of Gore

An absolute must-read for all who enjoy their horror with gallons of blood, lashings of guts, and dollops of severed body parts!

Madame Gray has personally selected a plethora of blood-soaked tales of terror and gruesome demise, each one brutally crafted to chill the soul and turn the stomach of even the most hardened fans of the macabre.

Prepare to have your senses assaulted by...

Frederick Pangbourne, R. L. Meza, Drew Nicks, Gerri R. Gray, Travis Mushanski, Tylor James, Stephen McQuiggan, Jon Douglas Rainey, Max Carrey, Carlton Herzog, Eamonn Murphy, Alexander Nachaj, John Mara, J Louis Messina, John Robinson, James Harper, B.M. Tolkovsky, Bryan Miller, Jason Krawczyk, Cecily Winter, David-Jack Fletcher, Matt Martinek, Edward Ahern, Dr. Chris McAuley, Shannon Lawrence, Bryan Holm, and Michael Highgrove

Madam Gray's Creepshow

A veritable smorgasbord of twenty-three deliciously terrifying treats, each one simmered to blood-curdling perfection and seasoned with just the perfect amount of gallows humor.

From murder and madness to monsters and the downright macabre, the stories awaiting you within in this superlative anthology push the boundaries of horror to the next level... and way, way beyond!

Featuring stories by: Juliana Amir, Ross Baxter, Norris Black, Matt Bliss, Scot Carpenter, Max Carrey, Josh Darling, James Dorr, Gerri R. Gray, Chisto Healy, Carlton Herzog, Scott McGregor, J Louis Messina, Drew Nicks, Cooper O'Connor, Brett O'Reilly, Lisa Pais, Frederick Pangbourne, Clark Roberts, Rob Santana, Kelli A. Wilkins, and Scott Bryan Wilson.

The Amnesia Girl

Filled with copious amounts of black humor, Gerri R. Gray's first published novel is an offbeat adventure story that could be described as One Flew over the Cuckoo's Nest meets Thelma and Louise.

Flashback to 1974. Farika is a lovely young woman who wakes up one day to find herself a patient in a bizarre New York City psychiatric asylum. She has no idea who she is, and possesses no memories of where she came from nor how she got there.

Fearing for her life after being attacked by a berserk girl with over one hundred personalities and a vicious nurse with sadistic intentions, the frightened amnesiac teams up with an audacious lesbian with a comically unbalanced mind, and together they attempt a daring escape.

But little do they know that a long strange journey into an even more insane world filled with a multitude of perilous predicaments and off-kilter individuals are waiting for them on the outside. Farika's weird reality crumbles when she finally discovers who, and what, she really is!

Gray Skies of Dismal Dreams

Prepare for an excursion into a gloomy world of shadows, where the days are never sunlit and blithe, and where the nights are wrapped in endless nightmares.

No happy endings or silver linings are found in the clouds that fill these gray skies.

But what you will find, gathered in one volume, are the darkest of poems and tales of horror, waiting to take your mind on a journey into realms of the uncheerful and the unholy.

An amazingly surreal collection of short stories and the darkest of poetry, all interspersed with stunning graveyard photographs taken by the multitalented author herself - an absolute must for every bookshelf!

Blood and Blasphemy

If you enjoy your horror dipped in buckets of blood and sprinkled with generous amounts of blasphemy, then you've come to the right place!

Blood and Blasphemy is a collection of over thirty of the most sacrilegious horror stories ever written. Within these irreverent pages, you will encounter a priest that keeps his deformed spawn chained in a root cellar, a convent where a poisonous species of salamander is worshiped, a demonic altar boy, possessed religious relics that kill, blood-drinking clergymen, a Son of God who feeds on sin, an unsuspecting couple who run afoul of religious lunatics in a small town, the divine (and deadly) turd of Christ, and other terrifying tales guaranteed to make church ladies faint and nuns clutch their rosaries.

**A HellBound Books LLC
Publication**

www.hellboundbooks.com

Printed in the United States of America